MEGALODON BLOODSHED

A NOVEL BY MICHAEL COLE

SEVERED PRESS
HOBART TASMANIA

MEGALODON: BLOODSHED

Copyright © 2022 by Michael Cole
Copyright © 2022 by Severed Press

WWW.SEVEREDPRESS.COM

All rights reserved. No part of this book may be reproduced or transmitted in any form or by any electronic or mechanical means, including photocopying, recording or by any information and retrieval system, without the written permission of the publisher and author, except where permitted by law. This novel is a work of fiction. Names, characters, places and incidents are the product of the author's imagination, or are used fictiously. Any resemblance to actual events, locales or persons, living or dead, is purely coincidental.

ISBN: 978-1-922861-07-8

All rights reserved.

CHAPTER 1

Atlantic Ocean. One mile northeast of Palm Beach, Florida.

"We cannot get any closer. Coast Guard and Navy aircraft have intercepted us twice. However, Janet, we're close enough for everyone to see for yourselves. The USCGC Omega Fury has been destroyed."

"Honey, what's wrong?"

It was the third time Cassie Bodi asked her husband that question, and the third time it went unanswered. The natural assumption she jumped to was that the jerk was ignoring her. From the aft deck of their luxury cruiser, she couldn't hear whatever radio broadcast he was listening to.

Miller Bodi kept his ear to the radio. Beads of perspiration took form at his receding hairline. Not since September 11th had he been so glued to the media. A Coast Guard cutter sunk nine miles southeast of Islamorada? This could not be an accident.

"Babe?"

"Oh! You're talking to me now?"

Miller looked down at his wife. She was stretched out on a towel, getting her tan on.

A splash of water hit her butt, sparking a jolt. Before she could turn to their seventeen year-old son Codi to chastise him, a sixteen-inch sheepshead slapped the deck beside her face. Cassie leapt three feet off the deck like a cat, much to the pleasure of her teenage child.

"Damn it, Codi! You could've sunk the hook in my neck."

"Oh, Ma. Have a little humor." Codi continued to laugh while he removed the hook from his latest catch. He looked to his father to see his reaction. Usually, Miller joined in on the laughter during these situations. This time, he hardly seemed to notice. In fact, he looked troubled, as though he just saw a ghost and was on the lookout for it, should it appear again. Whatever he was looking for, it was out in the water.

"You alright, Dad?" No reaction. "Dad? Dad? Hey, DAD?!"

Miller snapped out of it. "Oh! Uh, yeah. I'm good." His eyes returned to the horizon. There was nothing out there but a single sailboat about half a mile straight east. "Nice catch, bud. Keep at it. I'm gonna talk to your mom for a sec."

Cassie squinted. "You sure you're alright, Miller?"

"Just come up here, please."

"What's going on, Dad?"

"Just something in the news. Won't interest you. Just keep fishing."

"Oh, news! What are you paying attention to them for? You know they sell nothing but propaganda." He placed the fish in the livewell and baited his hook.

Miller sat at the helm. He needed to. He was too exhausted to stand. His heart raced as though he had just finished a hundred yard sprint.

The water was always a place of Zen for him; a place where he could recover from the work week and enjoy nature. No matter how stressful things got at the office, he could always look forward to being on the water. Something about the ocean lapping against the hull on a sunny day was therapeutic.

But today, that water was a veil that concealed something horrible.

Cassie ascended the ladder to the flybridge. "What's going on?" Miller waved her over to the radio and turned the volume up slightly.

Some high-ranking military official was making a press statement from Cielo Nublado.

"We urge all vessels in the area of Key Colony Beach all the way up to the Treasure Coast to head inland immediately. We cannot yet confirm how many creatures are in the area, but we can confirm that they are dangerous and destructive."

The next voice was a reporter's. *"Admiral, there are reports that two Coast Guard helicopters have been brought down by one of the sharks. Can you confirm this?"*

"It was two response boats in addition to the Omega Fury and one rescue chopper," the Admiral said.

"Have you spoken with the local police chief?" another reporter asked.

"He's assisting in evacuation efforts. We will be using Cielo Nublado as a base of operations while we combat the threat. We also have top scientific minds assisting us. This is an unprecedented situation."

"Have you confirmed the size of the creature that brought down the cutter?"

"Negative."

"Do you know its present whereabouts?"

A pause. *"We're working in conjunction with the Air Force. Pave Hawk helicopters are flying at low altitudes to see if any of these creatures can be sighted from the air. We've got three sentinel-class cutters moving in from Key West to assist in the situation. At least five sharks have been identified."*

"Can Dr. Denise Reta make a statement?"

"The doctor is working with us presently," the Admiral said.

"Is this situation in any way related to the Miami bank robbery that resulted in a half-dozen murders?"

"That's not my jurisdiction. My understanding is those men were killed by the eighty-footer that attacked the island. That particular shark is now dead, but there are multiple other threats."

It only took two seconds for Cassie to get as pale as her husband. "Is this for real?"

"Sounds like it," Miller said.

"Sharks?! Freaking... GIANT sharks?!" She shook her head. This had to be a joke. Such a thing was impossible. No way could giant sharks exist, and it was even less possible that they could bring down a Coast Guard cutter. Despite how unfeasible it seemed, part of her believed it. Enough so that she was now watching the water. All she could see was the horizon, the infinite stretch of blue, and the white sailboat in the distance. Things that usually provided great levity were now distressing. The peaceful serenity felt deceiving. The Admiral stated that all boating activity should be suspended all the way up to the Treasure Coast, an area they were in. Did that mean there were shark sightings in this area? Or was it just a precaution?

She touched her husband's arm. "Should we head in?"

"I'm starting to think that's a good idea."

"Oh, come on!" Codi said. He had another fish on the line. He reeled it within six feet of the vessel and flung it high over the guardrail. The mackerel hit the deck behind him and flopped. "I don't know what you two are freaking out about. All I heard was giant shark. Don't know what all the fuss is about. It's not that big."

"Codi, you don't understand. This is a very serious... Wait. How do you know how big it is?"

Codi laughed at his mother and pointed to the port quarter. "Don't you see the dorsal fin? It's over there!"

Cassie put her hands to her face and started to scream. "Oh my God! We're going to die! Miller! Start the boat! Get us out of here!"

"Whoa! Holy shit, Mom!" Codi said. "It's a little extreme to freak out over a blue shark, isn't it?"

Miller grabbed his wife by the shoulders. "Hon, chill. You're not helping." Together, they watched the ten-foot blue shark calmly swimming along the surface.

Cassie took a deep breath. The tension eased its ugly grip for a moment. Just a regular shark. Her imagination had run wild after hearing the report. All she could envision was a towering dorsal fin and an enormous mouth lined with white teeth.

Codi threw another cast.

"Alright! Last one, kid! Then we're heading in," Miller said.

"Last one? But we've only been out here for a half hour. Bad weather on the horizon?"

"No, there's a…" Miller debated on whether he should alarm his son. After a moment of debate, he concluded on telling the truth. Codi was going to learn one way or another anyway. "Codi?"

The teenager winced. If anything alarmed him, it was his dad's weird behavior. "What?"

"Don't be afraid, but there's a situation near the Keys. There's reports of sunken boats, including Coast Guard vessels."

"What? Are we at war?"

"No. The news is saying there's enormous sharks swimming in the water. Megalodons. One was reported to be eighty feet long."

Codi glared at him for a full minute, awaiting the punchline for what had to be a joke. The fact that one never came was even more hilarious to him. He fell on his knees, threw his head back, and burst into laughter.

Miller felt as though he could snap the guardrail with his bare hands. "It's not funny! People have died. The government is informing all vessels to dock immediately."

"Oh, yeah! Like I'm gonna believe THAT!" Codi shouted. He tapped a hand against his chest while he caught his breath. "Oh, good lord. Oh, the pains in my stomach. My eyes are tearing up. That was a good one, Dad. Well played."

"Son…"

"Dad… the idea that you would believe anything the government says is less realistic than monster sharks roaming the ocean. There's nothing out here but us!"

"We're heading in. You don't get a say in the matter," Cassie said.

"Oh, come on! He said one more cast! I'm on a roll!" Codi held his rod up and made a childish pouty face.

Miller inhaled deeply. He needed to get the anchor up anyway. "Fine. One more, then we're heading in. Hurry it up."

Codi turned around and launched the hook about sixty feet off the stern. The mackerel had practically been fighting each other for his bait this morning, so it was likely that he would only have to wait a few seconds for the next bite.

Miller climbed down to the main deck and pulled the winch lever. The anchor chain rattled as the machine hoisted it into the boat. As soon as it was all the way in, he was back up to the flybridge. He sat at the console and reached for the ignition.

No key. In his shirt pocket, go figure.

Why do I always do that?

He dug a hand into his pocket in search for the little sliver of metal. Every other time, he always found it instantly. This time, when he was in a hurry, of course it was buried under his wallet and a half-eaten breakfast bar!

"Honey?"

"I'm getting it started. Just hang on."

"Honey?"

Cassie's voice was trembling this time. He turned to look at her. She was staring into the horizon. Her expression displayed puzzlement as much as it did fear.

Miller followed her gaze to the ocean. His expression matched hers. There was nothing but blue out there. The speck of white had vanished.

"Where's the sailboat?"

"Oh man! There it is!" Codi shouted.

Both parents looked ahead of him, then felt foolish to realize he wasn't referring to the boat, but to the fish at the end of his line. This one was a bigger catch. An Atlantic salmon.

"Oh yeah! Now there's your giant fish!" Codi said. The fish went deep. Being thirty-inches in length, it put up a much greater fight than the mackerel. "Oh, no you don't. I don't care how big you are, you're coming aboard this boat the same as your tuna friends."

"The sooner the better," Miller said under his breath. With the key in hand, he turned to start the motor. The sight of lapping water, the usual source of comfort for him, made him freeze with anticipation. The blue shark was darting away, as a predator would when chasing a meal. Or as prey would flee when a predator arrived.

It was heading straight west, toward the shallows.

"Codi! Let it go! We're leaving."

"Hang on! I'm about to make my final move!"

Miller begrudgingly waited. The fish was just a few feet from the stern. It'd be quicker to let the kid fling it onto the boat than argue. He couldn't gun the engine anyway. The way Codi was leaning over the rail, the sudden motion of the boat going forward would send him head over heels into the water.

The teen gripped his rod with both hands. "Alright. This'll take a little extra muscle on my part, but it's worth it when I'm hauling aboard my biggest catch yet!"

He yanked with all his might.

The ocean erupted. A wall of water embraced the boat, but there was no barrier thick enough to obscure the fourteen-foot extended jaws. Baring eleven-inch teeth that looked to be shaped from Hell's grindstone, the megalodon raised its mighty head.

Its bulk came down like a mighty hammer. Codi was crushed under its belly, while the entirety of the flybridge was caught in its jaws.

Cassie's screams were lost by a rush of water and wreckage. All she saw was darkness. Her imagination went into overdrive, envisioning the pit of red hot acid that was the creature's stomach as she and her husband were swallowed whole.

CHAPTER 2

Palm Beach, Florida.

For the Ferrisburg family, it was the first vacation in four years. Parenthood was a blessing, but it also had a way of throwing a wrench into one's established routines. In their first two years of marriage and the three years of dating leading up to it, Eric and Marly Antonio always took a week in the summer at a beach resort. The goal was to sit, relax, drink, and forget about the world. Then little Joey came into their lives. On the day he was born, family members were quick to spout the typical supportive phrases. "If you need any help, anyone to babysit, don't hesitate to call." It should have come with no surprise when Eric and Marly did make those requests, they were declined. "Oh, no. Sorry. I don't have time."

Right away, they learned they needed to temper their expectations regarding vacations. Four years ago, they came to Coconut Haven, their favorite beachside resort with a two-month old in tow. Every meal, every attempt to suntan, every spa session was cut short or interrupted by a wailing baby. Marly's alcohol intake was heavily limited due to her breastfeeding at the time. The week of rest proved to be more work and frustration than had they simply stayed home. So, for the following three years, they did just that. It was a good decision too. Joey went through the terrible twos and threes. Bringing him here would have been a disaster.

By his fourth birthday, the little guy had mellowed out. It took him a while, but he had finally entered that cute stage that parents could not get enough of. It was the end of July, going into August. He would be starting preschool in a month. If he was ready for that, he was ready for a week at the beach resort.

The sand was heaven on Marly's feet. The rest of her was stretched out over a towel. Eric was in a reclining chair with a Kindle in one hand and a tablet in the other. In his cupholder was a thermos filled with coffee. In two hours, it would be replaced by a beer or margarita glass. Joey was in his glory, tossing handfuls of sand into the water.

It was a full day on the beaches of Coconut Haven. Nearly a thousand people occupied the couple hundred yards of sand in front of the resort. The restaurants were starting to transition from breakfast to lunch menus and the tiki bar staff were wiping their counter tops and shelves.

The busiest area was the ocean itself. It was a hot summer day, and the crystal blue water was a welcoming sight. Much of the older folk and less adventurous types remained in the shallows, while the more energetic crowd branched further out. By ten o'clock, the ocean was alive with rafts and swimmers.

"Mommy!"

Marly looked up from her towel. "What is it, sweetie?" The little guy's eyes were on the activity in the water. He held his floaties in his hand. Marly already knew the answer. "Can we wait a little longer to go swimming?"

"Can we go?"

"Baby, what did I just say?"

"That we can go!"

She pressed her face to the towel and laughed. How kids could be simultaneously cute and irritating was a mystery that surpassed the deepest reaches of the universe.

"How 'bout we wait a little longer?"

Joey shook his head. "Noooo!"

Marly nodded. "Yes!"

"Nooo! Let's go swimming."

She looked at the water. It was only twenty feet from her location, with a clear line of sight. He probably just wanted to splash around in the shallows. It would be a simple matter to enjoy her tan while keeping an eye on him.

"Here. I'll put your floaties on and you can splash around. How 'bout that?"

Joey shook his head. "Nooo! I want out there!" He pointed to the rafts further out.

Marly dropped her head a second time. "Oh, come on, buddy. We don't want to go out that far."

"I want out there." He repeated the phrase five more times before Marly broke.

"Why don't you go with your dad?"

"Nuh-uh! The last two days, I was on parent duty," Eric said. "I'll go with him later, but right now I'm not budging from this seat."

"Fair enough." Marly took a moment to consider her blessings. There was no joy like having a child who saw you as the greatest celebrity ever. Moments like this shouldn't be wasted. She personally knew people who resented themselves for not taking advantage of their children's younger years in pursuit of self-comfort. It was something you could not take back. She smiled at Joey, touched her nose to his, then kissed his cheek. "You wanna go swimming?"

Joey nodded enthusiastically. "Yes! Swimming!"

"Alright. I'll sit in the water with you." He shook his head. Marly winced. "No? We're going in the water! Isn't that what you want?"

He pointed far out at the rafts. "Out there!" He ran past his mother and grabbed her inflatable raft from behind Eric's chair. "Come on! Let's go!"

Eric sniggered. That was a pure imitation of him. Every time they were running late, he'd be at the doorway saying that same thing.

Marly stood up and took the raft. "We're not gonna go too far out."

"Oh, you guys will be fine. As long as he keeps those floaties on, you guys could cross the Atlantic if you wanted to."

"Yeah-no, I'm good. It'd take too long to get to my next alcoholic beverage."

Eric watched her figure as she stretched her back. "I'd rather you stay as well. On this side of the ocean, it'd be easier to persuade you to join me for some 'physical therapy' while the kid naps."

Marly rolled her eyes in exaggerated motion, projecting the illusion that she hated the idea when in reality she was thinking of ways to get Joey to nap sooner.

Good thing he's in the mood for a swim. Maybe we will go further out. Exhaust the little guy.

"Mommy. I want swimming!"

"Alright, we're going." She took the raft and led the kid to the waterline. The sun had warmed the ocean to the perfect temperature. There was no need to ease into it.

Once she was in three feet of water, she laid herself onto the raft. Joey paddled alongside her, his floaties doing their job marvelously. They swam in the shallows for a while before he felt brave enough to swim deeper.

"Careful, Joey." She paddled after him, rocking the raft back and forth to achieve decent strokes. The kid was a natural. There was no hint of fear. He couldn't see the bottom, nor did he care. He was part of the ocean now, swimming past several adults into deeper waters.

Marly was regretting her decision to let him roam free. There had to be at least fifteen feet of depth underneath him now. Her imagination went nuts with potential scenarios. Those floaties were holding fine, but what if there was a tear in the nylon strap? He could slip out and sink to the bottom! Or what if they lost their air? Same horrible result. Or what if the clip somehow broke? Possibilities that seemed impossible five minutes ago now dominated her mind. Marly was not a great swimmer. She would never find him if he sank.

The worst part was he was a fast swimmer. Really fast, and still had no fear of the ocean in front of him. Marly started to resent her husband's remark about swimming across the Atlantic, for it seemed Joey had taken that statement quite literally.

He was ten feet ahead of her with no sign of slowing down. His little hands and feet paddled like little propellors. How he wasn't exhausted, she would never know. Kids tended to have infinite energy for some reason, and Joey was no exception.

"Come on, bud! Slow down."

Through the sound of chatter and splashing water, she heard Eric's annoying belly laugh from the beach. She looked back, amazed and frightened to see that she and Joey had already put nearly two hundred feet of water between them and the beach. Eric was still in his chair with a hand over his eyes, taking great joy in watching his son drive his wife insane.

Yeah, so much for that 'physical therapy,' asshole.

Eric crossed his legs and turned his eyes back to his tablet. The book on his Kindle failed to hold his attention, so it was time for some casual scrolling through the internet. The tablet chimed as an alert appeared at the top of the screen. Eric only had a moment to read the headline before it disappeared.

Coast Guard on the hunt for large predators near Keys. East Coast on high alert.

He swiped left to find the article. By the time he tapped it with his finger, another alert popped up.

EMERGENCY! Navy orders all boating activity to be suspended between Daytona Beach and the Seven Mile Bridge.

EMERGENCY! U.S.G.C Omega Fury sunk near Islamorada.

Eric read each headline three times to make sure his eyes weren't playing tricks on him.

"Hey!" someone shouted. "You guys see that?"

Several sunbathers stood up and approached the shoreline. A series of pointing fingers aimed out to sea. Next came screams. Lifeguards blew their whistles, while one with a bullhorn shouted to the crowd.

"Out of the water immediately! Everybody get out of the water now!"

Eric stood up, only to get knocked back into his seat by a fleeing swimmer. By the time he stood up, he was jolted by another. Everyone had the same look of terror on their faces. They retreated from the sea as though the Devil himself had revealed his ugly face.

He jostled his way through the crowd until he finally got a decent view of the ocean. Then he saw it.

It wasn't the Devil. It was worse.

A dorsal fin rose twelve feet over the waterline. Sixty feet behind it was a semi-circular caudal fin propelling a titanic mass toward the crowd of terrified swimmers.

There were still hundreds out there, the furthest being someone on a purple raft chasing a little green floatie.

Eric dropped his devices and screamed, helpless to watch as a monstrous shark approached his wife and child.

In the chaos of chasing Joey, Marly mistook the screams around her as young people goofing around. Many of them rode their floatation devices into war with their friends.

The echoes of bullhorns was the first true realization that something was wrong. She looked behind her and saw the crowd racing to shore. Every movement was frantic.

For the first time in her life, Marly witnessed pure panic. When she turned her eyes east, she *experienced* it.

First she saw the fin. Then the bulk that carried it. A pointed snout, dark grey in color, contrasted with the pale-white eyes. She felt a shock of realization and the adrenaline rush that followed. This was real, an honest-to-God giant shark. And it was coming straight for her and Joey.

He stopped swimming and watched the monster approach. Marly abandoned her raft and swam after him.

"Joey! Joey!"

The kid was oblivious to the terror around him. He raised his hand and waved at the approaching cave entrance lined with teeth.

"Hi, Sharky!"

Marly grabbed him and pulled him back. Immediately, they were lifted by the surge pushed by the creature's mass. The snout towered above them, blocking out the sun. The lower jaw angled under their feet. The hot stench of its throat embraced them like a dragon's fire breath.

 She tucked her son close and screamed.

Another rush of water lifted them, followed by a sudden drop, and another, gentler rise. The sun was on them again.

By the time Marly opened her eyes, the huge dorsal fin was already a sliver on the horizon. For whatever reason, the creature was moving out to sea with intent.

Joey was smiling ear-to-ear as he waved. "Bye-bye, Sharky!"

****

Research vessel Anderson Ernest

Dr. Trevor Zenner watched the viewing monitor. The drone, operated by his assistant Mark Eurupe, hovered over the leviathan. Even six hundred feet below the camera, the megalodon's immense size barely fit within the frame. The shark's weight and length had already been recorded a week ago, after he had first discovered it feeding off whales east of the Bahamas.

"Going... Going..." the Nigerian assistant said. "It's already a half-mile from shore, Doctor."

Trevor threw his hands up as though he'd scored a touchdown. "It works! It's moving away from a full buffet."

Mark shook his hand. "Well done, sir. Who knew that your device would be applied toward prehistoric sharks."

Both men turned their eyes to the briefcase-sized electronic box on the deck. This was the second major test of the Porpoise on O'Brien, and so far, the most noteworthy.

"Well, its original designer did hope to attract great whites and other species away from populated shorelines."

"Oh. Protecting the public, I see."

"Ha! No, she claimed she was protecting the sharks!" Trevor pulled up the wireless speaker mic from the water. "In that case, she would use the signals as a deterrent and force them away from the fishing grounds. She never would have guessed those same signals would be used to attract the big ones."

Mark nodded, then steered the drone back to the vessel. "Should we alert the Admiral?"

"Not yet." The doctor attached a different speaker to a cleat on the transom, then tossed it into the water. "I want to run a few more tests first. Let's continue drawing this fella south, make sure it continues to respond to the signal. Besides... I don't want to answer questions as to why we put civilians at risk."

"Fair enough. Sir, we probably should have tested the device when O'Brien encountered that boat."

"A handful of measly bite-sized people against a whole smorgasbord on the beach? It wouldn't have been a definitive conclusion. For a shark as large as O'Brien to abandon a dinky boat in favor of a possible whale, that would just be obvious. But to abandon a huge platter that's right in front of him?" Trevor pulled a beer from the cooler, chugged half of it, then put the can to his forehead. "We had to do it for the sake of our research. You know this, Mark."

"Y-yes, sir."

"Is there a problem?"

"Just feel a little guilt, sir."

"Those people should have headed in when they received the alert," Trevor said. "More to the point, our research is saving many more lives. With this device, we'll be able to lure these sea creatures wherever we please. Now, is the tracker still functional?"

Mark opened a laptop and faced the screen toward the doctor. The image displayed a radar view of the Treasure Coast and a small red blip slowly moving away from it.

"Good. Applying that thing to him was a bitch. Don't want to do that again."

Trevor finished his beer. Drinking this early wasn't a regular habit, but he needed something to sooth the stress. Should the Admiral find out about the lengths he took to test the Call Beacon, it would mean a lifelong sentence in federal prison. The Admiral believed in solutions, but he was also an idealist. A patriotic American military commander who believed in the call of duty.

Results are results. If those people didn't die, it would have been someone else, and in greater numbers.

Nothing would come of it. If anything ever came up, he would simply say he and Mark did not have eyes on O'Brien during the time of the boat attack, and that their drone was on an intercept course at Palm Beach.

Trevor shook the thought from his mind. Right now, he had to focus on the new issue. O'Brien was now coming in his direction. Time to haul ass south and test the secondary speakers, or else he would be in the same predicament as those boaters.

"Anchor's up. Turn us sixty degrees starboard and take us to thirty knots."

"Yes, sir." Mark was already up on the flybridge. With a twist of the key, the engine roared to life. Mark pushed the throttle to the max and drove the *Anderson Ernest* south, while keeping an eye on his own tracking monitor. Five miles of distance meant little to a hungry hundred-and-twenty foot megalodon, especially if it believed it was tracking a ninety-foot juicy whale.

CHAPTER 3

Cielo Nublado, thirteen miles east of the Overseas Highway.

The Excedrin rattled in Nico Medrano's hand as he lifted it from his jacket pocket. It had been several days of little-to-no sleep, and judging by the escalating situation, it was only going to get worse. It didn't help that he was still swollen from his tussle with the Miami bank robbers Ed Thatcher, Kris Hebron, and Allen Lo. Just the memory of those pricks was enough to trigger a headache.

If there was any good news to this scenario, it was the fact that the families of their victims took great comfort in knowing those killers got the justice they deserved. There was no drawn out court proceedings, no nonsense defense pleas from attorneys, and no risk of some criminal-sympathetic judge accepting an insanity plea.

Nico knew how they felt, for he felt the same. He could still hear the gunshot that took Cameron Royle's life. Part of him even considered them responsible for the megalodon's rampage. The death toll was still yet to be determined. How could one account for people when they were being eaten by the half-dozen. Had those thugs and the criminals on that seaplane not fired on the fish, perhaps they wouldn't have triggered its fury. It was evident that the shark had been near the area for at least a couple of days prior. During that time, it mainly focused on larger targets, namely whales and boats. It was still a threat that needed to be stopped, but until it saw humans as a threat, it steered clear of the shallows.

He swallowed the pills dry and turned his attention to the chopper pad. The lines of people with briefcases were only half the size they should be. He always knew that the island had a proud population, but never knew the true extent of that pride. The visiting population were quick to get on the planes and helicopters. As of eight-thirty yesterday evening, all tourists—except those who fell victim to the eighty-foot megalodon's reign of terror—were flown off the island. The transports transferred them to the Keys, where public busses transferred them to Miami where they could catch flights back home.

In addition to Navy and Coast Guard personnel, several U.S. Marine units were deployed to the island. Their tasks were to assist the local police in the evacuation efforts, then provide security while the top brass developed a plan to destroy or remove the creatures.

"Chief!"

Nico turned around. Dalton Mayberry, a local café owner, approached with the swagger of a cowboy eager to enact a duel.

"Yes?"

"How can you approve of this? This is insanity. An overreaction!"

"Dalton, you are aware of the situation, yes?"

"Yes, I understand that there are big sharks around here. But to evacuate this island? Does the military have that authority to begin with?"

"It takes a special order from the President and Governor, which have been given," Nico said. "And believe me, I agree with it."

"Come on, Chief. Look at this!" Dalton pointed at the various military choppers flying overhead, then at the Sentinel-Class cutter *Red Nova* which was anchored a half mile to the east. "People live on this island. I get that the military want to use it as a base of operations, but why do we have to leave?"

"We don't take kindly to being forced from our homes," another local said. Nico recognized her from the local physician's office. She worked as a front desk clerk. Usually, she was a very friendly person, so friendly that Nico almost didn't recognize her with that narrow gaze. He knew not to hold the emotion against her. Like many middle class people, she needed the money, and probably had to utilize her vacation time to make up for the loss of revenue. If she had any vacation time left, that is. Who knew that giant sea creatures would show up out of nowhere and spur the government into ordering an evacuation?

"It's not my call," he said.

"You have pull with the mayor," Dalton said.

"I'm not undoing this order. The situation is worse than you know. It is not safe here on this island. You *must* leave. By tonight."

Dalton groaned and returned to his vehicle. "Over my dead body, Chief."

The desk clerk followed, muttering something under her breath. Nico put his imagination to use. *"You're a swell guy, Chief. And handsome! If only that Denise woman wasn't in town..."* He managed to chuckle. Any cheerfulness, no matter how minor, was welcome at this point.

For his first time as police chief, it was the residents themselves who gave Nico an issue. Some of them left willingly, but others, like Dalton Mayberry, refused to evacuate. "What danger is there? Sharks cannot come on land," many had said.

If only they saw the aerial footage of that octopus.

Nico checked his watch. Eleven-oh-nine, almost thirty-six hours since the sinking of the *Omega Fury*. The mayor convinced the military officials to let Nico in on the briefings. For all of Zahn's faults in handling the first meg, his mind was in the right place when it came to this issue. It allowed Nico to be on the same page as the military, something that came in handy when dealing with the public.

When he first saw the footage of those gigantic tentacles rising over the *Omega Fury*, he truly believed it was a computer simulation. Such a sight felt impossible. Megalodons, as mythical as they seemed, were at least proven to have existed at one time. It was common knowledge. But a Kraken?

After the attack, the creature disappeared. Navy and Coast Guard vessels were dispersed along the Keys and the Strait of Florida. There was no sign of it on sonar, no visual from the various aircraft patrols. In the meantime, the military had to focus their attention on the multiple megalodon sightings.

"Alright, this chopper's full. Go ahead and lift off." Renny Jackman shut the fuselage door and waved the flashing baton at the crowd, backing them away from the aircraft. Even after working tirelessly and receiving numerous insults from the typically friendly public, the guy managed to keep a humorous tone in his voice.

"What? You expect us to wait outside in the blazing heat?!" one resident said.

"Hey, welcome to my world! My wife makes me do it all the time whenever she's pissed at me."

"I can attest to that!" Carley Amburn shouted. She stepped from the police tent at the edge of the lot and tossed her partner a water bottle. "Better watch it, Renny."

He held his hands up. "What'd I do?!"

"I saw how you were eyeing that Navy sailor at the beach."

"Sorry. Not my type."

"Including the brunette?"

"Oh, *her*... I hardly noticed..." He watched Carley reach for her phone. "Oh, come on! I'm helping to save the world right now from giant monsters. The good scenery helps sooth my aching soul."

"Aching soul my ass. I saw how you've bragged about having the bed to yourself this morning. With the missus staying at your in-laws' house in Austin, you're having the time of your life, aren't you."

"No. Of course not. I'm sad and lonely."

"You're so full of shit." Carley sipped on her water bottle and looked at the incoming choppers moving in from the west.

Watching her, Nico could sense the lack of energy. He understood people enough to know when they were stressed from intense worry rather than overexertion.

He approached her. "How are you feeling, Carley?"

"I'm alright."

"Your husband still on the island?"

"He left yesterday afternoon."

"Good. He with your mother on Islamorada?"

"No. Coincidently, his dad is undergoing chemo in Iowa. He went to go see him. They caught it fairly early, which is good."

"I'm glad," Nico said. "What about your mom? How's her condition?"

Carley chuckled. It was one of those situations in which if you weren't laughing, you were crying.

"Go figure her heart had to take a turn for the worst now of all times," she said.

"She needs you there," Nico said. "I'll make arrangements with the Navy. Finish this phase of the evacuation, then go home and pack a small bag. I'll have you flown over there tonight."

"No, Chief. There's work to be done. I can't abandon this post. We're short staffed as it is, even with the help of the county."

"Carley, within a day or two, this island is going to be overrun by military personnel. Who knows how long this situation will last? I've already had some of our officers ask me for a letter of recommendation."

"Can't be surprised about that. Who wants to work around sea monsters for forty grand a year?" Renny said.

Carley snorted. "You do! You crazy dumbass."

"Hey, I rescued five crewmen from that sinking ship," Renny said. "You should be saying something like 'oh, my hero!' while swooning over me."

"I'd rather lick an octopus tentacle."

"Alright, you two! Jesus!" Nico squeezed his eyes shut and rubbed his forehead. Of all the crazy events taking place around Cielo Nublado, that mental image was the most disturbing.

To Renny's credit, there were probably a few wives in the world that probably would swoon over him and call him their hero. As soon as the Mayday signal got out, he was the first one in the air. Poor guy, it had been a whole day of chaos, tracking down the bank robbers, to battling the megalodon and witnessing several friends and innocents killed in the process, then to managing the public aftermath, to saving his ass from Denise's sinking research boat. He didn't even get an hour of rest before he was back in the air again. Renny Jackman might have been a goofy officer, but the reality was that any department could only dream of having such a dedicated man on their team.

A sudden downdraft interrupted his thoughts. When Nico opened his eyes, he saw the three Navy helicopters zipping past overhead. All three were armed with hellfire missiles among multiple other armaments, and judging by their speed, they were flying with purpose.

"Looks like they're going east," Renny said. He gripped his sidearm and looked at Nico. "Should we join them, Chief?!"

He chuckled. "I've been in the air more hours in these last few days than my entire career. Let the Navy and Coast Guard handle whatever the problem is."

"It's a three-figure formation," Renny said. "Something's got their attention."

"Could just be a precaution," Carley said. "If something was going wrong, we'd hear it over the radio."

"Can't be any attacks. All cruise ships have been ordered to dock. There shouldn't be any civilians over that way. The only ones I can think of are..." He felt his chest tighten and stomach compress. "Denise's chopper."

"She's out there right now?" Carley asked.

"Yeah, tracking the triplets. Shit, if that chopper got low enough, those damn fish could..." The dreaded thought only worsened his anxiety. In the darkness that clouded his world during the last few days, the only ray of light was getting Denise back in his life. The thought of anything happening to her was unbearable. Crushing. He'd lost his son already, then lost his wife. No way was he gonna get her back only to lose her again immediately after.

He switched his radio to the chopper frequency. "Search Baker, this is Blue Tin."

The delay in response nearly made him grab Renny and drag him to the department helicopter. Before he could humiliate himself, the response came through.

"Hey, Nico. Everything alright?"

He breathed a sigh of relief. The pilot recognized his voice and simply had Denise get on the radio, hence the delay.

"Just dandy. I thought I'd check in. How are things over on your end?"

****

Denise adjusted her headset and gazed through the fuselage window of the Navy Sikorsky S-97 Raider Recon. The fuselage was spacy, allowing her to operate three different computers while she observed the behaviors of the three sixty-foot megalodons below.

"Not bad at all. Just keeping an eye on our new friends."

"What are they up to?"

"Well, they're traveling in unison. Dash is at the front of the group. As usual, he's the energetic one, hence the name. I'm worried Webb is gaining an infection in that little wound he has." She lifted her binoculars to look at the lacy, semi-circular laceration above the shark's left pectoral fin. Her theory was that the shark encountered either a trawl net or a drift net, got tangled, and had to tear itself free, cutting its flesh in the process. The result was an injury that resembled a spiderweb.

"What about Bruce?"

"He's being his normal self. Oh, there he goes right now! Living up to his name." The slowest of the triplets stopped in place and allowed itself to sink. Denise laughed. "I don't know why he does that. Maybe it's a way of resting for a moment. Then he kicks up speed again and runs after his brothers."

"Eh, I still think you should've named them Moe, Larry, and Curly."

Denise laughed. "Oh, imagine a world if you were a marine researcher, Nico. I can only imagine you naming a new species."

"Instead, I've come across an old one."

"It's an amazing thing. I wish Cameron was here. He'd be having the time of his life." She regretted mentioning his name. It had only been two days since those thugs murdered him. If anything brought Denise satisfaction, it was firing two flares into Thatcher, forcing him to jump overboard, where he got pancaked by the megalodon's tail. She didn't usually celebrate death, but everything had an exception.

Dash angled off to the left, his motions replicated by his slower brothers.

"They're turning north. Keeping up with the routine of the last twenty-four hours. Fine with me. Makes it easier to track them."

"You sound as though you enjoy their company."

"I do! Is there a problem with that?"

"Hey, I get it, hon. You're a scientist. But these things have caused major damage and have killed God knows how many people."

"The eighty-footer did, and the sixty-footer the *Omega Fury* encountered. As far as we know, these things might be relatively docile."

"Really? Docile? Those big sharks?"

"Nico, would you compare all of humanity to people like Thatcher and Kris? Is the rest of civilization responsible for the violent crimes of a few crazy idiots?" The lack of a reply meant her message was sinking in. "Then why should we apply the same standards to these sharks?"

"Here you go getting philosophical on me."

"You could use some philosophy." She watched the triplets continue moving north for a quarter-mile. "The triplets have maintained a spiral formation. They don't quite have a sense of direction, probably because they're used to deeper waters. I wonder if they're still adjusting to the sunlight."

"The eighty-footer didn't seem to have much of a problem."

"Hard to say, unfortunately. What I can say with certainty is that the first one was more mature. Maybe its brain reached a higher point of development. And who's to say it had completely adapted?"

"Sounds like you have a theory in mind."

"The theory is I don't think all of these sharks are as violent as we believe. The government is treating this as a large scale disaster, and in a way, that's justified. But there's word about exterminating all of these sharks."

"Denise, babe... I hope you won't be pissed at me for saying this, but I'm in that camp."

"I don't begrudge you that. I know you've fallen in love with that island, and it pains you to see what's become of it. But I don't think destroying all of these creatures is necessary."

Another pause. Denise knew her ex-husband well enough to know when he was trying to avoid an argument. At least he respected her feelings on the matter. At the end of the day, it didn't matter whether he believed the sharks should be hunted down. He didn't have the authority to make any calls on the matter. He was focused on his role, which was overseeing the safety and evacuation of his people.

"Any idea when you'll be back?"

"Funny he should ask," the pilot said. The chopper veered to port and doubled its speed.

Denise checked her compass. They were going northwest.

"Something wrong?"

"We've got an alert. One of our choppers spotted a group of fishing vessels heading this way. They're refusing to respond to radio instructions and we've been ordered to intercept."

"Who the hell are they?"

"Local fishermen from Georgia. We're not sure of their intent as of yet, but considering that they're hightailing it toward the Straits, my guess is they're hotshots in hopes of scoring a megalodon trophy. Sorry, Doctor. We're running point on an intercept course. You'll have to keep tabs on your sharks using the tracking devices."

Denise looked at the silver case which held the high-powered rifle. It took a little persuading to get the military to install tags on the sharks instead of gunning them down with miniguns. The sharks hardly even flinched when the tags were attached. With skin as thick as theirs, anything less than a Barret M82 anti-material cartridge would have bounced off. The device themselves were essentially a bullet cartridge with a waterproof transmitter inside. With one embedded in the flesh of each shark, their whereabouts could be tracked at all times.

She buckled herself in and fixed her headset mic. "Nico, I'm gonna have to go. Looks like there's a situation developing."

"Ten four. Yeah, we're getting word on our end. Stay safe. I'll see you when you get back."

"Sounds good." Now she was the one feeling nervous. If things got bad, he would be back in the air for the hundredth time to assist any rescue effort. "Be safe, okay?"

"You know me."

She could tell he was running.

****

Nico got in his squad car, then waited for Renny.

"Want me to come?" Carley asked.

"No, I need you to continue overseeing the evacuation," Nico said. "Get these people out of here. Tonight, the Navy's gonna start going door-to-door. I'd like to get as many out peacefully as possible before it gets to that point."

Once Renny was in the passenger seat, he flashed the overheads and floored the accelerator.

"Did I hear the report right? Local fishermen from Georgia?"

"That's right." Nico completed a series of turns until he was on the main road. The command tent was on the north beach. There, Admiral Vince Heston of the Navy and Rear Admiral Jon White from the Coast Guard Mayport Station were likely receiving aerial footage of the situation.

Nico was fine with letting them be in charge of the overall operation, but he wasn't okay with being told to 'standby until called upon.' Five miles around the island of Cielo Nublado was police jurisdiction. If something was occurring within that radius, he wanted to know about it.

The tent looked like a small building. It was a rigid-hulled structure, like that of a Zodiac inflatable, weatherproof, and capable of holding an entire command crew.

Admiral Vince Heston was standing outside near a Jeep, speaking to a younger officer. A man nearing his seventies, he had what Nico thought of as a gentle 'grandpa' demeanor. His voice sounded relaxed even giving instructions. It kept his men on their toes, while assuring them that their boss was in complete control.

Heston faced away after finishing his exchange with the other officer. When he saw Nico approach, he raised a finger signaling for him to wait. In one hand was a personal phone, in the other was a two-way radio. He barked orders into both.

"I want the carrier on the twelve-mile line and refueling planes at every Coast Guard and Navy base on the southeast coast. I want aircraft searching every square inch of water between Key West and Cuba. If there's anything bigger than a bluegill in these waters, I want to know about it." He lowered the phone and switched to the radio. "This is Heston. Have Choppers Seven, Eight, and Nine diverted course?"

"That's affirmative, Admiral."

"Copy. Make sure they move fast. Sounds like these civilians are asking for trouble." He lowered the radio and shook hands with the Chief. "Is it safe to assume you've been paying attention to the feed?"

"Aye-aye, sir," Nico said. "We're ready to get in the air if you need us." He and Renny followed the Admiral into the tent. The inside looked like a large conference room, with a big screen at the back end relaying footage transmitted by one of their choppers. To the side were various smaller monitors, most of which were tacking some of the megalodons in the surrounding area.

"So far, you can keep your feet on the ground, Chief," Heston said. "There hasn't been an attack yet."

"That can change in an instant," Renny said.

"Unfortunately, it looks as though these idiots are counting on that," Heston said. "Look. See the guy on the aft deck? They're chumming. They're intentionally luring the fish to their boats."

"How many are there?"

"Three standard fishing trawlers. Fifty-feet long, three man crews on each."

"Have your people spotted any weapons?" Nico asked.

"We haven't gotten a close enough view to confirm exactly what they have, but by the looks of it, high-powered rifles and possibly some dynamite."

"So they mean business," Renny said. "No wonder your guys don't want to get too close."

"Correct, and it's pissing me off. Chief, if you don't mind, we're gonna put your jail to use once we have these people apprehended. I don't know for sure what the motive is, but it looks to me like they're shark hunting."

"Anything you need, Admiral. I'm pissed off too. My ex-wife is on one of your birds."

"We'll get her back in one piece." The Admiral turned to face the screen. "Alright, Chopper Five, use the loudspeaker. Let these idiots know we aren't playing."

Nico eyed the rifle in the hands of the center boat's operator, and the long trail of chum that stretched behind it.

"I don't think they are either."

CHAPTER 4

"Warning! Civilian vessels, you are heading into restricted waters. You are hereby ordered by the U.S. Coast Guard to return to port at once."

Arthur Pen didn't pay any attention to the two helicopters circling about, except to gauge their positions and distance. He knew they wouldn't attempt to board unless absolutely necessary. If anyone was going to attempt to infiltrate his vessel, it was the large ship on the southeastern horizon.

His attention was on two things; the sonar, and two photographs pinned to his console. One was of a five year old girl blowing candles out on her birthday cake. The other showed the same girl doing the same thing at twenty-years of age.

Hellen would have turned twenty-one in two days. Instead of the usual gathering with cake and ice cream, her boyfriend Kevin had arranged something different, but only with dad's permission. Both of them had finished their Associate's degrees two semesters early, and with flying colors. After three years of dating and with plans to get an apartment together, Kevin felt he was ready for the next step.

Arthur liked the young man, and happily approved the proposal. No way would he intrude on such an event. Kevin was right; this called for a special trip just for the two of them, and Arthur knew just the place. Cielo Nublado was a place with beautiful white beaches, deep blue waters, deep sea fishing, and fond memories. He had brought his family there on five separate occasions, with intentions for future visits, mostly due to Helen's constant insistence. Each visit, no matter if she was a small child or a mature teenager, she was always reluctant to leave. What better place for Kevin to pop the big question?

Friday morning, he got a picture text of the two lovers on the north beach, smiling ear-to-ear and showing off the ring. The question had just been asked and the right answer given.

Several hours later, breaking news filled every television and smartphone in the country. A then-unspecified attack had struck the island, resulting in mass casualties. That afternoon was spent sending nonstop phone calls and texts to Helen and Kevin, with no answer. Calls to the island police station went on hold. His wife scoured the news footage of people on the beach, desperate to catch a glimpse of their daughter safe and sound on dry land.

Then came the dreaded phone call from the Monroe County Police at two in the morning. Some of the remains had been identified. Helen was found mangled on the beach. She and Kevin had been swimming on a raft when the shark attacked. When it passed the net barriers, it struck her with its caudal fin, breaking every bone in her body and launching her onto the shore. The only reason she was identified was the ring she wore, which was paired with a box which was on the beach along with their belongings. Kevin was never found.

Arthur saw red. In that moment, he became a changed man full of rage. He was a fisherman by trade, but he always respected the sea, and made sure to pray to God to thank Him for the gifts provided by the ocean. Now, he cursed Him for allowing such a fiend to inhabit the waters. The news of the megalodon's death brought little comfort, especially after more of them had been spotted.

The species was guilty by association. Besides, he saw no proof that the meg responsible for Helen's death had been terminated. Sleep only came in tiny intervals. Rest was not an option, not until he knew every single one of those devils lay dead on the ocean floor. He didn't care about the other strange sightings, including that of a tentacled creature that supposedly brought down a Coast Guard cutter. His hatred was directed solely on the megalodons. Anything else that rose from the depths were not worthy of his attention.

His local fishing community felt the same. Fellow fishermen Caleb Turner and Matt Leau were the first to offer their support when the news broke. As further reports of possible other megalodon sightings hit the internet, Arthur vowed to see them all dead. The final straw were press conferences from the science communities and even some politicians about preserving the species. With no faith in the federal government to see the job through, Arthur vowed to destroy the creatures himself.

With his wife's blessing, he set out on his vendetta.

The bow of his vessel, the *Pelican*, hit a wave. Salty mist swept over the vessel like a fog.

Arthur glanced back at the main deck. The metal drum was covered, the supply inside protected from the moisture. He was no expert on explosives. The only knowledge on dynamite came from a brief lesson from the mining foreman he purchased it from. Light the fuse and let it burn to the stick was all he cared to learn.

A long brownish-red line stretched from the transom to the horizon. His fishing hand, Paul Faye, tirelessly chucked scoopfuls of the mixture from the big grey tub. They had fished for sharks in the past, though nothing remotely close to this. Paul didn't care, nor did Hans Archer, who stood at the port quarter with a 30.06 rifle in hand. Both hands had grown close to the Pen family over the years, and felt the same lust for vengeance as Arthur.

Two other chum lines ran parallel to the *Pelican's*. To the vessel's eight o'clock was the *Great Dane*, run by Matt Leau and his first mate.

Matt was up on the flybridge, shotgun strapped over his shoulder, while his man tossed chum over the stern.

On the starboard side was the *Brass Lightning*, piloted by Caleb Turner. He was the oldest of the three captains, and the only one to express the idea of letting the military handle the situation. It wasn't until the politicians started running their mouths that he lost faith in that idea.

Each captain offered money to their usual crews to join in this personal mission. Those who saw it as suicide opted out. The rest, whether for financial gain or personal glory, were now traveling southeast.

"This is your last warning. Turn around, or prepare to be boarded."

Caleb's voice came through the radio. *"Pelican. Looks like we've got more than the Coast Guard out here. Look to your ten o'clock."*

"I see em," Arthur said, eyeing the three Navy Seahawks hovering in the distance.

"Is it usual for the Navy to conduct in these kinds of operations?" Paul asked.

"No. Watch their altitude. They're providing fire support," Arthur said.

"Fire support?"

"He means cover," Hans said. "They're watching for the megalodons."

"Good. I don't care who kills them. Just as long as it's done," Arthur said. He increased speed, then grabbed his rifle by the barrel. "We're in the area where they've been inhabiting. Any minute now, we'll see one. Keep your eyes open."

"What about the cutter?" Paul asked.

Arthur looked to the southeast. The hundred-fifty foot piece of steel was now less than a half mile away. He had underestimated its speed.

"We're maintaining course. I'm not going back until all of those sharks are dead."

One of the Coast Guard choppers gradually started to descend. The pilot was clearly operating with caution, the crew watching the boats through the open fuselage door and reporting all activity. They had seen the weapons and were not eager to approach too quickly.

"Lower your weapons and raise your hands. You are about to be boarded," the pilot said.

Arthur raised his middle finger, then his gun. He didn't point it at the chopper, but his point was clear all the same. He had no intention of being boarded.

The chopper backed away. Now, the fuselage was open all the way. Sniper crews were taking position.

"Oh, shit," Hans said.

"Keep chumming. They're not going to fire unless fired on first," Arthur said. "You had the option to stay home. I made it clear what you were committing to. This is for Helen."

"What's to stop that cutter, though?" Hans said.

He had a point. Arthur foolishly believed he could outrun that vessel, for his was smaller and lighter. In his hubris, he failed to consider that he was going up against forty-three hundred kilowatt engines.

The boat grew increasingly monstrous as it neared. The next voice to echo across the water was from the bridge.

"Drop your weapons and surrender. Failure to comply will result in deadly force. You are under arrest."

A new anger flooded Arthur's mind. Who cares if he was entering restricted waters? This was *his* life! He understood what he was getting into, as did his fellow fishermen. Nobody had the right to stop him, not even God Himself.

"What do you want to do, Arthur? We're with you all the way," Matt said. Arthur could see him giving a two-finger salute from the bridge of the *Great Dane*.

Suddenly, the choppers broke formation. The Navy choppers pointed their guns to the northeast. The cutter angled to starboard, the crew gathering on deck. Many of them were on the starboard side, as though searching for something in the horizon.

"Something's happening," Arthur said. "What's over there?"

"I don't see anything," Matt said. *"Whatever has their attention is UNDER the water."*

Arthur smiled. His perseverance had paid off.

"It's here."

****

"Sonar reading. Bogie at one thousand yards, moving in at seventy-kilometers per hour. One hundred feet deep. No visual from Sea Rock. Do any chopper units have a visual?"

"Negative," Lieutenant Wilson, the Sikorsky pilot, replied. He looked at his co-pilot, Ensign Charley Ortmeier. "Anything on that side?"

"You sound like my wife whenever we're stuck at an intersection," Ortmeier said.

"Answer the damn question, smartass."

"Negative, Lieutenant. No visual."

Denise Reta pressed her forehead to the glass. The water below was a perfect glassy blue, with gentle waves moving out from the *USCGC Sea Rock*. The vessel had turned, its Bushmaster cannon rotated to greet the threat.

A thousand feet out, a dim cloud appeared under the water. It moved like a torpedo speeding for its target. For a split second, that target looked like it would be the *Sea Rock*.

"I see it," she said into the mic. "It's running deep. It's passing under the cutter." She crossed the fuselage and looked at the fishing boats. "It's come for their bait."

"Bridge to Dr. Reta. Which megalodon is this? Is this one we've been tracking?"

Denise double checked all of her computer monitors. "Negative. This is an untagged one. We have no data."

No data meant no knowledge of its size, temperament, and age. Three factors that were crucial in combatting these creatures. The larger ones had thicker skin, thus were harder to kill, even with anti-material projectiles. It was as though nature had designed these beasts specifically to be weapons of war. And war was here. The fishermen below had set the terms of engagement.

As she predicted, the megalodon passed under the vessel. Only once it emerged on the other side did it begin to surface. The dorsal fin pierced the air, the white eyes visible against a dark grey snout.

Hopefully they will live to regret it.

****

"Arthur! I see it! I SEE IT!"

The only time Arthur ever heard Matt so excited was when he came home at noon with ten-thousand dollars' worth of tuna. Ten thousand dollars for four hours work was a good day, and it planted the seeds of possibility that tomorrow would bring the same luck. Today, he was about to complete the greatest challenge of his life—killing a giant shark.

The dorsal fin rose eight feet into the air. Thirty-five feet behind it was the half-moon shaped caudal fin. It waved to-and-fro, pushing the fish toward the three chum trails.

"That's it for the chumming. Get the dynamite ready. Paul, toss me up a bundle." A moment later, the crewman tossed a six-stick bundle to the captain. Arthur reached into his pocket and pulled his cigar lighter, a gift from his daughter, and held it close to the fuse.

The *Great Dane* and *Brass Lightning* moved further out, their crews preparing their own explosives and weaponry.

"This is the Coast Guard. Do NOT engage the shark. Allow us…"

Arthur pointed his rifle up and fired a shot, cutting off the speaker and forcing the chopper to bank right.

"Fuck off."

The megalodon passed behind the *Great Dane*, slowing as it reached the chum trails.

Arthur lifted his speaker mic. "Caleb, it's closest to you. Have your crew dump the bait. I'm circling your way. *Brass Lightning,* hold position at two-hundred meters." He cut the wheel and looked to his men. "Ready with that dynamite?"

"You got it. Let's make some chowder."

"These bastards were supposed to be extinct. Let's correct nature's mistake." He turned the boat a hundred degrees port and pointed the bow at the *Great Dane,* which had slowed to two knots. Matt Leau's first mate, a man with the physical form of a Greek statue, lifted a two-hundred pound steer carcass. Two buoys were attached to it for floatation and to allow the fishermen a visual.

The crewman tossed the piece of meat overboard then dumped a bucket-full of chum after it.

Immediately, the dorsal fin turned.

Arthur tapped his foot on the deck as though dancing to a beat. His bloodlust had turned to pure excitement. He was only a couple hundred feet from the *Great Dane*, which was now turning east. Matt Leau had his eyes on the fish and a bundle of dynamite in his hand.

"It's going for it."

As he spoke, the grey pointed snout lifted. The jaws peeled back, revealing the white daggers lining the gums.

The *Great Dane* finished hooking left, now pointed south and parallel with the *Pelican.* It passed east of the megalodon, while Arthur took the west side.

The fish made short work of the bait and was searching the water for more.

"Now!"

Both captains touched a lighter flame to three inches of fuse, let it burn halfway, then chucked their explosives thirty feet at the fish. Before the dynamite even hit the water, both men were already speeding away.

Two fiery explosions shook the Atlantic. The flash was brief, like that of a firecracker, but with five-thousand times more destructive force. Water stretched to towering lengths, nearly reaching the Coast Guard choppers above.

The Navy birds were now circling, searching for any clear shot of the fish.

Arthur circled back to see the results. The water was simmering, the waves having completed their fall. The *Great Dane* was coming toward him, its captain and crewman watching for the fish.

Arthur moved within shouting distance. "You see it?!"

"Not yet."

"You see anything? Any blood?"

"I do, but I'm not sure if it's the chum, or the fish."

The water returned to its normal state, the only disturbance caused by the boats and the choppers' downdrafts. They were looking for it too, with no success.

Matt Leau smiled. "I think we got it, Arthur."

"I think so too." Arthur looked to his daughter's photographs. "We did it, baby. We got one. And I did it for you."

The sound of gunfire erased his smile.

"Holy shit! There it is!" Paul yelled, pointing west.

The fish emerged two hundred yards west. Eyelids slid over its eyes, rendering its entire face grey—except for its white teeth. The crew of the *Brass Lightning* fired a few more shots at the incoming snout before giving up and retreating forward.

Caleb Turner gunned his engine, but it was too late. The megalodon's jaw closed on the aft deck, its chin snapping the propellors like toothpicks. The bow reared, catapulting its captain backward. He landed face-down atop the shark's head.

Miraculously, he managed to hold on while the fish shook his boat back and forth. The men aboard were tossed about like dice in a cup. The megalodon released its grip and let the boat sink. A swing of its caudal fin pushed it over the submerged deck. The jaws opened, intent on snatching the two bleeding humans aboard.

It had underestimated the reach of its snout.

The two crewmen's screams were abruptly silenced as they were pancaked against the cabin.

The next scream came from Caleb Turner after the shark pulled back and unveiled the two mashed corpses. Flat as pancakes, they stood against the structure like wall decorations, oozing blood.

Sensing the pest on its head, the shark tried looking up. It could feel Caleb, but could not see him. Cruising along the surface, it tucked its snout down, then snapped upward.

Caleb was tossed straight up, legs kicking. The scream didn't start until he realized he was falling. Like his crewmen, that scream was quickly silenced. This time, the shark's jaws were on point, snatching the human snack out of midair like a dog catching a treat.

Arthur accelerated at the fish, his joy reverting to anger. His tactic had failed, inflicting nothing but minor burns on the devil. Maybe he and Matt didn't get the explosives close enough. Maybe the fish dove too soon. Maybe he needed a two-second charge instead of three.

"Cap, what are you doing?" Hans said.

"Finishing the job."

"To hell with that! Let's get out of here."

"Shut up! These things killed Helen! Now they killed Caleb." He picked up the mic. "Matt. We're going in again."

"Right behind you. Payback time."

The *Great Dane* was a few dozen meters back from the starboard quarter, going full-speed at the target. The muscular crewman had a rifle in hand, locked and loaded.

The fish was still moving along the surface in search of any remaining fleshy tidbits. Sensing the vibration from the oncoming boats, it turned east.

Paul and Hans unloaded the dead steer from the *Pelican's* deck. As soon as it splashed down, Arthur veered to port, putting distance between them and the *Great Dane*.

The plan was the same as before. Pass by the shark and hit it with explosives.

It zeroed in on the buoys, drawn by the scent of blood. Matt Leau's crewman prepped his explosive. In a count of five, the shark would reach the bait. This time, it would not have the opportunity to grab it and run. The explosive would land as soon as the fish made contact.

One... two...

He touched the lighter to the fuse, reared his hand back...and screamed. The shark did *not* go for the bait. Instead, it went for the *Great Dane*.

It did not raise its head or part its jaw, for it now understood that blunt force was needed to crack the rigid hulls of these non-organic 'creatures'. The snout punched five feet into the portside, splitting the hull, and knocking the crewman backward.

Matt Leau fell to his knees and looked backward. The fish dove under the boat, its caudal fin whipping briefly above the water. His eyes went to the damage, then to his crewman. He was lying flat on his back, next to the drum, dynamite bundle in hand.

"Fu—"

Forty-sticks of dynamite discharged at once, instantly reducing the *Great Dane* to shrapnel. Razor sharp slivers of steel, ranging from a few inches to several feet in length, soared in all directions.

****

"Evasive maneuvers. Everyone pull back." Wilson was already banking to port as he spoke.

Denise tucked her head down. Shrapnel clanked against the steel hull. Somewhere behind her, a window cracked. Warm, salty air invaded the chopper.

"This is U.S.C.G. One-One-Four. We have rotor failure. No way around it—bracing for crash landing."

Alarms echoed from the cockpit.

"Doc! If you're not already strapped in, do it now."

Denise leaned forward and grabbed her three computers. The alarms and the pilot's instruction meant one thing: USCG One-One-Four was not the only one suffering from rotor failure.

The chopper danced in mid-air, smoke billowing from the top rotors. The inflow of air turned into a full wind, carrying the stench of diesel and TNT. She sealed all three waterproof containers then clipped her harness.

"Oh, shit. Oh God." She took a deep breath and focused on comforting thoughts. "Nico…"

Wilson continued his countdown. "We've lost control. Touching down in three, two, one…"

CRASH!

****

Command Central. North Beach, Cielo Nublado.

"Search Baker is down," a Navy radio operator said.

"Do we have eyes on the shark?" Admiral Heston said.

"Viper One. We've lost visual."

"This is the USCGC Sea Rock. Sonar reading shows the target is still in the area. Probably circling underneath."

"Probably driven down by the explosion," Heston said. "I want all three Seahawks to arm hellfire missiles. Let the Coast Guard unit pick up the fallen crews first. Provide machine gun fire should the target surface." He rubbed his forehead. The situation was out of control. He knew beforehand that these sharks were dangerous, but seeing it with his own eyes made him feel the gravity of the situation.

"Contact! Pull up!"

The Admiral watched as the second Coast Guard chopper lifted away from the Sikorsky floating wreckage. The megalodon had half its body in the air, jaws snapping shut within inches of the underside.

"It's gone berserk," the second lieutenant said. "It's those damn fishermen and their dynamite. Now it thinks we're all out to get it."

Heston maintained his calm demeanor. Underneath that shell was an angry storm. *Damn these bastards for causing this.* A meeting with Congress was inevitable at this point. There was plenty of debate on whether the creatures should be destroyed. For the last few days, Heston was on the fence, but now, he was ready to pick a side. If one shark could cause all of this, what would happen should the others turn out to be aggressive?

"Sir, we can't get close. Shark's trying to jump out at us."

"Viper One. We don't have a shot. Target's too close to Search Baker. There are survivors in the aircraft. I repeat, I have a visual of survivors in the aircraft."

Heston heard running feet behind him. When he turned, Chief Medrano and his officer were gone. At that moment, he remembered that the fellow officer was his chopper pilot.

He rushed out of the tent. "Chief! Do not interfere. We have more choppers on route…"

The police Interceptor spun back and raced inland. Straight for the department's helipad.

****

For a moment, everything had gone black. It took a smack by the chopper pilot and the bitter taste of saltwater to snap Denise back into reality.

She opened her eyes and reached out. Lieutenant Wilson was cutting through her straps with his knife.

"You awake? How many fingers am I holding up?"

"Two."

"Right answer." He helped her out of the seat. That was when Denise realized that the chopper was resting on its portside. Standing on the bulkhead, she looked 'up' at the starboard side, where the copilot Ortmeier was propped on one of the seats. He pulled the door open, letting in a rush of water.

"Just a wave. Climb on up."

Wilson gave Denise a boost, then followed her up the seats. With her foot on the headrest, the marine biologist reached up to Ortmeier. Seated on the door, he hoisted her out of the fuselage.

"Oh no!" Denise looked down. "My computers!"

"Can't do anything with them," Wilson said. He climbed out of the aircraft and looked to the surrounding ocean.

The dorsal fin was less than a hundred feet from the tail rotors.

"There's important data on there," Denise said.

"What kind of data?"

"I've been monitoring these sharks," she said. "There's information on which ones exhibit aggressive tendencies, migration patterns, analysis on the residue samples found on the *Omega Fury*."

"Can't do it, Doc. You'll have to live without it."

The Coast Guard chopper descended, its rescue diver harnessed and ready to jump down to them. Once again, they were forced to ascend. The megalodon bit at the air, as though guarding its prize from greedy scavengers.

"We can't get close to you, Search Baker. We're pulling back. Your Navy friends are gonna have to lure the fish away."

The Coast Guard chopper moved away to make space for the three Seahawks.

"This is Viper One. Might wanna duck back into the chopper, guys."

Machine guns swiveled, pointing their muzzles at the water.

The megalodon turned and raced west, passing the last remaining fishing boat.

"What the?" Ortmeier watched the shark dart several hundred yards into the distance. "Is it…"

"Retreating?" Wilson said.

"Well, that was surprisingly easy," Viper One said. *"Tell the Doc that these fish might be smarter than we give them credit for. Clearly, it didn't want to be in front of our M134."*

Denise shook her head. "That's not possible. This thing wouldn't retreat, unless…"

Wilson looked at her. "Unless what?"

"Unless it sensed a larger predator in its vicinity."

****

Arthur's ears were ringing. The world around him had plunged into chaos. One moment, the *Great Dane* was there, the next, *boom!* Reduced to pieces which were still hurtling high in the sky like volcanic debris. Black smoke rose from the blast area, as though an underwater volcano had erupted.

Next thing he knew, helicopters were dropping out of the sky.

Down below, Paul was on his knees. Blood was trickling from his left ear. "Captain… ARTHUR!"

Hans helped his friend up and articulated what he couldn't. "We're getting out of here, Arthur. We wanted to avenge Helen's death. We loved her too, man. But this is too much. Now Caleb and Matt are dead."

"We discussed the risks," Arthur said.

"We did, but there was a confidence of success," Hans said. "Turn back, or I'll take the wheel and do it myself."

Arthur watched the megalodon splashing near the downed Navy chopper. All of a sudden, it turned west and swam off. His eyes went back and forth between Helen's photo and the dorsal fin. He couldn't let it get away. To hell with the consequences and the risks. A father's loyalty to his child was far greater than his friends.

He pushed the throttle to its max and chased the beast.

"No, you stupid idiot!" Hans said.

"Get the dynamite ready."

"No way."

"I need to kill one. Just ONE! I can't live knowing this was all for nothing," Arthur said.

Hans peeked around the structure and watched the fish. It was arching its body, turning back.

Like mosquitos, two of the Navy Seahawks hovered above it. Machine gun fire peppered the ocean.

The fishermen could not tell if the weapons were inflicting injury, but it was enough to make the shark turn around.

"Fine!" Hans shouted. He and Paul pulled stacks of dynamite from their barrel. Neither of them were enthusiastic about this, but if they could kill this shark in the next five minutes, it'd spare them from starting a mutiny.

Paul lifted his stack and cut the fuse. He froze, his eyes locked on the water to the starboard side.

"Um, guys?"

"What?" Hans said.

"Is the shark still up ahead?"

"Yes." Arthur looked back at him. "Why?"

"There's something over there, under the water," Paul said, pointing north.

"Wait... there's something on the portside. Like an eel or something."

Like massive earthworms, the new arrivals raised their heads from the ocean. Arthur looked at the two 'creatures', his heart feeling as though it were trying to escape through his throat. Like his crewmates, it didn't want to be here either.

He knew what these things were. The suckers, the three-foot hooks protruding from each one, the cobra-like heads. Tentacles.

The Kraken was here...

He looked at the fish finder. The entire screen was blazing green. It was underneath them.

More tentacles towered above the boat. Like the fingers of an enormous fist, they closed over the *Pelican*.

The three fishermen screamed in unison before their bodies were imploded along with the vessel.

****

"Can't this thing go any faster?" Nico said. He hooked his harness to the fast rope, which the Coast Guard had graciously installed after the *Omega Fury* sinking.

"I'm pushing it to the max," Renny said. "Trust me, at one-eighty, it'll only take a couple minutes to cross four miles."

"Hey, Blue Tin! What the hell's going on? I saw the chopper dart off. What's this business in flying away without me?"

"Oh Carley," Renny said, shaking his head. "Sorry, woman. This is a boys only club today."

"Oh, the nerve. Your wife is totally gonna get an earful, Renny!"

"Nothing I'm not used to. Like I said earlier, I have the house to myself. By the time I see her again, anything you say will have blown over."

"Oh, is that right?"

"Damn straight! Like I said, considering all the lives I've saved recently, there's nothing she'll be mad about that'll override her joy of reuniting with her hero!"

"Let's put that to the test, mister."

"Fine."

"Good, because your ownership of twenty Victoria's Secret catalogues is about to become public, my friend."

"Oh… you know about those."

"Don't forget, I'm often the one in charge of the department's mail."

"Hey, can we switch to the Coast Guard frequency and deal with your guys' nonsense later?" Nico said. "You forget that Denise is in the water right now with a giant SHARK?!"

"Right. Uh, Carley, I gotta go. And, uh… for your information, I only get those catalogues for the articles."

"Right. Sure."

Renny turned the knob to sixteen. Immediately, a flurry of traffic assaulted his ears. "Holy crap! I think it's safe to say we missed something in the last couple of minutes."

"Can you make out what's going on?"

"Something about a bogey and that the last fishing boat is down. Give me a sec, I'll get caught up."

The two men listened to the transmissions.

Nico cleared his throat. "So, you're using the department mailbox to collect *Victoria's Secret* catalogues?"

"I thought there were more important matters at hand?"

"Just curious."

"Isn't the love of your life at risk?"

"We're on our way to the rescue," Nico said. "In the meantime…"

"As I told Carley, I only get them for the articles. And I didn't make any subscription. They just sent them to me."

"Oh." Nico cracked a grin. "I see."

"Hey, look at that!" Renny pointed straight ahead. "I see the cutter. We're here."

Nico watched the hot zone come into view. Towers of smoke twisted and expanded as they elevated, resembling black tornadoes against the blue ocean. The second Coast Guard chopper had moved to its companion.

"Chopper One-One-Eight, can you give me an update?" Nico said.

"One-One-Seven's crew has reported multiple injuries, including a man unconscious. Sorry, Chief. Must prioritize them first."

"I copy. Any other choppers in the area?"

"Got three coming in from Mayfield, plus two more cutters. Should be here in a few minutes."

"They don't have a few minutes. We'll take Search Baker."

"Viper One to Sea Rock. Bogies are moving fast. Closing proximity. They're going for each other."

"Bogies? Another shark?" Renny said.

In the next ten seconds, they passed over an additional several hundred feet of water. As they neared the downed Sikorsky, the thrashing tentacles came into view. All eight of them.

In the middle of the writhing mass was a rounded body that made Nico think of a grass spider. The two black eyes bulged from the creature's face, furthering its arachnoid appearance.

"Oh, shit. That's no meg."

****

The seventy-footer turned south. Despite the assault on its senses, its lateral line ciphered the motions created by the arch-nemesis of its species. The tentacled creature was a mature and experienced one. Its body mass alone matched its own. With the tentacles, it was a true giant that dwarfed anything it came across.

Its jet propulsion method of travel surpassed the meg's speed, so outrunning it meant certain death without obstacles to distract it. It didn't have the underwater mountain ranges of its original habitat or the natural darkness the lack of sunlight provided. The cephalopod was large and fast, but clumsy during a prolonged chase. Here, though, there was nothing but shallow water.

Diving was out of the question, for there was less than two-hundred feet of depth in this region. It only got worse the further west it went, so retreat was impossible.

It could see the Kraken moving parallel on its left side. The shark was already worn down by its encounter with the mechanical opponents. It had led these creatures on chases, and pursued smaller members of its species for its own nourishment, for miles at a time. Right now, the meg did not have miles to its advantage.

Only one option remained: attack.

The megalodon parted its jaws and moved in. The Kraken had tucked its arms in and inflated its mantle, using the buoyancy to keep it afloat. There, it waited for the fish to advance.

There was no strategy other than move in and inflict a fatal blow. The rounded mantle made for an easy target.

Its eyelids slid over its eyes, the caudal fin thrashing with maximum intensity. A seventy-foot bullet, it zipped along the surface. The jaws extended. One big mouthful of flesh could end the fight.

A rush of water slowed its advance. The invisible force brought to mind the raging currents that followed the impact by the rock that drove it from its habitat. Except this was concentrated, a tunnel of water that met the megalodon head-on.

Its jaws closed over nothing. The fish opened its eyes and saw nothing but air bubbles and slimy residue where its enemy had been. Beyond this grimy underwater mist was a trail of the same residue. The trail arched to the left, like the tail of a comet orbiting the earth. The shark had been baited by the mantle and fell right for the Kraken's trap.

Signals from its lateral line alerted the confused shark of an advancing mass coming in from the left. By then, it was too late.

The mantle was concealed behind an umbrella of tentacles. In the middle was a massive beak, protruding a pink tongue. That twenty-foot eel of flesh was lined with teeth as sharp and coiled as the hooks on its arms.

Immense arms coiled over its body. All range of motion suddenly ceased. The weight of its attacker was now on its back, the arms wrapped under its body like a brace.

The two predators rolled along the surface, the fish shaking its head and snapping its jaws. Internal pressure built up as the Kraken hugged it tighter. Its cartilage skeleton compressed its internal organs. The hooks protruded from the suckers like nails from a cat claw. All at once, fifty of them dug into the megalodon's sides and belly, drawing blood.

Then came a piercing pain from above, this one far more intense. Like scissors, the beak sheared the dorsal fin from its back, then continued to slice along its head.

****

"My God! You see that?" Ortmeier said, pointing at the mountain of water rolling to the east. Behind the twisting waves was two bodies, grey and red in color, locked in combat.

The way they moved had the appearance that they were one body. Denise's marine biology education kicked in. The shark was not rolling like a crocodile voluntarily. The cephalopod had it locked in its grip. Considering its advantage in size, strength, and leverage, the fight was quickly coming to a close. The megalodon was not long for this world.

"Pay attention," Wilson said. When the downdraft swept over them, Denise finally noticed the helicopter. This was not a military unit, but a black and blue department vehicle. On the side read *Cielo Nublado Police Department*.

"Nico."

The fuselage door opened.

"Hold it steady!" Nico shouted to his pilot.

"Nah, I thought I'd swing it back and forth," Renny replied.

Nico descended on the fast rope, landing on the Sikorsky. "Pizza delivery service! You guys ordered the pineapple, correct?"

"Ha!" Denise threw her arms around him. "More like anchovies, today."

"You like anchovies?"

"Well..." She shrugged.

Nico handed the stepladder to Wilson. "Get your asses on the bird. Hurry it up." Wilson eagerly climbed aboard, his co-pilot right behind him. The Chief looked at the battle taking place behind them, then pushed Denise toward the ladder.

"Let's go. We'll discuss your weird pizza tastes on the ride back." As soon as she was up, he grabbed the ladder bar and followed. "Alright, Renny. Lift off gently."

The predators lurched, the octopus creature's body resembling a giant blimp. Two black eyes stared at the people dangling from the black helicopter.

"Don't need to tell me twice."

Renny ascended gradually. Nico and Denise entered the chopper, slammed the fuselage door shut, then watched the bloodshed ensue.

Red froth expanded from the chaos. The Kraken rolled over, exposing the megalodon's underbelly. The caudal fin curved to one side and spasmed. More blood filled the ocean.

As quickly as it began, all motion stopped. The tentacles released their grip on the upper body, except for a couple which had it by the tail.

"Oh, Christ," Denise muttered. The shark's head had been reduced to ribbons of flesh which dangled like tendrils from a limp grey body. It disappeared under the waves with the Kraken.

The Navy Seahawks closed in.

"Viper One to all units. All personnel are out of the water. Open fire. Turn the bastard to calamari."

A series of explosive flashes tore into the ocean as a dozen hellfire missiles launched from their pods.

"What is that?" Renny said. The ocean darkened. At first glance, Nico believed it to be blood.

"Does that thing bleed purple?"

"No," Denise said. "It dispersed ink."

Nico brushed his sleeve over his wet brow. In just a few seconds, that ink cloud covered a one-thousand foot radius.

"Sonar contact. Target moving east." A moment of silence. *"It's gone. We lost it."*

Nico took a seat, completely spent. "Renny, take us back."

The pilot didn't bother with any quips. He turned the chopper southeast and sped for home, all the while trying to shake the image of that freakish beast from his mind.

"What the hell is that thing?"

CHAPTER 6

"It is a distant relative of the giant Pacific octopus. A very distant relative." Denise clicked the button on her remote to move the slide. The projector flashed the image of the modern day cephalopod against the wall of the police briefing room.

Seated around the table was Admiral Heston, Coast Guard Rear Admiral Jon White, Lieutenant Commander Gordon Hobert of the *USCGC Sea Rock*, Lieutenant Commander Jim Davidson of the *USCGC Richard Denning*, and Lieutenant Commander Bradley Pine of the *USCGC Red Nova*, among others. There were two Florida senators, a congressman, a half-dozen other people in suits, the Monroe County Sheriff, and Nico. Some chose to stand at the opposite wall, either to exhibit a sense of importance, or simply from feeling too uncomfortable to sit.

The briefing began with footage of the recent incident and the attack on the *Omega Fury*. Many of the viewers were left in a state of shock. They were used to rival nations and terrorist groups. It was easy to grasp man being capable of such bloodshed. But deep sea organisms, whom they didn't believe existed three days prior? It was too much to take.

"Doctor, is there any scientific record of this thing?" the Admiral asked.

"Only their claws. They've been occasionally found over the last fifty years along the coastlines. I believe they wash up the same way as megalodon teeth do." Denise scrolled through a few slides until she found a grainy photo from the 1980s. "This was taken on a beach in Maine. This hook has the same calcium structure as present day squids, adjusted for size of course. As you can see, the specimen in this photograph is roughly eighteen inches long."

"There's never been any sightings, though? Something that big, it's hard to imagine nobody's ever seen one."

"You'd think people would have seen these sharks, but they haven't until that meteor strike and the geographical consequences that came with it. Namely, the earthquakes in the Puerto Rico Trench, which are widely believed to have been triggered by it," Denise said. She read the room, half-anticipating a question about the major earthquakes which took place shortly after the meteor landing. Before the arrival of species thought to be extinct, the science community was baffled by sightings of deep sea organisms retreating to the surface from the trench. Most of these creatures were smaller in scale and non-violent, hence they hadn't made the headlines.

"You think there were creatures which emerged from the trench as well?" Heston asked.

"Not sure," Denise said. *Fascinating. He knows about the earthquakes. An education man. Makes sense.* "Fact of the matter is the ocean's a deep and mysterious place. After all the deep-sea exploration conducted over the years, we thought we had an idea of its secrets. Once in a while, nature throws us a curve ball."

"And who's to say there hasn't been sightings?" Nico said. "Let's not pretend we've forgotten all the tales from old merchant ships. The classic sketches of a big squid attacking a boat."

Denise, having anticipated this point, brought to view a slide of the famous Pierre Denys de Montfort drawing of a giant octopus attacking a ship.

"It's possible that we might have encountered these creatures before. Of course, we're talking about the pre-satellite and internet days. Back then, all we had to rely on were the eye-witness testimonies of sailors. And well, people simply chalked it up to wild imagination."

One of the Senators straightened his tie. "So, what are we doing about this? The public's getting nervous. The state authorities are running patrols all along the shoreline. The White House is getting nervous, and the rest of the world leaders are using this as propaganda to imply that the U.S. cannot handle its waters."

"My cutters are expanding their search," Rear Admiral White said. "Navy's got Destroyers along the eastern edge of the Strait, going all the way up to the Mid-Atlantic Trench. Submarines have reported movement twenty-miles north of the Bahamas, but nothing that matches the movements of this Kraken. The *Red Nova*, *Richard Denning*, and *Sea Rock* have expanded their search to a thirty mile radius. The only movements we've identified are from megalodons and local… 'normal' wildlife. Bottom line, I'm starting to suspect the Kraken has moved out of the area."

"We thought that after the sinking of the cutter," Nico said. "We might want to consider that this thing is as smart as we are."

White turned to look at him. "Beg your pardon, but this is a military operation. Mind if I ask why a local police chief is in on this briefing?"

"This is *my* briefing room, hotshot," Nico said.

"Gentlemen, let's not waste time with this nonsense," Admiral Heston said. He looked around the room. "Here's a question: is there anyone in this room that has killed one of these giant creatures? Shark or otherwise?" Only Nico raised a hand. "Case and point. He stays. Plus, his wife here is one of the most knowledgeable people on this matter. Frankly, we could use all the help we can get."

The sheriff scratched his head. "Isn't it *ex*-wife?"

"That's a little complicated," Nico muttered.

"Back on topic," White said. "I still believe the Kraken has left the area. There's nothing to indicate that it's still here. No heat signatures, no sonar readings."

"It could be resting on the seafloor," Denise said. "As for the heat signatures, I believe this creature is cold blooded. Its body temperature will match its surroundings. You won't find it that way."

"Even so, there's been no physical sightings. The Navy has deployed over two dozen unmanned underwater drones throughout the area," White said. "Even in an area as large as this, we should have spotted the thing by now."

"You're not dealing with a mindless killing machine," Denise said. "This thing is an intelligent killing machine with many different tricks up its sleeve. One of which is camouflage. Your drones have probably passed over it a dozen times and never knew it. That thing looks like a part of the ocean floor. You'll never find it by sight."

"Why would it be hiding?" the second senator asked.

"Two reasons. One, it's feeding on the megalodon that it killed. Second, it's probably avoiding your ships, choppers, and drones."

The senator chuckled. "No disrespect, Doctor. I can understand it avoiding the cutters, but certainly this thing doesn't understand that the drones are part of the search operation."

"What makes you say that?" Denise said.

"Well... it's an animal."

"A very intelligent animal. Intelligent, incredibly strong, and as we saw today, really damn fast. It's capable of using jet propulsion to travel hundreds of yards in the blink of an eye. All it needs to do is pause for a moment, fill its mantle with enough water to fill a baseball stadium, then it's off for another several hundred yards. That's only if it chooses to flee. God help you should the creature choose to attack. Cephalopods are capable of lifting over forty times their body weight. Their tentacles are pure muscle. It crushed your cutter like it was a soda can. It's worse now, because it *knows* it can do it."

"So... you believe this creature is currently... strategizing?" Heston said.

"You fail to understand that cephalopods are among the most intelligent creatures on the planet. Research has shown that octopuses are capable of complex tasks. There was one experiment in which a small octopus was sealed inside a closed jar. The thing had been raised in captivity and had only seen the inside of an aquarium. In less than two minutes, it figured out how to unscrew the top and free itself."

"That is impressive, ma'am, but it's a long way between opening jars and understanding brand new technology," the senator said.

"It's in a strange new world," Denise said. "This thing has risen from a much darker place and is seeing all of this for the first time. Believe me, it's studying this place. It's watching your ships. It probably witnessed the *Omega Fury* kill the second megalodon and saw it as a rival predator. Next thing it knows, all sorts of other mechanical oddities are in the area, hunting for it."

"Is that why it was initially here? You believe it was tracking the megalodons?" Admiral Heston asked.

Denise nodded. "It was probably tracking them after the meteor crash. Then the chaos with the eighty-footer created distant vibrations that drew the others into the area. Sharks are drawn by distress motions and erratic heartbeats."

"Even from one of their own?"

"Like they care," Denise chuckled. "Being as large as they are, the megalodons need to eat whatever they can to sustain their mass. That includes each other if necessary."

"So, they are not acting in unison?" asked Lieutenant Commander Pine of the *Red Nova*.

"No. They're just like regular sharks, traveling on their own, the only exception being the triplets," Denise said.

"That brings to question," Admiral Heston said. "We've got numerous megalodons traveling along the east coast. How many of these giant octopuses might there be?"

"That's a good point," White said. "What if there's more than one? That would explain the infrequent sightings better than it simply hiding."

"I'm inclined to believe it's just the one," Denise said. "Considering its size, and comparing its hooks to the fossils we've acquired over the years, I estimate it's a mature adult. Most probably only reach two-thirds of its size. It might even be hundreds of years old."

"I'd go as far as to say the meg and the Kraken are ancient rivals," Nico said.

"That's highly possible," Denise said. "Brute strength vs. intelligence. They've probably been going at it for millions of years."

"Millions of years of evolution doesn't make these creatures impervious to modern day weaponry," White said. "These monsters have directly caused hundreds of deaths, including eight guardsmen. Now add two injuries from my chopper crew earlier today. It's only going to get worse. I'd advise we conduct an operation to draw these things out and kill them."

"We have trackers on several megalodons," Lt. Commander Davidson said. "Should be a simple matter to draw them to the surface with bait and blast the hell out of them."

"Whoa, hold on!" Denise said.

"You have an objection?" White said.

"I do. I agree, the eighty-footer had to be killed. I was right there in the middle of the bloodbath. Believe me, I don't want to see anyone else killed. I also agree on the Kraken. As spectacular of a creature as it is—a miracle of nature, in fact—I acknowledge that it is a rampant killing machine that must be stopped. That said, I don't think it's necessary to kill the other megalodons."

"And what would you propose we do with them? Build a giant aquarium?" the Sheriff said. "Doc, I'm in charge of the safety for everyone along the Keys, and they're extremely uncomfortable knowing that these predators are only a dozen miles from their shores."

"There's zero chance of an attack," Denise said. "The Keys are way too shallow. The sharks would be scraping the bottom before they reached the shore. The Kraken, on the other hand, is the one they should be concerned about. If it's anything like regular species of octopus, it can come on land."

"We have one cephalopod and maybe eight tagged megalodons," Davidson said. "Not to mention all the ones unaccounted for. We should assume they are the greater threat."

"It's a proven fact they go after boats," the congressman said.

"The eighty-footer did," Denise said. "In case I didn't say it loud enough before, I don't think all of these megalodons are aggressive. Let's not pretend THIS didn't happen." Tensing, Denise tapped a few keys on her computer until she brought up recent drone footage of the triplets. The three sharks traveled in their standard formation, with Dash at the lead. Coast Guard choppers circled above them, ready to intercept, for a civilian sailing yacht was in their path.

"Watch." She pointed at the screen. The sharks circled the yacht, studying it. After several passes, the creatures moved on, disinterested. "They probably thought it was a whale at first, or something similar to whatever they fed on in the past. Bottom line, they left it alone."

"That time," the sheriff said.

"Who knows? They probably weren't hungry at the moment," White said.

"Considering their metabolism, I'm inclined to disagree," Denise said. "Listen, we can bait them. Keep them in this area until we can figure out a method and a destination to relocate them."

One of the senators stepped forward. "Doctor, you were hired by the government as a consultant. Not to fulfill your own agenda with military resources."

"How is it fulfilling an agenda to state that this is wrong?" Denise said. "These creatures are new to this part of the world. Yes, some are dangerous, but as I've proven with this video, I don't think all of them are."

"Tell that to the people near Palm Beach," White said.

"Palm Beach? What happened at Palm Beach?" Denise said.

Nico stepped forward. Being a cop, and someone who was closer to Denise, he knew how to express the concerns more delicately.

"There was a sighting in that location this morning. A megalodon moved into the shallow waters and attacked a populated area."

Denise stood silent. What could one say when her whole narrative had been shattered? She could read the room. Nico's two sentences had more impact on the military leaders and politicians than her entire briefing.

"This is the first I'm hearing of this," the sheriff said. "How many fatalities?"

"On the beach? None, thankfully," Nico said. "According to reports, the shark turned around and moved out to sea. However, we have confirmed—"

"So what's the alarm?" Denise said. "You just admitted that the megalodon didn't kill anybody."

Nico paused until the interruption cleared, "…confirmed that the shark is directly responsible for the destruction of four small vessels in the area. Two small sailboats, a cruiser, and dinghy. We're still waiting on the details, but the death toll is looking like a minimum of ten."

"That far north?" White said. "Do we have any tracking on that fish?"

"The Navy has a man on the job," Heston said. He leaned back in his seat, deep in thought. While Rear Admiral White was responsible for the Coast Guard function, the overall command of the operation was in his care. "For the short term, we're going to keep the megalodons confined to this area. The priority is the Kraken. The megalodons are dangerous and I'll consider whether or not to destroy them, but for now, we open fire only when necessary. The Kraken is a massive threat and must be eliminated. Admiral White, alert all cutters in the area to open fire on sight once they have a confirmed sighting of the beast. I'll alert my carrier and destroyers. Chopper units will continue their search. God only knows what other deep sea giants have been awakened by that damn meteor. Chief, how are evacuations?"

"Almost complete, Admiral. My officers will have to track down a few stragglers."

"Do it, please."

"Bear in mind, sir, there are people who have to stay. The power grid doesn't operate itself."

"I understand, but everyone else has to relocate by tonight. As the Professor said, that octopus can come on land. I'd hate for it to come ashore with a civilian population. Go door-to-door if you have to, but see to it that everyone is aboard a Navy chopper. Then you and your people can move out."

"I'll get right on it. And, if possible, I would like to remain and possibly provide air support if you'll allow it."

The Admiral thought about it. "We have several choppers available, Chief. We appreciate the assistance you've provided thus far, but do remember this is a military operation. I can't be responsible for putting non naval or Coast Guard personnel in harm's way."

"You still need Dr. Reta to study the sharks, correct? And you'd like another pair of eyes in the sky to search for the Kraken?"

"True."

"I can provide her air transportation and let your boys focus on the hunting and gunning."

After a few additional moments of consideration, the Admiral nodded. "Okay, Chief. You have a deal. Now, if you'll excuse me, I need to get back to the command station and speak with the President."

All members stood up and filed out the exit.

Denise stood in stunned silence. It was as much of a surprise to her as anyone else that Admiral Heston backed her on the preservation of the sharks, even if it was warily.

A minute later, only Nico and Denise remained in the room.

She smiled at him. "Don't think I don't know the real reason you want to stay."

He winked. "Is it that obvious I wanna have the local bar all to myself?"

"Right. You're a cop. You wouldn't sneak a bottle of bourbon."

"If only you knew the perks of being chief here, Doc. At least eight business owners have given me the key to their shops." He glanced at the still image of a giant octopus on the projector. "You think that thing really is capable of coming on land?"

"I do. It's a creature of the deep. Up until recently, it didn't even know a world above the ocean existed. All it needs to do is learn that it can."

"In that case, I better get back to work. There are a few stubborn people refusing to leave." He went for the door. "Will I see you later?"

"I'd like that," she said. "Hopefully I won't have to work too late."

CHAPTER 7

Eight-thirty P.M.

Stationed in the local high school, Denise watched various monitors. On the right were blood-pressure and heart rate readings. Beside each one was the name and length of the megalodon assigned to that tag.

To this moment, she was grateful for her university for flying the tags in on their own dime, and for their help in convincing the Coast Guard and Navy in tagging the creatures.

From Cielo Nublado, Denise could monitor their stress levels, body temperatures, heart rates, determine whether they were hunting prey or aggressively in combat. Technology had come a long way from simple tracking tags which only displayed the specimen's location. Just from a couple of days looking at these monitors, Denise learned more about these creatures than her predecessors did physically tracking specimens in the field. She learned which ones were ill, which ones were healthy, average speeds, feeding patterns, and so much more.

According to the irregular heart patterns and poor blood pressure, the sixty-three foot specimen, whom she named Albert, was battling some sort of illness. The fish did appear underweight during her flyovers, possibly due to an inability to catch sufficient prey. She spotted two tears in his caudal fin and what appeared to be small lacerations on its upper tail. Her guess was that it had an encounter with the Kraken or another meg and narrowly escaped. The downside was that his range of motion was limited. It was a miracle the Kraken hadn't located the shark yet. One way or another, Albert wasn't long for this world unless he got sustenance.

Denise jotted notes into her tablet, then began looking up fisheries.

"Let's see… What would it cost to get some food?"

The door opened behind her. "With a charming guy like me? Free!"

Denise smiled and looked at her ex-husband. In his hand were two pizza boxes. The odor of sauce, pepperoni, and freshly melted cheese filled the room.

"Wow, when you said pizza delivery service earlier, I didn't realize you were serious."

"I stand by my word," he said. "Unlike you! You'd rather spend more time with these oversized guppies than me!"

Denise looked at the clock. "Damn. Sorry. I guess time got away from me."

"Nah, I'm just giving you a hard time. Fact is, time almost got away from me as well. Spent all day going house-to-house and finishing up with the evacuation. Can't say it made me feel good. Felt like a damn stormtrooper."

"Renny staying?"

"On condition that the government give him a significant raise. The kid probably never thought his helicopter pilot's license would pay off so well." Nico cleared a table with his free hand and placed the pizzas down. "Hope you worked up an appetite."

"Where did you get those pizzas? If everyone's gone, then there's nobody to make it at the shop."

"Ha! Clearly, you thought I was kidding when I said a bunch of the shop owners trusted me with keys to their stores," he said.

"You helped yourself to their pizzas?!"

"And their kitchen!" He waited a moment in hopes that her probing stare would go away. "Oh, relax. I left him a note and a couple twenties in his office."

Denise chuckled. "Good. I'm no looter." She pulled a chair up to the table and opened one of the boxes. "Jesus! Went a little nuts on the sauce, did ya?"

"Better than not enough. No anchovies, though."

"They're just salty fish," Denise said. Nico shook his head and stuck his tongue out. "Fine. More for me." She pulled a slice free. "I will admit, you did a pretty good job. If I didn't know better, I'd say there was still a crew at this pizza joint."

"Not the first time I've done this. One time, I had a hankering for a midnight snack. Unfortunately, the shop closed at eleven, but nothing else sounded good at the time. So…"

"Let me guess. You went ahead and helped yourself to his kitchen without asking."

Nico shrugged. "I guess I have a hankering for not asking permission. When I want my way, I get it."

"Like staying here?"

"Someone's gotta keep an eye on you, Denise." He took a bite of his slice, then quickly leaned forward to keep from spilling his extra sauce. "Okay, it might be possible that I went a little overboard."

"We'll survive."

"I hope so." He wiped his face clean, then looked at the red smear on his napkin. "Frankly, I'm surprised we have the stomach to eat this, after everything we've seen lately."

Denise shook the memory of a beachful of body parts from her mind. "It'll get better soon."

"Not sure about the 'soon' part. More sharks. A giant octopus-thing. It's a miracle we've kept them contained so far."

"We'll figure something out."

"I hope so. The Navy can only bait these things for so long. Giant sharks require a hell of a diet. Sooner or later, they'll branch out in search of real food."

Denise quietly ate for a few moments, silently reflecting on her recent studies. "I'm optimistic about this, Nico. I'll come up with something."

Nico shrugged again, breaking eye contact. "If you don't, the Navy will."

"Heston agrees with me."

"For now."

"You think he's reluctant?"

"When I look at him, I see a man with a lot on the line. I know a gambler's face when I see one."

Denise wiped her face then leaned back, staring at Nico as a suspect would an interrogator. She didn't like what he was getting at, considering his feelings on preserving the sharks.

"And what is he gambling? His reputation?"

"That, and lives. If we've learned anything today, it's inevitable that those sharks are going to kill someone else." The next sound was that of him chewing. Denise's silence brought a feeling of regret. Nico was good at reading people, except sometimes her. Spouses had a way of being ambiguous sometimes. All throughout their marriage, Nico found it amazing that he could accurately analyze people he had only known for five minutes, but with Denise it was still hard to get a read. Maybe it was his emotional investment in her feelings. Right now, he was feeling protective of that investment, having just gotten her back in his life. "I'm not trying to start a fight."

"Yet, you're so good at it."

"Hey! I made you pizza!"

Her smile brought a sense of relief.

"That you did. Even if the cheese is swimming in sauce. You probably should've brought forks." She parted a second slice, stopping briefly after hearing a fluctuation in one of her monitors.

"Something wrong?" Nico asked.

"Just an elevated heart rate," she said. She waited a moment until it settled down. "It stopped. Pete probably found something to eat and went after it."

"Hopefully not something with arms and legs," Nico said.

"No, Nico, I can assure you that's not the case. Nobody's swimming around here, remember?"

"Could be going after a boat."

"The heart rate would still be up, considering the amount of effort the shark would need to apply." She put her slice down and pushed the plate away. "Nico, you really think I would prioritize these things over human life?"

"Of course not. I'm just worried you're blinded by discovery."

"I'm mesmerized a bit, sure. But not blind. I saw both sides of the equation. I was there, right by your side, when the megalodon attacked. I know it killed many of your officers. I saw the bloodbath on the beach. And I saw what the Kraken did today."

Nico nodded. "Good."

"I also saw the triplets the night you and Renny went out to assist with rescuing guardsmen from the *Omega Fury* sinking," she said.

Nico tapped a finger on the table while staring. Twice already, he had scolded her on the stupidity of stealing a police boat and taking it out on hostile waters. Her intentions were good; she was trying to help with the rescue efforts, rather than idly sit by.

"It's a miracle you weren't killed."

"You can say that all you want, but I know what I saw. I saw the triplets for the first time that night. Don't get me wrong, they practically gave me a heart attack at first. They circled the boat, curious about it, then moved on."

Nico toyed with his pizza slice, then turned his eyes to the monitors.

"Probably moved on to easier prey. Like the crew of that cutter."

"Give me a break, Nico. Those megs could have attacked me, but they didn't. They *chose* not to. And they went nowhere near the sinking. Same thing with the others. The point is, they are predators, but not all of them are monsters. Not unless we turn them into monsters."

Nico considered a counterargument to that fact. As far as he was concerned, the megalodons evaded the sinking because of the Kraken. Some of the bridge crew survivors even reported that the nearby megalodons had retreated when the Kraken arrived, meaning they were directly avoiding it.

The images of the megalodon jaw gaping at him, the sight of his police cruisers in pieces, the red water, the bodies on beaches, all haunted his memory. The safety of the public was his responsibility. He had failed too many people up until now. With the advanced weaponry in the military's arsenal, the problem could be taken care of in a day. If it weren't for Denise's efforts, it probably would be over already.

He swallowed the urge to make that point. They had already gone too long with this topic, which he wanted to avoid entirely during this dinner.

"What's on your mind?"

"Hmm?" He turned his eyes back to his ex-wife. She was studying him as if he were a specimen in her lab.

"I'm worried about you. You look stressed."

"Maybe a little. I'm worried about *you*. You've barely slept the last seventy-two hours. Hell, aren't you on a two-day stretch with no sleep?"

"I took a nap this morning."

"Oh. A nap! That sounds healthy."

Denise laughed. "Sorry. This is the biggest thing I've ever been a part of. Haven't you had anything to make you feel this important? You're a police chief, formerly a detective. Certainly, something had to make you feel so special that you wanted to devote all your time to it."

Nico leaned forward, cupped his hands on the table, and looked her in the eyes. "One thing."

A calm warmness swept over the tenseness from their debate. Denise shared a long, silent moment with him.

"I suppose I could use a little break from all of this," she said, tilting her head to the monitors. She stood up and started shutting them down for the night. She tapped a few keys on her tablet and smartphone, then packed them into her bag before looking back at Nico with a purposeful grin. "You have any suggestions where I can stay? I think the hotel's closed."

"I might know a place."

CHAPTER 8

Anderson Ernest
Eighteen miles southeast of Key Biscayne.
0523 hours.

"Yeah... uh-huh. Yeah, he just got here... Hey man, these are the risks you play if you want to test this thing. I'm aware of what happened... I'll do my best to keep it from happening again.... Right. I'll phone you at oh-nine-hundred. Out." Dr. Trevor Zennor ended the call and clipped his phone to his waistline, shooting a glance at his assistant, Mark Eurupe. "Guy asks me to play with fire and apparently is surprised when someone gets burned in the process."

"So he knows about the—" Mark positioned his hand into a slant, then slowly moved it down like a sinking ship.

"Yeah, they found it. After the sighting at Palm Beach, it was easy for the local authorities to connect the dots."

"Found what?"

Trevor looked to the captain of the *Salt Mine*, Besson Cross. By his tone and questioning stare, the contractor was not aware of the sinking of the Ferrisburg vessel, or the disappearance of the other sailing boats in the area. It took a little persuading from his employer to transfer the test subject to the *Anderson Ernest*. Even if he had not received word of O'Brien's recent attacks, he was more than aware of the recent chaos surrounding Cielo Nublado.

"Nothing. Just a quirk in the device. Nothing to worry about."

"The device?" Besson looked to the water in search of a dorsal fin. On dry land, the guy often tried giving the alpha male impression, projecting confidence and fearlessness. Now here he was, given a hint of danger, and he was already cracking like an egg. With that in mind, Trevor wished he'd thought up a better lie.

"It's fine, Besson. For the love of God, pull yourself together."

"Dude, if the device wasn't working, you think we'd still be out here?" Mark said.

Besson took that point into consideration, then nodded. "Fair enough." He took one more glance at the water. "Where is it, exactly?"

"A little over a mile northeast," Trevor said.

"Underwater speaker?"

"On and off. We don't want to overdo it. The fish needs to associate the signal with food. If it keeps getting drawn to the thing, but finds nothing, then it might start ignoring it."

"It can hear it from over a mile away?"

"Several miles away," Trevor said.

Besson resumed watching the water. "How do we know we're not attracting any other sharks?"

Trevor chuckled. "What makes you think we haven't?" Besson turned toward him, his hand gripping the helm of his boat. "Oh, relax. It's not here anymore."

"Where'd it go?"

"Scattered across the Atlantic floor," Trevor said. "O'Brien didn't like having a competitor in the area. Unfortunately for the second meg, O'Brien had over thirty feet of length and six-thousand pounds of weight to his advantage. It wasn't much of a fight."

Mark stepped to the side and stood on his toes to get a look at Besson's main deck. "I know I'm not running the show, but if we can get started sooner rather than later…"

"Sounds good. First, we need to install the miniature speaker to the harness and run a quick connection test before we conduct the experiment." Trevor snapped his fingers at Besson. "Hand over the package."

Besson climbed down to his main deck and joined his crewmate. They clipped a cable to the strap ring of a seven-foot stretcher, then elevated it.

Trevor and Mark gazed at the bottlenose dolphin. Its temperament was mild, the mammal offering no resistance to its handling. Having worked with humans all its adult life, it was used to such transfers. The only question was the task its human companions had assigned to it. So far, there was nothing around these boats but open ocean. However, it did recognize the recording device the crewmate brought to it.

Probably thinks it's going on a scouting mission. It's correct, in a sense.

"I'm told his name is Rico," Besson said.

Trevor smiled. "Good to meet your acquaintance, Rico."

Trevor looked at his assistant. The longer Mark watched the dolphin, the more he appeared to shrink. Guilt was eating away at him. Five years ago, he immigrated to the U.S. with the goal of pursuing marine research. He was ready for the physical and mental demands of pursuing a PhD. What he did not anticipate was the assault on his conscience.

"I warned you when you signed on with me," Trevor said.

"Yes sir. I know."

"You're not getting cold feet on me, are you?"

"No, but if I may speak freely, sir?"

"Won't change anything, but go ahead."

Eurupe scratched his neck while silently debating whether he should bother getting his concern off his chest.

"Don't you think this is wrong?"

Trevor shook his head. "Things like this are always done in the name of research. You ever hear the term 'lab rats'? Or animal testing in general? There are always sacrifices made for the greater good."

"But this isn't medicine," Mark said. "Nor is this really for the betterment of mankind."

"Some might disagree with you," Trevor said. "This technology will protect the North American coastlines. Prevent more tragedies."

Mark planted his elbow on the gunwale and sunk his chin onto his palm, watching his superior in his peripheral vision.

"I'm not an idiot, Doctor. I know that's not what this whole thing is about."

"Sounds an awful lot like cold feet to me, Mr. Eurupe," Trevor said. "If you prefer, I can call our sponsor and inform him that my assistant has opted out of this project. Granted, you will never see a doctorate, and the hundred grand of student debt you've accumulated will never be paid off. You'll be stuck working in zoos, instead of studying the migration patterns of sea turtles. That's your passion, correct? Sea turtles?"

Mark nodded.

"So?" Trevor picked up his phone. "Looks like I have a signal."

Mark stared at the water. He remembered moving to the U.S. as a ten year old. His family had to barter for passage on a private ship. His father did not own many possessions. For much of his life, he worked on fields and in government buildings, emptying wastebaskets and maintaining equipment, all for peanuts. They lived without electricity most weeks, with most of the money being saved for food and medicine. The most valuable possession, other than his wife and two children, was a crystal amulet of a sea turtle.

In Nigeria, the sea turtle was symbolic of wisdom and heroism, as well of creative trickery. Specifically, a trickster that will manipulate his way out of any bad situation. Mark considered the sea turtle as his father's spirit animal, for he was willing to do whatever it took to get his family to the land of opportunity. With the cash falling short, it was the sea turtle amulet that fulfilled the Eurupe end of the exchange.

Ever since, it was sea turtles that Mark wanted to study. It was a way of honoring his father and preserving the species whose spirit had helped his family through great hardship.

Killed for their meat, their skin, shells, and their eggs, and also facing habitat destruction, the sea turtle population had severely dwindled over the last forty years. Mark felt more than admiration toward these amazing creatures, he felt an obligation to them. It was their spirit that allowed his mother to receive treatment for her lymphoma, and for his younger brother to open a business and make a living, and for his father to save for retirement. During the excruciating process of obtaining American citizenship, the Eurupe family reminded themselves about the spirit of the sea turtle.

Mark watched the dolphin. As opposed to the turtle, its species was prosperous, their numbers blossoming. Nowhere near endangerment. Mark was still not comfortable with the action that he was taking part in, but maybe the greater goal was worth it.

The spirit of the sea turtle was, after all, a tricker's spirit.

I know that includes manipulation. Does that include sacrifice? Would they look down on me for this?

He shrugged.

They're just animals. Fascinating animals, but at the end of the day, just animals.

"Forget I said anything," he said.

"Good." Trevor tucked his phone away. "Alright, Besson. Let me get the equipment over to you."

"Okay. Are you going to give me an opportunity to get far away from here before you start your tests?"

Trevor shook his head. "To be frank, for the next couple hours, the safest place you can be is right here with us. I'd like a controlled environment for this project. Two hours should do the trick."

"Fine. Better not take any longer."

CHAPTER 9

It wasn't the sound of an alarm which shocked Nico from a deep and pleasant sleep, but the frantic way in which Denise jumped out of bed.

"Whoa!" He sat up and checked his phone. Five-fifty-one a.m. "So much for sleeping in." His hopes for the morning would be to sleep in, gradually wake up, enjoy a fresh cup of coffee, and reflect on the pleasant 'interchange' with Denise which lasted much of the night. Instead, he was watching her digging through her bag, buck naked. She pulled out her tablet and switched it on.

"Oh, shit."

She placed it on the nightstand and started throwing her clothes on.

"What's the matter? Leave the stove on?" Nico said, chuckling. Denise did not pick up on the humor. He leaned over and peeked at her device. On the screen was the squiggly line representing an elevated heart rate and stress levels. He looked up at her. "You've got these readings on your freaking tablet?"

"It allows me to monitor them one at a time. Much more difficult than working in an office with multiple screens, though. So I programmed it to alarm me if any of the megalodons experience distress."

"What, are you like their counselor or something?"

Denise did her best to fix her hair quickly, then collected her phone and other belongings.

"For a reading like that to occur, it means they're experiencing some kind of major discomfort. The kind that a rival predator would bring."

"Or a Navy chopper?" Nico said.

"Precisely." Denise threw her bag over her shoulder and went to the door.

Nico chuckled. "You planning on running to the command center?"

"Nope. You're gonna drive me."

"Oh, am I?!"

"Yep."

"Right. I'm sure the Admiral is eager to be woken up by a passionate scientist intent on telling him how to run his operation. Just let it go."

"Nico." She had her hands on her hips, a look he saw many times in their married life. Her stance and stare did all the talking.

"What if I say no? I'm not in the mood to be chewed out, you know?"

"Plenty of places for me to sleep tonight, mister."

He was ninety-nine percent sure she was bluffing. Unfortunately, that final one percent had the vocal strength of an opera house.

****

It was a few minutes past six when they arrived at the command center. Communication technicians were at their desks, relaying information to the Coast Guard and Navy ships patrolling along the Strait.

Four Seahawks patrolled to the east, while a Coast Guard tactical squadron consisting of three Sikorski MH-60 Jayhawks raced to the northwest. Half a mile north was the Coast Guard Cutter *Red Nova*.

Before Nico put the vehicle in park, Denise was already opening her door.

"Hang on. Let me do the talking, please. He's more likely to listen to me."

"The island's evacuated, Nico. Your authority left with the local population," Denise said. "Not to sound mean, but you've officially been moved to the science division. Meaning I outrank you now."

It was nothing Nico did not already know. Still, it stung to hear it said out loud. He looked at his jeans and black shirt.

"At least I don't have to wear the uniform." For good measure, he kept the badge on his belt for identification purposes. Without it, he would look like an unauthorized citizen.

Denise checked with the sailors guarding the tents. "Is the Admiral in?"

"Affirmative."

"Good." She flashed her government-issued badge and proceeded, waving for Nico to follow her.

He sighed and walked to the tent. *Hope you're not expecting me to provide moral support.*

Inside the command tent was Rear Admiral Jon White and Admiral Vince Heston. Both men were in conversation, their eyes fixed on an aerial transmission of the triplets.

"Excuse me, sirs," Denise said. They looked back at the biologist.

"Dr. Reta, if you need to get in touch, you know the line number," Admiral Heston said. His voice was gentle with a hint of sternness.

"Admiral, Dash's readings indicate a major spike in stress. It's no coincidence you guys are focused on them right now. What's going on with the triplets?"

"Ma'am, the sharks were moving too far northwest, toward Key Largo. So, I had my Seahawks drive them back with their M60s."

"You shot at them?"

"That's generally what you use M60s for." Heston was a patient man, but he was visibly not in the mood for having his orders questioned by a civilian. "Doctor, no serious harm was done to the sharks. I don't want to be remembered as the guy who destroyed the megalodons. That said, you need to let me run my operation the way I see fit."

"Admiral, with all due respect, we're only making the situation worse by firing on them," Denise said. "There are other ways to draw them back."

"We tried baiting them," Rear Admiral White said. "It drew them back momentarily, but then they continued northwest. I don't know if they're getting wise to our act, or if we're not supplying ample sustenance. I suspect the latter, considering their size and metabolism."

"If they're getting hungry, they'll go where there's food," Heston said. "Probably why they keep moving toward the coast."

"They're exploring," Denise said. "As I stated yesterday, sir, they likely won't go all the way to the Keys. It's too shallow."

"Technically, it is deep enough for them make it to shore. Barely, but possible. I'm not risking it," White said.

"Sir…"

"Denise!"

She looked over her shoulder at Nico. His keen stare said it all. *Don't push it, babe. You're not making the situation better. You're coming off as a crazed activist.*

She gave a subtle nod. Even after three years apart, he knew her like the back of his own hand.

"I apologize, Admiral. It's not my intention to interfere."

"No apology necessary, ma'am," Heston said. "Trust me, I see a value in these creature's existence as well. We're doing our best to track any others swimming on this side of the ocean. If we do, we'll tag them with the equipment you've provided."

"Thank you. But sir, if you're worried about them moving too far out, just give me a call. I'll bait them myself."

Heston shook his head. "That's a negative, Doctor. I'm not risking your safety a second time. It was a mistake yesterday to send your chopper to the boating situation. You almost got killed. I'm not risking a repeat."

"Sir, what happened yesterday couldn't be predicted. Those boats were loaded with explosives," Denise said.

"That's the problem. *None* of this can be predicted," Heston said.

"I won't use a military helicopter. Nico and his flight crew will assist me." She glanced at Nico. "Right?"

He nodded, unenthused.

"We can work on luring them."

"Negative, Doctor. Your role is observation and analysis, not interference. Leave that to our personnel," Heston said.

"Is there another way we can herd them?" White asked. "If we're not going to exterminate them, we need more methods of containment. Baiting won't work much longer."

"What about lights?" Nico said.

Denise shook her head. "We can try it, but I'm confident it won't work. We've observed that the Kraken is capable of bio-illumination flashes. Considering its original environment, those lights were used for luring prey, particularly smaller sharks. The big boys got wise to the act, hence their age."

Both men watched Denise, waiting for a new tactic. Her mind frantically searched for possibilities like a computer search engine. After several seconds, she understood it was best to leave. Heston was a fair man, but Denise violated one of the basic rules of professional conduct. She barged in on a meeting and essentially told these experienced commanders they were wrong. She was lucky not to have been thrown off the operation yet. Such a thing would be a disaster, for a replacement advisor could be a government person more interested in climbing the administrative ladder than scientific study. To climb that ladder, they could possibly advise that it was better to exterminate the megalodons, then claim that their 'scientific input' helped saved hundreds if not thousands of lives.

Denise wanted that more than anything, but not at the cost of broad extermination of a species that a month ago was not even aware of man's existence.

Right now, she needed to give the admirals their space, but not without offering them something with substance.

"I'm not sure yet on the sharks, but Rear Admiral White might be onto something with the lights. The Kraken might possibly be drawn to them. Cephalopods, the more common ones, are attracted to colors." She chuckled. "You can call this Operation Disco, because you might need a big underwater disco ball to produce the lights that might attract it."

Heston smiled at the statement. "We'll discuss it. Now, if you'll excuse us."

Denise and Nico stepped outside, leaving the men to resume their work.

"Well, I suppose that could have been worse," Nico said.

Denise was out of breath. The reality of the situation was starting to weigh on her. Resources were dwindling. The sharks were reacting less and less to the chum, forcing the Navy to resort to more drastic means of herding them. She needed to come up with something fast, before repeated machine gun strikes triggered aggression in the megalodons. As they learned with the first one, their aggression was unmatched.

"Damn, I need to think of something," she said.

"You need a chill pill," Nico said. "Or a drink."

"Too early," she said. She stood by the car and stared into the horizon. "Light's won't work. Chum is losing its touch. Sooner or later, they'll go deep again and branch out. Then the government will believe they have no choice but to kill them. Heston's holding out, but God knows how much longer he'll be able to continue."

"What about sound?"

"I don't know what they'll react to. I need something from their original habitat."

"They feed on whales, don't they?" Nico said. "Don't some whales dive deep for their prey? I'm sure the megs are familiar with whale calls."

Denise rubbed her chin, considering the idea. "It'd have to have amplified signals, not just a blind speaker. I'd need a device that could... son of a bitch! The Porpoise! Why haven't I thought of that before?"

Nico raised an eyebrow. "Dolphins? Not sure how they will help... unless you're thinking about feeding them to the sharks. That might do it."

"No!" She slapped his shoulder, triggering a laugh. "That's terrible, you freak! I'm not talking about the animal, I'm talking about a device I worked on with the University of Florida."

"You named a device after a dolphin?"

"It's a device capable of releasing amplified soundwaves, based on the calls of various sea mammals. We're able to augment the soundwaves in order to attract a species, or repel them—which is what I had in mind when I joined the project."

"It mimics echolocation?"

"Correct."

"What would you repel with echolocation?" Nico asked.

"Anything that species eats," Denise said. "What I had in mind specifically were great white sharks. My hopes were to move them away from populated coastlines and from fishing grounds."

"Did it work?"

"Our initial tests showed promise," she said. "Unfortunately, I didn't get to see it through completion. The meteor landed in June, and once the initial chaos was over, I was assigned to study the effects it had on sea life. You know the rest of that story."

"So, what's the idea? Use it to steer the megs toward the island?"

"Lure them, to be exact," she said. "What would scare off a great white might attract a megalodon. And maybe even a Kraken."

"The Navy will be pleased to hear this. Where is this thing at?"

"Should be at the University. You think Renny is willing to fly us to the mainland?"

"His only role now is to fly a chopper. I'll give him a call," Nico said. "What if this thing isn't there?"

"It should be, unless one of the other scientists on my team found some use for it."

CHAPTER 10

Anderson Ernest.

Rico the dolphin was in the water. The microphone was intact, the camera rolling.

"Connection is good," Mark said. He made the mistake of glancing at the dolphin. It was swimming around the boat, happy to be in the open ocean. He imagined the freedom it felt, much like his parents felt the day they legally immigrated to the U.S.

"Good. Let's get started." Trevor stood at the transom and held his finger up. The dolphin recognized the signal and looked at its new handler. "Good." He tossed it a fish, which it gladly accepted.

"I take it you've done this before?" Besson said.

"I've done training for the Navy," Trevor said.

"Dolphin training?"

"Yes. They use dolphins for various reasons, some of which are top secret. Now, if you please…" He looked at Mark. "Is the drone ready?"

Mark held up the four-rotor standard drone. Dangling from its center was a green softball. Following the professor's commands, he started the device and steered it toward the transom, positioning the green softball within arm's reach of Trevor.

The professor patted the ball, then held up a fish for Rico to see.

"Bring it down to him."

Mark hovered the drone a meter over the surface. The dolphin studied the green object dangling a foot over its head. Fluttering its tail, it lifted its head and battered the softball.

"Excellent!" Trevor tossed Rico the fish.

Besson chuckled. "At least we know that if your career fails, you can always make a living at SeaWorld."

Trevor ignored him. "Mark, take it five hundred feet out." Mark did so, keeping the ball twelve-inches over the water. The dolphin received Trevor's hand signal and followed the drone. Once at the location, it tapped the ball and raced back to retrieve its reward.

Trevor tossed the fish then knelt by the device.

"Fifteen hundred feet."

"You sure?"

"We don't have time to instruct this dolphin to travel a couple miles out. Besides, the goal is to attract the meg." Trevor turned a few knobs, amplifying the frequency.

Mark closed his fists, cursed himself for doing this, then followed through. He took the drone near the dolphin, waited for Trevor to give the hand signal, then took it further out.

Trevor activated the device. Soundwaves echoed from the speaker, traveling twice as far and as fast through the water than the air.

Both men's eyes went to the tracking monitor.

"It's working," Trevor said. "O'Brien changed direction. He's going toward the sound." He rubbed his hands together and smiled. "Give Rico a good run. Change course and go east. Let's see if O'Brien will keep pursuing."

"Once he sees where it's coming from, I don't think you'll have to worry about him not pursuing."

****

Rico followed the flying manmade object. The soundwaves emitting from its harness made it slow momentarily. It recognized them as whale calls, which were no threat, then resumed the chase. It did not question the purpose of this exercise, for it never questioned its trust of its human companion. Over the course of three years training with Trevor, it built comradery and trust. As far as Rico was concerned, there was no risk in any instruction provided by its trainer.

Whatever the reason was for whale calls to come from the speaker in its harness, Rico was not concerned. Trevor never once put it in harm's way.

This exercise was rather fun for the dolphin. It was simple and yet, it still tested its ability to focus. It was like a natural predator in the wild, chasing after fish for sustenance, only without the frustration of failure. Just tap the ball and go back for its next treat.

The flying thing changed course, now darting right. Rico followed, and as soon as it closed in, the thing moved left. Through the years, Rico learned persistence. There was clearly a motive for this. Regardless, Rico accepted the challenge because harder tasks brought greater rewards.

Fluttering its tail, it closed in on the drone. With a bounding leap, it cleared the air and tapped the ball.

Splash!

Success! Rico swam in a series of loops. It did not matter that its trainer was not in sight. Rico understood that, through technology, Trevor knew it had completed its task.

It was time to head back. The series of twists and turns had gotten Rico turned around. No problem. A few blasts of echolocation would solve the issue. The dolphin sent out a few pings.

The excitement evaporated and a rising fear took hold. Something large was moving in from the north. Normally, such a large organism turned out to be a whale, except whales did not increase speed while coming at it. Rico may have spent much of his time in secure Naval pools, but he knew the movements of a predator when he saw it.

A dark shape took form in the distance. It was only a silhouette, but Rico recognized the pointed snout and the vertical-shaped tail. A shark! It was impossibly big, dwarfing even the largest of whales Rico ever swam alongside. And it was coming his way. Comparatively, Rico was the equivalent to the fish Trevor rewarded him with.

A few heartbeats later, it was no longer a silhouette, but a grey fiend with white ghastly eyes. All doubt was gone; this thing was here to feed.

Rico turned and put all his energy into his fluke. He went west, going deep to hopefully blend in with the seabed.

It did not work. The shark was still closing in. Each swing of its caudal fin generated more thrust than ten waves of the dolphin's fluke. The fish was big, but it had the muscle to propel such mass with ease.

The fish neared, opening its jaws to swallow its prey whole.

Rico darted to the side and ascended. He broke the surface with a leap that dwarfed the last one. In midair, he spotted the boat. His master was at the transom, watching through a set of binoculars. Behind him was the partner, with a headset on, standing over a piece of technology.

He could not comprehend the equipment, but he knew the body language. They were watching. Spectating.

The soundwaves coming from its harness now made sense. They were whale calls, and even sperm whales would be prey for such a shark. They were blasting these soundwaves to *attract* the shark.

Sadness and fright formed a perfect storm in Rico's brain. What had he done to deserve this? His master, whom he worked with loyally for years, had sent him to die.

Despite all of this, the dolphin's sense of loyalty still prevailed.

After splashing down, Rico danced on the surface, chirping and waving his flippers. It was both a warning and a plea for help.

The shark emerged from underneath it. Its jaws clamped down on Rico, splitting him horizontally down the middle.

****

"Oh, DAMN!" Besson said. He was on the flybridge of his boat, hand on the ignition. "Dude, I thought you'd said it'd be further out."

Trevor removed his eyes from the binoculars and held up his hand at the contractor. "Relax! Don't make any unnecessary vibrations." The splash of O'Brien's head smacking the ocean made him return to the glasses. He watched the megalodon turn away, Rico's blood leaking from the gills. "It works. It zeroed in on the signal."

"Congratulations," Mark said.

Trevor gave thought to making a remark about his partner's low spirits.

Maybe later. Right now, I have more important things to take care of.

He kept his eyes on O'Brien. The tip of the dorsal fin was cruising along the surface, appearing as though it were that of a normal great white. The fish turned eastward, and after traveling a few hundred feet, suddenly turned forty-degrees to the right.

"What's it doing?" Besson said, watching through his own binoculars.

"It's circling us," the crewmate said. "Let's get out of here."

"Hold on. Don't turn on that boat," Trevor said. *Freaking high school dropouts.*

Mark was standing by his side, squinting as he traced O'Brien's motion with the naked eye. "What is he doing, exactly? Doesn't appear like he's circling."

"No, it doesn't," Trevor said. The shark gradually picked up speed, then suddenly stopped. Before it sank, he watched it turn right again until it was facing the boats."

Mark checked the monitor. "He's still a few hundred feet out."

"He's not interested in us," Trevor said. "O'Brien doesn't waste time. If he wanted to sink us, we'd be at the bottom of the ocean by now. Something else has his attention." He rushed to the flybridge and checked the sonar.

A large blip that was the megalodon occupied the northeast part of the screen.

From the south, another large blipped moved in.

Trevor looked to the sea. "Oh my God."

It was close to O'Brien's size, perhaps falling short by a few meters. The dorsal fin was thin, transparent, and running the length of its back. The other detail that stood out was the creature's shape and bodily motion. It was not like a shark, for sharks swung their tails side-to-side to move. This visitor wiggled its entire body like a snake.

"Holy sweet savior!" Besson cried out. "It's… it's a sea serpent!"

"An incredibly large species of eel, more specifically," Trevor said.

For both Mark and Besson, his tone was as surprising as the creature's existence. Noticing the stare from his assistant, Trevor realized how unsurprised he sounded—as though he'd seen this species before. "Ever since the first Kraken attack, it was speculated whether other large species were driven from the depths."

"Looks like we have the answer to that question," Mark said.

A bead of sweat formed at the tip of Trevor's widow's peak. He felt foolish for not keeping a closer eye on the sonar, especially having previously lured one other megalodon with the Porpoise. No doubt this eel was following the signals of the speaker. As far as it knew, it was tracking a whale, and found two whale-sized objects near the source of the soundwaves.

The eel creature slowed to a stop, its upper body bending in the shark's direction. Like a cobra, it raised its head. Crocodilian jaws lined with twelve-inch fangs turned toward the boats, inspecting the bites of meat on board.

Despite his best efforts to remain calm, Trevor's heart rate started to climb.

"Aw, shit!"

His brief display of urgency put Besson over the edge.

"To hell with this! I'm out of here!" He started his engine.

Trevor raised his hands. "No, no, WAIT!"

It did not matter at this point. The sound of the motor drew the eel in like a magnet. Like the cobra it resembled, the creature lashed at the port bow of the *Salt Mine*. Its closed jaws, hard and rigid as bone, punctured the hull like a lance. The impact pushed the vessel to starboard, smacking it into the *Anderson Ernest*.

All four men lost their balance, the crew of the *Salt Mine* suffering the worst. The eel pried its jaws free then bit at the edges of the wound it created. This 'whale' was not comprised of flesh, but the creature did not seem to care. It had come here to kill, and would not stop until it completed its purpose.

Trevor pulled himself to his feet. There was no choice now. All he could do was speed away and hope for the best.

"Sir?" shouted a terrified Mark Eurupe. He was already pulling up the anchor. He didn't even need to voice his concern, for it was obvious in his voice.

"Yes, we're going!" Trevor twisted the key. The engine turned over slowly, failing to spark. Trevor could feel his composure starting to slip. That damn impact must have damaged something. He tried again. Same result.

Again.

"Come on, you bastard." As though it sensed his anger, the *Anderson Ernest* roared to life. Trevor placed his hand on the throttle and began to push.

CRASH!

For the second time, the *Salt Mine* was thrust into the *Anderson Ernest*, instantly killing the engine and breaching the hull.

Trevor clung to the controls as his vessel rocked and spun in place. When he looked to the *Salt Mine*, he saw the eel slithering over the bow, its head rising over the flybridge. Besson was on his knees, hands raised high, resembling a man pleading to a god.

His murmurs erupted into a scream. The eel lunged, its jaws snapping shut on the human treat. A series of chomping motions followed, reducing

Besson to a mixture of ground meat, bone pellets, and tattered fabric. All of it was welcomed into the creature's gullet.

Before it finished swallowing, it was already looking at the crewman. He had a pole in hand, raised like a baseball bat. Adrenaline had him bouncing on his toes as a boxer would in a ring before a fight. The macho attitude vanished in the split-second before the creature struck.

Like his captain, the crewman was mashed in the eel's jaws. His right arm, still clinging to the pole, detached and plopped on the deck.

The *Salt Mine*, driven by the creature's weight and that of the inflowing ocean, plunged into the Atlantic. Water rushed over the upper deck, erasing it from view.

The eel inspected the floating remains, then turned its gaze toward the *Anderson Ernest*.

Trevor tried starting the engine. This time, it refused to respond at all. They were dead in the water. They had nothing to fight with. Rescue could not possibly arrive in time. Even if he and Mark hid below, it would only take the eel a couple of minutes to dig them out.

Only one thing was capable of fending this creature off.

Trevor glanced back at the megalodon. Its dorsal fin was fully exposed, still a few hundred yards away. It was keeping a distance, monitoring the situation. Right then, it became clear that O'Brien was not a creature that picked a fight unnecessarily. Only when something directly threatened it or was in competition for its meal, as was the case when it battled the other megalodon. O'Brien was not interested in the *Anderson Ernest*, therefore it did not see the eel as competition.

We'll have to change that.

"Mark, get the speaker into the water right now, then activate the Porpoise."

"You mean, draw the meg in?" Before Mark could comment that this action was suicide, he saw the eel closing in. That's when he comprehended Trevor's plan. Make O'Brien interested in attacking the *Anderson Ernest*, see the eel as something trying to steal its meal, and fight it off.

He tossed the speaker over the side then knelt by the device. With the twist of a knob, he sent out several high-pitched pings.

O'Brien responded immediately. The caudal fin sprayed water with several wide swings, launching the shark like a bullet at its target. For the first several hundred feet, O'Brien was on a direct collision course for the *Anderson Ernest*. With less than one hundred-fifty meters to cross, it sensed the second predator making a move at its prize.

O'Brien was not one for sharing. It turned twenty degrees left, maintaining speed. It parted its jaws and closed in on the eel.

The serpentine creature had its head above the water, ready to snatch the helpless humans aboard the vessel. With a mighty jolt, it was dragged under. Its entire hundred-plus feet of length flailed like a kite in the wind.

The plan worked. The creatures were locked in combat.

From the upper decks of the *Anderson Ernest*, the creatures were nothing more than two black shapes twisting and turning under the water. The thinner, more flexible body of the eel was constricting around the shark. Whether it was trying to pin O'Brien down, or crush him with a squeeze, it failed to slow the shark.

O'Brien was dragging the eel in tight circles. Within moments, a red cloud was rising to the surface.

Blood had been drawn.

Mark turned his attention to the breach in the hull. "Doctor. We're taking in water. We don't have long."

"Such is my luck. Hold tight. Get that device ready for transfer," Trevor said. He picked up the speaker mic. "This is the *Anderson Ernest* issuing a Mayday to any nearby Coast Guard units."

****

"Let me get this straight," Renny said, keeping his eyes on the instrument panel as he sped the chopper northwest. "You built this dolphin robot to scare sharks away from the coastline? And now, you're hoping to use it to steer the megalodons in whatever direction you want?"

"That's the gist of it," Denise said. She leaned on her armrest and watched the ocean through the window. Whenever she wasn't staring outside, she was watching the computer monitor in the next seat.

Nico was sitting across from her. "Man, if only a woman would look at me the way you look at that monitor."

"Trouble in paradise?" Renny said.

"No," Denise said.

"Like we'd tell you if there was," Nico said.

"Suit yourself. I'm good at relationship things. I'm like a guru."

"Don't you spend half your nights on the couch?" Denise said.

"That's a gross exaggeration," Renny said. "And the times I do, you can thank Carley for. She takes great pleasure in getting me in trouble. And, sometimes, I wonder if my wife enjoys it too. Women enjoy a power trip, sometimes."

"Oh! Generalizing now, are we?" Denise said.

"Hey, I'm not the one looking to control a dozen giant sharks," Renny said.

Nico watched Denise's body language shift from relaxed to defensive. Her legs were no longer crossed, she was sitting up straight, her eyes like a predator's. The Chief understood Renny's way of speaking to understand he was simply kidding around. Denise, however, was not taking it that way. If she wasn't so emotionally involved, she probably would have seen the remark for what it was. Unfortunately, this situation was the equivalent of a stick of dynamite with a rapidly burning fuse.

"Alright, you two. Settle down." He leaned toward Denise and lowered his voice to a whisper. "Babe, just chill. He's pulling your chain."

Denise turned her eyes back to the monitor, then began shifting through the various files. All stress levels and heartbeats were level. For now. That could change any moment.

On her phone was a speech from one congresswoman speaking on the issue of 'man-eating predators roaming the waters near Florida'. The only thing more annoying than the braindead politician—in other words, *most* politicians—was the wavering internet signal. It was the one time she actually cared to listen to any of these idiots talk, not for their insight, but because they unfortunately wielded influence.

This particular one made the point that the sharks needed to be destroyed.

"We cannot make room for another catastrophe such as the one that occurred at Cielo Nublado. After the attack in Palm Beach and the sinking of the nearby vessels, I say enough is enough. Some of my colleagues say we need to preserve this new species, rather than drive them to extinction. My point is this: just because we kill the ones we know about, doesn't mean we'll drive these creatures to extinction. I'm sure there's plenty other megasharks still in the deep ocean. My concern are the lives of people who fish for a living, who live on the coast, and anyone else I may have left out."

"That's like exterminating a whole pack of wolves because one of their members bit somebody," Denise said.

"A hundred-plus people dead is not the same as a bite, Denise," Nico said.

"Huh. Never thought I'd see the day you agreed with a politician," she said.

"I concur—with both his point, and that observation," Renny said.

Denise's body language shifted back to defensive. She stopped herself from telling him off. The guy did not have to be here. In fact, the only reason he was here was to help her. In fact, he was helping her right now with this trip to Miami.

Damn. Maybe I am getting a little too obsessed.

"With a little luck, we'll have the best of both worlds," she said. "With my device, we can protect human lives—which I acknowledge is the number one priority—and preserve these sharks."

"We'll still need a place to send them," Nico said.

"Working on that. But at the very least, as long as we've got them tagged, we can track their movements. Every time one lingers close to a populated area, we sound off a whale call and lure it away."

Renny looked over his shoulder and raised a finger to his mouth. "Hey, guys! Shush for a sec!"

Denise and Nico each put on a set of headphones. When a jokester like Renny Jackman was alarmed, they knew something was up.

"...I repeat, we are taking on water. Location is two clicks southeast of the Dust Valley wreck. Any Coast Guard unit monitoring this call, please respond."

"Copy, Anderson Ernest, this is Mayport Coast Guard Station. We'll be sending chopper units immediately. How many bogies you say are in the water?"

"Two. Hurry up. We've got maybe five minutes."

"They said Dust Valley wreck. No way the Coast Guard will get there in time," Denise said. "Renny, you know where that is?"

"Affirmative. Changing course. Coast Guard, this is Blue Tin from Cielo Nublado. We're near the location of that Mayday and will be responding."

"Copy that, Blue Tin. Be advised, our units will still be en route. Keep us updated."

"You betcha." He turned the chopper northeast and pushed it to full speed. "I'm rescuing so many people from killer sharks, there should be a movie made about me."

****

The waterline was inches from spilling over the top of the *Anderson Ernest's* transom. Mark Eurupe tossed the available mics and portable hard drives to his boss, who secured them in a bag on the flybridge. All that was left was the Porpoise.

Trevor could not make out the status of the fight taking place below. Every few moments, the two creatures appeared as one body, only to dip out of view again. Even if he had not caught these glimpses, it was still evident that the shark and eel were locked in combat. Their violent motions were powerful enough to stir twenty-thousand square feet of ocean, as though an earthquake was occurring underneath.

The *Anderson Ernest* rocked in the swells, the bow tilting up and to the left.

Trevor fell to his knees and reached down along the ladder. Mark stood on one of the lower bars, pushing the large device up to him.

"Come on, man. A little further!" Trevor shouted.

"It's heavy, boss." Mark rested the Porpoise on his right shoulder like a huge, seventy-pound pizza, then grabbed the next ladder bar with his free hand. Straining, he stepped higher, found his balance, then used both hands to push the device closer to Trevor.

The professor found the nearest side handle and pulled. At last, the Porpoise was atop the main deck. Right away, he searched the skies for any aircraft. That 'Blue Tin' unit stated they were close. Being from Cielo Nublado, they had to be coming from the south.

"Any time now…"

Mark was halfway up the ladder. "Where are they, sir?"

His question was answered by a tremendous impact which rocked the vessel and the two men aboard. Mark's face smacked against the ladder, loosening his grip. He plummeted to the main deck, splashing against the water that was now freely spilling over the sides.

Trevor did not even notice his assistant had fallen, for his eyes were glued to the chaos behind them.

The megalodon and eel cleared the water in a unanimous leap. The shark, still wrapped in the eel's constriction, corkscrewed in midair. Its jaws were latched on the eel's throat, forcing its snout to the left. The serpentine creature bit at the air, unable to angle its jaws at the shark.

Both creatures disappeared under an eruption of water. Trevor backed to the console, tensing as the tsunami fell over the *Anderson Ernest*. The force of the wave pushed the sinking boat further south, the crest drenching Trevor and his equipment.

The Porpoise's shell was water resistant, but that did not stop the scientist from folding himself over it like a parent protecting his only child. Moments later, the wave cleared, unveiling the next stage of the clash.

The megalodon and eel had separated. They circled each other, blood trailing from the injured serpent's wounds. Any other creature would have attempted to flee at this point. Perhaps this thing was an alpha predator in its own right. Like the Kraken, it also battled the megalodons for supremacy of the deep.

Or maybe it's just pissed off.

That theory was supported by the eel's next action. It ceased its circling motion and made a straight line toward O'Brien. The shark met its opponent head on. For a moment, its head lifted to the air, then closed down over the eel's snout. The creatures tossed and turned, the eel's body waving like a flag. Once again, its jaws were positioned away from its target, with no range of motion to inflict a bite.

O'Brien kept its grip like a dog with a bone, the teeth piercing the eel's rigid crocodilian head. The thing smacked its tail against the shark, failing to inflict sufficient pain to break its grasp.

The shark shook its head, the teeth sawing the flesh. The slicing of nerve endings caused surges of pain which made the eel's entire body spasm.

Trevor watched in fascination. In any moment, the megalodon would inflict the final blow.

A brief, but blinding flash forced him to throw his hands over his eyes. Sparks flew off the metal hull. He heard Mark down below shuddering uncontrollably, his voice ululating. It was the same sound he saw someone make in a documentary regarding electrical surges.

When he looked down, he saw his assistant twitching in the water. The spasm lasted a moment, leaving him unconscious against the ladder bar.

O'Brien released his grip and darted away from the eel, immediately circling back to finish the fight. The fish repeatedly opened and closed its mouth, as though the roof of its mouth had been burnt.

The eel drifted along the surface, having lost significant blood and energy. Still, it had no intention of giving up the fight.

"Good Christ. An electrical surge," Trevor said to himself. A droning sound in the sky made him turn around. Rescue had arrived. "About damn time." He slipped the backpack on and picked up the Porpoise.

He gave one last glance at the sea monsters. They were closing in on each other, jaws extended, baring white razor-sharp teeth.

****

"Am I seeing what I think I'm seeing?" Renny said. His two passengers crowded the cockpit, watching the spectacular showdown ahead.

"You referring to the big snake-thing, or the fact that that megalodon is WAY bigger than the others?" Nico said.

"Either one. Denise, you have any thoughts?"

"Only that there's more about the deep than we ever thought we knew," she said.

"Let's focus on the matter at hand," Nico said. He pointed at the boat. "The stern's completely under."

"I see the guy on the bridge," Renny said. He lowered his aviators. "What the hell is he holding? Looks like a really big game console."

Denise leaned forward. "Is that—Dr. Zenner?!"

"I wouldn't know, ma'am," Renny said.

"I worked with him. We were actually on the team that designed the Porpoise." She grabbed a pair of binoculars and aimed it at the large object in Trevor's hands. "That's it!"

"That's what?"

"The Porpoise!"

Renny perked up. "The shark luring device thingy?"

"Shark repellent—never mind. Get down there."

Renny lowered the chopper to the flybridge. Dr. Trevor Zenner was practically standing on the rear wall at this point. The stern and middeck was completely submerged, the water now at the flybridge's edge.

Nico opened the fuselage door and threw the ladder down. "Come on, Doc. Climb up!"

Trevor propped the device atop his shoulder and tried to reach for the bars. His balance quickly wavered, forcing him to secure both hands on the Porpoise.

Nico looked to the north. The shark and the eel collided once again. Tails swiped the air, fanged mouths biting repeatedly.

The eel finally secured a bite, sinking its teeth near the meg's left gill slits. Its grip was quickly lost after the meg turned to the right, prying itself free. Its caudal fin swung high over the air, connecting with the eel's snout with an ear-shattering *CRACK!*

The creature reeled backwards, huge scarlet raindrops spraying from the many wounds in its neck and face.

A dozen meters below the water, the megalodon pointed itself at the enemy. It charged at an upward angle. Eleven-inch teeth plunged into the leathery flesh, twenty feet below the eel's jawline. The momentum did not stop with the impact. Both creatures were airborne again.

The megalodon was in complete control of the fight. Though the eel snapped at its nose, it failed to induce enough pain to free itself. Its attempt to bite the megalodon degraded into mindless flailing as new pain consumed its nervous system. Racing along the ocean's surface, the megalodon thrashed its rival left and right. With each motion, its teeth sawed at the flesh, widening a hundred incisions.

Chomping motions followed, creating new wounds. The megalodon chewed, gradually mincing the eel's neck.

There was no slowing the fish. With the eel clenched in its jaws, it raced across the water. Every several hundred feet, it swiftly changed direction, the eel's dying body trailing beside its own.

Nico watched the violent conflict slowly draw to its resolution. He hoped that the eel would die and that the megalodon would simply drag it to the depths and feed.

Instead, the megalodon changed direction again. Now, it was racing toward the *Anderson Ernest*.

His blood rushed. It was not clear if the shark was intent on ramming the eel into the boat for a final death blow, or if it had merely gone berserk. One thing was clear; there was no sign of it stopping or altering course.

"Chief?!" Renny said.

"I know." Nico reached down. "Come on, Professor!"

"Take this!" Trevor said.

"Forget it. Get aboard!"

"No! Take this, goddamnit!"

"Chief?! I'm gonna have to move in about five seconds... four," Renny said.

The countdown showed he was not being figurative. Nico ran through a series of possible actions in his mind. "Screw it." He grabbed a ladder bar and flung himself out of the chopper.

Denise threw herself to the doorway. "Nico!"

A few feet down, he got close enough to grab the Porpoise by its side handle.

Relieved of the object's weight and bulky mass, he was finally able to get a firm hold of the ladder.

"Guys, we gotta go!" Renny called out.

"They're good," Denise said.

"Hope so." Renny pulled up on the joystick. The chopper lifted, the chief and professor dangling from the rescue ladder.

A colossal impact shook the ocean below them. Fragments of the *Anderson Ernest* took to the sky, nicking the chopper's landing struts. Nico shut his eyes and accepted the possibility that one of those fragments would knock him off the ladder. Five seconds later, he was still in midair, unharmed except for the strain in his shoulder.

He looked up and saw his ex-wife reaching down at him.

"Nico, don't let go!"

"I should tell you the same thing," he replied. He looked down at Trevor. The professor was clinging tight, more concerned about making sure his backpack was intact rather than his own well-being.

A hundred feet below them was a swirling ocean. In the middle of the whirlpool was the bow of the *Anderson Ernest*, and the wreckage that was the stern and mid-deck. The boat twisted with the waves, then vanished below them.

Coursing through the middle was a twelve-foot dorsal fin. The meg dragged the eel through the debris field. Though nearly dead, the thing was still trying to bite at its captor.

As if fed up, the megalodon arched backward, lifting the eel. It loosened its jaws, only to secure a new hold on the throat. From there, it whipped to the left, then to the right. The ocean turned red.

The battle was finally over. The eel fell away, its body rippling during its descent to its final resting place. Only a chunk of its throat remained in the shark's jaws. Over the next few moments, it was reduced to ground meat.

After swallowing its catch, the megalodon dove, likely in pursuit of the rest.

"Nico." Denise was reaching for him. "Hand it to me."

Nico strained as he raised the device up to her. She grabbed it by one of its other handles and dragged it into the fuselage. Nico and Trevor soon followed, the latter slamming the door shut behind them.

"Son of a gun! Thanks a hell of a lot!" Trevor said. He rested on the floor, catching his breath. He perked up after glancing at his former colleague sitting across from him. "Dr. Reta?"

"Dr. Zenner."

"Fancy seeing you here."

"What the hell is going on? What are you doing with the Porpoise?"

"Before we get to that, there's a more important question," Nico said. "Dr. Zenner, was there anyone else aboard your boat? I don't want to leave anyone stranded."

Zenner pulled himself onto a seat, then watched the floating wreckage below. He shook his head. "No. Just me."

"Alright. Renny, go ahead and take us back."

"Looks like we saved this bird a few miles," Renny said. He pointed the chopper south. "Heading for home."

****

When Mark Eurupe opened his eyes, he was underwater, surrounded by wreckage. The last thing he remembered was lying on the deck after falling off the ladder. Right as he recovered, he inexplicably went into a spasm before blacking out.

A few strokes returned him to the surface. The *Anderson Ernest*—the parts that floated—were all around him. There was nothing to identify it as a ship, just useless remains no more advanced than the iceberg that sunk the *Titanic*.

He looked to the sky. A single helicopter glided above him. Mark waved and shouted, but the bird had already shrunk in the distance. He was alone in the water, abandoned.

Mark clung to a piece of wreckage, only for his weight to pull it below the water. His limited strength gave out, leaving him to sink with the debris. Before he could close his eyes, he saw movement. This was way smaller than the meg. Smaller than a man even. Two flippers extended from a dome-shaped object.

A sea turtle had graced him with its presence. His family's spirit animal, the motivator for his father bringing his family to America, the sign of a better life. The reason he studied the ocean to begin with. Perhaps the ocean was forgiving him for sacrificing Rico to the shark.

He is a manipulator who gets out of bad situations. This has to be a sign. I'll find a way out of this.

The sea turtle ceased all motion. As though paralyzed, it sank with the debris around it.

A sensation of rushing water drew Mark's eyes beneath him. From the black depths emerged two rows of white teeth quickly separating. Attracted by his rapid heartbeat, O'Brien closed in on the human snack.

Mark's eyes returned to the sea turtle. It was relaxing its heart rate, meanwhile using Mark as a decoy to save itself.

A trickster.

The jaws slammed shut, reuniting Mark with Rico.

CHAPTER 11

Cielo Nublado.

When the chopper arrived at the CNPD helipad, it was greeted by a military Jeep. Its only occupants were a driver and its passenger, Admiral Vince Heston.

"Look at that. We have a welcoming party," Renny said.

"Interesting he's here," Nico said. He looked at Trevor. "You familiar with Admiral Heston?"

"That I am. He's the one who recruited me for this project."

"What project?" Denise said.

"That's classified," Trevor said.

"Classified? Really?" Denise pointed at the Porpoise device. "What use could the Navy have with this that would warrant classification?"

The chopper set down. Nico opened the fuselage door and stepped out. The Admiral was already approaching.

"Is the professor okay?"

"Yes sir." Nico pinched his finger and thumb together. "Came this close to being shark food, but we yanked him out just in time."

Heston smiled. "Having you guys on my team has more than proven to be a good investment."

"Investment, huh?" Denise stormed onto the helipad. "You had him working with you all along?"

"That's correct."

"I don't get it. What's the point of having me here if you're just going to use Trevor's research? These past few days, you've asked me for ways to lure the megalodons, even though you already had the Porpoise."

"It's standard practice to have multiple science consultants," Heston said. "Zenner's responsibility was to test the soundwaves and their effects on O'Brien. Yours is to help me understand the megalodons' attack patterns. What? You thought you were the only scientist doing research for us? I informed you yesterday that I had another team tracking a shark further north."

Denise reconsidered her intended filibuster. "I suppose that's true. But what about the Porpoise? You obviously knew about it."

"That I did. I knew Dr. Zenner headed the development of this device three years ago. So I asked him to test it on the megalodons to see if they would respond to the signals." The Admiral looked to Trevor. "You okay, Professor?"

"Had a close call."

"Where's your assistant?"

"Assistant?" Nico grabbed Trevor by the collar. "If you made us abandon someone out there…"

Trevor forced his hand away. "Mark Eurupe was killed by the eel creature before you guys arrived."

"Really? You said it was just you."

"Meaning I was all that was left. You really wanna do this, Chief?"

"Knock it off," Heston said. "Chief Medrano, stop rushing to conclusions, please. Dr. Zenner, show some damn gratitude."

Trevor nodded. There was no effort made to thank Nico or his crew, but it was not an issue Heston was in the mood to pursue. The Admiral put his hand on Denise's shoulder then walked with her to the Jeep.

"Thank you for saving him and the Porpoise. What were you guys doing on the copter? Our readings show the registered megalodons to the south and east sides of the island, not near the mainland."

"We were making a trip, ironically enough, for the Porpoise. I thought it would lure the sharks away from populated beaches," Denise said. "Apparently, you were already aware of the project."

"Correct. Dr. Zenner has made several findings with his research. With this device, we hope we'll be able to lure any megalodon in the area to this island."

"I'm not sure that's such a good idea, sir," Nico said. "You should have seen the one that sunk their boat. It's almost as big as a Sentinel-Class cutter. BIG! Good luck picking out a name for that one, Denise."

"Already done," Trevor said. "We call him O'Brien."

"O'Brien? Interesting choice," Denise said.

"Well, I almost went with Willis, but it made me think of Bruce instead of my intended reference," Trevor said. He chuckled. "It's fitting. We really are living in the age of monsters now."

"No shit. After seeing that sea serpent thing, I'm inclined to agree with you," Renny said. "What the hell was that thing anyway?"

"Obviously another visitor from the depths," Denise said. "I don't recall seeing any record of its existence, but it has all the physical characteristics of eels. My guess is that it's a member of an evolved species that made its home, probably living in caves in the ocean depths."

"Lovely," Nico said. "First giant sharks, then a pissed-off octopus, now a big ass eel."

"Electric eel," Trevor said.

"Electric?" The Admiral stopped and turned to face him.

"I saw it. It let out a charge during its fight with O'Brien."

"An animal large enough to fight him has got to produce a charge strong enough to light up a city for a day."

"Ha, I don't think it was quite that strong, but it was enough to shake him loose," Trevor said. "It was a quick zap. Sadly, we won't get to tag the specimen and examine it. From what I saw, it couldn't muster up a second bolt. Maybe they can only produce so much electricity, or perhaps that eel was a juvenile."

"I'd rather not think about that," Nico said. "Shit, that would mean an adult would have to be well over a hundred feet long."

"Too bad the thing didn't solve the issue of the super-meg for us," Renny said.

"We might not need to kill it," Denise said. "Now that we have the Porpoise, we might be able to steer the megalodons somewhere else. I might be able to find a place that's suitable for them."

"First, there's more research to be done here," Admiral Heston said. "Dr. Zenner, get in the Jeep, please. Bring the device."

Trevor lifted the Porpoise and loaded it into the back of the vehicle. "We're gonna need more speakers."

"Already got a crew on it." Heston got into the passenger seat, then nodded appreciatively at Nico and Denise. "We'll be in touch."

Denise approached the vehicle. "Admiral, if I may say so, I was part of the project that developed the device."

"I understand that, Ms. Reta, but I want you to focus your efforts on the Kraken and the other megs. Particularly the triplets."

"Why are you so interested in the triplets?"

"Because they act as one unit," Heston said. "Naturally, that would make them more dangerous should they choose to attack one of our ships. Report to the Command Center at thirteen-hundred to help me supervise our next operation. The *Red Nova* will be testing your theory on the Kraken's attraction to bright light."

"Okay sir, but be advised, if this works, the beast in all probability will go after the cutter."

"We'll have five Seahawks in the air ready to turn it to chowder," Heston said.

"Where would you like me to be?" Nico said.

"Just remain on standby in case we need you." Heston fixed his sunglasses. "Corporal, take us to the command center."

"Aye-aye, sir."

Nico, Denise, and Renny watched the Jeep pass the open gate and turn northeast.

"Something's off," Denise said.

"I'm sensing a bruised ego," Nico said.

"No, it's not that. I mean, I'm a little pissed that Trevor is in charge of operating the Porpoise, but that's neither here nor there. What's weird is that the Admiral is eager not to discuss the issue."

"Why should he?" Nico said. "He has a plan, and you're not a senator or a ranking military officer. He doesn't have to discuss his plan with you."

"No, it's like he didn't originally want me to know he was using the thing. That's valuable information, considering part of my objective is to find ways to steer the megalodons wherever we want them to go. And why does he not want me to scout suitable, unpopulated areas for the sharks to reside?"

"I don't know, hon. Probably because he had bigger fish to fry. Or rather, calamari."

"Speaking of which, I'm gonna grab some brunch," Renny said. "If I'm gonna have to rescue more people from a giant octopus that's giving them a yum-yum face, I'd rather not be doing it on an empty stomach."

CHAPTER 12

USS Makin Island (LHD-8)
South China Sea, thirty miles southeast of Taiwan.
2317 hours.

"Flight graphics and DVRs are checked and running. Checklist complete. Turboprop is started. Awaiting the go-ahead."

"Stand by, Noble Three. Awaiting instructions from the captain."

LTJG Dayton Grissum kept his hands on the joysticks. When he entered the Navy's drone operation academy, he never expected to be placed aboard the second shipboard ground control station. It was his third year as drone pilot and his sixth month operation the new Northrop Grumman Mq-4C Triton. At twenty-eight years old, he had flown over two hundred surveillance missions, covering Navy SEALS in various regions in the Middle East before moving on to top secret projects in the Mediterranean and Iranian waters.

Such projects brought a pay raise to 0-2, a promotion to Lieutenant Junior Grade, and a government order to never speak about such projects under penalty of treason. Grissum never took issue with such things, nor the pressures of such high-risk assignments. The risk did not come in the form of bodily harm, as being a drone pilot, he operated from the safety of the control room. It was mainly the boots on the ground that carried the personal risk. For Grissum, the stress came from the probability of failure. In many cases, he was flying past international barriers, spying on and sometimes eliminating targets the U.S. was not officially at war with. Should his drone be shot down and its remains identified, or any of the ground forces he was covering be killed or captured, the results could mean all-out military confrontation. Official war, the kind that made headlines and got politicians talking.

It was even worse when tensions between certain nations were already high. When Grissum got word that he would be serving aboard the *USS Makin Island* near Taiwan, he knew the mission had something to do with China. He assumed it was surveillance, considering the current situation with Taiwan. At first, he was correct. Day after day, he monitored the locations of Chinese Naval ships, had his sensor operator calculate their distance from Taiwanese territory, and made several notes about the flight patterns of Chinese Coast Guard Patrols.

That's when he suspected this was more than surveillance. His suspicions grew after being instructed to take high-altitude patrols along the Taiwan Strait. This was not surveillance; he was practicing a specific route.

At twenty-hundred hours, he received an order to meet with the captain of the *Makin Island*. Behind closed doors. No recordings.

There, the truth came out, or at least part of the truth. Tonight, he would conduct his flight route, but below radar. High risk mission. Such flights usually indicated some kind of attack was inevitable.

At the time of the briefing, his drone was being outfitted with something simply referred to as the 'package'. He was assured that it was not an explosive or any other weapon of war, but also was instructed that there would be no mention of it outside this control room.

Success would bring him back to his normal ground control base back in the States, and a promotion to LT/0-3. The only thing said about failure was that it could be catastrophic.

Grissum watched the telemetry monitor. The map image showed the aircraft carrier, and the little red triangle that was Noble Three's drone.

"Night vision's activated."

Grissum glanced to his sensor operator, Ensign Kelsi Penn. "Not gonna need it, considering the altitude we'll be flying at."

"Flight deck to Noble Three. Package is secure and ready for drop off."

"Copy."

"Noble Two, standing by for a landing check."

"Copy. Good to go. Nine-knot gust factor so had three."

"Copy. Moving from seventy-two to seventy-five.... Flaps, neutral. I have rudder control. Kick in left rudder... leveling out... touching down."

"Offset left, then turn right. Alright, you're good."

"This is Noble Two, manual is off."

Grissum felt his palms moisten the joysticks. The first drop had been successfully completed. Once the ground crew cleared the deck, it would be his turn.

"This is the captain. Noble Three, you have the green light."

"Copy that." Grissum licked his lips then started the engine. "On we go." He watched the two upper monitors. One was a camera from the ship's bridge looking down at the deck, the other was the Triton's forward cam. He mainly watched that one, watching the ship's deck scroll down until it was replaced by ocean. "Takeoff complete. Following course Bravo-Two-Five."

"You're at twelve meters," Penn said. "Decrease nine."

"Got it. Decreasing nine." He adjusted the altitude. "Level. Ensign, keep a sharp eye on that gauge. Not much margin for error, especially at this speed."

"Copy that. Steady on course. Continue at two-three-five. I'll instruct you on when to turn."

The north flight lasted fifty-minutes, all of it at twelve feet above sea level.

"Approaching turn," Penn said.

"You make it sound like a fork in the road."

"To us it is. Steady, in fifteen seconds, turn forty-degrees port." She watched the map and the clock. "Three, two, one."

"Copy. Forty-degrees port." He adjusted the drone, taking it northeast along the Taiwan Strait.

"USS Makin Island, this is the USS Milius. Be advised, we are picking up increased air activity in Quanzhou."

"This is Captain Moore of the Makin Island. Please elaborate, Milius."

"Four J-20s have departed Quanzhou. Moving south at five-zero-zero. Approaching Mach one."

"Noble One to Makin Island, please be advised, Chinese Destroyer Taiyuan has just turned south. Current position; forty miles southeast of Wenzhou."

Grissum and Penn looked at each other. Both saw the same suspicion in the other's eyes.

"They're on to us," Grissum said. "Noble Two to Command, abort or proceed at the next turn?"

"Proceed, Noble Two."

Grissum bit his lip. He was hoping for the other answer. "Copy that. Steady on course. Increasing speed to three-two-five. Maintaining altitude."

"Chinese drone must've spotted us. Or maybe they've secretly placed sensors along the Strait," Penn said.

"Sounds like they don't trust us. Gosh, I wonder why."

Penn chuckled. Sometimes, the only way to maintain composure during such missions was to treat it like a joke.

"Starboard, fifty degrees. How far away are we from the drop off point?"

"Let's see, forty miles."

"Those J-20s are going to meet us before we get anywhere near."

"Attention. U.S. Naval ships, you have an unmanned drone entering restricted waters. You have one warning. Turn back immediately."

"Case and point." He went over his available options, then sighed. "Damn it. Pushing speed to three-seven-five."

"This is the USS Makin Island responding to the Chinese Navy. We only have one drone in the air, flying above Taiwan at ten-thousand feet."

"Negative. We have eyes on a drone, moving northeast at attack speed."

"Great. Caught in a lie. That's sure to make this situation look better."

"Alert," Penn said. "We're being targeted. J-20s are locked on to us."

"Distance from drop zone?"

"Nineteen miles. Eighteen now."

"Command to Noble Two."

"Go ahead, Captain."

"Just received word from the Pentagon. Green light. This is close enough."

"Copy that, sir." Grissum looked to his partner. "You're up."

She typed in a code on her keyboard then pressed a button on her joystick. "Package deployed." Her eyes returned to the telemetry. "Missile incoming. One thousand meters. Five hundred."

"Turning around." Grissum tugged on the joystick, performing a sharp turn to port at sea level. At a hundred-eighty degrees, he saw a speck in his night vision. That speck grew larger and more fiery with each passing second. He turned right into the path of the missile.

Blank.

"Noble Two down," Penn said.

"Noble One confirms. Noble Two down."

"This is the USS Milius. We've got increased Chinese Air Force activity in Shekou and Nantong, and two more squadrons departing Guangzhou."

"We have two destroyers moving east from Sanya," Noble One said.

"Copy. I need all destroyers on alert. I'm gonna place a call to the Admiral."

"Oh great." Grissum leaned back, hands over his eyes. "So much for that 0-3 promotion."

"First time you've lost a drone?" Penn asked.

"Yep." He uncovered his eyes and listened to the increased chatter by both U.S. and Chinese naval forces. "Also the first time I started World War Three."

CHAPTER 13

Islamorada General Hospital
Noon CST

It had only been one night and already Carley Auburn's back was sore from sleeping on the hospital sofa. That was nothing compared to the mental strain of seeing her mother, Valerie May, on the hospital bed. Every fluctuation in the heart monitor made Carley's own heart jump. Coronary artery disease was no joke. What Mom had was something commonly called the 'widow maker'. Her left anterior descending artery was ninety-five percent occluded. It was beyond the point of stints; the only medical option was for doctors to harvest saphenous veins from her thigh to bypass the part of the coronary artery that's damaged.

Surgery was scheduled in three days. The procedure would be a coronary artery bypass graft. It they couldn't get between the ribs—most of the time they can't—they would have to crack the sternum and go right in.

In other words, open heart surgery.

First they needed to optimize her, which meant get her blood pressure right, blood sugars and electrolytes where she needed them, keep her hydrated, among a few other corrections. All of this would improve her odds of surviving surgery.

Seeing her mother in the hospital bed made Carley feel horrible for not leaving sooner. Mom was quick to correct that mindset. "Had you left last week, you would not have been around to save Nico." With age came wisdom, and her mom had a lot of both.

Carley was grateful the Chief negotiated pay with the leave. Technically a layoff. All of this depended on the length of the military occupation. If it did not last longer than a month, she probably would be able to go back. Then again, it didn't really matter. After everything that happened, Cielo Nublado would be a ghost town for at least a decade. Perhaps it was time to start looking for other employment. She knew Nico was already thinking of resigning to live with Denise.

It was a stressful thought. She and her husband enjoyed the simple island life. Most people knew each other, the culture was a good one, and they had the privilege of meeting visitors from all over the country. Now, instead of Cloudy Heaven, it should have been named Shark Island.

The gentle piano music playing on her mother's phone helped put her mind at ease. Valerie loved these instrumentals. Carley did not know the artist. It was just some Russian YouTuber who performed licensed piano covers for various songs. She was good and the music was soothing, so if it worked for Valerie, it worked for Carley.

The only issue with the music was that it made it difficult to hear the news broadcast. Not that it mattered, it was the usual talking heads regurgitating stuff that was not really the truth. It was rather infuriating whenever they brought up the topic of the megalodon situation. Trying to sound smarter than what they really were, some of these talking heads discussed the local handling of the situation. Some brought up the fact that the police chief had evidence of danger after a dead whale washed ashore with bite wounds. Then of course, many of these people brought up the timeline of events, with the boat disappearances—disregarding the fact that the Klingberg-Dan Huckert incident had all the makings of an altercation escalating into a boat crash. There was even evidence that Huckert even shot one of the guys. But leave it to news people to leave out details if they had somebody they wanted to crucify. If anything, Carley was surprised it took this long for the blame game to start.

Then came all the people taking advantage of the situation to advance their own agendas.

Carley made the mistake of settling on CNN where some bonehead member of Congress was 'boldly' claiming that the megalodons rose to the surface due to climate change.

"You know, Don, it's very clear that our use of fossil fuels, the melting of the ice caps, and the dumping of trash in the oceans have now come back to bite us. These creatures can't live in their natural environment any longer because of climate change, and it's our fault as a society."

"Yeah, yeah, yeah," Carley muttered. "'And the solution is to raise taxes, regulate your lifestyle, while we the government live high and mighty on private jets, eating meals that cost an average joe's yearly wage to prepare, and think of the next talking points to make you peasants keep voting for us.'"

"Something wrong, sweetie?"

Carley looked at her mother. "Oh, Mom. Go back to sleep."

"I've slept enough, and come next weekend, I'll be doing nothing but sleeping." Valerie's eyes went to the TV. "Oh, lovely. The news."

"At least, that's what they call it."

"You trying to trigger another heart attack? I have to spend my possible last days looking at this garbage? If that's the case, get me a Philly cheesesteak and let me be done with it." She smiled and closed her eyes. "Mmm, I miss those. That wouldn't be a bad way to go out."

"Oh, Mom! Don't talk like that!"

"Kid, I'm seventy-two. I've lived a good life. Frankly, I'm not too thrilled on this vegan thing the doctors are trying to push on me."

"Yeah? Guess what: you're gonna get used to it. Make it through this, and I'll get you a chilly cheesesteak or any other calorie infested meal as a yearly Christmas dinner."

Valerie smiled. "I guess I can live with that. If your father were here, he'd be bringing me one now to shut me up."

"He had a way of bending to your will."

"He better had. I bent for his will plenty of times. How do you think you came into this world?"

Carley stood up, her face wrinkled. "Holy shit! Mom!" She turned away and slapped a hand over her eyes, sparking laughter from her mother. "Wh---why?! Why was that necessary?"

"They say laughter is the best medicine, and I wanted to see your reaction." She closed her eyes longingly. "Mmm, those were good times, though. Being young and wild, and—"

"Okay, now I no longer feel sorry for not coming here sooner. Nor do I feel bad for not calling more often anymore." She rubbered her forehead as though in physical pain. "Good God! That image is burned into my brain!"

"Hey, I'm old. Not dead."

Carley shook her head. "You know what? Maybe I will get you that Philly cheesesteak." Her phone buzzed in her pocket. It was Renny. "Gotta take a call. But first, I'm gonna give you a little payback. I believe your favorite show is still on…"

"What favorite show?" Valorie gritted her teeth when she recognized the channel number. "Oh, don't you dare! If you put on *The View*, I swear to God I'll haunt you after my heart decides it's had enough. I got plenty of self-important cackling old hens with pea-sized brains in my personal life!"

"Sorry! Gotta go!" Carley tossed the remote on the sofa and stepped into the hall.

"Carley? Carley! That's it! Erin's my favorite child!"

"Hmm, I was sure you'd pick Michael," Carley said. She closed the door, chuckling after hearing her mother groan and sneer at Whoopi and Joy. She answered the call. "You've got perfect timing, Renny."

"That's what all the ladies say."

Carley stopped and lightly tapped her forehead against the wall. She had traded one crude knucklehead for another. "Why am I surprised? And I'll have to let the missus know about the ladies plural thing."

"I'll have to remember that next time I think to call and check on you. How's your mommy?"

"Driving me crazy, as always."

"Really? I always thought she was a hoot."

"Makes sense that you guys would get along. Anyhow, it's the usual stuff. They're getting her electrolytes balanced, all that other optimizing stuff so she's ready for the big operation."

"Aw. She's a tough cookie. She'll be fine."

"Yeah, such is my luck." They shared a laugh. "Enough about me. What's going on with you? Calling from home or some shark's gullet?"

"After today and yesterday, I'm really tempting fate."

"Jen still mad at you?"

"She's always mad at me. You don't help with those matters. But I did get a text asking when I'm evacuating."

"You do know Nico would let you leave, no questions asked, right?"

"I'm aware, partner. But this is too much fun. Who knew I'd get to do battle with giant sharks?"

"Wait, you've engaged in combat with them? When did this happen?"

"Okay, it's more like pulling people out of the water before they can get snatched, but 'doing battle' sounds cooler. Either way, that's how I'm framing it in my resumé update."

"Resumé, huh? You thinking of leaving the island too, once this is all over?"

"Maybe. I'm just focused on the here-and-now."

"What's going on there-and-now?" Carley asked. "All I can see is the crap on TV."

"This shit's getting weirder, Carley. There's more to this than even I know. You should've seen this big ass eel thing we encountered earlier."

"An eel?"

"Yeah. An electric one, apparently. It was throwing hands with a hundred-and-twenty foot megalodon."

"What?!"

"You heard me right. You were smart to leave. The megalodon killed it, so luckily we shouldn't have anything to worry about on that front."

"Yeah, assuming there's no other ones. What about the Kraken?"

"The Navy and Coast Guard are about to test one of Denise's theories, actually. They're going to use big lights to see if Squidward responds. If it does, they'll blow it to kingdom come."

"Hope it works. Are you going to—hang on a second." She pressed her phone to her shoulder after seeing two nurses rushing down the hall, right toward her mother's door. "Everything alright?"

"Valerie just paged us. She says she's experiencing horrible discomfort and needs immediate response."

"Renny, I gotta go."

"Keep me updated."

"Thanks." She hung up and followed the nurses into the room. Her mom had her hands over her eyes, baring teeth, and groaning.

One of the nurses went to the monitor. "Same as our feed. A little stress, but nothing too drastic."

The other nurse went to the patient's side. "Valerie? What's the matter dear?"

Carley's heart thumped. "Mom? What's wrong?"

Valerie uncovered her eyes and glared at her. She pointed at The View.

"*That's* what's wrong! Get that off or I swear I'll have a heart attack right here just to spite you."

The nurses stepped away, relieved. One was mildly frustrated, though the other found the antic amusing.

"Oh, you little devil. Don't scare us like that again." She grabbed the remote, switched it back to CNN, then handed it to Carley on her way out.

Valerie sulked, glaring at the boring news report. "Not much of an improvement. And why did she give it to you and not me?" Carley didn't answer. Instead, she was glued to the screen. "Oh, when did this happen?" Still no response. "Carley?"

Carley continued to watch. For once, the *Breaking News* banner actually meant breaking news.

"Tension increases as Chinese Naval Forces close in on U.S. Naval ships near Taiwan. We're getting more information, but according to sources near Beijing, a U.S. Naval drone was shot down. Chinese officials are claiming that the drone was flying below radar level. Another is stating that it supposedly dropped some unknown object into the Strait, sixteen miles from the coast. The White House is yet to comment."

Carley flipped to another news network.

"We're seeing increased movement in the air. The Chinese Air Force is on high alert. Their Coast Guard is doing a sweep of the waters. They haven't officially stated, but it's believed they're concerned about explosives being dropped near their populated areas."

"If the drone really was flying below radar level, I'd say our boys were doing something they didn't want to be caught doing."

"Oh, look at that," Valerie said. "I might live long enough to see our government get us into another war. Good for the career politicians. Of course, they didn't get close enough to plant the bombs in the shipyards."

Carley shook her head. *If they dropped bombs, they would've gone off by now, and they wouldn't be using just one drone.*

"What the hell would they want to put in the water?"

CHAPTER 14

USCGC Red Nova

Lieutenant Commander Bradley Pine stood in the bridge of his vessel, binoculars in hand, watching the Sikorsky approach.

"Stop at four-hundred feet. Descend to thirty meters and lower package."

"Chopper One-Five to Red Nova. Copy that. Lowering to thirty."

"*Red Nova* to Command, we are initiating operations. Is the consultant on standby?"

"This is Admiral Heston. That is affirmative. Proceed with caution. Should the hostile appear, weapons free."

"Affirmative, Admiral. Will do, with pleasure." He lowered the radio and binoculars, then glanced at the Petty Officer First Class standing nearby. "How's it feel being the extended hand of the Navy?"

The Petty Officer grinned. "They'll take all the credit when this is over. Gotta love the President for giving the order."

Both men turned their attention to the Seahawks hovering in the air. There were five of them now, forming a tight perimeter around the kill zone.

Pine was back on the radio. "I want an eye on that sonar screen at all times. Gunners, have the Bushmaster ready. Let's show our overlords who really takes care of business around these parts."

"Aye-aye, sir."

"Chopper One-Five here. We're in position. Ready to lower package."

"Proceed."

The Coast Guard Sikorsky lowered a cable. At its end was a large round ball. The sight of it made Pine laugh.

"If you told me eighteen years ago when I first joined the USCG, that I'd be lowering a big ass disco ball for giant squids, I would've suspected the whole branch was full of cocaine junkies."

The Petty Officer chuckled. "Are we sure that this thing will even show up?"

"I hope it does," Pine said. "I knew Captain Grade. Between you and me, he was a bit of a blowhard, but he was still a friend of mine. I'd like to report to his folks that the tentacled coward that killed him got what it deserved."

"Aye-aye, sir."

"Light is on. Ten meters deep."

"Copy. Pan it around a bit," Pine said. "If the big boy is here, we'll know soon enough."

****

Naval Command, North Beach, Cielo Nublado.

Even after a few days, it was hard for Denise to believe this giant rigid tent could hold so much technical equipment. On the central monitor was a feed of the operation. To its right was a satellite image. The various other monitors had footage of the megalodons that were at surface level.

"We've got Akira and Lang near the *Jacques Grave* wreck site. Galileo is roughly four miles south, heading northwest. It's consistent with his usual pattern. Drill is two miles northwest of the test site, and Old Albert is west of us, swimming north near *Sea Rock*."

Admiral Heston stood, arms behind his back, watching the monitors at Denise's desk. On her main laptop was a satellite image of the island and surrounding waters. The little red dots indicated the tagged megalodons' positions.

"And where's O'Brien?"

"I've patched into the tag Dr. Zenner had placed. He's about ten miles north, gradually moving south towards us."

"Good. That's how we want to keep it."

Denise watched his radar blip. "I'm wondering if he senses the presence of the other megalodons," she said.

"It's possible."

"Possible, maybe. Unless something else is luring him here. Like maybe high-frequency soundwaves, like those from a certain device I helped rescue." She waited for an answer from the Admiral. "Is Dr. Zenner operating the device?"

"Periodically," he said. "We need to use it sparingly, or risk further agitating the other megs."

"Further agitate?"

"Dr. Zenner discovered that certain frequencies can cause aggression in them. Or rather, in O'Brien, at least." He pulled up a seat next to hers. "Dr. Reta, I've never expressed my thanks for your assistance in this matter."

She shook her head. "That's not necessary, Admiral. This is an opportunity most scientists can only dream about. Honestly, it is I who should be thanking you."

A sailor approached the table with a cup of green tea. Heston accepted, then looked to his consultant. "May I offer you a cup?"

"Sure. Good for the heart."

"That it is. Keeps you young. May I offer you with some lemon?"

"No thank you."

"Okay." He nodded at the sailor, who left like a waiter for Denise's cup. He cupped his hands around his own tea and watched the monitors. "What is the triplets' location?"

Denise turned to look at the laptop screens on her left. "Three miles east of the island."

"Three miles…" Heston did some math on his notebook, glancing at a printout of the island map and surrounding waters. After doing a few measurements, he put his pen down and began sipping his tea.

"Something wrong with that?"

He shook his head. "Simply curious about how far away they were from the operation."

"You've been very curious about them," Denise said.

"Most of the other sharks are rogues. These ones stay together. I want to know if that increases the risk factor."

"I personally encountered them. They're not deadly," Denise said. "There's one I named Drill, a seventy-two footer. He's a real piece of work. It's evident by the scarring on his head that he's been in plenty of fights with other megs. I personally witnessed him get into a tussle with one of the others. Drill might be a threat that, I hate to say, might have to be put down if we can't redirect him. Right now, he's a couple miles southeast of here, not too far from where Nico and I killed the first megalodon."

"Good to know."

Denise noted the slight disinterest in his voice. She chalked it up to him being focused on luring the Kraken.

"What's the word from the White House about all of this?" she asked.

"What do you mean?"

"All I see are political know-it-alls on the television. I know they're just putting on a show for the cameras. What does the government *really* want to happen regarding these creatures?"

"There's a great deal of debate about that," Heston said. "Nothing's really changed. The talking points are generally the same. The White House is too afraid to commit to any kind of action. The Greenpeace crowd is really hitting them hard, and a few other scientific organizations have spoken out to preserve these animals. None have offered a solution regarding the 'how', however."

"What about you, sir?"

"What about me?"

"Certainly you have an opinion on this matter. You're very interested in the megalodons. So interested, you've asked me to gather as much data as possible. Metabolism. Speed. Aggression. Feeding patterns. The triplets' unity."

Heston shrugged and lifted his mug. "Ma'am, I'm a man who studies what he's up against. We've already suffered enormous casualties from these creatures."

"Then why not destroy them?"

"You advocating I do that?"

"Oh hell no," Denise said, smiling nervously. She paused while the sailor brought her the mug of green tea. She nodded in thanks, then continued. "You're the man in charge around here. I'm not experienced in military operations, but I've always wondered how you expect someone in the middle of the country to call the shots, when you're the one out on the field. Doesn't it get frustrating listening to someone several thousand miles away?"

"It's called the chain of command for a reason, Professor," Heston said. "Yes, perhaps I know better than they do, but should the Commander-in-chief make a decision, I have to honor it. That's why it's my job, and that of those working below me, to obtain as much data as possible. I'm sure it works similarly with your university."

"Sort of." Denise sipped on the tea. Bitter, but tolerable.

"One thing that's certain is that the Kraken is the number one threat," Heston said. "There's been a small outcry to preserve it as well, but the government is a little firmer on its stance. I guess having a military vessel destroyed is enough to let the ties, dresses, and pantsuits of the world see some common ground."

They sat in silence for a minute.

"You never did state your opinion on the sharks," Denise said. "Just curious. You do have a lot of data to work with."

Heston finished his tea and pushed the cup aside. "They're dangerous, capable of vast destruction. They are an armament of nature, with the free will to unleash their fury. My job is to see if they can be controlled. Hence, I hired you and Dr. Zenner. It's the only way to preserve them, Professor."

Denise nodded. "Understood."

****

Cielo Nublado Police Station.

"Tension increases as Chinese Forces mobilize along the southern coast. Concerns are mounting in Taiwan, South Korea, and Japan. Australia's armed forces have been put on red alert."

Nico watched the livestream coverage on his computer, shaking his head as he watched the footage of Chinese military forces hustling on the unrestricted parts of their Navy bases.

"What the hell were they doing?" he muttered.

"I don't know, but they're using this as their excuse to advance on Taiwan," Renny said.

"That they are, but I still don't get it," Nico said. "What were *our* people doing? Nothing about this operation makes sense. Why fly a drone that low?"

"Chief, they do all sorts of shit we don't know about. I can't relate to any of it. Can you?"

"No. But if they make a move, Australia won't stand for it. They can't afford to let the Chinese have total control over that sector. The Japanese certainly aren't thrilled about this. Relations between those two nations have never been good."

"That's what happens when you occupy an entire nation," Renny said.

"Doesn't justify someone else doing the exact same shit to the other side three generations later." Nico listened to more coverage, then exited the tab. "No sense in stressing out about this."

"Plenty to stress out about. All it takes is for one of those guys to get pissed off and release a hellfire missile."

"I am curious to know how this will affect things here."

"Oh, politicians will do their usual flexing…"

"No, I mean here on this island. We have a leading Navy Admiral here. Destroyers patrolling just a few miles off our shores. An aircraft carrier near the Bahamas. They might have to divert if things get more tense."

"It'll fall into the hands of the Coast Guard," Renny said. "Who knows? The Admiral might have to leave within the next day or two." He stepped out into the briefing room and gazed down the hallway at the dispatch office. "I'm not used to it being so quiet in here…" He opened the lounge refrigerator. "But on the bright side, at least Travis won't complain about me stealing his lunch this time! What have we got here, oh yum!"

Hearing the sound of tinfoil, Nico stepped out of his office. Renny froze, sandwich in hand, bits of lettuce and turkey dangling from his lips.

"That's *mine*."

Renny swallowed. "Oh…" A mayo-stained smile took form. "Want it back?"

"I'd rather skinny dip in toxic sludge." Nico returned to his chair and adjusted the radio volume.

"Chopper One-Five to Red Nova, are there any readings yet?"

"Negative. We'll let you know."

"Should we adjust the depth?"

"Twenty meters. Maintain position."

Renny walked into the office and sat in the second chair. "Feeling a little sidelined, are ya?"

"More bored than sidelined. Military service was never one of my grand ambitions," Nico said.

"I always figured you were the go commando sort."

"Huh? What?"

Renny replayed the last sentence in his mind and realized how he sounded. "Oh, NO! I didn't mean that. I'm sure you wear underwear. I mean, if you don't that's up to you. Just for the love of God keep your shirt tucked in, because if you bend over and it rides up…"

"Good God Almighty, this rabbit hole ran deep," Nico said.

"Sorry." Renny laughed. "What I originally meant was, I thought you were the kind of guy who'd like sailing the high seas and battling evil."

"I took down enough evil in Waco," Nico said. "And no, constant travel was never really my liking."

"Hmm, I hope you've considered that," Renny said.

"Beg your pardon?"

"Once this is over, you and Reta will make up for lost time. But to do that, you might have to tag along in her research. You know this prehistoric shark issue is going to be a lasting one."

"Yeah, I suppose it is." Nico slumped his chin onto his palm.

"You worried about how this might come in-between you two?"

"No… maybe a little."

"You still think they should be destroyed?"

"The families of the officers we lost certainly thought so. Be grateful you didn't have to knock on their doors and inform them of what happened, that their bodies couldn't even be recovered for a damn burial because they were in the gullet of that thing."

Renny looked away. He knew those people. Despite his attempts at humor, the image of blood splattering from the chopper rotors occasionally flashed in his mind.

"I didn't knock on the doors, but don't you forget I was right there in the bloodbath with ya."

"You've got a point." Nico clenched his jaw and stared off into the distance, tapping a pen against his desk. "Sorry, I guess I've been a little self-absorbed, lately."

"Nah. It hasn't been the best week for any of us."

"That's an understatement." Nico needed something to change the subject. "How's Carley? I'm assuming you've spoken with her."

"She's alright. Her mother's driving her nuts as usual. I'd be lying if I said I didn't take pleasure in knowing that." Renny scooted his chair closer to the Chief's desk. On the computer screen were black and white images of war torn country. The highlighted tab above read *Korean War: Battle of Old Baldy*. It was the other tab that most interested him.

Admiral Vince Heston, U.S. Navy Admiral.

"Doing some homework on the Admiral?"

"Yeah. Just curious about a few things. Got nothing better to do. It's hard for me to enjoy movies and books with everything going on."

"Hmm." Renny looked at the Korean War image. "I didn't realize the Admiral was that old…"

Nico laughed. "He's not. He was born in fifty-three. His father served during World War Two in the Pacific, and then in the Korean Conflict. He was killed in action. The Admiral wasn't even born yet. His mother was pregnant with him."

"Oh. That sucks," Renny said.

"I'd say so. Guy served three years in World War 2, saw all kinds of action, just to get picked off a few years later. Probably what inspired him to join the Navy, if I were to venture a guess."

"Jesus, Chief, I'm starting to think I need to get a violin. So much depressing bullshit in this office today."

Nico exited out of the tabs then shut the computer down. He leaned on the edge of his desk, chin in palm, staring at his reflection in the black screen. The waiting around was worse than the constant flights and rescue missions.

"What's on your mind, Nico?"

"Probably the same as what's on yours."

"Tacos?"

Nico looked at him. "How can you think of tacos when you have a belly full of my sub sandwich?"

"I've worked up an appetite. Besides, I'm always thinking ahead. Sometimes I think of dinner as soon as I wake up. Sometimes I plan my next date, think of options should Jen decide to dump my ass, and sometimes I think of what I'm going to do next in life." Renny scooted his chair next to Nico's. "That look you have on your face is the one I have when that last one comes up."

"You think you're *Dr. Phil* or something?"

"Maybe. 'How do you feel about that?'"

Nico rolled his eyes. "If you and Carley are thinking of splitting from this department, I'll write a good letter of recommendation. In your future employer's case, probably a small cautionary letter too, letting them know what they're getting into."

"Appreciate that," Renny said. "What about you?"

"I already know. I'm done. Maybe it's time to take an early retirement."

"Good. For a while, I was worried you were going to piss away a good thing." Renny clapped his hands in a mock applause for the Chief. "I just hope you don't let those megalodons come between you and your future ex-ex-wife."

"This is Red Nova to Naval Command. We've got movement coming in from the west. Three bogies, moving fast."

"Three… the triplets." Nico turned up the radio. "Speaking of megalodons…"

CHAPTER 15

"Prep the fifty-cals. All hands, we are on Orange Alert."

Lieutenant Commander Pine kept his binoculars to his eyes, watching the three dorsal fins moving across the water. Studying the distance between them and the caudal fins, he estimated these creatures were a little over sixty feet in length. "Naval Command, I believe the triplets are paying us a visit. Can you confirm?"

"Confirmed. Bogies are triplets."

"Copy. Rotate Bushmaster thirty degrees." All at once, the sharks descended. "I lost visual. Chopper One-Five, do you have visual of the sharks?"

"Affirmative, sir. They seem to be circling the light... whoa!" The cable tightened, the Sikorsky wavering in the sky. *"One of them is biting the light. They're dragging us down... Stand by... I think they let us go."*

As he listened to the crewman, Pine watched the cable ease back up. Relief took over. "Thank God. Looks like they were just checking it out."

"They're continuing to circle. They're moving slowly. They're obviously drawn to the light."

"Naval Command? Does our advisor have anything to say about this?"

"This is Dr. Reta. I concur. They're interested in the light. Just hold position, don't make any sudden movements. They'll move on shortly."

"As you wish, Doctor." Pine lowered the radio and looked to his Petty Officer. "Hope that woman knows what she's talking about."

The Petty Officer shrugged. "I think it's okay, sir. She seems to understand these things pretty well."

****

"I don't understand," Denise said, watching the screen. She could see the sharks under the water, their bodies distorted into hazy grey shapes. "They were three miles away. How the hell did they see the light from that far out?"

Heston was on his feet, hands clasped behind his back.

"The light's pretty bright," he said.

"Not that bright," Denise said. "Even at night, there's no way they could have seen the thing from that far out." She checked her watch. "It's only been twelve minutes. It's no coincidence; they came directly for that light. Unless they followed something here. Do we have anything on sonar? Any movement at all?"

"One bogie coming in from the west. *Sea Rock* reported movement about six minutes ago," one of the sailors announced.

"Old Albert. They're not following him. He came from the opposite direction," she said. "Any unidentified signals?"

"Negative, ma'am."

"I thought maybe the Kraken was moving in. That would have made sense."

"Red Nova here. We've got movement. Sharks are breaking away from the light. Viper units? You still have visual?"

"Viper One to Red Nova, sharks are moving toward you. Increasing speed... Red Nova, brace for impact!"

Denise stood up. The hazy shapes took definite form as they neared the surface. All at once, they collided into the *Red Nova's* portside. The ship rocked to starboard, the men on deck scattering.

"Red Nova to Naval Command, we are under attack."

****

Lieutenant Commander Pine staggered backward, nearly falling over one of the bridge consoles. Alarms echoed across the bridge. The sonar operator was scrambling to return to his chair, fixing his crooked headset.

"Hostiles are circling. We've got one coming in on the port bow. Impact inevitable."

The ship rocked again.

"Weapons free. Eliminate all hostiles—shit!"

One of the triplets struck the port quarter, turning the *Red Nova* counterclockwise.

The Seahawks narrowed the distance. Machine gunners opened fire on the megs.

Dash was racing northwest, angling a hundred meters ahead of the cutter. It dipped, then angled up. The shark was airborne, in a direct collision course with Viper Two.

The Seahawk narrowly dodged the attack with a left bank.

Gravity pulled the megalodon back to the Atlantic, but not before it twisted in midair. Its massive caudal fin swung wide, the upper lobe nicking Viper Two's underside.

"Fuel line damaged. Rotor control lost. Can anyone get a shot?"

"Not without killing you," Viper One responded.

Pine put the binoculars to his eyes. The chopper fishtailed in midair, smoke trailing from its tail rotor. The pilots' attempts to keep it airborne were futile. Viper Two smacked down with a tremendous splash.

"Right rudder. All ahead full. Get those sailors out of the water." He lowered the binoculars. "Should've blasted those damn sharks when they first arrived."

"Sir! We have incoming. Shark that took down the Seahawk is closing in. Impact in three... two... one..."

CRASH!

CRASH!

Pine would have managed to stay on his feet had it not been for the immediate second impact. As the shark named Dash struck, one of its brothers rammed the keel.

"Sir, we're losing rudder control," the helmsman said.

Pine crawled to the end of the bridge where his radio had slid. "Engine room, report."

"We have a rupture in the—"

Another impact ended the transmission prematurely.

Pine's patience had faded, as well as his temperament. "What the hell's going on? Why are they going after us?" He stepped out onto the bridge deck for a better view.

The guardsmen on the middeck were propping their machine guns on their mounts. One of the units opened fire to the port side. The megalodon disappeared as soon as the bullets stung its flesh.

Up above, the Seahawks circled for a clean shot, which none of them could obtain.

"Viper One to Red Nova, they're hanging too close for you. Cannot use incendiaries."

"Don't worry about us. Have one of your guys pick up the sailors. Hurry." He looked to stern in time to see one of the sharks closing in. On its back was a little red scar shaped like a spider web.

The sailors on the aft deck screamed. The shark lifted its head high above the transom like an anaconda, clamping its jaws over the bite-sized humans aboard. It veered right, pieces of blood-soaked uniform spitting from its gill slits as it veered to its right. Webb hit the water, leaving a big red smear on the crumpled deck.

One of the Seahawks attempted to chase it. Miniguns, firing three-thousand RPM, tore into the ocean. The fish managed to evade by diving deep.

Up at the bow, Pine's crew began shooting at one of the other sharks. It was not Webb, for it lacked the scar. It wasn't nearly as fast as Dash.

What was the third one's name?... Bruce! She named it Bruce because he tended to stop and sink.

In the blink of an eye, the shark dipped under the water. There was no splash from its caudal fin, no dramatic angling of its body. The shark basically dropped.

Through his binoculars, he could see the creature. It descended ten meters, then flung itself at the keel.

Pine clung to the guardrail, spitting curse words with each breath. It seemed he could not keep his balance for more than ten seconds. The sharks were pelting the *Red Nova* like hornet stings.

Again and again, they struck the vessel.

"Hostile off the starboard bow."

Pine did not need a radio signal to know the shark had appeared. He saw the cone-shaped snout rise over the edge of the ship. Its chin slammed down like a hammer, pancaking his machine gunners to the deck. The fish wildly snapped its jaws, angling its head to scrape the minced meat with its teeth.

Before the Navy Chopper could align a clear shot, the fish was back under the water.

Pine rushed down to the main deck, while shouting into his radio. "Engine room, status report?"

"We're taking a beating, sir. The hull is cracked. We have sea water entering the lower compartments."

"What about the engine? Can you get enough power for us to limp to shore?"

"Barely, sir."

"Do it. Bridge, set a course for Cielo Nublado's northwest beach. We can anchor in the shallows."

Without waiting for a response, he sprinted for the second machine gun unit. The Bushmaster had opened fire at one of the megalodons, the fish managing to stay a step ahead of the rounds.

It was heading southeast, crossing the port bow.

"Out of the way," he said to the guardsmen. He took the machine gun, pointed it at the dorsal fin, and squeezed the trigger. He watched pellets of water spurt along its fin. After several dozen rounds, those splashes began to turn red.

That's right. I'm hurting you, you big bastard. Time I showed these Navy pukes how it's done.

The dorsal fin turned toward him. The snout rose, revealing the ghostly white eyes. A dark protective layer, a nictitating membrane, slid over them. The shark charged, mouth hyperextending. During the next split-second, Bradley Pine saw its many teeth come into view.

He hit the shark with everything he had, his bullets barely scraping its thick flesh.

Dash burst from the water and closed its jaws over his target. The next thing Pine saw was the back of its throat.

****

"Red Nova bridge crew, can you confirm? Is the Lieutenant Commander gone?"

"Confirmed. He's KIA, Admiral. Engines are operational, but we're taking on water. We're following his last order and heading toward the island."

"Copy," Heston said. "Proceed with your course. Order all crew below. The megalodons have learned they can pluck them off the deck. Give us a chance to get a clear shot at them. Vipers, you copy?"

"Viper One copies. But Admiral, I do not have visual on the targets."

"Viper Two confirms. No visual."

Heston looked to Denise. "What's their location?"

She looked at her tracking monitor. "They're retreating. Heading northeast at ten miles per hour. Depth, thirty meters." She turned to the main screen and watched the severely damaged cutter limp away from the scene. The Seahawks maintained a tight group, like a police escort.

"Viper One to Command, you want us to go after them?"

"Negative," Heston said. "Continue escorting *Red Nova*. We'll have a team ready to bring the crew to shore. Be advised, however, we will be making a new gameplan. It's likely to be 'shoot to kill'." He looked at Denise and braced for any objection she may have.

Her face was a blend of disbelief, astonishment, and sorrow. She looked the Admiral in the eye, but did not offer resistance to his statement. How could she? Up until now, she had vehemently stated that the triplets posed no threat. Today, they were directly responsible for multiple deaths, and the near-destruction of an eighty-million dollar cutter.

The Admiral changed the channel on his radio. "Dr. Zenner, do you read?"

"Affirmative, Admiral."

"Meet me at Naval Command on the double."

CHAPTER 16

Palm Beach, Florida.

"Jeez, it's quiet."

Throughout the afternoon, Sam Travis could not keep his eyes off the long stretch of beach. No matter what day of the week it was, it was always jampacked full of bathers by now. Since the megalodon attack, it had been vacant. Even the safe area of the sand was untouched, as though it was dangerous merely by being associated with the water.

"Let's keep going," his partner said. Kevin Chase made it clear the moment they got on the county boat that he did not want to be on the water a moment longer than he had to. It did not help his nerves to know the job he was tasked with was as useless as boobs on a bull.

The shark barrier stretched far to the north, with another few miles to go. He slowly steered the tugboat south, the winch gradually unwinding the net.

"Stop," Sam said. "Anchor drop." He splashed the anchor down and let the net fall with it. He fixed his goggles and rebreather, then lowered himself onto the diving platform. "Gotta love the diligence of the county. Clearly, this net should have no problem fending off a hundred-foot shark."

"It's a blind response to the public outcry," Kevin said. His voice was monotone. It was the same stupid conversation with each anchor drop. It was a symptom of both men wanting to be anywhere but here. It was a long and boring task. Not only that, but it was tense. While Sam studied the beach, Kevin watched the open ocean. His eyes played tricks on his psyche, creating illusions of a giant dorsal fin coming at him.

He eased the boat to a stop, then dropped anchor. "Hurry up, man. I wanna be on dry land as soon as possible."

"You know how this works, wuss," Sam said. He dropped the net anchor into the water and pulled his goggles over his eyes. "At least they were nice enough to pay us triple time for this."

"Triple time doesn't do much if we're swallowed. Hurry the hell up, will ya?"

"Aw. Worried a shark's gonna come bite ya?" Sam said.

"This isn't a joke, man." Kevin turned the knob on the radio.

"...Rescue crews are surrounding the craft as we speak. We're waiting for a report from the Navy and Coast Guard Admirals, but it does appear

that the Coast Guard Cutter Red Nova has been attacked by a group of megalodons. We don't have word yet on any casualties..."

He turned the volume down. "Case and point. Hurry up."

"Wait—they downed a cutter?"

"Damn straight."

"Jesus. Talk about war machines. Still, I don't think we have much to worry about. They're all down there."

"We don't know that," Kevin said.

"We've been out here a few hours. No oversized guppy has shown up. I think we're good."

"Will you just shut up and get it over with?"

"Alright, alright, I'm going. Holy shit, you wuss." Sam placed his rebreather in his mouth then dropped into the water.

He entered a crystal blue world. It was thirty feet deep, with hardly a single fish in sight. There was something special about being the only one in this alien place. Only a few seaweeds below offered him company. Like tendrils, they waved back and forth, absorbing the sun's rays.

Sam lowered himself to the anchor and began bolting the stakes into the seabed. With a simple tool, they could be easily extracted, but for a shark attempting to plow straight into it, the anchors would have no problem keeping them at bay.

Normal sharks, at least.

Sam wanted to laugh. Did the local government seriously think the public was this stupid? Sure, the net would help to ease nerves in the aftermath of a normal shark attack, but not a freight train with teeth.

At the end of the day, it did not matter. He was being paid to install the thing, not question its practicality.

He installed the first stake, then lifted the rotary hammer drill. It was a pain to hang on to the thing while he pulled the second stake from his pouch. Go figure, the thing slipped from his grasp and fell into a nearby grouping of weeds.

Go figure.

Sam could not afford to give in to the temptation of disregarding it. Even though the county was willing to pay triple-time, they were still cheap enough to supply the bare minimum of supplies.

The next couple minutes was spent at the bottom of this alien world in search of his dropped stake. He dug into the weeds, smacking the leaves aside like mosquitos. The drill dangled in his right hand, the tip hovering a few feet above the bottom.

Thump!

He felt a vibration run through the tool. With soundwaves much more distinct underwater, it was obvious that it had struck something metal.

What the hell's behind these weeds?

He brushed them aside and peered at the large object. Three legs, insectoid in appearance, jutted out of its side.

Sam gasped, then jumped back, the rebreather falling from his lips. The sensation of water in his mouth forced him to calm down and find the rebreather. He put it back in its rightful place, then turned to look at the weeds. The thing was lying there, motionless. Light reflected the 'shell'. It was metal, not living.

He approached and bent the seaweed down for a better look.

The object was a meter wide, tilted on its right side. At its rear was something that resembled a box fan. Propellors.

Holy shit. Somebody lost a drone.

Studying the way it was lying, he initially assumed it was resting atop a rock.

Wait. He got on his knees and shone a light. The thing underneath the drone was not rock. It was metal and rounded, somewhat flat. *A stereo speaker? Is this for real? Why the hell would somebody attach a speaker to some high-tech drone?*

Kevin turned the radio volume up. The news channel had gone from the situation near Cielo Nublado to talking about the escalating situation with China. In a way, it was worse than the news about killer sharks.

Warships had been sighted near Alaskan waters. The U.S. Coast Guard and Navy were on high alert, the Air Force doubling its air patrols. Simultaneously, Australian, Russian, and Japanese forces were reportedly putting their military on Orange Alert. NATO had announced it was finally shifting funding into their defensive capabilities. Tensions were high. All it would take was for one unruly idiot to fire a shot, and World War Three would officially start.

"What the hell were they doing dropping off bombs in the Taiwan Strait?" Kevin assumed they were bombs. What other secret device could Navy drones be planting?

A spout of water to the northeast made him perk up. Six hundred feet out, a mound of water rose and fell. The rest of the ocean was calm. It wasn't the wind that did that. That water was moved by a large body.

He saw another one. This time, he saw the grey mass under the wave. There was an animal in the water. A *large* animal, and it was coming toward them.

"Oh, hell. Holy Ghost. Holy Mary. Holy *shit!*" He ran to the transom and looked into the water. "Sam! Where the hell are you?!"

The creature was approaching. It was only three hundred feet away now, traveling a couple meters under the surface. With this close view, he confirmed its length and color. Fifty feet at least, and grey—the same color as the megalodons.

He looked at the water. "Sam, hurry up!" After a count of five, he gave up on his partner and rushed to the controls. He sped the boat forward, out of the creature's path.

It collided with the net, entangling itself. Flippers and a huge tail slapped the water.

For the second time, Sam was screaming underwater. His attention had been so fixed on the weird device, that he never noticed the large organism approach until it was a few feet away.

The net bent, then twisted. Large fins flapped like the wings of a giant bird. They were white, contrasting against the creature's dark flesh. Then he saw the body and the lack of a dorsal fin. It had no teeth, no white eyes, and the tail was horizontal.

A whale.

Once again, Sam replaced the rebreather and caught his breath. The tension had not let up. The water rushed around him like a violent storm. The creature was in panic mode now, entangling itself further into the net.

Sam swam to the surface, only to see that his partner had fled several dozen meters. "Hey!"

Kevin spotted him and circled back.

"You dumb idiot. I waited till the last second, but you never came up." He grabbed his partner by the hand and hoisted him aboard. Both watched the writhing behemoth tear up the ocean.

"What the hell's going on?" Sam said. "Why the hell did a whale swim up this shallow?"

"I don't know... LOOK!" He pointed behind the netted creature. Another one of equal size was approaching the net a few feet to the north. "No, no, NO! Oh, shit!"

The creature tried to stop once it neared the net, but had too much momentum. Its attempt to turn left resulted in its flipper getting snagged.

"This isn't good," Kevin said. "I gotta get in touch with the Coast Guard. If these things suffocate, they'll pin it on the county... and *us*."

"I might be able to help cut them free," Sam said. He watched as a third took a breath a few feet beyond its entangled friends. It managed to stop short of the net, then swam in circles. A good family member, it refused to abandon its fellow whales. Looking further into the ocean, he saw others approaching. It was a whole family of whales. "Well, at least I was right."

Kevin looked at him, radio in hand. "Right about what?"

"It wasn't megalodons we had to worry about."

CHAPTER 17

Cielo Nublado. Command Central.

Admiral Heston tired of video conferences with people who had no clue what they were talking about. In his private quarters, he had several screens erected. On each one was a Senator, a congressman, and some of the President's Chief of Staff.

"We've lost two cutters to these creatures so far, Admiral," the Louisiana congressman said. *"As far as my constituents are concerned, this is a national security issue. If those creatures bypass the Keys and enter the Gulf, the death toll could be even more catastrophic."*

"It's a good thing we have them confined to this island, then," Heston said.

"But for how long? These aren't creatures you can control," the Chief of Staff said.

"General David agrees with that assessment," the Secretary of Defense said.

"With all due respect, this is a matter for the Navy and Coast Guard," Heston said.

"Admiral, we need you back in Washington," the Secretary of Defense said. *"You're obviously aware of the escalating issue with China. As dangerous as these sharks are, we believe the situation in the Taiwan Strait takes precedence."*

"I agree," one of the senators chimed in.

"We're still awaiting answers regarding how this situation even occurred," another said. *"The Chinese have found the downed drone. It's definitely American Navy. What was it doing there?"*

"Surveillance," Heston said, coldly.

That did not satisfy the many officials electronically covering his wall.

"Admiral, with all due respect, the Chinese would not likely shoot down a drone flying at surveillance altitudes."

"What the hell are you talking about? They do it all the time," Heston said.

"Admiral, don't get smart…"

"Or what?" Heston said. The congressmen and senators trembled in their seats. Their illusion of power failed to strike any sense of intimidation into him. "Boys and girls, some of you weren't even born before I took office. Some of you are nothing but community organizers and bartenders who fooled the public into putting you in a position you don't understand. I've been toe-to-toe with China, North Korea, and Russia more times than the lot of you had birthdays. Believe me, I'm handling this situation with China from here. I've been in constant contact with our ships and know every little detail that's developed over the last twenty-four hours. Things are bad, but we're not at war. Let the president kowtow to them, and maybe this will deescalate. In the meantime, I have my ships under control."

"Nice speech, Admiral. But if you had this under control, this situation would not have happened in the first place."

"With all due respect, or lack thereof to be honest, I'm in perfect control. I'll be here for another couple of days, then I'll take a plane to the South China Sea."

None of the officials dared to continue the conversation. It was clear that Heston was a hardheaded and experienced Naval officer who did not believe he had to answer to a bunch of science majors.

Only the Secretary of Defense dared to speak. *"The President will likely take issue with this."*

"He knows how to get in touch with me. Now, excuse me, I have an operation to run." Heston switched off the feeds. "Politics. I'd rather slam my nuts in a car door."

He stepped outside, overhearing the radio traffic from boat units who were picking up the surviving crew of the *Red Nova*. The vessel was docked on the west side of the island. Towing vessels had been barred from hauling it to the mainland due to obvious risk. For the meantime, welding crews placed patches over the breaches to prevent the cutter from sinking.

Dr. Trevor approached from his right, looking as amused as though he had witnessed a pro-wrestling match.

"Those megalodons pack a punch, don't they?"

"That they do. Those triplets like to work as a team. It's terrible, but fascinating."

"What does Dr. Reta have to say about this?" Trevor said. Heston tilted his head to a dock a few dozen yards to his left. She was standing at its edge, looking out to the water. Even from this distance, it was easy to figure out what was on her mind. "A bit distraught, huh?"

"Who can blame her? She's infatuated with these creatures. You're a scientist. You obviously understand."

Trevor showed no sympathy. "What's next, Admiral? The government asking you to kill these sharks?"

"The public wants them gone. Who can blame them, really? But there are a few groups and politicians that are advocating for their preservation. I suppose a proper middle ground can be reached. Tomorrow, we'll do our best to steer them into open sea and lure them to a more... suitable... environment." He glanced around, gauging the distance of the nearby personnel, then looked at Trevor. "What's the present location of Alpha One?"

"Far enough away for now. Turned southwest this morning."

"How long until it reaches us?"

"Two days. Hence it's important we get this underway tomorrow. If things go right, we can have them all far away from the coastal areas."

"Then that's what we'll do," Heston said. "Right now, I have something else to take care of." With that said, he marched to the dock where Denise stood. Like an older brother eager to witness his sibling get in trouble, Trevor followed him.

Denise Reta was in a trance, her mind repeating the sequence of events that claimed at least a half-dozen guardsmen.

Was it my fault? I told them the triplets were not hostile.

She could not make sense of it all. The triplets attacked the cutter, but not her when she was on a much smaller boat. Were they not hungry when she first encountered them? Even so, why did they not attack during any of the other occasions? Then there was the question of why they appeared in the first place. Minutes prior, they were three miles away.

"They could not have seen the light from that far out."

"Excuse me, Dr. Reta?"

Recognizing the Admiral's voice, she turned around. He stood formally, hands behind his back, chest out. She knew the demeanor; she wasn't going to like whatever it is he had to say.

"Yes, Admiral?"

"Doctor, your research and insight has been invaluable to me. I personally want to thank you for your contribution to our efforts."

"But?" Her tone was not hostile, but it did prompt Heston to skip the ritual and get to the point.

"It is time you and Chief Medrano depart this island. Your services are no longer required by the Government of the United States, or its Navy."

Denise smirked. "Let me guess. *He's* staying." She nodded her head at Trevor.

"That he is," Heston said, his tone apathetic to her point. "He's worked with us for years. He'll be in charge of the Scientific Division."

"Is this because of what happened, or are you just cutting back in general?" Denise asked.

"The situation with the *Red Nova* was not your fault, ma'am," Heston said. "I will prepare a transport to send you and Mr. Medrano to wherever you wish to go at first light. I will be getting in touch with him momentarily."

"I guess I don't have a choice in this matter," Denise said.

"That you don't," Heston replied.

"May I ask what your next step is? Obviously, you have something in mind."

"We're going to use the Porpoise to lure the megalodons out to open sea," Heston said. "After that's underway, I'll have to report to Washington to handle a more drastic situation on the world stage. You know what I'm referring to."

"What about the Kraken?" Denise asked.

"The Coast Guard will increase their presence and monitor these waters."

"Won't you want an expert here for that?"

His eyebrow raised slightly. It was barely noticeable, but nonetheless occurred. Same with the brief hesitation before replying.

"We have other experts," Heston said. "After everything that occurred, only federal scientists are authorized to be present on this island."

Denise *almost* believed him. Having been married to a former detective, she had learned how to detect a lie, even a convincing one.

"Where are you leading the sharks?"

"Dr. Zenner identified an uninhabited island seventy miles east of Trinidad. Operations are underway to get a military facility secured there. It's warm waters over there, far from densely populated areas, easy to monitor the creatures." The Admiral's radio crackled.

"Admiral, sir. We need you back at Command."

"Stand by," he replied. He turned his attention back to Denise and smiled. "Well, Dr. Reta, I guess this is it. Thank you for your service to our nation and Navy. I assure you, I will do whatever's necessary to preserve the megalodons."

"Even after what they did to the *Red Nova*?"

He sighed. "If we can steer them away from the U.S., perhaps the general public will be satisfied. We can only hope. With that said, your service is no longer needed. Be at the helipad at oh-eight-hundred tomorrow morning for departure. Thank you, and be safe."

Heston walked to shore and marched to the command tent. Trevor was a few steps behind him, but not before shooting Denise a smug look.

His ego was at Hollywood levels. *Look at me, I'm the chosen one. I'm more important than the lowly civilian consultant who only got hired because she happened to be in the right place at the right time.*

Denise refused to give him the satisfaction of occupying her mind. Besides, it was Heston that made her suspicious.

Something was going on and the Admiral did not want her to know about it.

"Admiral on deck."

"As you were." Heston approached the lieutenant who radioed him. "What's the big news?"

The lieutenant sat in his chair and brought up a grid on his computer screen. "I've been monitoring the tsunami warning system during the attack, and I found something peculiar." He played back the log then pointed at one of the points on the grid. "Watch this buoy." He rewound the time to 1325 and let the feed play. Several seconds later, the buoy let off an alert.

"How far is that from us?" Heston said.

"Roughly four miles," the lieutenant said. He pointed to another point in the grid. "Now this one...there." The next buoy let off a ping. It was making a straight line for the *Red Nova's* location during the operation. "There's one more thing." The lieutenant snapped his fingers at a corporal, who brought an image from a reconnaissance drone to the big screen.

In one moment, there was nothing but ocean and sunlight. Then the screen came alive with a gargantuan shape. Its presence was brief, but freeze-frame images captured the presence of tentacles.

"There it is," Heston said.

"Interesting," Trevor said.

"More than interesting. It's useful," Heston said. "We know for sure it was heading for the *Red Nova*. Something about our plan worked."

"Couldn't have been the light," Trevor said.

"No. I think Dr. Reta's assessment was correct. The bastard is simply too smart for all of our tricks. But *something* drew it in." He looked at the doctor questioningly.

"I think I know," Trevor said. "It's the same thing that led it to the *Omega Fury*. Conflict. It's as much a scavenger as it is a hunter... it moves to the point of conflict and hopes to pick off the winner after it's been exhausted."

"You think it would follow a large gathering of megalodons?" Heston said.

"It's highly possible," Trevor said. "Other than the triplets, none of them share pack instincts. The Kraken likes to feed on them. If we can get a large group of them to gather and move as a group, the Kraken might follow."

"We still need a way to track it." Heston tapped the desk, brainstorming ideas. An imaginary slideshow of all of Denise's data played in his mind. Finally, a lightbulb went off. "The shark Albert. We can put him to use."

"The sickly one?"

"That's right." Heston lifted his iPhone and typed in a code, which brought a blueprint image of a machine which resembled a deep-sea Triton submersible. "We'll put these babies to use."

Trevor leaned over to look at the blueprint image of the Zeus-Class U.C.D (Underwater Combat Drones).

"They fire electric darts. You intend to zap Albert?"

"Zap him, start a fight," Heston said. "Maybe the Kraken will pick up on the disturbance and close in. Then we can plant a tracking device on it. If so, we'll know if he's following our megs to the final objective point."

Trevor chuckled, realizing what the Admiral was thinking. "That's mean, sir, using that poor ol' shark for bait like that."

"He's living on borrowed time anyway," Heston said. "I'll make some calls and we'll give it a try tomorrow. Get the Porpoise ready."

Trevor bowed like a servant before his king. "Your wish is my command."

CHAPTER 18

Nico rummaged through his closet, stuffing his clothes into two large duffle bags. Before Denise arrived, he had already received the call from the Admiral personally thanking him for his assistance, but informing him it was time to evacuate the island. On the bright side, the Admiral informed him that the federal government would provide a year's worth of pay to both him and Renny for their services, and three months' worth to all the Cielo Nublado Police Department officers and staff.

If nothing else, it could afford Nico an extended vacation.

Denise would be paid a similar sum for her services. He wasn't sure the amount, but because she was doing scientific research directly for the Admiral, it was probably significantly more. Because of this, it took him aback to see her stressed out about leaving.

It was three in the afternoon. The last half-hour had been spent griping about how Trevor was remaining in service, how the bastard was using the Porpoise, and the fact that the Admiral knew about the device and never said anything.

"Don't you think it's strange?" she said. "He had me here for research. Why would he not let me in on the loop that this device was being used on the creatures?"

Nico threw some shirts on the mountain that poked from his duffle bag. "Don't know, sweetie." He cupped both hands on the shirts and did CPR compressions on the pile, gradually cramming it down until he could get that zipper shut.

"Aren't you concerned about all of this?"

"Not really. We talked about this before, I was already fantasizing about moving on. If this continues long enough, the federal government will buy out this property. Saves me the trouble of having to put it up for sale."

"They'll screw you over," Denise said. "Pay half what it's worth, if you're lucky."

He shrugged. "Dunno. If this island becomes a Navy base, Heston might see to it we're paid twice what it's worth. Trust me, the federal government throws around money without a care in the world. Humans tend to do that when they aren't the ones providing the funds. The cost of buying all the properties on this island will be like pocket change. Probably sneak it into a healthcare bill that nobody will read. At least this time, some of it will come back my way for once."

"You're not curious as to what's going on around here? I thought you were a detective?"

"Emphasis on the 'were'. Not even a chief anymore. Actually, I'm unemployed now."

"Maybe, but don't pretend certain things don't add up," Denise said.

"They don't, but it doesn't matter. There's ONE detail I have my eye on."

"The money. I know."

"Oh, shut up." Nico stepped out of his bedroom. "You seriously think that little of me?"

Guilt weighed her down, right onto one of the dining room chairs. "You're right. I'm sorry."

Nico went to the fridge and pulled out a beer. The last drink he would have in this house, might as well enjoy it.

"That one detail is control. I have *no* control over what happens here. There's another detail I should mention, and that is the government's tendency to silence those who ask the wrong questions."

Denise nodded, then extended her hand. "Got another one of those?" Nico pulled out a second beer and handed it to her. She took a slug, then looked at the house where her ex had lived the last few years. "Maybe it is out of our control. But it's got me nervous. Why would they want us out of here?"

"For security reasons, I guess."

"That's the official answer, but what's the real reason? They're gonna try to move the sharks tomorrow. Why is it important to have us gone by morning? Just three people?" She took another drink of the beer, then rested the bottle against her forehead. "Gosh, what's been happening? This summer has been nuts."

"Tell me about it. The meteor and tsunami, the Miami bank robbers, Cameron getting murdered, prehistoric fish and squids showing up everywhere, oversized eels that can shoot electricity, this shit with China... Oh, and now whales are going apeshit, swimming into shark nets." He scoffed then drank his beer. "Stupid bastards, laying out a regular shark net to repel a megalodon."

Whales... electricity... Denise stared into the distance.

"Everything alright?" Nico asked.

"You remember Maxwell Island?"

It took a minute for Nico to remember what she was referring to. "Oh, that! Jeez. So much has happened around here, I haven't really paid much attention to that."

"It was a Fourth of July catastrophe," Denise said.

Both took a minute to reflect on the new reports circulating through the TV and computer screens several weeks back.

Maxwell Island was in the vicinity of Georgia. Much like Cielo Nublado, it relied heavily on the tourist industry, with part of the population consisting of fishermen. Most people, except vacation goers, had hardly heard of the island until it started showing up in the news.

It began with a yacht explosion on the night of June 30th. Four young people were reportedly shooting off fireworks from the flybridge of that vessel when suddenly the yacht exploded. That same night, another small boat went missing, only for one of the occupants to eventually be found dead under the beaches. She had been bitten in half, the rest bloated from being under the water for so long.

The following day, a speedboat towing a skier ran aground, the skier nowhere to be found. Soon, reports started emerging from a local researcher regarding oddly increasing water temperatures in random locations.

In the next couple of days, a fishing vessel was sunk. Witnesses confirmed that a sixty-foot sperm whale rammed the vessel, sinking it. With things on the island going to hell fast, the island government requested the Coast Guard to help. According to the Lieutenant Commander in charge of the cutter, there was no choice, they had to put the whale down.

That put the locals at ease. Even allowed them to continue with the Fourth of July festivities, in which some big company was going to have a big show. Several yachts were in place near one of the island beaches, where they would launch a glorious display of fireworks over the water.

It all led to disaster. Two of the boats were lost in enormous explosions, as though they were hit with hellfire missiles. Flashing lights were reported by witnesses and police, though there was too much chaos for anyone to understand exactly what was going on. At the end of it all, numerous people including law enforcement were dead.

The Coast Guard moved in with full force. Federal investigators declared the catastrophe to be the results of deliberate sabotage. Numerous people were tracked down and arrested. Names and histories were released to the public. The chief of police resigned and refused to comment on the matter.

"You remember it?" Denise asked.

"Yep."

"Any of the details sound familiar?"

"A little."

"I didn't believe that bullshit when it was first reported," Denise said. "There's almost no record of sperm whales attacking boats."

"I agree, but a few things don't add up about that event," Nico said. "The other odd circumstances involve boat explosions, one that took place around June 30th, then the fireworks fiasco a few days later. It's fair to speculate whether a megalodon was involved, but that said, sharks don't have incendiary abilities. They can't blow up boats like that."

"Yachts don't blow up like that on their own," Denise said.

"They didn't. Sabotage, remember? Psychos who infiltrated the company boats," Nico said.

"And the yacht that exploded July 1st?"

"They were shooting fireworks off, with a propane grill on deck."

"And you believe all of that?"

"I didn't say that," Nico said. He looked at his ex-wife and saw the inquisitive look on her face. "Look, I have no way of finding out if it's connected to what's going on around here."

"Why don't you talk to the police chief?"

"She resigned."

"What about the new one?"

"It's not like we're in a club," he said. "I don't think he'll take kindly to me sticking my nose in his department's business. And besides, what would I use the information for? I'm not a cop right now. Even if I was, I have no power to investigate the government. I'd be suicided, and given our personal history, believe me they'll be able to conjure up a convincing story."

Denise got up and tossed her beer bottle into the trash. "I'm telling you, Heston's up to something. And he's throwing a bunch of money at us to gain our good favor."

"Nothing we can do about it," Nico said. "That's the way of the world. It's a hard pill to swallow, I know. But swallow it, you must. Try to look at the positive. You've made a grand discovery. You'll be featured in university textbooks for decades. Not to mention your Porpoise device is helping to steer the sharks away."

"Yeah, seventy miles from Trinidad." She made air quotes.

"What's wrong with Trinidad?"

"There are no islands in that region. Nothing but deep ocean."

"Wait… He lied to you about where he's taking the sharks?"

"Yeah."

Nico opened the fridge. That last beer was about to come in handy. He twisted the cap off and held the neck to his lips, his eyes in a trance during the entire process.

"Why would a Navy admiral lie about that? They're just sharks."

"Why would he lie about anything?" Denise said. "Why does anyone in power ever lie?"

"To promote their image, to prolong their career…though I doubt Heston is the type to worry about those things." Nico only knew one answer. "Because they have an agenda."

"I wonder what the Admiral's is."

"I don't know. Again, it really doesn't matter. There's NOTHING we can do about it. We're powerless. All you can do is focus your energy somewhere else. Do something positive."

Denise put her head on the table. "Like what?" Her phone rang, making her jump. She recognized the number of her university. "Hello?... Uh-huh... yeah, I'll be heading out tomorrow... Where? I figured I'd head home... It's that bad?... Yeah, I saw it on the news but was too preoccupied... Sure, I'll head up there... I'll try to get a flight... Yep, thanks. Bye." She lowered the phone and walked past Nico into his bedroom.

"Mind telling me what that was about?"

"That was Dr. Noah from the University of Florida." Denise went through the cabinets, taking the few clothes she had stored there and stuffed them into a small bag. "He's asking if I can go to Palm Beach to help with the humpback whales. One's tangled pretty damn bad and has severe lacerations. There's a good chance that infection will set in."

"There you go!" Nico clapped his hands. "What did I tell you? You just needed something to drop into your lap. Some good conservation work will get your mind off all the weird shit going on around here. What time were they hoping you'd get there?"

"Soon as possible," Denise said.

"As in, this afternoon?"

"Yep. What's Renny up to?"

"Probably packing everything he owns." Nico groaned when he understood the point of her question. "No, come on. He's not our own private airline pilot. He has a life too. Besides, all we have to do is make a call to the Navy, and they can send us over."

"You seriously want to leave your department helicopter here with them?" Denise said.

Nico scratched the back of his ear. "Not really. Why's it so important, though?" Denise cracked a tiny grin. Nico backed up a step. "You're smiling."

"What? That a bad thing?"

"At ten at night, you and me sitting near a fireplace with a glass of wine in hand, a smile is a great thing. But we're talking about trips to the mainland and using my helicopter. What exactly do you have in mind?"

"You know as well as I do that whales don't make b-lines straight to shore," she said.

"I don't know. I seem to recall a sperm whale doing the same thing last week. Then again, it was being chased by a megalodon... ohhhh..."

"Uh-huh!"

"You think there's another shark up in that region?"

"It's extremely likely. It'd be insane to assume we've identified everything that's come out up from the depths. Between the meteor strike and the earthquakes in the Puerto Rico Trench, we've seen a lot of large organisms come to the surface."

"And you want the chopper to do some meg hunting." Nico crossed his arms. "You forget that Renny has a life too. I doubt he's in the mood to spend the rest of his summer flying across the Atlantic in search of overgrown fish."

"No, Nico, you don't understand." Denise stepped out, bag in hand as though she was ready to head out the door that instant. "If we find any megalodon swimming up there, we can plant a tag on it. Then, when the Navy leads the sharks out, we can figure out where they're going."

"For what purpose?"

"To expose the truth."

"Okay. Again, for what purpose?"

Denise dropped the bag and crossed her arms. "Because it's the *truth*. Because it's the right thing to do. Cameron would do it, if he were alive. You've been a cop your whole life. I figured you of all people would be up in arms about learning the truth."

"I was putting away criminals. Not investigating government and military conspiracies." Nico sank into the dining room chair. "Sorry. I like my head where it's at."

Denise leaned on the opposite end of the table, her eyes burning deep into his soul. "So, the truth means nothing to you. Good to know. I guess you really aren't a cop anymore."

Nico had a thousand replies, all of which he kept to himself. Instead, he settled with, "I guess I'll give Renny a call." He got up, unclipped his smartphone, and walked outside.

Denise absorbed the quiet, then shut her eyes. *Why'd you say that, you dumb bitch? You just got back with him, and you're ruining it. And for what? Scientific passion?*

There was no point in saying anything now. It had been a grueling week in which they faced life-or-death situations like comic book superheroes. Both were unnerved and exhausted. Maybe a day or two on the mainland would help ease the tension.

Nico stepped back inside. "Grab your stuff. Renny's already packed. Smart devil knew this day was coming. He'll meet us at the station. I'll give a call to the Command Center and let them know the change of plans." He grabbed his duffle bags and took them to the truck, stopping briefly at the door to look at her. "You coming?"

Denise nodded. "Yes." She picked up her bag and followed him out.

CHAPTER 19

Islamorada General Hospital

"Australia's Naval forces are gathering near the Territory of Ashmore and Cartier Islands in response to heightened Chinese aggression. Around noon U.S. eastern time, nineteen Chinese fighter jets flew into Taiwanese airspace, prompting the Taiwan Air Force to scramble their jets. Other nations, such as Japan and Germany, have released statements, threatening military action should China launch an invasion."

Being in the hospital room was torture. Carley's life was nothing but a cycle of non-events, watching the world spiral out of control on the television. She should have known better; her mother was a news hog, even if she questioned whether it was the truth. With the remote in her hand, she stared at the television, while the IVs did their thing.

Carley slumped on the sofa in a trance. This was life as she knew it until she could finally get out of here. She had used up some of her spare time talking to her husband on the phone and wandering about the Key. The sunshine helped a bit. Still, it didn't change the fact her day was mostly comprised of sitting and waiting. The constant questions from her husband and mother about the status of her job didn't help. It was the same answer every time. 'I don't know.'

It was sometime after five when her phone rang. To her delight, it was Renny Jackman. Compared to listening to the endless string of news media, his voice was angelic.

She answered it. "Hey. Gimme just a sec." She stood up and walked into the hallway.

"Where you going?" Valerie asked.

"Renny's on the phone," Carley replied. "I'm heading out to the lobby."

"Him again, huh?" Valerie winked and smiled.

"EW! NO! Not to mention, have you forgotten I'm married? HE'S married!"

"Doesn't stop you guys from…"

Carley shut the door before her mother could make the crude hand gestures. She took a breath. "Oh…my… GOD!"

"Everything okay?" a nurse asked.

"Physically, yes. Mentally, I'm not sure if the finest surgeons can fix what's wrong in that woman's head." The nurse laughed and went about her day. Carley stepped out into the lobby and sat down.

Nothing needed to be said to Renny for him to get the full picture.

"That bad, huh?"

"You don't want to know," Carley said.

"I actually kinda do," he said.

"Good God. You and Mom are a match made in heaven." They both chuckled. "So, you doing alright? It's getting scary. I heard another cutter got smashed up."

"The news already got wind of that, huh?"

"It's all Mom will have on the stupid television. I guess, in her defense, there's a lot happening in the world right now. What with potential war and all."

"Could get worse for us. Technically, we're still young enough to get drafted into the service."

"Oh, God. If you're the best the U.S. has to offer, we're really screwed. On that note, what's going on at Cielo Nublado? Doing more scientific research for the Navy?"

"I have no idea. We're not there anymore."

"Huh?"

"We got the boot today. According to the good admiral, our services are no longer required. On the bright side, I'm getting a year's worth of pay. Sticking around to help out kinda paid off."

"What? They're paying you a full year's wages?"

"Damn right."

"Son of a bitch. I'm gonna have to give Nico a piece of my mind for sending me out early. All I got is no pay and a week of hanging with my mother."

"Oh, don't be so mean! Your mom's cool! And you're not walking away with nothing. Nico said you'll be getting three months' pay. All paid for by the U.S. government."

"Hmm. I suppose that's better than nothing. Where are you guys now?"

"Palm Beach. Nico's soon to be ex-ex was requested to help out with the humpback whale situation. I flew her and Nico over. She's at the beach area now. Nico's getting checked into a hotel. I'm sorta hanging out. Thinking of starting a new career as a chopper pilot."

"I bet the missus is giving you an earful."

"No more than the usual amount. On the plus side, we're officially talking about moving."

"We've been discussing the same thing," Carley said. "Kinda sucks how everything has changed so quickly. I guess people go their separate ways sooner or later."

Another several seconds of awkward silence passed. It was the first time both of them realized they might not see each other again on a regular basis.

"Uh, speaking of moving. Are there talks of evacuating you guys to the mainland?"

"No. Some people have headed north, but there's been no formal talks of clearing the Keys," Carley said. "All the experts are saying the waters are too shallow for the sharks to pose any real threat. The folks at Palm Beach might disagree with that, but I digress."

Soon, the topic of current events was too much for both of them. They shifted the subject to sports, gossip about Nico and Denise, stories of police work, until it all came back around to the hospital.

"I know it's a scary surgery. Let me know if there's anything you need."

"Thanks. Not that you can do much. You're a couple hundred miles away."

"Hey. I got a helicopter, remember? I can go wherever I want. I'm like Superman. I can fly over, save the day, and you'd be clinging to me saying, 'Oh, my hero!'"

"There you go again with that nonsense. Not gonna happen." She chuckled and looked at her watch. "Oh, hell. I'd better get back to mom's room. Wish me luck—she'll likely accuse us of having phone sex."

"Ha! You wish!"

Carley squeezed her eyes shut. "I'd tell you to stay out of trouble, but I'd just be kidding myself. So, instead, I'll settle with stay safe."

"You too. Bye."

She hung up and returned to her mom's room. A shit-eating grin creased Valerie's face.

"Damn. It's been almost forty minutes. That stud must have a voice smooth as ice."

"Mom, another crude statement from you, and I'm going to ask the surgeon to sew your mouth shut."

Valerie shrugged. "Just say'n." She turned her attention back to the television screen. CNN was showing footage of the Kraken's attack on the *Omega Fury*. "That's a big ass octopus."

"Oh really. You think?"

"Hope that sucker doesn't venture this way."

Carley sat on the couch and laughed. "Mom, we're on land. I think we're in the clear."

"Hard to say, pumpkin. I've seen one of those things climb onto a dock ten feet high. Pretty damn fast too. If that big sucker's strong enough to bring down a Coast Guard cutter, believe me he's more than capable of slithering ashore wherever he wants." She took a sip of her juice. "Let's just hope he doesn't get any bright ideas."

"All you need to do is talk, Mom. Trust me, your monologues are more than enough to drive that octopus back to the depths." Carley leaned her head on the armrest and shut her eyes. "Maybe the Navy should hire you."

She heard a delighted 'mmm' from her mother. *Oh no. I triggered a memory I really don't want to hear.*

"Ah, the Navy," Valerie said. "I remember meeting this sailor back around eighty... before I met your father. Oh, man... what a man. He laid eyes on me, and that night we were..."

Carley cupped her ears. *Why is this happening to me?!*

CHAPTER 20

Palm Beach, Florida.

With permission from the local police department and airport security, Renny was able to land the chopper at Palm Beach International Airport. There, an Uber awaited, arranged by Denise's dean at the University of Florida. The Uber took them to the beach area where the whales were netted.

Two of them were tangled, while a few others swam a hundred feet further out, refusing to abandon their companions. The ones netted suffered bad lacerations and were showing signs of infection. Denise was immediately on a boat to tend to the situation.

It was beyond Nico's range of expertise. With nothing to do, he and Renny checked into a hotel. It was another small bit of good fortune that fell into his lap: this 'hotel' was actually the Marriot Singer Island Beach Resort, and the University was paying the fee. It wasn't a bad view from his room. He could see the ocean from his window, and the boats gathering near the shark net.

The trip had been a quiet one. He and Denise didn't speak much except about the current situation. He buried his face in a book for much of the trip. He was in no mood to read, however. Denise's remarks about him not being a cop anymore hit their mark. He could tell she felt bad about it, but it didn't matter.

For a half-hour, he flicked through the channels. It was either news or a bunch of programs he had no interest in. He had the option to order a movie, but for the price offered, he may as well go to Walmart and buy the Blu-ray. Besides, he was in no mood. All he could think about was the past several years.

He did a good job in Cielo Nublado. The staff and people liked him, and he liked them. But he wasn't there because of passion. It was a change of scenery, a chance to get away from the tragedy that rocked his world. Now, he was wondering if the time spent there had made him careless.

The 'Wolf of Waco' was sprawled out on the hotel bed, staring at the ceiling.

"Yeah, I'm not a cop anymore. What does she expect me to do? Investigate a Four-Star Admiral with nearly fifty years of military service? Yeah, sure." Sure, he had investigated more than his fair share of coverups, though most were local to Waco, Texas. He had more than his fair share of cases that took a dramatic turn, but as far as the world outside of Waco was concerned, they were nothing earth-shattering. The worst scandal he uncovered was a prosecutor who falsified evidence to put a defendant in prison, bribed by the actual perpetrator of the crime. Nothing federal or state government related. Certainly not military.

Fed up with the silence, he turned to grab the remote for another round of channel surfing. His arm rubbed against the mattress, his hand grazing his watch which was on the nightstand next to the remote.

Zap!

"Yeow!" Nico withdrew his hand and shook it. That zap got him good. It even managed to produce a spark. He sat up. *Gosh, now I feel like the megalodon... what'd they call him... O'Brien. When the sucker got zapped by that eel.*

His memory went to the time they landed at the helipad and Admiral Heston heard about the creature's presence.

"Son of a bitch didn't seem surprised that such a thing existed. Nor did Dr. Zenner. Unless they already knew about it. But why would they keep that secret?"

Doesn't matter. The thing's dead anyway.

Unless there's another one they were worried about...

He hated moments where his mind debated itself, especially when he voiced some of the thoughts out loud. It made him feel as though he belonged in a mental asylum.

The other reason he hated these moments was because they always led to him uncovering something. It was his investigative mind at work.

Curiosity got the better of him. Nico got on his laptop, got onto the hotel's Wi-Fi, and typed in 'Maxwell Island accident. *Dream Wrecker* explosion.'

It happened a few days prior to the fireworks show disaster. Photos of the vessel found their way to the internet.

Right on first glance, Nico knew something was off. *Those are burn marks on the hull. Like someone put a giant torch to the underside of this yacht.* The top was pretty much gone, the vessel having exploded from the inside. *A propane explosion wouldn't have caused that.*

"It's more like the fuel tank ruptured. Even a fire on deck wouldn't have done that. The fire would've had to make its way through the fuel cap." *Or a massive electrical surge hit the boat.* "But that'd have to be a freaking bolt of lightning."

The more details he looked up, the weirder the whole situation appeared. People had been going missing in the days prior to the Belanger Fireworks Festival. A jet skier was confirmed missing by her fiancé. A pod of dead orcas was discovered by the former chief of police. The orcas were said to have suffered severe burns and heart failure, as though exposed to a high-voltage current. In her initial statement, she explained that during the investigation, her lieutenant was killed by some large organism under the water. Later on, she changed her statement, explaining that it was a great white that had come to feed on the dead orcas.

"What was he doing in the water to begin with? I doubt he was going for a nightly swim."

Only logical reason would be he was somehow knocked off his boat, or his boat was sunk.

"You're not gonna convince me that a typical great white sank a police boat."

Then there was the mainstream narrative that domestic terrorists sabotaged the Belanger Fireworks Festival.

Really? Hundreds of more high profile events taking place across the country, yet they pick THAT one? On some vacation resort? Why not one in New York, or one of the ones in Texas? Somewhere a little more densely populated. Not some borderline obscure fishing community.

He looked over the recorded history of the suspects. It was the typical mumbo jumbo, filled with unsubstantiated nuggets of violence that apparently nobody took notice of until now. Every article mentioned violent social media statements from these suspects, though interestingly enough, none were ever shown. The media and a few politicians made their unfounded remarks, attempting to link the suspects with opposing political groups. Never let a tragedy go to waste.

Nico laid his head against the pillow. It was all interesting stuff, but nothing to go on.

Wait. Who responded to this crisis?

He ran a new search through the web.

The *USCGC Richard Denning*, commanded by Lieutenant Commander Jim Davidson responded to the whale incident, and was called back after the attack on the festival.

Nico's mind flashed to the briefing. "Son of a bitch. I was in the same room as the guy."

Interesting that he and his crew just so happen to be involved with what's going on around Cielo Nublado.

It was an odd coincidence. Still, it technically wasn't substantial that something sinister was going on. The only way he could make a connection was by speaking to the Maxwell Island Police Department.

He looked up the number and picked up the hotel phone.

"Oh, God. Why am I doing this?"

Before his mind could answer and stall him, he dialed the number.

****

Maxwell Island Police Department.

It had been another late day for Chief of Police Royce Boyer. Unlike his predecessor, he was ready for the demands of the job. Just not the circumstances that came with his start.

The department's staff had been cut in half, with many of them quitting over the course of the month. Some did not want to be near water after the event, leading them to relocate to somewhere dry. There had been several funerals lately, which proved to be too much for many of the officers. Then there were the federal arrests of 'conspirators'. Every day, he faced questions from the remaining staff about the status of three officers who were arrested by the Coast Guard.

Things were only now starting to balance out. The island was quieter than ever, which in a way, helped. The job was rinse and repeat, with little to worry about now that the media and military had departed. The current mayor was happy with the situation, despite the fact that local business owners were not. Obviously promises were made, handshakes were exchanged, and now she was waiting out the clock.

Whatever. So long as things stay nice and quiet around here.

It was nearing six. The afternoon shift was out on patrol. Few calls were coming in. After the cancellation of several August reservations, it looked like the typical busy time of the year was already coming to a close.

He shut down his computer and stood up, grabbed his keys, and went for the door. He called down the hallway to his dispatchers. "I'm heading out. Give me a holler if you need anything."

"Okay, Royce. See you tomorrow," Cindi, the dispatch supervisor replied.

He reached the door and was halfway out before she called for him again. "Hey Chief?!"

Royce chuckled and stepped back inside. "Wow. I didn't expect it to be so soon."

Cindi chuckled. "I have someone on the line asking to speak with you."

"Is it important?"

"They didn't elaborate."

"Then it can wait." He reached for the door again, but stopped himself. "Who is it?"

"The Cielo Nublado's Chief of Police," she replied.

"Cielo…" Royce's voice trailed off as his mind connected the dots. *Cielo Nublado… that's where the megalodon attacks occurred.* "Transfer it to my office phone, will ya?"

He returned to his office and sat down. At the first ring, he picked up the phone.

"Chief Boyer speaking."

"Good afternoon, sir. My name is Chief Nico Medrano of the Cielo Nublado Police Department. I'm calling to consult with you regarding current events that are taking place around my island."

Royce hesitated before responding. "Yes. You're the officer who killed the megalodon. I heard you took out those maniacs who robbed that bank in Miami."

"Well, the shark had a hand in that... or a tooth.... Never mind. Listen, I'm trying to figure something out. My island is now occupied by the Navy, who are about to launch an operation to relocate the sharks."

"Oh, good," Royce said. "Forgive me, but what does this have to do with me?"

"One of the cutters involved is the USCGC Richard Denning. I believe you've had some experience with that vessel."

"We have. We had an unusual circumstance regarding a sperm whale. Sad situation, really. They were forced to put it down. Creature got really violent, went after ships."

"Did it?"

Royce hesitated again. "I assure you it did."

"Are you familiar with Rear Admiral White of the Coast Guard?"

"Never heard that name."

"What about Admiral Heston of the U.S. Navy?"

Another hesitation. "No." The next hesitation came from the other end of the line. A cop like Royce knew his lie had been detected. "What's this about, Chief? I'm not a fan of being interrogated over the phone."

"I'm connecting some dots, and I think you and the former chief might help me," Nico said.

"Help you with what? The sharks? Sounds like the Navy has that under control."

"That's possible. Except they've lied to me and Dr. Reta about where they're transferring the sharks. Funny, you don't seem curious as to HOW they'll be doing that."

Shit.

Royce gave thought to hanging up. He looked at his phone. It would not be surprising if it was tapped.

"Forgive me, Mr. Medrano. I've had a long day, and I'm eager to head home. I really hope things improve with your situation."

"I'm not sure it will. First megalodons, then a giant octopus, and then there's the eel that emitted electric currents that appeared out of nowhere."

"I... where?"

"Not far from the mainland. It's dead, though. Killed by one of the megalodons."

"It's dead?"

Another pause.

"You're familiar with this creature, aren't you, Chief?"

Once again, Royce recognized his failure. He should have acted astounded to hear that this creature could even exist. Hearing his own tone and that of Nico's, he knew he made it obvious that he was indeed familiar with this creature. There was relief in the news that it was dead, until he recalled one little detail.

"You said ninety feet?"

"Correct." Nico was concerned by that question. *"You sound underwhelmed."*

"Listen, let the Navy handle this. Keep your nose out of it. You hear?"

"Are they forcing you to stay quiet about this?"

"Do you not hear me? Do yourself a favor. Take a vacation. Get a new job. Keep your head in the sand."

"What's the endgame, Chief? Why would the Admiral want to keep news of these creatures silent? And what of the one that attacked your island?"

"I never said one did."

"Was it an electric eel? Please tell me it wasn't bigger than the one I encountered."

"Don't know what you're talking about. Sorry, sir. I have to go."

"Alright, I'm reading between the lines. One last question. Where's the former chief?"

"Silvia relocated after the festival tragedy. She's dealing with some severe physical ailments right now."

"Where, if I may ask?"

"You may ask. You know I'm not at liberty to disclose that information."

"Can I at least have a phone number?"

I swear this guy's trying to get us killed.

"No. She won't want to talk to you, anyway. Take my advice. Stay in your lane. Don't do anything stupid." He hung up.

****

The dial tone blared in his ear. Nico hung up and watched the ocean through the window. Though he did not personally know this Royce Boyer guy, he did not strike him as someone who was clumsy or easily pushed around. Though not a veteran, Nico had been around enough military guys in his career. Chief Boyer's voice and demeanor screamed Marine Corps. It was just a guess, but one Nico felt confident in.

The call failed to retrieve the information he hoped to obtain. However, enough slipped through the cracks to convince Nico not only that the two incidents were connected, but that Heston was behind it all. Royce had even explicitly warned him against treading this ground.

Words spoken by a man who had been given a strict warning by someone very powerful.

And who was paying for the former chief's medical bills? A bribe, perhaps? Maybe they were given a choice. Take the money and be quiet, or we'll make you disappear.

I wonder if those cops that were arrested were about to go to the media.

It was still speculation. Not enough to pin anything on Heston. Part of him was tempted to take Royce's advice. But the alarm bells were ringing too loudly.

The Admiral knew of the Porpoise, but did not say anything. He wanted them off the island, right as they were planning to conduct their operation. There was a sea monster attack on Maxwell Island that was being covered up. Heston lied to Denise about where he was luring the creatures.

Why all these lies and coverups? And is it a coincidence that it's occurring at the same time the Navy was caught dropping something in Chinese Naval territory?

****

"Did you run a trace on that number?" Royce asked.

Cindi nodded. "Palm Beach. A resort called Marriot Singer Island Beach Resort."

"Wonder why he's calling me from there."

"Not too far from where Silvia lives," she said.

"Yeah, but he doesn't know that," Royce said.

"You sure? Also, are you sure this guy is who he says he is? Maybe he's some media hack."

"No, he's definitely a cop," Royce said.

"What's he so curious about?" Cindi asked. "Is it about what happened?"

Royce didn't answer. Being in this office, Cindi had the luxury of not being present at the incident, therefore it was easier for her to follow the narrative.

"Write the number and hotel down for me, please." He waited for her to jot it down on a notepad, then took the sheet. "Thank you."

He returned to his office, switched his computer back on, and looked up the address. It was a fifty minute drive from the former chief's new address. Likely a coincidence. Still, he was tempted to check in on her.

He scrolled through his phone and found her new number. She had changed it two weeks prior, and only shared it with him.

Send.

****

Goldville, Florida.

Silvia Remar gasped, the pain in her lower back sending shockwaves through her entire body. Even after nearly a month, her back was not looking much better. The disc, which had been degenerating since her early twenties, was herniated completely now. Her usual exercises did little to shift it back into her spine.

She was living in perpetual agony, with no relief from painkillers. Had it not been for the epidural, sleep would be impossible. Simply lifting her head from the pillow was enough to trigger another lightning strike.

In this case, she turned it to look at her ringing phone. Looking at the number, her nerves began to light up. Stress always triggered the pain.

Why is he calling me?

Clenching her teeth, she pulled her phone off the nightstand. "This is Silvia."

"Hey. It's Royce."

"Yes. I recognized the number. Why are you calling me? Turns out you can't handle the job after all?"

"Looks like I've caught you in a mood," Royce said.

"I'm always in a mood."

"I recognize that. To answer your question, the job is fine. Quiet, actually. Very quiet. I have a feeling it'll stay that way for a few years. I'd ask how you're feeling, but I think I already know the answer."

Silvia rolled on her side and stretched her free arm. Sometimes this position helped, sometimes it hurt more.

"What do you want?"

"Has anyone called you?"

"Huh?"

"About the… incident."

"No. Why?"

"Just had a guy call me. The Chief of Police at Cielo Nublado. A guy named Nico Medrano. He just called from a hotel in Palm Beach, inquiring about what occurred here on Maxwell Island."

Silvia sat up… too fast. She shrieked, sat still for a moment, then returned the phone to her ear.

"And?"

"He saw one."

"A meg? No shit, they're all over the place down there."

"No. One of…"

More pain, stress induced.

"It's back?"

"Don't think so. Not the same one, at least. It's too small, according to what he told me. Probably not mature enough to exhibit its full capabilities, if you know what I mean."

"Anything else?"

"Heston's down there. According to this police chief, he's getting ready to move the sharks. If they're using the method I think they are, then it'll be more than megalodons they'll be luring."

"Does this guy know about what really happened at our island?"

"Not officially, but he suspects. He's not dumb. He's putting the puzzle pieces together. What he plans to do, I don't know. Anyhow, that's why I'm calling you. I wanted to give you a heads-up and make sure you didn't spill the beans on anything."

"Nobody's called yet. What'd you tell him?"

"To turn the other cheek and forget any of this is happening."

Silvia looked at her television remote and her desktop. The latter was still on, an article still on the screen. *Cargo ship reports mysterious underwater electrical activity in Nares Plain.*

Another article read *Party Yacht Accident: Boat mysteriously catches fire twenty miles northeast of the Bahamas. Authorities baffled. Are megalodons responsible?*

"How can anyone turn the other cheek? Least of all you and me?"

"Nothing we can do about it. I just wanted to make sure you were aware that somebody's snooping around. Don't give in to the temptation and say anything to anyone. You know you're being monitored."

"I know."

"So, any improvement on the pain?" Royce asked. Silvia groaned. "Hmm. I get the idea. Has the surgery been arranged for you, at least?"

"Next week. Wish it was three minutes from now, instead. Then several months of physical therapy."

"Well, at least something good came out of this. Don't mess it up. Like... Jay and Corey..."

"And Terry."

Officers Jay Noel, Corey Wiebe, and Terry Graft... three names that haunted her memory. She considered them better people, better cops, with a higher level of integrity. They weren't going to be bought. The truth was most important. Too bad they were going up against an unbeatable opponent. They had not been heard from after the Coast Guard arrested them two days after they attempted to go to the media.

"Thanks for the heads-up, Royce."

"No problem. Feel better, alright?"

"I'll do my best. Bye."

Silvia ended the call, then planted her face in her pillow. In just a few short hours, night would be here. If the muscle relaxers were good for anything, it was helping her pass out hard.

Think of the money, she told herself. *You're set. And your back is going to be fixed up. Considering your circumstances, this is a pretty swell deal. Just don't pay attention to reality.*

She looked out the bedroom door into her living room. She could see the edge of her treadmill near the window. Walking didn't do much nowadays, but nevertheless, she needed the exercise. If nothing else, burning the energy would make it easier to sleep.

Slowly, Silvia stood up, strained to put her back brace on, then went to the device.

The constant spikes in pain, and the desire to make it all end, easily quelled the temptation to do the right thing.

CHAPTER 21

The humpbacks were free, their bodies given a proper dose of disinfectant, their wounds sewn with a biodegradable thread that would dissolve over the course of the month.

Denise brushed her hands together and smiled. "At least something good happened today."

"It's weird that they're still lingering this close to the shore," the boat driver said. They watched the family of whales swim in a group. Flukes rose over the water with grace. Some of them waved their flippers as if thanking the humans for their assistance. For several minutes, Denise watched them.

The driver was right. They weren't planning to go anywhere. Before, it made sense why the others remained. This was a dedicated group who would not abandon their injured companions. Even with their members freed and treated, they still were not moving on.

"At least they're giving us a nice song," the boat driver said. He smiled and pretended to dance to the steady chorus that the family provided.

Denise shook her head. "They're not singing."

"They're not? Awfully sounds like it."

"They're not singing. They're calling."

"Calling? Like, long distance?"

"Sort of," Denise said. "They're looking for another whale." She looked at the net, then at the driver. "Where are those workers who witnessed the whales approach?"

"Oh! Sam Travis and Kevin Chase! They're on the beach. Catching some overtime like me. That time and a half goes a long way…"

"I want to talk to them."

"Alright." The helmsman took the boat to shore. The evening sun assaulted their eyes like an angry demon. Even Denise's sunglasses were not enough to block its glare.

After they got close enough to fall into the shadows from one of the hotels, Denise could finally see again.

Dozens of people had grouped on the beach to watch the humpbacks. Many stood with smartphones out, recording or livestreaming the 'songs' and dances.

On the sand was one of the other maintenance boats. Two workers stood next to it, both yawning incessantly. She couldn't blame them. She worked her own share of double shifts and usually did the same toward the end.

The helmsman brought the boat onto the sand and snapped his fingers at the two men. "Hey! Sam. Kevin. This lady wants to speak with you."

The two workers stepped forward. The one named Kevin immediately raised his hands defensively.

"Hey, we didn't know those whales were going to hit the net…"

"Relax," Denise said. "I just want to understand what happened."

Kevin eased up. "Not much to explain. We started setting up the net early this morning. Gradually placed the anchors. Dipshit here…" he pointed his thumb at Sam, "took a thousand years to set one up. While I'm waiting, I see this huge shape coming right at us. I gun the engine and get us out of the way. When I looked back, these whales were plowing into the net we had just laid out."

"Wait… they were coming right *at you*?" Denise asked.

"Yeah."

"As in, your general direction, but a few dozen yards out to the side…"

"No, they were coming at us directly," Kevin said.

"Probably heard you whining and were sick of it. Just like me," Sam joked.

"Oh yeah? Is that why you took a thousand years to place the anchor?"

Sam turned to face him. "I told you, bean bag, I was inspecting that drone someone left under the water."

"Bean bag? What the hell kind of insult is that?" Kevin said.

"I'm curious to know the answer to that too!" Denise's helmsman said. "He's definitely too big to be tossed. And he definitely wouldn't fit into any small spaces!" He and Sam broke into laughter.

"Oh, yeah?" Kevin replied. "Speaking of small spaces, I seem to recall the last Christmas Eve party when your wife was giving me the 'mmm-hmm' face."

"Might've been that piece of pie you were hogging up."

"Could explain why the whales were coming at us," Sam said. "They thought they were visiting one of their own kind!" He and the helmsman laughed again.

Denise felt her neurons flash like sparking stars. She looked at the water. "Oh my God! That's it! That's why they're here!"

The two men's laughter doubled in intensity. Kevin sneered at the marine biologist. "Thanks."

"Even the scientist agrees!" Sam said.

"What? No! Jesus!" Denise waved her hands. *Gosh, these immature idiots. What did I walk into?*

"What did you actually mean?" Kevin asked.

"Sam, you said you saw something under the water?" she asked.

"A big drone with some sort of stereo speaker attached to it," he replied. "Didn't get a good look at it. Was too busy trying not to get eaten by whales."

"First of all, they wouldn't have eaten you. They're baleen whales," she said. "More importantly… a speaker?"

"Yeah. Lodged in the weeds," Sam said. "It was hidden pretty well. I wouldn't have found it had I not dropped my tool on it by accident."

Denise pointed a finger at the gap in the net. "And it was directly below where the whales got snagged?"

"Correct."

For the next several moments, Denise's eyes were locked on the Atlantic. The two maintenance men waited in silence, until finally Kevin spoke up. "Uh, is there a problem?"

"Can you take me there?" she asked.

"Beg your pardon?"

"You mean, you want to *dive*?" Sam asked.

"Correct. I want to see this thing," Denise said. "I'll get some diving gear and be ready to go in fifteen minutes."

"Yeeeeaah…" Kevin looked at the setting sun. "We'll be out of daylight by then. Not to mention our boats are going to be busy retracting the net…" His voice grew bitter. "Undoing the morning's work."

"Since your new friends are hanging around, we don't want to risk them getting caught in the net again," Sam said. He nodded at the biologist. "How 'bout first thing in the morning?"

"Seven-thirty sharp," she said.

"Seven… uh, sure," Sam said. "Frankly, I was hoping to sleep in a little, but alright."

"Good. Meet you here tomorrow."

****

The day finally caught up with Denise when she entered the Marriot Singer Island Beach Resort. She stopped in the lobby, seeing Renny on one of the sofas with his phone in hand.

Probably talking to his wife.

"Yeah, I'll catch a flight out of here tomorrow," he said.

Yep. Definitely his wife.

He looked at her and smiled. "Hang on a sec," he said to the missus, then lowered his phone. "Hey, Doc! How are the whales? You save the day?"

"That's what I do," Denise said. "Is Nico down here or is he in our room?"

"He's been hiding in that room since we arrived."

"He never came out?"

"Nope. But don't worry, no hookers have been sent up there to my knowledge." He smiled mischievously.

Good God. Did a wave of immaturity consume this whole area while I was working?

"I feel so much better," she joked back. "So, what brings you down here? Bad reception?"

"Just waiting on a pizza," Renny said.

"Hope it's better than the one Nico made me recently."

"It's the thought that counts. At least, that's what I'm told," Renny said. "Speaking of thoughts, what do you think is the next step for you and the Chief?"

"I don't know," Denise said. "We haven't discussed it yet. A lot has happened in a short amount of time."

"Is that doubt I hear in your voice?"

"No… I don't know," she said.

"I'd imagine the next step should be simple. Have him move in with you. Maybe he'll find a job in the local police department where you live. Hell! Make him work with the campus police!"

Denise smiled weakly. "If only things were that simple. My job requires a lot of travel."

"It didn't before?"

"No. Nowadays, I'm working all over the place. There's years' worth of research that needs to be done. The meteor impact and subsequent earthquakes have created a lot of ecological changes. I'm not sure if Nico's a fan of the idea of being a traveling husband."

"He's a big boy. He'll get over it," Renny said. "Besides, he's not the kind of guy to fall in love with a place."

That warmed Denise. "Thanks, Renny. And also, thank you for all the help. And for saving my ass yesterday. I gave Nico all the credit, but didn't offer his trusty pilot any."

Renny smiled and lifted his chin heroically. "Us heroes never seek credit. Unless when we're going out to dinner and the waiter brings the bill…"

Denise laughed. "On that note…" she took out her wallet, "pizza's on me." She tossed him some cash and went to the stairs.

"Hey, thanks!" He looked at the bill. "Hey! This is only ten bucks! The tab's twenty-five. Plus the tip!" Denise was already up the steps. "I'll remember that next time you need to be rescued!"

Denise made her way to the hotel room. Having gone straight to the beach after arrival, she never had the chance to get a key card. Nico had texted her the room number and floor.

Seeing the door ajar made her smile. Nico was always a very considerate man. It brought to mind moments of their past when he'd run to the grocery store for some items and return with a twenty-ounce coke for her. Little things like that always added up.

She stepped inside. "Hey. I'm back..."

To her surprise, Nico was already passed out on the bed with a laptop on his lap. *Poor guy must've been bored out of his mind.* She admired his sleeping figure for a moment, then gently lifted the laptop from his lap. She placed it on the desk, plugged it in so it could charge overnight, then brought up the screen to make sure nothing needed to be saved. The password was still the same from years past.

Such an experienced lawman, and he still falls for the most basic security goof-ups.

The screen lit up. Front and center was an image of Admiral Vince Heston. The text below was a detailed summary of his early life and military career.

Joined the U.S. Navy in 1971. Completion of bachelor's degree in 1973. Promoted to Captain in 1974.

Yadda, yadda, yadda.

She moved the mouse to the exit icon, stopping after seeing that Nico had seven tabs open. Five were about the Admiral, one had something to do with Maxwell Island, the last one containing a scientific article about strange ocean temperature fluctuations.

"The hell?" She clicked on the last one.

'Mariners Avoiding Bizarre Hot Zone in Northern Cape Verde Basin. U.S. Naval ships sighted near area. The crew of the Cargo Ship Arthur Wales, after wandering too close to the area, reported strange flashing lights under the water. According to one, it resembled a lightning storm under the waves. An esteemed scientist from the University of Florida has stated that the reports are exaggerations from mariners with too much imagination.'

Denise only knew one PhD from the University of Florida that would make such a statement. The same marine biologist with a connection to the Navy.

She went to the next tab, which outlined the mysterious events that occurred near Maxwell Island. This article was pieced together by a conspiracy theorist. Not somebody Nico would turn to for information, but after scrolling through down the page, she understood why.

'As you can see here, there's clearly something moving under the water.' Under the text was a photo, taken at night, showing what appeared to be an angular snout just underneath the water. *'Is the U.S. government covering up the involvement of megalodons during the Belanger Fireworks Festival at Maxwell Island?'*

Denise stared at the image for several minutes. The thing in the water was obscured by night and the reflection of lights from boats and fire, but it was definitely there.

"That's not a megalodon. Their snouts are cone-shaped. This one's jaw looks more... crocodilian," she said. *Just like the thing we saw when we rescued Dr. Trevor.*

She scrolled through the other tabs whose information centered around Admiral Heston.

One was about the Battle of Old Baldy in the Korean War. After a summary of how the conflict played out, the article listed notable American casualties. Among them was Lieutenant Ralf Heston, killed by Chinese artillery units.

Heston? The Admiral's father?

That led to the next article, which was also about Heston's personal history. A very long segment was about his mother's struggle. Two years after Ralf Heston's death, she remarried to the vice president of a grocery chain.

Probably in hopes of financial support for her kid.

Reading on, Denise learned of the divorce, following claims of physical and mental abuse. Police records show that the second husband, Curt Lewis Rhonda, was arrested, charged, and convicted of battery. Sadly, the misery did not end there for Mrs. Heston. For over a decade, she suffered through a series of jobs in mills and groceries, trying to make ends meet. The stress resulted in a drinking problem, and in June 1963, she took her own life.

"Jesus." She went to the next tab, which was another article about the Admiral's biography. The first section outlined the life of his parents, with several paragraphs dedicated to the late Ralf Heston's military career. The top of the article was full of black and white pictures from 1941 in Burma, featuring Mr. Heston and the First American Volunteer Group training in Burma, formed to oppose the Japanese invasion of China. By May the following year, the Flying Tigers were disbanded, the AVG moved into the Fourteenth Air Force. Over the course of World War 2, Ralf Heston flew several combat missions in Indonesia, the South China Sea, and moved on to providing support during the island hopping campaign.

Ralf Heston remained in the service after World War 2, reached the rank of Captain, and flew bombing missions in the Korean War. In the second engagement of the Battle of Old Baldy, Captain Heston was shot down by Chinese forces who had overwhelmed the 23rd Infantry Regiment and gained a foothold on the east finger of Old Baldy.

"Hey."

Denise turned around and saw Nico smiling at her. "Hey."

He rubbed his eyes and stretched. "I guess I dozed off. How'd you do with the whales?"

"Good," she said. "I'm making a dive in the morning, though. One of the workers stated he saw a drone under the water, and I want to check it out."

"A drone?"

"With a speakerphone attached to it."

Nico sat up. "Interesting. A speaker like that would have to be remotely operated."

"Just like the ones we used for the Porpoise."

"Interesting. What a coincidence, a speakerphone is lying under the water, exactly where a megalodon and a pod of whales arrived. Didn't you say the Porpoise uses amplified whale calls to either attract or deter sea life?"

"Correct." Denise felt a chill run up her spine. She looked at the water. "God, I hope that feeling in my gut is wrong."

"Depends," Nico said. "How far can whales hear each other's calls?"

"Miles," Denise said. "Many, many miles."

"Would a Porpoise signal designed to attract a pod of whales also be able to lure a hungry hundred-twenty foot shark?"

Denise sighed heavily. "Yes. But why did they place one here?"

"Same reason they're covering up whatever happened at Maxwell Island," Nico said. Denise looked at him, curious. "I spoke with the current chief. He refused to give any concrete information. To sum it up, he's scared. Not of what's in the water, but of retaliation. For someone to strike such fear into a guy like that, it would need to be someone with a lot of power. Either in government, or..."

"The military," Denise finished. She looked at the image on the conspiracy article. "This was long before the megalodons started showing up. If what we suspect is true, why would they cover up the existence of this thing?"

"Probably the same reason they would lie to you about where they plan to locate the sharks," Nico said. "Either they're responsible for bringing it to the east coast, or they see military applications that they don't want the rest of the world knowing about."

They both sat on the bed and stared into the distance, lost in thought. They were taking an awful big risk in pursuing the truth.

A knock on the door made them both jump. The sound of it creaking made them stand up in alarm.

Were they discovered? Was this someone sent to make sure they stayed quiet? Did the Maxwell Island Chief sell them out to save his own skin? The University used a credit card to book the hotel. It would not have been difficult for some government official to figure out their location.

The door swung open.

Nico and Denise eased at the sight of a clumsy Renny Jackman stumbling into their hotel room with a pizza box, two subs, and a two-liter Pepsi.

"Hey. I saw you left it propped open, so I figured no hanky panky was going on."

Denise looked down and smiled. She forgot that she left the prop in place when she came in. *Thank God we weren't doing anything.*

"Just thought I'd offer you guys some pizza. My empty stomach got the better of me and I ordered too much," he said, extending the box forward.

Nico stood up. "You know what? Don't mind if I do."

"Great. Just so you know, I'm an anchovies guy."

Nico's hand stopped short. "Why am I not surprised?" *Aw, hell.* He took a slice.

CHAPTER 22

It was night and she could hear the loud cracks from the other side of the island. To the exhausted mind, they sounded like distant artillery blasts in a warzone.

The sound mingled well with the sight of death floating around her. The smell of charred flesh permeated the air. Blood coated the water's surface like oil. Large bodies, originally white and black in color, had paled from the loss of blood.

Silvia was no scientist, but one didn't need to be to know a pod of killer whales was not something that was easily killed. Yet, here they were, an entire family of death.

Terror struck with the speed of the white flash. As though Zeus and Poseidon were at war beneath the waves, the flashes were everywhere. Perfect zig-zagged lines of pure heat reached across the water. Shock and panic stifled her. The second police boat burst into flames, its occupant diving into the water.

Wet hands grasped Silvia's.

"Pull me up!"

Silvia bared teeth as she put all of her strength into lifting the officer. She leaned up, hoisting him to the gunwale.

Then she screamed.

It was as if her spine had shifted out of alignment. Nerves soared through her lower back and left leg. All at once, her energy vanished, and she fell forward against the gunwale, losing her grip.

The sound of splashing water filled her ears. Then a bloodcurdling scream.

She could see the thing shaking him in its jaws like a hungry dog. Her screams turned to cries.

"No! No!" She collapsed on the deck, lost in a heap of mental and physical torture.

Silvia woke up, the sudden motion spiking nerve pain. The only thing worse was the torment going on in the depths of her mind. It was a pain that could not be cured with surgery. Booze either suppressed it or made her dwell on it even more. Same with pills.

She eased herself out of bed and looked at the clock. Five-forty in the morning. The sun was starting to creep over the horizon, shining through the windows and displaying the interior of her new house.

Every day, she justified taking the payment. What would speaking out do? She'd just end up like the others, anyhow. Vanished, her reputation tarnished... more than it already was.

People died, yet she profited. They were people she knew. People with bright careers, who did really good in the world. People like Adam Henry, who did more than coast through a job they didn't like. She remembered the letter she found in her office mailbox. He was leaving the low stress—*then* low stress—life of policing on Maxwell Island to investigate human trafficking at the U.S. southern border.

It should've been me in that thing's jaws. Not him. What did I do all day? Sit in an office and wait out the day, resenting my life circumstance while other people achieved real goals.

It was the daily debate she conducted against herself every morning. It was as much a part of her routine as getting on the treadmill and walking. It was the only way to unstiffen herself. Every step hurt, but not moving was worse. Besides, after the surgery, she would be doing plenty of laying around.

Attached to the treadmill arms was a laptop tray. The computer was already there and opened. She turned it on and started the machine, gripping the ends of the handlebars to keep herself upright.

She tried to avoid national news, especially now with her stress already high. Local news was usually more honest and, around here at least, did not contain the usual drama that state or national coverage got. Better yet, they often had good stories. For instance, she read one in which a police officer literally saved a cat out of a tree. It was good for a laugh and the warm and fuzzies.

The first article to appear on her screen brought her walk to a stop. It wasn't necessarily local, though it almost was. Palm Beach was less than an hour away.

'Pod of humpback whales freed by marine biologist.'

Palm Beach. The same area Royce said that police chief called from.

A police officer seeking out the truth, even when the powers that be are working against him. God, I couldn't even stand up to the mayor's office.

In sixteen years of law enforcement, all she achieved were a few lucky breaks that led her to a job she didn't deserve. She was exactly what Mayor Marsh needed, someone who would easily bend to her will and not make waves. It was a quality that caused her not to listen to her gut when the strange series of events started.

She so badly wanted to be viewed as a good cop, but settled as an obedient one.

Nico Medrano, Royce said his name was.

A good cop, much like Adam Henry. He was someone she could only dream to be.

But what will it gain him? What did it gain Adam? Adam's dead. Graft, Noel, Wiebe? How'd doing the right thing fared for them?

Silvia had no idea whether those cops were alive or dead. What she did know was that the Admiral was extremely well connected, and would not take well to learning that this Nico Medrano guy was doing some digging.

For the millionth time, she looked at the large empty living room. Paid for by the people who bought her silence.

She turned her eyes to the tablet. Grimacing, she looked up national and international news coverage. It was an endless series of videos and articles about the events in Cielo Nublado and in the Taiwan Strait.

This Nico guy doesn't know what he's up against. He'll get himself killed if he keeps prodding.

It was not mentioned what the Admiral's intentions were during her meetings. The pain made it easy for her to not care. But the very fact that he was willing to go to such extreme measures to keep it quiet made it obvious that his intentions were sinister and illegal.

Then, like an angel on her right shoulder arguing against the devil on the other, a counter-argument filled her mind. *Or maybe he'll blow the lid on what the Admiral is doing... something I should've done.*

Another glance at the house brought her face-to-face with the only antidote for her dilemma. She had to do something. The right thing. But what was the right thing?

After a few moments of consideration, she settled for warning Nico. At the very least, she could keep the guy from screwing up his life. It worked for Royce. It especially worked for her. In just a week, she would finally receive the operation that would spare her of her daily agony.

"It's the least I can do, Mr. Medrano," she said aloud.

She stepped off the treadmill, changed her clothes, crying out with every spike in back pain. She grabbed her truck keys, went outside, and carefully lifted herself into the vehicle.

After receiving her route instructions on MapQuest, she backed out of the driveway.

CHAPTER 23

Palm Beach, Florida.

Seven-thirty came bright and early. To Denise's relief, Sam Travis and Kevin Chase were right on time. She half-expected the former to be in his own diving gear, but judging by his plain-clothes attire, he had no intention of returning to the water.

"Good morning."

"It will be," Sam said, raising his thermos, "after this is in my veins."

"More like your bladder," Kevin said. "I don't think the good whale doctor will take kindly to you pissing in the ocean while she's swimming in it."

Denise turned her focus to the ocean. The whales were still present, though their calls had ended. They were much further out this time, having given up the search for the one they were calling for.

Kevin stepped aboard the boat. "You sure you want to do this, Doc?"

"Yes. Why? You afraid a giant shark will appear and eat me?"

"You say that as if it's not possible," Kevin said.

"Technically, that big one that showed up didn't actually eat anybody… well, not here at least," Sam said. "Scared the piss out of some woman who was swimming after her kid though. Don't know if you saw the footage."

"Actually, I didn't," Denise said.

"It was weird. It was two seconds away from swallowing them, then all of a sudden, it turned around and headed to the open sea," Kevin said.

"Were they too shallow?"

"Don't think so. They were pretty far out," Sam said. He could practically see the gears turning in the biologist's head. "I'm guessing that's not normal."

"To abandon food that's right in front of it? I'd say not," Kevin said.

"Why would it do that?" Sam said.

Denise boarded the maintenance vessel. "The answer's out there." Sam followed her aboard and took a seat, while Kevin steered the boat out to where they nearly had a collision with the humpbacks.

****

USS Vandervoort, Two miles northeast of Cielo Nublado.

The sky was alive with Navy Seahawks. Armed with hellfire missiles, they performed routine patrols on each side of the island in search of any nautical threat. A trio of choppers had descended within a hundred feet of the water. Large red chunks of meat fell from the side as the crew dropped bait for Albert the sickly megalodon.

"Shit. Even I feel a little bad about this," Trevor said, watching from the starboard bridge wing of the *Vandervoort*.

Admiral Heston lowered his binoculars and looked at him. "You're feeling bad about *this*?"

Trevor shrugged. "A tad."

"Not about your assistant? What was his name? ... Mark Eurupe? Nigerian descent, correct?"

"Yes." Trevor raised his own binoculars. The Admiral wasn't stupid. A potted plant could see the scientist was hiding his eyes.

"I haven't seen a hint of remorse about him. How long had he worked for you?"

"He should've moved faster to get to the bridge," Trevor said. "Besides, who are you to be lecturing me? After what you..." He lowered his voice and looked around to make sure nobody was listening. "After what you set up."

"I'm making the world a better place," Heston said. "Sadly, that required me to make certain tests to make sure the plan works. Now that the tests are complete, I have the utmost faith in this project. Feel good about yourself, Dr. Trevor. You're helping to make the world a much better and safer place."

Trevor looked at his tablet. A satellite map of Cielo Nublado and the surrounding waters appeared on the screen. Numerous blips sparkled near the island's northeast coast, with one isolated blip moving toward them. It was no easy task to lure Albert this far out without also attracting the other megs. So far, his strategy worked. Albert followed the bait trail toward the *Vandervoort* while the others were drawn to a low-frequency signal from the Porpoise. Once Albert got a little closer, Trevor would set off a separate low-frequency signal from the device to keep him in the area.

The captain of the ship, Stephan Bey, joined the men on the wing. He was over twenty years the Admiral's junior, and rougher around the edges in his outward demeanor. He needed to be, considering his destination and mission.

"We certain this is going to work?" he asked.

"Fairly," Trevor said. "The trick is to agitate the shark and create enough of a ruckus to draw in the Kraken. With a little luck, the tracker will get in its system undamaged."

"We have snipers ready just in case, ready to plant additional tags," Heston said. "Then we can finally monitor the bastard."

"What are the chances we'll agitate the creature?" the captain asked.

"You mean, what are the chances it'll attack this ship?" Trevor clarified. Bey nodded. "I'm confident it will keep a distance. Especially with easy pickings like Albert close by. Then, once we draw the sharks away, the Kraken will follow."

Heston straightened his sunglasses and stepped inside. Trevor and Bey followed him down the passageways until they emerged outside on the center deck. "We have eyes in the air. I'll watch from Command Central. Once we're done here, I'll have meetings in Washington to attend to. Maintain radio contact with my personal channel, you got me?"

"Aye-aye, sir," Bey said.

Admiral Heston saluted, then headed to the flight deck, where his chopper awaited.

****

Palm Beach, Marriot Singer Island Beach Resort.

Nico headed down into the lobby. If anything worked in his favor, it was the quality of the hotel room and the sleep he got. He had to give Denise credit for getting up bright and early to conduct her dive. It was a quarter to eight when he got cleaned up.

Down in the lobby, he found Renny, cozied up in his hotel robe.

"Good morning, Chief."

"Enjoying yourself, aren't you?"

"How could I not?"

"Does your wife know you're enjoying a little mini-vacation without her?"

"I just told her I was going to be in a hotel," he said. "Never said Florida University set us up in this nice resort."

"I guess the next question is: does Carley know?"

"Nope. I know better than to disclose that info," Renny said. They both laughed. Renny sipped on his coffee and looked at the openness of the lobby. "Too bad they only paid for one night."

"They wanted Denise close to the beach in case any other issue came up during the night," Nico said. He sat down. "She's out there again right now."

"It's cute," Renny said.

"Beg your pardon?"

"The way your individual qualities have rubbed off on each other," Renny said. "You've become an amateur marine biologist through her, and she became an amateur detective through you."

Nico watched the window and the peaceful blue sky that embraced the lobby. How long would that sky remain so peaceful, with the world on the brink of war? Multiple nations, all armed with nuclear arsenals, were baring their teeth. All it would take was one leader to say 'screw it' and push the button. One would lead to others, and next thing the world would know, that sky would be bright white, then orange, then black.

Less than a mile away, a marine biologist was trying to uncover how the megs fit into the big picture.

His ringing phone broke his train of thought. It was the hotel's number. "This is Nico."

"Hello, sir. Sorry if I woke you."

"No, ma'am. You're good. I'm actually sitting in the main lobby."

"Oh, good. I have someone here at the check-in desk asking for you. She already knew you were here, but I'm not at liberty to give your room info out. I didn't know if you were expecting anyone."

"Who is it?"

"Her name is Silvia Remar."

Nico stood up. That name was familiar... *the former police chief at Maxwell Island.* She must have spoken with Royce Boyer.

"I'm on my way over." He hung up and walked away.

Renny spun in his chair. "You got a new lady friend I don't know about?"

"You remember that electric eel we saw yesterday?"

"Oh, that thing. The big meg killed it."

"Yeah, I think it's just the tip of the iceberg."

"Wait, you're still investigating this thing? Come on, Chief. You're not a cop right now. Even if you were, there's no need to uncover this great mystery and save the world. You've done enough."

"And if 'enough' falls short?" Renny had no answer to that. "Listen, you've helped a lot. I'm not asking you to get involved. But there's something at play here that might affect everyone. And we might be the only ones that can bring a stop to it." Nico walked off, leaving a baffled Renny Jackman in the lobby.

He arrived at the check-in desk and waved at the clerk. She nodded to a woman leaning against the wall near the door.

Silvia Remar was not what he expected. Even standing still, she looked strained and stiff. She wasn't elderly, but her posture was like that of someone thirty years her senior who had done a lot of heavy lifting.

"You've asked for me?"

She turned around at the sound of his voice. "Mr. Medrano?"

"Nico will be fine."

"Nico, we need to talk."

"About the megalodons? And the sea serpent I saw?... Admiral Heston?"

Silvia shook the way someone with chronic pain did. "You need to be careful. If the Admiral finds out you're prying into whatever he's doing..." her voice trailed off. "It won't be good."

"You came all the way over here just to warn me of that?"

Silvia nodded. "He's trying to control the sharks with some kind of electronic device, isn't he?"

"That's right." He looked at her posture. "You alright?"

"I've had disc issues since my early twenties. I'm awaiting surgery, which I'm not sure I'm gonna get now that I'm talking to you."

"Let me guess, a bribe from Heston to keep you quiet," Nico said. Silvia nodded. *Explains why she came here in person. Her phone's probably bugged.* "Tell me what happened at the island."

"In a nutshell, there were no bombers. No saboteurs. It was a huge creature, one that I never thought could possibly exist. Its body is a natural conductor of electricity. It came across my island at the start of the month and immediately started wreaking havoc. They seemed like accidents at first. Strange accidents, but accidents all the same. Then on the night of the fireworks festival…"

"What was Heston's involvement?"

"He arrived the morning after," she said. "He and another scientist, who used some kind of long-range underwater frequency device to lure the thing away. They created a cover story, one that the Coast Guard commander of the *Richard Denning* went along with. Some of my officers tried to speak the truth, but were abducted by God knows who. My natural assumption was government agents, but now, I'm not so sure."

"Possibly mercenaries," Nico said. "This scientist, was he a fella about my age? A bit of a snarky wise-ass?"

"Oh, yes."

"Dr. Trevor Zenner. He's working with the Admiral down on Cielo Nublado." He could feel his own bit of sciatica acting up as the gravity of the situation began to weigh on him. "So, everything we were led to believe at Maxwell Island was a lie. All to cover up the existence of a giant electric-spitting eel. It's probably safe for me to assume you weren't told why."

"Correct," Silvia said. "Nor did I ask."

"Sounds like you were more than happy to remain quiet," he said. His tone was as judgmental as his expression. Silvia resented it.

"You don't know me, Mr. Medrano. Let's just say, I haven't been blessed with great genetics. I've been dealing with chronic pain since I was twenty-one. It got worse with working as a patrol cop. Being stationed at a desk for most of my career didn't help much, for the pain or for my self-esteem. I caught a few lucky breaks, made chief of police at Maxwell Island, and planned to ride that job out until retirement. Then everything came tumbling down around me in a matter of days. Then here comes Admiral Heston, with a promise of a surgical operation on my back and a significant amount of money. I can't work right now to begin with and I don't have any other skillset, Mr. Medrano. Pain kinda got in the way of everything."

Nico felt *some* sympathy, though not nearly to the extent Silvia was aiming for. He knew when someone was trying to justify something immoral.

"We all have our personal issues, Ms. Remar. I don't envy you yours. But it seems, nowadays, that people are eager to justify their shortcomings. I can't blame you too much—I almost looked the other way myself. But I realize what's at stake."

"There's nothing you can do about it. The power does not tilt in your favor. I came here to make sure you didn't end up like my officers," she said. She turned and started walking to the door. "I thought I was doing a nice thing. But it's clear you're intent on digging yourself into a deeper hole. Besides, what am I supposed to do? Go to the media with my story?"

"Sure. That's a start," Nico said.

"Oh, I see. With just my word, right? With no proof to offer?"

"Oh, there's proof alright."

Silvia and Nico looked to the doors. Denise, her wetsuit still dripping with water, stormed inside, holding a briefcase-sized mechanical object in her hands. She ignored the clerk's attempt to stop her from ruining the floor and approached Nico.

The device was undoubtedly an underwater drone. Attached to its back was a speakerphone and an antenna.

"What is this?" Silvia asked.

"It's the same model as the speakers we designed back in the University of Florida," Denise said. "They're made to retrieve signals from a bioacoustics device called the Porpoise. Our plan was to use orca calls to move sharks and other species away from populated beach areas. Dr. Zenner changed the acoustics to mimic calls of large baleen whales to lure the megalodons."

Nico pointed at it, his eyes wide. "This was in the water?"

"Exactly where the megalodon appeared," Denise said. "Those whales had responded to the signal from somewhere else and tried to meet up with what they thought was another humpback."

That sciatica was hurting a little bit more now.

"Oh, God," Nico said. "The electric eel was the first test of the device. Hell, it's use is probably what lured the megalodons to the East Coast to begin with. Over the course of the month, he probably had people building more of these speakers."

"Why would he have one set up here?" Silvia asked.

"To test it," Nico said. "To make sure the shark would zero in on specific areas." A revelation struck him and Denise simultaneously. "The *Red Nova.*"

"That bastard," Denise muttered. "He rigged a device on the cutter. That's why the triplets attacked it."

"The Admiral arranged an attack on a U.S. cutter? Why would he do that?" Silvia asked.

"To make sure the megs would attack," Nico said. "More importantly, to make sure they'd cause an adequate amount of damage. He didn't want to waste any more time on this scheme if the sharks weren't good against military vessels."

"If that was a test, then what's the real target?" Silvia asked. She felt stupid for asking the question. Anyone who had even glanced at a TV or computer screen in the last couple of days could piece together that answer. "The Chinese Navy. I can't believe it. Our government is actually trying to get us into a large-scale war. This'll make Afghanistan and Iraq look like picnics."

Nico turned around, hands in his pockets, his eyes pointed at the floor.

"I'm not sure the feds are involved in this one," he said. He looked back at them. His voice shook, the weight of this knowledge at crushing levels. "I think this is a scheme run by the Admiral himself."

"What?"

He looked at Denise. "You read his history. Basically spent all of World War Two helping to liberate China from the Japanese. Fast forward seven years and he's killed by the very country he helped. The grief and havoc that caused his mother. Shit rolls downhill. I doubt he had a pleasant childhood. And he blames all the misery his family suffered on them." He waved a hand at the underwater drone. "The drone that was shot down; it was carrying one of these."

"Wouldn't it have been easier for them to simply move them in under the surface. Underwater drones this small would not likely be detected. Why use a large, unmanned aircraft?" Denise said.

"Because he *wanted* it shot down," Nico said. "He wanted to draw much of the Chinese Navy near the Taiwan Strait. Now, he needs to maintain a standoff until he gets the megalodons, the electric eel, and probably the Kraken close enough. Then, he'll activate the speakers, and all at once, the Chinese Navy will lose multiple ships in a day. Give the U.S. an advantage in a war, that's for damn sure."

"Not to mention plausible deniability," Silvia said. "These are biological organisms with destructive capabilities. If they can steer it in whatever direction they please, they can eliminate nautical targets and then deny any involvement. It was the creature's fault, *it* attacked. As long as the Chinese government is unaware that the Navy is using this device."

"Assuming they even care," Nico said. "The Chinese might get desperate and launch a full scale assault, feeling their backs are against the wall."

"God help us," Denise said. "We need to stop him. It doesn't matter how this will start, war with China will be inevitable. Russia will head westward. Iran will get involved. The whole world will delve into this hodgepodge."

"Literally World War Three," Nico said. "In the nuclear age, that's not good. The Admiral doesn't care. I think the only reason he even joined the Navy was to wipe that country off the face of the earth. Damn the collateral damage."

Silvia squeezed her eyes, her face tensing with regret from getting herself involved. All she wanted to do was warn these people and keep them out of Guantanamo Bay, or any other federal facility where they may never be heard from again. But no, the pieces were all coming together, yet these people were even more determined to intervene.

Denise walked past them, then cupped her hands to yell into the lobby. "Renny!"

He stood up and hastened over, his body language conveying complete lack of interest. It was obvious by the urgency in her voice and the fact she was standing in the resort dripping wet, that she was making an aviation request.

"Whaaaaaaaat?" he said, as though responding to a nagging spouse.

"I need your help."

A sardonic smile took form. "Need me to chip in for lunch?"

"Tell you what—fly us back to Cielo Nublado, and I'll buy *you* lunch."

Renny didn't know whether to laugh or cry. "Wait, wait, wait! I don't know what's more insane; the fact that you want me to take you into a militarized no-fly zone… OR the fact that my only incentive is lunch!"

"Renny, please! We have to try and stop Heston," Denise said.

"Stop him? How? What exactly is the plan?" Renny said. "Tell me there's more to this than fly down there and wag your finger at the Admiral."

"We need to get the right peoples' attention," Nico said. "We need to speak with Rear Admiral White of the Coast Guard. He'll be able to do something about it."

"And if that fails?" Silvia said.

"You can help," Nico said.

She stepped back. "Me?"

"You can stand here and do nothing, or you can do what's right," Nico said. "Go to the nearest news station. Tell them what you know. Get the public's attention. You're a former police chief, you know how to call a news conference on short notice."

Silvia looked away. She was breathing heavily now.

"I don't know…"

"Don't know? You realize what's at stake?" Denise said.

"It's speculation," Silvia said. "Maybe his plan will work. If the creatures attack the Chinese Navy, and no connection is found between them and the Admiral…"

"Or it could go south really quick," Nico said. He looked at Denise. "Maybe I should stay."

"No, you need to speak to White and help me convince him of what's happening," she said. Her eyes turned to Silvia. "Please. Help us. Talk to the media, get the public… and government's attention."

Silvia wanted to cry. Her back was on fire at this point. Now, she truly regretted with all of her being for coming here. The worst part was that she knew they were right. There was more at stake than her own personal struggle, no matter how unbearable it felt. She already was hounded by grief for what happened at Maxwell Island. Maybe she could do the right thing this time.

"Okay." It was barely audible. She tried again, louder. "O-okay. I'll go."

"Thank you." Nico looked at his watch. "That operation's about to start. We need to leave now."

"You say that as if I've agreed to take you," Renny said.

"Renny, for heaven sake," Denise said. "The Admiral is trying to use the megs in Naval combat, which could escalate into a large scale conflict. We are literally the only ones with any chance of stopping it."

A trounced Renny closed his eyes. That stupid conscience had a way of ruining a relaxing day.

"Fiiiiiiine!" He pointed a finger at Denise. "But you're buying me a freaking seafood buffet when we get back!"

CHAPTER 24

USS Vandervoort

The machines had the same shape as typical triton submersibles, and were equal in size. To the laymen, they were practically the same thing. Dr. Trevor Zenner and Captain Stephen Bey knew these machines were not instruments of science, but of war.

"You sure these will do the trick?" the captain asked.

"To question that would be to question the Navy's engineers," Trevor said. "You trust the people who built this battleship?"

"It's a destroyer."

"Same thing."

"No… they're not." Bey decided not to go down the rabbit hole of explaining the classes of Navy ships to someone who clearly did not care. It was clear the doctor saw typical Naval warfare as beneath him. He was interested in developing the next generation of nautical combat. It was a combination of new technology and biological warfare. The best part was that he didn't have to go exploring to find the biological component. Nature was kind enough to raise it from the depths for him.

Progress required sacrifice. Trevor did not see Albert the megalodon as completely useless. Despite his poor health, he would still serve a higher purpose. The fish cruised several hundred yards out, its enormous dorsal and caudal fins cutting across the water like boat sails.

Trevor turned his eyes to the two Zeus-Class U.C.Ds (Underwater Combat Drones). Under the ballasts were twin-barrel launchers, ten feet in length, attached to a magazine system. As their name suggested, the U.C.Ds were not armed with typical bullets, incendiaries, or harpoons. Instead, they were loaded with electrified darts, each one containing a highly electrified charge that could send even a seventy-foot shark into a spasm.

"The Admiral said something to me about this shark having a bad heart," Bey said.

"Yes."

"You sure this is the best route? Might put the shark into cardiac arrest. I doubt a dead megalodon would suit your purpose."

"They've been loaded with lower voltage projectiles," Trevor said. "Enough to throw him into a fit without stressing him too much."

"Depends on how long the torture lasts. One bee sting might not kill ya, but if you're jabbed over and over again."

"Captain, with all due respect, let me handle the science-y stuff."

Bey raised his radio. No need to display his contempt for the doctor. *'All due respect.' Yeah, sure.*

"Lower the U.C.Ds." The submarine combat drones touched down. The cables detached and retracted into the winch reels. Bey turned to the bridge. Inside, stationed with the bridge crew, were the U.C.D. operators. "Zeus One and Two, you're a go."

"Zeus One copies."

"Zeus Two copies."

The drones submerged and accelerated toward their target. Albert was roughly two hundred yards out now, showing no interest in the destroyer. One of the Sikorsky helicopters dropped another helping of dead whale.

As far as the shark was concerned, today was a good day. It wasn't often he had the pleasure of a full stomach. Whenever he detected the smell of blood or the struggling motions of injured prey, one of the younger, healthier megs always beat him to the punch. All he had managed to eat were scraps, provided by the humans riding in the flying machines.

Today, he was getting full portions. None of the other megs were around to steal them. Though he was old, his metabolism still worked as quickly as the others. He was still fueling a seventy-foot, sixty-ton mass. Albert followed the flying mechanism above the water, waiting for it to drop more.

Reality sank in as deeply as the thing that stabbed his left gill slit. Albert was not as concerned with the object that pierced him as much as he was the sudden loss of motor control. His tail slapped the water, his head quivering violently. As quickly as it began, the charge stopped.

The fish sank several feet, stunned. After a few seconds, senses and motor control returned. He fluttered his tail, circling rapidly, biting the water. The fish was confused and alarmed, a dangerous combination for whatever dared to attack it. Albert was old, but a vicious predator nonetheless.

Natural instinct went into overdrive. Its lateral line went to work detecting any movement around it.

Two objects were approaching from the north. Albert turned, jaw parted, ready to bite into the nearest one. They were over a hundred feet away, one flanking to his right.

For most of his adult life, especially in later years, the fish was a docile creature, preferring to feed off already dead organisms rather than partake in aggression. It was not a comprehension of morality or acts of kindness. The fish simply did not care to waste energy attacking things that were not food or a threat. This became more so after age and illness set in. The shark did not have the intelligence to identify the problem, but its instinct served as its voice. It knew something was wrong and that it was physically inferior to most other predators. If a threat appeared, Albert preferred to retreat.

This time, the attackers were much smaller than itself. Though there were two of them, they were maybe a third of his size. Fast and agile, but still smaller. It was not a scenario like when he evaded a pod of orcas. There were only two attackers.

Albert made his move, jaws extended. He closed within a few yards of the nearest enemy.

Bubbles exploded from a small hole under its glassy head. A split-second later, Albert felt pain under his snout. He immediately forgot about that pain due to the current that sent him into another spasm. The shark convulsed, each motion sending vibrations that alerted every predator for miles.

Trevor was inside the bridge with the captain, watching the camera monitor from Zeus One's POV. The megalodon had fallen for the trap.

The captain was on the radio with Command Central. "Units have engaged the fish. Underwater cameras and sensors are in place. All sniper units, stay alert. The objective could arrive at any moment." He lowered his radio and looked at Trevor. "I hope this plan of yours works."

"Oh, I'm confident it will," Trevor said. "The Kraken is the kind of prick that likes to get involved with everyone else's fights. And we just started a serious brawl. He'll show."

****

"Come on, come on! Can't this thing go any faster?" Denise said.

Renny looked over his shoulder at the frantic scientist. "Holy good Lord, woman! This isn't an F-16. I'm pushing this bird to its maximum potential. Now, if you please." He pointed up. Denise followed his finger at the seatbelt sign. "Those who don't comply can be removed from the flight."

"How far are we?" Nico said.

"Will you guys just trust me enough to fly the chopper?"

"How far?"

"Five miles out."

"We're within radar," Nico said. He moved up to the co-pilot seat and placed a headset on.

Renny watched his hand go for the radio. "Don't forget, Chief, we're technically trespassers now. They might not listen to a word you have to say."

"We didn't come here for the view," Nico said.

Renny looked at the water. "Why not? It's a pretty nice one." His eyes went to the horizon. A few dots took form in the distant sky. The decrease of distance provided form to those little dots. Rotor blades carried four Coast Guard choppers straight at them. "On second thought…"

"They found us," Denise said.

"Good." Nico adjusted the radio frequency. "This is CNPD Chief Nico Medrano hailing the U.S. Coast Guard. I require the immediate attention of Rear Admiral Jon White."

"Civilian aircraft, you are ordered to turn around."

"Damn, they really didn't listen to a word you had to say," Renny said. The choppers swarmed around them like hornets. The fuselage door opened on one. Inside, a sniper unit had his scope locked on their cockpit.

"Is this standard practice for the Coast Guard?" Denise asked nervously.

"Typically, no. But this is a Coast Guard under Admiral Heston's command. God knows what orders he's delegated to the Coast Guard," Nico said. He tried again with the radio. "I repeat, this is CNPD Chief Nico Medrano. This is an emergency. We must land on Cielo Nublado immediately. We are unarmed. We have an urgent message for Rear Admiral White."

"Negative. This area is off limits."

"Jesus, you stupid idiots!" Nico shouted. Civility was off the table. "It's about the Admiral's plan."

A few moments of silence followed. The choppers travelled parallel to theirs.

"Look there."

Nico and Renny glanced back at Denise, whose face was pressed to the portside window. They looked to the east. In the distance was a Naval Destroyer. Five hundred feet in length, it had its bow pointed eastward. In the water around it were numerous specks.

The use of binoculars helped Nico identify those specks as dorsal fins.

"They got the sharks gathered. They're getting ready to move them."

"Why haven't they done it yet?" Renny asked.

"Maybe they're waiting for more to arrive," Nico said. "Or, there's another task they need to complete first."

"U.S.C.G. to civilian aircraft."

Renny scowled. Civilian aircraft? Did the logo on the fuselage mean nothing? *I guess technically it doesn't anymore. Still, it hurts no longer being official.*

"Go ahead," Nico said.

"Follow our escort to Cielo Nublado Airfield."

Nico tapped fists with Renny.

"It worked," the pilot said. "They're listening to you…"

"You have disobeyed repeated commands to vacate the area. Upon arrival, step out with your hands raised. You are under arrest."

Their smiles vanished.

"Okay... this just got a little more complicated than we thought," Renny said.

"Shit." Nico tore his headset off, then raised a middle finger to the nearest chopper.

"Great. Just great," Renny said. "I'm used to being the one with the cuffs. Not the one who *gets* cuffed. Thanks, guys. I was planning on a pleasant morning with pancakes, eggs, and extra bacon. Instead, I'm gonna have to settle for jail food. And jail food sucks!"

"What's going to happen now?" Denise asked. "You think the Commander will see us?"

"It's not looking good," Nico said. "At the moment, it looks like our only hope is Silvia Remar."

****

West Palm Beach Florida News Station.

Silvia Remar sat in the parking lot. Her cell phone was in hand, the number to the station typed out, her thumb over the *send* icon.

The device shook in her hand. She could hardly sit still. The hour-long drive had played havoc on her nerves and disc. Looking at the dialed number worsened the stress, which in turn, spiked her pain even further.

The internal debate started. Would she even manage to get an audience? Would this agency manage to get the attention of larger news organizations? Would it have *any* effect on what was happening?

There was only one reality she could contemplate: If she got in front of news cameras, Heston would see it. She could kiss her payments and back surgery goodbye. She could get it herself, but be stuck with thousands of dollars' worth of medical debt. Getting that debt would require getting a job, and after her handling of the Maxwell Island incident, getting a good paying job would be no easy feat.

The conversation with Nico and Denise played through her mind. War with China, the Porpoise being used to lure the creatures into conflict, the possibility of Heston's plan being uncovered, further escalation... and the potential consequences.

This is the right thing to do.

She looked at the *send* button. It was the right thing. Still, she could not do it.

Pain made it impossible to sit still. Her eyes welled up. Adam Henry would have done the right thing.

But he wasn't compromised by pain.

Overwhelmed, she moved her thumb off the button. Already, the promise she made became a distant memory. She was willing to take the chance. Maybe Heston's plan would succeed. It would be nice for the U.S.

to have a dominate Navy, wouldn't it? After constant displays of weakness from timid, possibly anti-American presidents, maybe strength was the answer to the world's problems. More justifications followed.

Only one mattered.

I don't want to be in pain anymore.

She deleted the number and tossed her phone into the passenger seat. Turning her vehicle around, she headed for home. She wasn't a heavy drinker, but today, she would help herself to a morning mimosa.

Anything to bury her head in the sand.

CHAPTER 25

By the time the chopper arrived at the airfield, a dozen marines arrived in Jeeps. The sight of M4 Carbines with thirty-round magazines hammered in the point—don't do anything stupid.

There were a few other choppers in the airfield, including the damaged Navy ones from the recent megalodon and octopus showdown. Sailors and guardsmen, who were present to perform maintenance and repair work on the vehicles, stood aside to let the marines handle the unpleasant task of apprehending the trespassers.

Trespassers. Renny would have laughed at that paradox if he weren't the one about to be arrested. "Answer me this, Chief. How do you trespass on your own neighborhood?"

"Eminent domain," Nico said. "Which they haven't officially declared."

"And they're getting away with this, how?"

"Because we've become a complacent society," Nico said. "Government seizes power. The best thing they can hope for is for good people to do nothing."

Renny's eyes were on the rifles. "Who can blame them?" Begrudgingly, he brought the chopper down. The marine sergeant approached, weapon raised.

"Step out, hands high above your head."

"Damn, I'm used to being the one saying that," Renny said.

Nico opened the fuselage door and stepped out, hands raised. "I'm unarmed."

"Put that down!"

Nico looked over his shoulder at Denise, who stepped out with the drone. She placed it down and raised her hands.

"I'm Dr. Denise Reta. I'm a research consultant with Admiral Heston…"

"You've ignored an order to turn back," the sergeant said.

Nico glanced back and forth, hoping to see anyone with a senior rank. Near the county vehicles was a man in a blue Navy uniform. It was a chopper pilot uniform. Nico recognized the man's face. It was one of the pilots he rescued from Search Baker, the same chopper that carried Denise while attempting to intervene with the fishermen.

Shit, what was his name? Ortman? Ortmay? ORTMEIER! He was not anyone of significant rank, but maybe would get him in touch with the right people who in turn could provide an audience with the Rear Admiral.

"Excuse me?! Ensign?! I'm Chief Nico Medrano. Remember me? I saved your ass before you could be shark food."

The pilot looked away, hoping to ignore the situation as well as his conscience. That lasted ten seconds. He faced the former chief, unsure of what to say.

"We need to speak to Rear Admiral White," Nico said.

"Why?" Ensign Ortmeier asked.

"What Heston is about to do with the sharks… it's going to end in major catastrophe. White might be the only guy who has any chance of stopping it."

The Ensign approached, only to be stopped by one of the marines.

"This is a security matter. Step back," the marine said.

"Hang on, guys. I know this guy. He's good."

"He's unauthorized," the sergeant said. He looked at one of his men. "Cuff em, Private. We'll hold them in the local jail."

"Hang on, Sergeant." Ortmeier plucked his own radio from his belt. "Bravo-Three-eight, please report to the airfield. There's a situation here that needs your immediate attention."

"Is this about the unauthorized aircraft? Let the grunts work for once."

Ortmeier took joy in seeing the marines make a few snide remarks under their breath.

"Lieutenant, the situation is a little more complicated."

"Fine. I'm on my way."

"Your ass is mine if this turns out to be a waste of time, Sailor!" the marine sergeant said.

The sailor said nothing, and waited in silence with everyone else. What everyone hoped would be a few seconds turned into excruciatingly long minutes. During this time, nobody moved.

Renny, Nico, and Denise stood in a row, hands kept high. During that time, they watched the marines grow increasingly bored. Nico and Denise frequently watched the choppers flying in the distance. They were circling a specific area, watching what lurked below.

The sharks were still there.

"Why hasn't the Admiral moved them yet?" Nico muttered. "What's he up to now?"

"Keep your trap shut," the sergeant bellowed.

Renny's arms started to tremble. "Hey, do we have to stay like this? My muscles are starting to get tired…" He started lowering his arms.

Several marines converged, guns raised.

"Don't move, damn it!"

Renny's hands were back up. "Ooooookay! A simple 'no' would have sufficed." He waited in silence for another minute. "Okay, when is this snail of a lieutenant gonna arrive?"

"Who the hell called me that?"

Renny bit his lip, looked straight ahead, and kept his hands raised... all while pointing a finger at the sergeant.

Nico resisted the urge to step forward. As he had hoped, the lieutenant was Wilson, the other pilot he rescued from the crash. With no assigned aircraft, he was probably assigned ground duty until further notice.

"Lieutenant!" The co-pilot approached his superior.

"What the hell's going on?" Wilson said.

"It's *them*," the co-pilot said. The lieutenant looked in Nico's direction. Right away, he felt foolish for not recognizing the chopper, let alone the chief and marine biologist.

"Chief Medrano? What the hell are you doing here? I thought you were sent away," he said.

"I need your help, Lieutenant," Nico said. "Can you put us in touch with Rear Admiral White of the Coast Guard?"

"Uh..." Wilson clenched his teeth, fretfully. "Not without a damn good reason."

"We found this in the waters off Palm Beach," Denise said. She lifted the drone and revealed the speaker. "This is synced with the device they are using to control the megalodons. They used this to lure the hundred-twenty-footer to Palm Beach."

"We think they used it to make the triplets attack the *Red Nova*," Nico said.

The lieutenant shifted in place, unsure of what action to take. He was a man torn between his gut and the Admiral's orders. Intervening with this arrest could spell trouble for him.

Yet, though he didn't know the chief and doctor well, he doubted they'd come here if they didn't genuinely believe this information.

"Why would he do that?"

"Because he's taking the megalodons to China," Nico said. "For the same reason he covered up the attack on Maxwell Island. Those weren't terrorists that caused those boat explosions. It was another creature."

The news seemed to hit Wilson with physical force. He looked like a man in pain. He put a hand to his forehead, contemplating the urge to walk off and forget everything said.

"Wow. Entertaining this bullshit totally won't impact my career," he joked. "Listen, Chief. I'm gonna need something a little more concrete than that if I'm gonna annoy White. Almost everything you just said is speculation."

"Lieutenant, I..." Nico held back. His burning temper was not going to help the situation.

Denise stepped forward, keeping her hands raised to appease the marines.

"Sir, is the *Red Nova* still anchored?"

"Correct."

"Send divers to inspect it. You might find one of these attached to the hull. If so, it's what caused the triplets to suddenly attack."

The lieutenant sighed. He looked at Ortmeier. "You got your diving gear?"

"Y-yes. You're asking me to go out there? In the water? With those sharks around?"

"The cutter's in the shallows. The sharks are a quarter-mile to the north. You'll be fine." The lieutenant lifted his radio. "I need a Zodiac to meet us by the west docks. Hurry up." He lowered the radio and looked at Nico. "I appreciate you saving my ass, Chief. That said, you better not be wrecking my morning."

"Wrecking *your* morning?" Renny said. "You should've seen the breakfast menu I was about to order from before I was dragged over here."

****

Another electrified dart hit the shark, shaking its body with an electrified charge. Albert descended to the depths, twisting and turning in agony. His tail slashed about, his recent meal ejected in a red mist. Pain flooded his insides, his frail heart strained by the repeated shocks.

The fish attempted to flee, only to feel the mild sting of a dart piercing his caudal fin. Albert was stunned again before he could gain a hundred feet of distance.

The drones moved in, lining up for their next attack. As the dart spent its battery discharging its voltage, Albert sank again. His bowels and bladder ejected their contents, forming a second, more undignified cloud around the fish.

"Damn," Zeus Two's pilot said. "First time I ever made someone shit himself." He and the other drone pilot laughed.

"Stay focused," Captain Bey said. A sharp exhale followed the statement. He was briefed on the shark's physical condition. There was no glory in killing an ailing fish, no matter its size. It was the same disgust he felt as a teenager in Brooklyn when he witnessed a pair of street thugs beat up a sick old man for his wallet. And like these drone operators, those thugs were convinced they were the toughest dudes on the block.

To Bey's regret, another similarity was that he was complicit in both. Despite his attempts to distance himself from the lifestyle of his younger days, there was no denying he was a gang member who took part in many crimes. A minimal part, but was complicit nonetheless. When they got caught he was able to change the trajectory of his ways. Go to jail or join the service was something mostly seen in fiction. For Bey, attempting to break into a car which belonged to a rear admiral made that a reality.

At the time, Bey figured then-Rear Admiral Heston saw something in the kid he didn't see in himself. Maybe Stephan Bey could be useful after all. Turns out, he was. Just not in the way he thought. When he received his promotion to Captain of the *USS Vandervoort* on July 5th, his gut sounded alarms. It was time to repay Heston for keeping him out of jail and for giving him a fruitful career. It didn't mean he had to like it.

"Is there anything on sonar?"

"Not yet," the sonar tech said.

"Of course not."

"Give him a little more time," Trevor said. He tapped Zeus-Two's shoulder. "Hit 'em again."

"Don't overdo it, Doctor," Bey said. "You could stress the fish into cardiac arrest…"

Trevor pivoted to face him, hands on his hips like a professor talking down to an unruly student. "Listen, Captain, we decrease the assault, the shark could escape, which would make this a big waste of time. I'm monitoring his vitals. I'll let them know if we need to lighten up." He turned and leaned toward the screen, tapping the operator again. "Keep going."

"Aye-aye," the operator gleefully said.

Trevor glimpsed at Bey, then sniggered. "Cardiac arrest. Feeding the shark to a giant octopus, fine and dandy. Zapping him a little, 'think of the children!'"

They watched the shark on the screen. It had recovered from its recent hit and was diving deep. The drones followed it four hundred feet down, where it smacked into the seabed. Albert rolled over, his light-grey belly pointing upward. His senses were frazzled. It did not know which way was up.

The fish rolled on his side, and with a smack of his tail, was levitated off the seabed. A few more flickers generated momentum, like an aircraft taking flight.

Zeus-Two's operator moved his thumb over the trigger.

"What are you waiting for?" Trevor said. "I told you to hit him again."

The operator lined up the shot and pressed the button. The dart zipped from the muzzle and struck the thick flesh atop Albert's head. The barb failed to stick, the dart skidding over his back, and spiraling into the distance.

Albert turned in the direction of thumping motors and *thuds* which always occurred before the strange electric teeth zapped him.

"Oh, hell," Trevor said. He tapped the operator's shoulder repeatedly. "Fire again, you idiot." He looked at Zeus-One's pilot. "You! Zap him."

In the blink of an eye, Albert's jaws engulfed the screen.

****

The *USCGC Red Nova* stood on the water, unmoving, like an island composed of metal. Ensign Charley Ortmeier could not take his eyes off the smashed deck and railing. The *Red Nova* was practically a ghost ship in the eyes of many. No matter how much welding and repairs it received, it would forever be known as the location where numerous guardsmen were slaughtered.

Ortmeier had taken a leak before changing into his wet suit. Already, he sensed his bladder giving him fresh warning signals. He looked into the water to calm his nerves. He could see the bottom, brightly lit by the sunlight. It was only twenty-to-thirty feet deep around here.

Too shallow for the sharks… except for that big one in Palm Beach… GREAT!

"Such my luck," he said. "I survived an explosion and crash forty-eight hours ago, only to willingly serve myself on a platter."

"Quit bitching," the helmsman said. Ortmeier placed his rebreather, only to spit it right back out.

"Excuse me? Don't forget, I outrank you, Sailor."

The helmsman smiled. "Only for a couple more minutes, as far as we know."

Ortmeier stared, astonished to this guy's straightforwardness. "That's… MEAN!" He moved to the rear of the boat, and looked at him once more before fastening his mask and rebreather. "Well, dipshit. If I get eaten, I hope the shark comes up for seconds."

"Joke's on you. If I see a dorsal fin, I'm outta here."

Ortmeier tried thinking of a retort, only to lose focus after Lieutenant Wilson's voice barked over the radio.

"What's the holdup?"

"Heading down, sir." He tossed the radio back to the sailor. "Damn volleyball." He took one final unfiltered breath, then placed his breather and mask on. *I had Mexican last night. If a shark decides he wants to eat me, maybe I can provide a little heartburn.*

He leaned toward the water.

"Hey!"

He looked back toward the sailor, unable to speak. *What?*

"I just got that reference!... Wilson… *Cast Away*."

Congratulations. Ortmeier hit the water, then swam to the *Red Nova*. Its shadow cast a massive shape onto the ocean floor. It was perfectly black, contrasting heavily with the golden sunshine sparkling around it.

The world around him was crystal blue. He had a fairly clear view of his surroundings, except for the underside of the ship, which was shrouded in its own shadow.

Ortmeier arrived at the bow first. Nothing but dented steel where the triplets relentlessly bashed it. He swept the flashlight back and forth to be thorough. He had no intent for Wilson to order him back out here because he rushed the inspection.

He found welding plates, which were installed a little too late. Thousands of gallons of seawater had already made it onto the ship and had to be pumped out. Everywhere he aimed his flashlight, he saw damage. It was amazing to think of the power these sharks contained. He had seen impact tests on these ships' hulls. It was no small feat to damage them. And those triplets were only sixty feet in length.

Wasn't the Palm Beach meg a hundred-twenty? Good thing HE wasn't doing this.

He worked his way to the midsection. Nothing on the keel. Nothing on the sides.

He neared the stern, then froze. At first, he thought he was looking at some kind of enormous crab under the hull. Its shell reflected his light back at him. All of its components were grey or silver, except for a black object attached to its back.

What the hell?

****

It was like a transformation. There was no joy or remorse, no contemplation of shedding its docile nature. Man's violence had killed the gentle giant and revealed the monster under the flesh.

Albert clamped his jaws over his metallic foe, and drove it to the surface. The second one trailed behind, its projectile shooting wide. They were no longer fighting a slow-moving, nonaggressive scavenger. They were now in combat with a leviathan, whose species roamed the depths for millions of years, and survived thousands of conflicts with other giants. There were no alpha predators in its world. The megalodon's enemies, not even the Kraken, entered a fray with them without caution. Even the docile ones, when pushed, reverted to the most basic of instincts.

If they couldn't flee, they would fight. Even if they lost, the adversary would rarely leave unscathed.

Albert breathed the water, sub in mouth. He ignored the pain in his torso, instead fixated on the task at hand. His reentry into the ocean resulted in a tremendous wave which smacked the large ship.

Below, Zeus-One was hit by the vibration, skewing its aim to the left. Much to the frustration of its operator, the shot went wide. The shot from its other barrel bounced off Zeus-Two, which rapidly was coming right for it. Albert had no concept of shields. He was simply going after the second attacker while the first was immobilized.

Two more *clanks* vibrated off the hull as two more darts made impact. With the target on a collision course, Zeus-One veered to starboard.

Unwilling to lose its grip, Albert swiftly turned to the right, his caudal fin swinging wide. In a world of violence, even the most passive of creatures were born with instinctual combat skills. Its caudal fin struck the drone under its port ballast. Like a tennis ball, Zeus-One hurled for dozens of yards.

"Listen, you idiots, it's gonna get away," Trevor said.

"I warned you," Bey muttered.

"Nobody asked you," Trevor said. "Just run the damn ship, let me handle the sharks."

Bey wanted to laugh. The oh-so-brilliant scientist was happy to act high and mighty while he thought he was in control. Now that things were working against him, a childlike temper tantrum was brewing. He resisted the urge to pester him, and remained on task.

"Is Zeus-One still operational?" he asked its pilot.

"Port gun is inoperable. Starboard side still functional. Both rudders still working. Thrusters sluggish, but working."

"Turn it around. Hit the meg before it decides to flee."

"Command Central to Vandervoort. What the hell's going on over there?"

This time, Bey sniggered. Seeing Trevor's breakdown accelerate after hearing Heston's voice was too much.

"This is Captain Bey. Do you wish to speak with Zenner?"

"Put him on."

Trevor snatched the radio, then took a moment to get his temperament under control. "I'm working on it. Just a setback. We are dealing with large predators, after all, Admiral."

****

"Don't you lose that fish, Doctor."

Rear Admiral Jon White stood in the tent, watching Admiral Heston's body language. While there were no definite outbursts so far, the Admiral was considerably more emotional this morning. The cause for concern was somewhat justifiable. The mission, as he was told, was to bait the Kraken and plant a tracker on it, which would allow them to keep tabs on the creature during the attempt to lure it to the South Atlantic.

Seeing Heston on edge was unusual. Even when the *Red Nova* was under attack, his demeanor was calm and collected. It was a good trait for a military leader. It was the opposite of what he was witnessing this morning.

"Perhaps I should send some of my cutters to assist," White said.

Heston shook his head. "No. This will work."

"If I may, Admiral, I suggest you proceed with moving the sharks. The Coast Guard will devote all of our resources in locating the Kraken. Let's not risk losing the megs in the pursuit of locating this beast."

Heston slammed a hand to the table. Everyone in the tent looked at him, some lifting their headphones off to hear any outburst that might follow.

The Admiral could sense the attention. He turned to face the room. "You're all doing a good job. Continue your work." He looked at the Rear Admiral. "This is our one chance to bait the creature. If it follows the sharks, we won't know it unless we tag it."

White stood still, hands behind his back. "Aye-aye, sir." By order of the President, he was still under Heston's command. There was no wiggle room for argument.

They watched the footage provided by one of the choppers on scene. They could see the dark shape of the megalodon lashing about, the drone trapped in its jaws.

"It'll have to let go eventually," Heston said. "He's blocking the water flow to his mouth. He's wearing himself down." He was back on the radio. "*Vandervoort*, draw him to the surface. Our snipers need a clear shot when it attacks."

"One question, sir. Why not blast it with missiles? Why bother tagging it?"

That temperament which Heston was known for was gone. "Jon... not now."

White read between the lines. Still, he couldn't help but watch the Admiral. Twice, the man dabbed his brow and neck with a handkerchief. Either he was sick, or he was extremely nervous. Perhaps the events on the world stage were weighing on his shoulders.

He chose to remain quiet and watch the screen.

"Excuse me, sir?"

White turned around and returned the salute of the captain who entered the tent. "Yes?"

"One of our units have requested your attention."

"It better be urgent, Captain."

"Yes sir..." the captain looked in Heston's direction. "It is."

White stepped outside. A few yards from the tent, Lieutenant Wilson stood with Chief Nico Medrano, his department chopper pilot, and Heston's former research consultant. A man in a dripping wetsuit stepped forward—Ensign Charley Ortmeier. He held a mechanical device in his hand.

"Sir, I found this on the *Red Nova*," he said.

White squinted at the thing. "What the hell is it? What are you guys doing here?"

"Sir..." the lieutenant tilted his head at the civilians. "These people have information that requires your immediate attention."

White saw the device in the female doctor's hands. It was identical to the one held by the Ensign.

"I'm listening."

****

Albert pushed its victim to the surface, outmaneuvering its metal companion. His energy was waning, the adrenaline failing to compensate for the lack of oxygen. He chomped on the machine in hopes of dealing a death blow, his teeth chipping on the steel skin. With his body screaming for seawater, he finally spat the thing out.

Zeus-Two's situation did not improve much. It was immediately smacked by his tail and hurtled like a bowling ball under the destroyer's bow.

Albert swam a hundred feet south, circulating water over his gills. His blood freshly oxygenated, he circled back. Directly ahead, a few meters deep, was the other machine. It was facing him, attempting for another assault. The megalodon arched downward, then back up in an S-shaped path. The upward arch put him directly underneath Zeus-One. Like a trained dolphin playing with a volleyball, Albert struck the drone from underneath. A second tap took the drone to the surface.

Next came the instinct to swat it with its tail. Albert cruised along the surface until he was lined up with the machine. With frightening speed, he charged, mountains of water rolling in his wake. A mere three feet from impact, the fish turned around. For a split-second, his body was crescent shaped, like the strange bright object he sometimes saw in the night sky.

The caudal fin swung.

SMACK!!!

Zeus-Two was airborne.

"Holy shit, brace for imp—" Bey recoiled as the drone exploded across the *Vandervoort's* forecastle. A tremor swept under his feet. Even before he stepped onto the starboard bridge wing, he could hear the shouts of numerous sailors rushing forward.

There was nothing to identify the drone as a machine. Like a grenade, it had burst into shrapnel upon impact.

"Status on Zeus-Two?"

His answer came in the form of a distant echo. Bey looked at the water. Underneath the destroyer was a large torpedo-shape, moving like a large shadow. Its head was not pointed, but significantly round.

Albert charged the ship at a forty-five degree angle.

A second, stronger vibration shook the *Vandervoort*. Gripping the guardrail, Bey kept his eyes on the water. Pieces of Zeus-Two danced across the ocean like skipping stones, the drone having been smashed against the ship.

The shark wasn't done. A frenzy had been incited. Everything sharing the water with this fish was now an adversary, no matter the size or armament. A third impact—a ramming deliberately meant to damage the ship—forced Bey to grab the guardrail a second time.

He stumbled back into the bridge. "Damage report."

"Phalanx is unresponsive," a crew member replied.

"Two casualties from the U.C.D. impact," another said.

The fish struck the vessel again. The drone operators turned in their seats, their hotshot confidence gone, replaced by a sense of uselessness and confusion.

"That shark can't possibly damage this boat, right?" the Zeus-Two pilot said.

"You can bet he'll try," Trevor said. He was the only one on the bridge who seemed happy about this. It was easy for Bey to figure out why: the prick was only concerned with the shark fleeing, thus losing the chance to tag the octopus. With Albert attacking the *Vandervoort*, that opportunity was alive and well.

Bey had no plans to needlessly risk the lives of his men. He approached the weapon's control station.

"Target the shark. Blast it out of the water." The order left a bad taste in his mouth. There was no joy in killing the fish, especially knowing that up until fifteen minutes ago when they zapped the thing, it was nonviolent. It brought to mind the recording of the briefings given by Dr. Denise Reta, in which she had stated most of these sharks are non-aggressive unless provoked.

I think we just proved that theory.

"Sir, the target's too close. We can't use the torpedo tubes without damaging ourselves," the weapon's operator said.

Bey picked up the mic to communicate to the choppers. "Viper One, this is the Captain of the *Vandervoort*. Decrease altitude to twenty-meters. Use your M60 and see if you can draw the target away."

"Roger that, Captain."

****

Heston stood in Command Central, arms crossed, his teeth grinding while he watched the event play out on the screen.

"What's the status on the other sharks?"

The radar tech checked the computer screen previously used by Denise. "Still gathered a quarter-mile north. *Richard Denning* reports no changes, but they are getting riled up."

"And what's O'Brien's position?"

"Closing in, roughly two miles northeast of our location. At present rate, he'll be here in twenty minutes."

Heston placed a cigar in his mouth. "At least it's not a total bust so far."

"You sure about that?"

Heston turned around, his brow crinkling with anger. Rear Admiral Jon White stood at the entrance like a gunslinger about to draw on him.

"Excuse me?" Three other people entered the tent. Heston removed the cigar, grimacing at the presence of Nico, Denise, and Renny. "Chief, I see you managed to avoid arrest." He looked at White. "What are they doing here?"

"It's what *you're* doing here that concerns me," White said.

"I don't follow." Heston lit his cigar.

"I think you do," White said.

Heston lowered the cigar, smoke lifting from his lips like steam. "Jon, I'm sensing an accusation. I'd choose my next words *really* carefully if I were you."

White stepped aside and allowed Lieutenant Wilson and Ensign Ortmeier to bring in the drones. "Why don't you explain why one of these was found attached to the *Red Nova?*"

"And why I found one at Palm Beach, where O'Brien attacked," Denise added.

"I don't recognize this tech," Heston said. "Now, I want these people removed. MPs, get in here and take these civilians to the jail."

"Nice way to have us silenced, right, Admiral?" Nico said.

"Chief, I like you, alright? You've been a great help to me. Same with you, Dr. Reta. But you've disobeyed a direct order. If you cooperate, I'll only detain you for a couple hours until I have a unit available to fly you out. If you keep talking, you'll only make it worse."

"That what you told Silvia Remar and Royce Boyer?" Nico said. "What about those cops that were arrested? Noel, Wiebe, and Graft? Unwilling to follow your narrative about Maxwell Island, were they?"

Heston took another draw. In doing so, he realized he was making a mistake. The whole room could sense he was stalling, searching for a response.

Nico looked at the surveillance screen. "Is that the ship that's leading these things to China? Looks like they're having some issues."

"It's Albert." Denise kicked the drone, skidding it to Heston's feet. "You've done the impossible, Admiral. Made a killing machine out of something gentle."

"Get off your high horse, Doctor. These creatures are born killing machines. And you, Chief, I don't know what you're trying to insinuate. We are trying to lure the…"

"Yeah, yeah, yeah. Lure the Kraken and tag it and such," Nico said. "White filled us in. Except you're not taking these creatures near Trinidad."

"There's no island in that region," Denise said. "It's all a lie. We're on to what you're doing."

White stepped forward, his hands clasped behind his back. It wasn't formality—he was keeping himself from lashing out. "Is it true? Did you destroy my cutter and kill my men? All for some trial run? Make sure these things were effective?"

Heston's eyes shifted, catching glimpses of the personnel in the room. Every stare was directed at him, their gazes inquisitive. He felt like a man on trial.

Audio transmissions of gunshots drew his attention to the screen. They provided him a chance to stall while monitoring the operation.

Along with everyone else, Nico watched the screen. A Seahawk helicopter was shooting at the megalodon. The dorsal fin emerged near the starboard quarter and began following the aircraft.

Questions arose in his mind. *Obviously the Captain of that ship must be in on this, if he's deliberately leading the sharks to China. Odds are the crew is in the dark about their objective.*

With the Admiral's attention on the screen, Nico quickly leaned over to Lieutenant Wilson.

"Who's the Captain of that ship?" he whispered.

"Stephen Bey."

"Any connections to…?" He tilted his head in Heston's direction.

"Recruited him several years back. All I know," Wilson whispered.

What are the odds? Nico cocked a smile. *I should've been a detective.* Relieved he didn't voice that corny joke, he faced Heston. "We know everything. The electric eel… why you were so interested in the one we encountered yesterday. Wanted to ensure your secret weapon hadn't been compromised in any way, didn't ya?"

Heston snapped his fingers at the MPs. "I thought I told you to arrest them."

"And we know what your drones were dropping in the Taiwan Strait," Nico said. He tapped the undersea drone on the floor with his foot. "You've been setting up all of these throughout that area. Small enough to sneak up onto Chinese Naval ships and the shorelines. Now that you've run your tests in Palm Beach and on the *Red Nova*, you're confident your plan will work."

Heston maintained a stern gaze. If anything, he seemed more irritated at the MPs for standing by instead of following his orders.

Nico pressed further. "You're really willing to risk all-out war? And for what? To satisfy a personal grudge against China? To avenge your mother and father, and to get even for the crummy life it caused?"

Heston pulled the cigar from his mouth. Once again, he prevented himself from lashing out.

For Nico, the little ticks in his expression were enough to confirm his suspicion, though not enough to prove it to everyone standing around.

"It's all speculation and conjecture," Heston said. "You can't prove a thing."

Alright, time to pull out the big guns.

"Actually, I already did."

Heston smiled. It was clear he was thinking of the many ways he could, and would, destroy Nico when this was all over. Daily torture at some unknown military prison in the ass-end of the world, most likely.

Nico gave one last glance at the destroyer on the screen. *Oh, hell. Hope this bluff works.*

"Captain Stephen Bey just placed a call on a secure line, fessing up to his involvement in your plan. Figures, the guy running the ship would have to be in the know. Too bad he cracked under pressure when Albert attacked." He watched Heston look at the screen, then at his own phone in search of any alert from Bey. "Sorry, Admiral. You've been busted."

An immediate transformation occurred. The poised, self-assured leader vanished, his flesh consumed by a ravenous beast hungry for Nico's blood.

The MPs finally went to work, stepping in to stop Heston from strangling the chief.

"You should've taken the cash and kept to yourself, you meddling bastard! Get—get off me!" The two MPs grabbed him by the shoulders and pushed him back.

Heston's skill matched his rage. He stepped to his right, grabbing one of the MPs by the arm. There was a crack of bone and a pained shriek, followed by the thud of the man being thrown against one of the desks. The second MP stepped back, surprised by the near-seventy-year-old's display of physical strength and agility.

More security rushed in.

White raised his hand to gather their attention, while keeping his eyes on Heston.

"I'm sorry, Vince. We've known each other a long time. But I can't permit you to do this." He looked at the men. "I'm relieving the Admiral of his Command."

"Jon…"

"It's Rear Admiral White, and I'm taking control of this operation." He looked at comm station. "Get Washington on the line."

The MPs surrounded Heston, now prepared for possible resistance. He paid them no mind, seething while his burning gaze roasted the people that destroyed his plans.

"You weak, pathetic people. You don't realize what you just did."

"I know *exactly* what I just did," Nico said. "I stopped you from starting a large-scale military conflict."

"You didn't stop anything, Medrano," Heston said. "You think peace is going to last between us and China? Have you kept your eyes shut all these years? You think they've been expanding their Navy, threatening Taiwan because of some property ownership? They gain that territory, they gain control over all of the South China Sea. Then they expand. Control shipping lanes. Control the market long enough to drive Western economies down an endless spiral. You realize the world is facing a shortage of computer chips? And who makes them? Taiwan. And what's being run by computers nowadays? *Everything!* If they take Taiwan, they'll cut the U.S. off from that resource. That will result in crisis after crisis. Plus, they'll be able to cut off shipping lanes. They'll have absolute control over that region. You want us to go to war with them then?!"

"I'd rather it not happen at all," Nico said.

"Then you're a naïve idiot," Heston said. "Or a Chinese loving commie."

Nico's hands went in the air. "Oh, here we go. I'm surprised it took that long. Listen, Heston, not that I need to explain this, but I'm not sympathetic to China one slight bit. I'm aware of all the atrocities that go on over there. But you're proving a basic fact about war: it's usually a small handful of people who actually *want* the conflict, and everyone else is sent to fight. I can't believe I'm explaining this to an Admiral, but it'll take more than a bunch of sea creatures to defeat an entire nation."

"But they can cripple their forces." Heston clenched his cigar between his teeth. "You think the world doesn't notice the weakness our nation is currently experiencing? You think they won't take advantage? If I don't do something, our way of life as we know it will be obsolete."

"Don't make this seem like you're doing this for the greater good, Heston," Nico said. "You're doing this because of personal bloodlust. Your father fought to liberate the Chinese from Japan in World War Two, only to be killed by their military in Korea. Of course, it's a simplistic way of looking at it, but I guess when you've grown up watching your mother going on a downward spiral because of your dad's death, it's easy to see how you'd frame it that way."

Heston pulled a fresh cigar from his shirt pocket. "Doesn't mean I'm not right."

"Actually, you're wrong," White said. "You're betting the odds of our nation on weaponizing creatures that cannot be controlled. And how do you think other nations will react when they inevitably find out the U.S. Navy launched this attack?"

"They won't find out," Heston said.

"That's what thinking emotionally does—makes you forget details," White said. He pointed to the drone on the floor. "*We* found out. Weren't supposed to know you did that, were we?"

"You see this?" Denise said. She rolled the *Red Nova* drone on its underside. The legs which allowed it to attach to the hull were crumpled and scorched. "Like White said, emotion makes you ignore important facts. I think you designed these to detach from the targets once the objective is complete. Except, the sharks go right for the source of the sound. They hit the drone, disabling the sensor. It was literally stuck to the cutter, unable to disengage. The same will happen to the Chinese navy ships. This *will* lead to war."

There was no remorse or compassion in the Admiral's face. By now, it was more than evident that he wasn't only willing to risk war, but he cherished the thought. He salivated over it. The thought of killing thousands of enemy troops was a joyous one. Worth the price it would entail.

"Excuse me... Sirs?"

Heston and White looked to the radar analyst, who was not sure which admiral he wanted to address.

"What is it?" White said.

"I've received a ping on the tsunami warning system. I'm receiving alarms from the undersea motion detectors we've placed in Sectors Seven and Eight... heading straight toward the *Vandervoort*."

All eyes went to the main monitor. Centered on the screen was the destroyer. Near the lower frame, the meg was chasing Viper One.

On the upper right corner, a dark shape came into view.

CHAPTER 26

"Here, fishy, fishy." Viper One's gunner angled the M60 on its swivel, popping multiple bursts at the oncoming fish. The meg followed the sensation of the rotor drafts on the surface, confused as to why it could not find the source. "We're up here, fishy!"

"Stow it," the pilot told him.

"Central Command to Viper One. Arm hellfire missiles. You have a bogey moving in to your two o'clock."

As though he heard the transmission, the shark darted to the left. The gunner pivoted his gun and fired a spray at it, failing to regain its attention. He looked to the open sea.

"I don't see…"

As an apocalyptic asteroid approached a planet, a huge dark shape flew under the water—straight to the source of conflict. At first, it was somewhat narrow in shape, resembling a massive tadpole with a round head and a squiggly tail.

In one collective motion, that 'tail' broke apart into eight curved appendages. In that brief moment, the creature resembled a spider about to leap on an unsuspecting grasshopper.

The pilot initiated ascent, but the chopper never went anywhere.

Like the devil's claw reaching from a deep abyss, tentacles coiled around the tail and pulled. Viper One fell fifty feet, then hovered in place.

The Kraken's mantle emerged, forming a mountain riddled with spines and calloused flesh. In its grasp was the chopper. The beast twirled the machine as David did with his stone sling. And to the Kraken, the goliath was the metal beast to its north.

Having learned of the aircraft's explosive weaponry in its last encounter, the Kraken devised its plan of attack.

It threw the helicopter. Confident in its aim, the beast submerged, favoring pursuit in the megalodon over witnessing the fiery spectacle.

Viper One smacked down behind the *Vandervoort's* bridge. Four hellfire missiles and two Mark-46 torpedoes burst into a roaring ball of fire. Metal and flesh took to the sky, trailing smoke and blood. Sailors who weren't stunned by the concussion rushed across the parts of the deck that wasn't encased in flame.

In the bridge, alarms blared in Bey's ear. He was on his hands and knees, his head rattling. The crew were fighting to get a damage report, some simply resorting to looking outside than use the computers and radios. Half the equipment wasn't functional anyway, a telling sign of the *Vandervoort's* status.

"We're taking on water," someone said.

"Fire's spreading to the lower decks!"

"Water reported in level six and five. The hold is flooded."

"Hull is breached on both sides."

"Engines failing to respond."

"Weapons system unresponsive."

"We have men trapped in the engine room. Smoke is filling Decks One, Two, and Three."

"Captain, what's your order?"

Bey looked to his left. Dr. Trevor Zenner was on his knees next to the Porpoise. He lifted it up and carried it to the stairwell.

"I thought you could control that thing," Bey said. Trevor paid him no mind. Bey stood up and followed him onto the wing. "Doctor! You said you could lure the beast! That it would follow the megs!"

"What do you expect from me now, Captain? To give the octopus a talking to? Now, if you'll excuse me, I'm expecting a flight off this bird."

Bey went to grab him, but was distracted by a bridge crewmember who stepped out.

"Captain! What do we do?"

Bey looked back and forth between the doc and the bridge. Between violent desire and his duties. The latter was more important. He could track down Trevor and strangle him some other time.

He went straight to the comms station. "Get a Mayday out. We need immediate pickup." He turned to the sonar operator. "Where's the octopus?"

****

Even a predator as mighty as the megalodon succumbed to the imperfections of biology. For Albert, those imperfections were enhanced by age and disease, and exacerbated by fatigue. His energy had been spent on the man-made opponents, with little in reserve to flee when he sensed the superior threat approach.

His opportunity to escape, provided by the Kraken's distraction with the humans, amounted to nothing. Each swing of his caudal fin was slower than the last. A constricting sensation filled the space between his pectoral fins. Albert could not comprehend that his heart was giving out.

Even if he could, he likely would not have. His lateral line detected water distortion behind him. The scent of ammonia entered his nostrils. The light disappeared from view, overtaken by an immense shadow.

Having easily closed the distance with its jet propulsion capabilities, the Kraken hovered over the meg. Cunning and ruthless, the beast knew an encumbered target when it saw one. There was no escape for this shark.

It expanded its eight arms, taking the form of a massive umbrella.

Albert angled himself up at the enemy. Lacking the ego of the earth's more intelligent species, he felt no sense of honor, no terror, no apprehension of what lay beyond death, nor a desire for a warrior's death. Death was death, it all amounted to the same conclusion. All the fish had, all the fish *knew*, was a will to survive. Even in the face of certain doom.

The megalodon launched the last attack he would ever make. Slow and heavy, he was easily countered. A mild jet of water and a wave of tentacles allowed the Kraken to evade the biting jaws.

Albert's teeth intertwined, piercing nothing but ocean.

Tentacles seized him. The fish wiggled in place, the caudal fin entangled in the leathery clutches. The smell of his own blood and the stabbing sensation of three-foot hooks entering its body overloaded his senses.

One of the arms hooked around the neck, sank its hooks through the gill slits and under the chin, and squeezed. As a strangled outlaw would kick while dangling from a noose, the fish thrashed.

The Kraken pulled, maintaining its grip on the rest of Albert's body. Skin and muscle tissue stretched, then tore. Cartilage snapped like rubber bands. A cloud of blood burst and shrouded the Kraken in red, blinding it to its surroundings.

Its pleasure was unhindered, for the beast did not need eyes to enjoy the sensation of removing the megalodon's head from its body.

It released the twitching, headless corpse and let it drop to the seabed, instead holding on to the severed head. The jaw hung slack, the eyes even more pale than before.

Vibrations rippled through the water. The Kraken dropped the head, then ascended to the bright, glittering surface. Two black eyes strained in the waterless space above. It was a momentary inconvenience while gauging the status of its other enemy.

The metal beast was in ruins, the back end slowly dipping into the water. The pointed front was a few feet higher now, its insides filled with seawater. The Atlantic, minutes ago seeming peaceful and gleaming, was now a river of death inside that man-made beast.

Smaller metal creatures hovered in the sky. Their motions reminded the Kraken of large shrimp that scavenged in its original habitat. They belonged to one large school, but they acted individually, searching for food to sink their talons into. The beast had learned not to misjudge another creature based solely on size. It had witnessed one of its brethren swarmed by such creatures. Though only half the size of the Kraken, it was still many times larger than the shrimp. They had numbers and maneuverability on their side, and little by little, they sliced into the not-yet hardened mantle.

These flying beasts did not have the numbers of the shrimp, but they had a superior sting. Yet, as it witnessed from the humans' encounter with the megs, they would not fire too close to their own. They were not insusceptible to their own explosive weapons, a fact proven when the Kraken threw the flying thing into the big floating one.

For long enough, the creature remained hidden, watching the humans, studying their machines, while evading their patrols. With age came experience, and the beast knew when it was being hunted. Thus, there was only one conclusion. The humans were not food, but rival predators. In order to dominate this new habitat, all rivals would have to be extinguished.

The humans, the megalodons, *all* of them.

Filling its mantle with water, the Kraken submerged, aimed itself at the new target, then jetted.

It was time to finish what it started.

****

Trevor took the stairs to a series of passageways which led him to the deck. He paused to monitor the situation and ensure he had enough space to get around the fire and deck breaches.

"Move. Out of my way."

Trevor's words went unheard by the frenzied crew of sailors. Many were putting extinguishers to use, their grey fog mixing with the smoke. Others sprayed hoses, resembling everyday firemen but without the big coats and hats.

Won't see you assholes on calendars. A wave of residue rolled over him, forcing the doctor to gag for breath and eliminating his attempt to ease his nerves with humor.

The sight of charred corpses and scattered body parts were enough to disturb even him. The heat from the smoke, combined with his adrenaline, soaked Trevor in his own sweat, making his grip on the heavy Porpoise a slippery one.

Even more frustrating was Admiral Heston's apparent refusal to answer his call. The two had arranged that he would receive pickup in the unlikely event of trouble. Of course, by trouble, they were thinking of something more along the lines of a megalodon ramming the ship, not a Kraken literally using their own firepower against them. With the unlikely now an unprecedented reality, he was watching the skies for his chopper.

He was forced to stop near the DDG-51 Phalanx, cut off by an impossible stream of flame. While waiting for the sailors to extinguish it, he placed the Porpoise down, then hit the call button on his satellite phone. There was only one number programmed into it. Once again, he had to listen to the damn thing ring.

"Alright, Admiral. Any day, now…"

He looked aft to the sound of sailors calling out to each other. Many were pointing thirty-degrees off the starboard quarter, then turning around and racing up the gradually-increasing slope.

Trevor lowered the satellite phone, his watering eyes straining to make out the approaching shape, partially obscured by smoke and extinguisher residue.

"Oh, shit…"

At first, it resembled a tidal wave moving backward, the crest pointing away from the ship. Yet, the wave got larger. Only when it neared impact did Trevor recognize the spiked mantle plowing across the sea.

With only a few yards to go, the beast turned. Huge black eyes gazed at the deck and its many inhabitants. Two enormous arms grabbed ahold of the ship, then strained.

Trevor felt gravity shift, and heard the straining of steel as the *Vandervoort* took on sixty-five tons of added mass. The mantle, oddly rigid, yet simultaneously soft in its appearance, scraped the flight deck. Arms and tentacles felt its new surroundings. Its siphon, resembling the exhaust pipe on a car, spewed water and bits of dark-green waste. This was its first time being completely out of water.

Trevor tucked his phone away, picked up the Porpoise, then slowly backed toward the bridge. Though stricken with terror, it was fascinating to watch the Kraken adapt. Being out of water, gravity felt different to the beast. There was no buoyancy, no water to draw in through its mantle cavities, nor any pushback when the siphon expelled its contents.

Machine gun fire returned the creature to its violent, lively state. Sailors, two armed with fifty-caliber machine guns, and others with M14 rifles, stormed the deck, guns blazing. Wave after wave of bullets struck the Kraken, stinging its flesh, drawing blood from the softer tissue on its tentacles.

Trevor's fascination came to an abrupt halt. He turned around and raced back to the very bridge he had abandoned minutes ago. Only when he arrived at the superstructure did he look back.

Just as it did when it first emerged from the depths, the beast adapted to its new environment. On both occasions, it was a matter of survival. Its tentacle still bore the bite marks of a pod of killer whales who, despite being much smaller, thought the Kraken to be a viable source of sustenance. Unlike the mammals that swam near the surface, the Kraken was capable of retaliation. As it turned out, *they* were the source of sustenance, and the first indication that the Kraken could survive in this new world.

Now, it was these pathetic land-dwellers picking a fight with a larger foe. Their attacks were meager, their courage nonexistent in the Kraken's eyes. In its world, courage did not exist. There was only eat or be eaten, and creatures that tried to pick a fight they couldn't win only meant nature was serving up an easy catch.

The Kraken retaliated. Tentacles, surpassing the length of the megalodon they had just killed, uncoiled like busted springs. Their hooded tips found sailors, folded over them, and carried the dinky catch to the beak.

The gunfire persisted.

Impatient with eating them one-by-one, the Kraken resorted to lashing out. The physicality of these humans could not endure the force of its attacks. Some were smacked clean off the boat, every bone in their body busted. Some broke into pieces, limbs flying in separate trajectories from the bodies. Others exploded into red mush on impact.

Now, the humans seemed to realize their efforts were futile. Some had made the decision to retreat after the first few were devoured. Others held their ground for a little longer, retreating after the second wave of attacks.

They ran to the front of the ship, some disappearing into little holes in the structure.

Sliding to the middle of the ship, the Kraken set its eyes on the large, towering portion of the ship. Several men stood on an outside platform, watching it approach. This part of the ship was different. The Kraken sensed some kind of importance to this particular section. It thought of it as a head. Sever the head, rid the enemy of life. Though it knew this floating creature was not living, it still operated as one. Thus, the logic was the same. Go for the head, destroy the brains.

This new interest overrode its desire to pursue the sailors. The Kraken slid forward, fascinated by its body's ability to secrete slime which acted as a natural barrier between it and the deck. Despite its mass, it moved effortlessly, slowing briefly as it crossed the smoldering hot area where the flying machine had exploded.

More bullets struck its mantle, chipping its calloused flesh. Little gusts of wind brushed the tentacles.

More of those flying machines. Like the shrimp from the world below, they swarmed the Kraken. As it predicted, they refrained from using their explosive weapons. A seemingly unified species, they would not risk the harm of their brethren.

However, these near-invisible projectiles were stronger than the hand-held ones used by the sailors. They fired with greater force and a faster rate. The Kraken had to act fast, or else suffer severe injury.

It lunged at the nearest one, its tentacle falling short. The flying machines were wise to its act, having witnessed the destruction of the other. The Kraken never limited itself to a single means of attack. All of its life, it had learned to utilize its surroundings to its advantage.

All around it were pieces of the ship, loosened or broken free entirely. Improvisation was key to survival. It allowed the Kraken to discover new foods, and survive violent encounters. That was one of two secrets to its long survival: be the strongest, and the *smartest* beast in the ocean.

It grabbed a broken section of the boat and gave it a yank, snapping the little bits of metal that kept it attached. It raised the object back, then heaved it into the air.

Trevor reached the starboard bridge wing, where Captain Bey stood. He was looking past him at the creature, captivated by what he was witnessing. The ship vibrated as a piece was separated from it. Trevor turned around just in time to see the monster *throw* part of the MK99 missile control system at the choppers.

Crash!

Viper Two was hit square in the cockpit. The chopper, still firing its miniguns, spun out of control. The impact was followed by a hundred tiny *clangs* of metal in the span of an instant.

Viper Three was hit by its guns, the rotors smoking. Both choppers twirled during their descent. Two struck down first, immediately followed by Three.

The next piece to be thrown was one of the five-inch guns. Like the MK99, it was tossed at one of the Seahawks. The bird dodged the projectile by banking to port and lowering altitude.

The Kraken seized the opportunity, launching itself over the starboard side and lashing its tentacles into the air. Its clawed suckers attached themselves to the fuselage. The chopper attempted to pull away, but failed.

One of the crew, believing this bird would suffer the same fate as Viper One, took his chances by bailing. He felt the freefall, but never felt the splash of water. Instead, it was wet, putrid flesh. He survived long enough to regret his decision, before finally feeling that splash of water, and the snapping beak that was under it.

The dead crewman was not wrong in his suspicion.

Recognizing the way the beast maneuvered the Seahawk, Trevor and Bey raced into the bridge, the latter waving his arms at the remaining crew.

"Brace for im—"

The chopper hit the bow and exploded. Glass shattered, all lights went out, and fiery heat invaded the bridge. Moments later, there was smoke.

When Trevor and Bey looked up, they saw no forecastle. Only fire and smoke. There were a few screams from the unlucky crew outside who somehow survived the explosion.

Bey grabbed the doctor by the collar. "You maniac! You and the Admiral! Don't you see what you have done?!"

"You say that like you weren't in on it!" Trevor said. He attempted to pry Bey's hands loose, only to realize the captain was far stronger than him.

Bey threw the doctor against the instrument panel, stepped forward, then thrust a finger in his face. "If we survive this, I'm going public. You, Heston, I'm gonna spill the beans on *everything*."

"I dare ya," Trevor said. "You'll be dishonorably discharged. You willing to take the heat, Captain?"

Bey pointed toward the sound of screams outside.

"Nothing compared to the heat they're facing." He lowered his hand. "Certainly nothing compared to the heat you and I probably have ahead of us."

He raced below with two other crewmembers in a likely futile attempt to rescue any injured sailors.

****

USCGC Richard Denning

"What the hell is going on?"

Lieutenant Commander Jim Davidson watched the numerous dorsal fins from the bridge wing of his cutter. The sharks were going haywire. A couple of them had darted off into open sea, despite the Porpoise speaker still functioning perfectly.

"Are they fed up?" Petty Officer First Class Tom Elway asked. "They've been waiting around here for a while."

"I don't know," Davidson said.

One of the megs raised its head, spraying the ship with water. Its jaw was open, pink gums bared fully. It was racing at one of the other megalodons. There was another spray of water when the shark it pursued moved out of the way.

Davidson noticed the series of scars on the attacker's head. Drill. According to the files, he was a fairly aggressive meg who liked to start fights with others. The seventy-two footer turned to chase the other meg. It was one of the triplets. Dash, judging by the way it moved.

"Command Central, this is the *Richard Denning*. We've got problems. The megs are breaking off from our location. I repeat, they are diverging from our present location." He lowered the radio. "The Admiral's plan isn't going to work. Using the signals sporadically and using bait has worked thus far, but when the sharks are exposed to a continuous signal in a singular location for long enough, they see through the bullshit."

"You think they know they're being tricked?" Elway asked.

"Not in so many words, but these are whale signals they're using. Well, the sharks have been swimming around, and there's no whale. They're basically saying 'screw it' and moving elsewhere." The lieutenant commander groaned. "Dr. Zenner and the Admiral didn't think this through."

"In this one's case, he's *pissed*," Elway said, watching Drill make another go at Dash.

The sixty-footer dodged the attack yet again. Drill darted to the left to follow, only to be struck by a massive impact from underneath.

Bruce, the slower of the triplets who periodically let himself sink, intercepted the enemy meg. Though twelve-feet shorter, he managed to strike the fish hard enough to launch it clear out of the water.

Drill crashed down a few yards from the *Richard Denning's* hold. The crew retreated forward, some knocked down by the mini-tsunami that spilled onto the cutter.

"Arm the Bushmaster," Davidson said to the bridge crew before speaking into his radio. "Central Command, we're seeing aggressive activity from the sharks. Looks like the one named Drill decided to pick a fight with the triplets." He ducked down as Drill and Dash both smacked into the starboard bow. Like crocodiles, they rolled along the surface, biting at each other. Caudal fins struck the ship as they went under.

The impact rotated the *Richard Denning* to port.

"Central Command, do you copy?"

"This is Rear Admiral White. Richard Denning, you are ordered to depart. We are aborting the mission."

Davidson lowered the radio and watched the sharks resume their fight. The third triplet, Webb, darted at Drill and bit him on the right pectoral. The larger fish tried to bite back, only for Dash to sink his teeth into the left side of his neck. The ocean was alive with fins and teeth. A bit of blood and white foam altered the natural blue color. After a brief struggle, Drill broke free and raced past the bow, the triplets now pursuing him.

"Looks like he picked a fight with the wrong crowd," Davidson said. The sound of engines lifted his attention to the sky. A few Coast Guard choppers were speeding to the east. Following their trajectory with his eyes, he spotted the trail of smoke in the far distance.

"That doesn't look good," Elway remarked.

"No, it does not," Davidson said. Before the megalodons grabbed his attention, he had heard through the feeds that the Kraken was attacking. He lifted his radio, then ducked when the brawling megs plowed into the keel. Water spat high over the cutter with volcanic force. "Sir, what's the status of the *Vandervoort*?"

****

The Kraken beheld the results of its handywork. The big machine's rear end was completely submerged, its still-blazing front section now pointed skyward. There were still a few flying machines high above it. They were beyond reach of its arms and lining up for a fresh attack.

It submerged and discharged a cloud of ink, obscuring it from view. Now at the sea bottom, it moved west. Its suspicion proved accurate, for the ink laden area it previously occupied was hit with thunderous force. There was a flash of orange followed by a concussion strong enough to drive a creature of its size backward. The Kraken clung to the seabed and held position, watching the bright surface around the ink cloud.

The shockwave ran its course, leaving behind a hot section of ocean still billowing smoke. The Kraken waited for new vibrations given off by the flying machines in hopes they would descend low enough to be grabbed.

Instead, new vibrations caught its attention. They were faint, at least a couple miles away. But there was no mistaking these sounds, for they were identical to those that attracted it toward this area to begin with. The megalodons were in combat, either with each other or with one of the floating things. The sound of impact on metal was unmistakable.

It had defeated this metal beast, which was multiple times its size. The other ones were smaller. Experience brought confidence. The Kraken even knew it could operate above the water's surface. Its feeding grounds had been expanded two-fold, as were its means of attack.

Thousands of gallons filled its mantle and was immediately ejected, jetting the Kraken toward its next fight.

****

Command Central

White and Heston were on different radios, barking orders to squads individually. Current events had delayed Heston's detainment. His plan was forgone anyway. The *Vandervoort* was halfway sunk, as was its goal of luring the sharks into Chinese territory.

Smoke continued spewing from the ship's forward half, obscuring any decent view of its bridge.

"USCG Nine, what's your status?" White said. "There might still be men aboard that ship and they have minutes left at best."

"Does anyone have a visual on the target?" Heston said.

"Negative, Admiral."

"We've got men in the water. Survivors from Viper Two and Three."

"This is USCG-Nine, we're arriving on site. Eight and Ten will go after the crash survivors. My team will go for the bridge."

"Hurry it up," White said.

"I need every available Seahawk in the air in search of the Kraken," Heston said. "Fire on sight."

White, still barking orders through his radio, shot a disparaging glance in his direction. "Trying to save your image, Admiral? Have something to tell Congress? 'See? I tried to destroy the biologic.'"

"You seriously want to do this now?" Heston said.

"Yes, actually," White said. "You're officially no longer in command. MPs, see him to the local PD's jail."

The MPs slowly approached the Admiral, ready for another retaliation. This time, Heston went quietly. Words were not needed. His eyes, directed at Nico and Denise, conveyed the message perfectly.

Just you wait…

"Sir!"

White turned to the sailor monitoring the megs. "What's the matter?"

"It's the hundred-twenty footer. It's heading straight for the *Vandervoort.*"

White was back on the radio. "USCG Nine. You've got another biologic headed in your direction. Get those men off the ship and out of the water *now*!"

****

USS Vandervoort

God, I regret this treachery I have taken part in, and will do anything to atone for my evil.

The sight of the five severely burned sailors piling into the safety of the bridge further pushed the reality of the absurdity of Heston's agenda. Bey felt like he was moving in slow motion, not because of the weight of the man he carried, but the heaviness of his guilt. Every 'what could have been' scenario played out in his mind. All he had to do was say no to the Admiral. Then again, knowing Heston, he probably would have had Bey framed for something, and sent to some hush-hush facility. That consideration helped Bey justify his actions to himself in the days leading up to this. Today, he was staring at the direct consequences of attempting to weaponize nature.

Even when Bey stepped outside, he barely had any visibility. He managed to catch brief glimpses of the Coast Guard helicopters descending from the sky like angels from Heaven.

What was *not* obscured from view was the water climbing up the rear of the ship. It had nearly reached the bridge.

The forecastle was fragmented, the chain gun completely destroyed, the frame contorted into some Godforsaken shape that bore little resemblance to its original design.

A continuous gust dispersed some of the smoke, making way for the Coast Guard chopper.

"Thank God." Bey waved his arms. An aviation survival technician was already being lowered on a harness. Bey reached out to grab him and guide him over the guardrail. "Good to see ya."

"Lieutenant Talbert, here to save the day, sir. How many do we have?"

"Six bridge crew, four injured sailors, myself, and a civilian consultant." He waved his hand to the sound of screams and splashes all around them. "How many men we have in the water, I have no idea. I can't even give a casualty report at the moment."

"Don't worry about that, Captain. Let's get you out of here," Talbert said.

"I'll go first, thank you very much." Trevor happily bumped the captain out of the way, Porpoise in hand.

The AST jumper shook his head. "Sorry, sir. We need to get the injured personnel up first."

"This is more important than him," Trevor said.

"Lieutenant, you might wanna hurry it up. We've got another bogey on approach from the north."

Talbert cursed under his breath. "USCG Seven, head to the port bridge wing. Grab some of the sailors." He looked at the nearest injured sailor. His face was charred from fire, his uniform completely flaking off of his body. "You first! Let's go. Come on. Bridge crew, make your way to the port wing."

"What about me?" Trevor said.

"What about you?"

"I have to get this device to safety," Trevor said. "It's essential to keeping the sharks from coastal areas."

Talbert sensed the bullshit. The look on Bey's face practically confirmed that the scientist had some other motive. Unfortunately, there was no time to debate.

"How heavy is it?"

"Seventy-pounds."

"Those handles sturdy?"

"Sure are."

Talbert took two clips from his vest pocket, then attached one of the handles to the harness ring. It was an unconventional setup, but at least it ended the argument, while still allowing the injured man first dibs aboard the chopper.

He signaled to his crew to initiate hoist. The injured sailor and the Porpoise were pulled into the chopper, out of harm's way.

"You're next," Talbert said, pulling another injured sailor forward. The harness came down and was quickly strapped on the man's torso.

"This is the Sea Rock, ready to receive any passengers."

One by one, Talbert got the injured sailors into the chopper. As he did, USCG-Seven took position over the port wing.

"I'll go aboard that one," Trevor said. He went for the door, then jumped back as one of the bridge crew darted onto the starboard wing.

"Holy shit! Captain, it's coming! It's coming! It's coming! Get us out of here!" the sailor shouted, hands pointing to the north.

Bey went through the bridge and peered out the port wing. At first, the fin resembled a huge sail cruising in his direction. A gap in the smoke allowed a momentary clear view of its grey color, the mass underneath it, and the lapping of water pushed by its mass.

O'Brien, the hundred-and-twenty foot megalodon, had arrived.

In the water directly ahead of him were a half-dozen sailors who were now regretting their decision to jump clear of the vessel. O'Brien's upper jaw lifted over the water, exposing teeth as white as his eyes.

With no regards to the massive object behind his victims, the fish accelerated. In a single gulp, it swallowed all six of them before plowing against the side of the boat.

The ship shuddered and angled to starboard.

Next thing Bey knew, he was lying *on* the wing wall, looking *up* at the bridge. The *Vandervoort* was rolling to its side. The captain tried to stand up, but was weighed down by something tugging on his uniform.

To his left, Dr. Trevor Zenner was frantically pulling on him. The idiot, having been leaning on the wall during the impact, was now teetering over the side, his feet kicking wildly.

"Captain! Captain! Don't let me..." His hand slipped— "FAAAAALLLLLL!"

Bey reached for him but was too late. All he could do was watch Trevor hit the thrashing water. The ship, still swinging with momentum from the meg's impact, passed over him.

If he was hit by the bow, then he's a pancake.

"Let's go! Let's go!" Talbert barked. Like a drill sergeant, he hustled the remaining sailors. The two choppers worked fast to haul the rest of the crew from the ship.

After a few minutes which felt like hours, Bey was the last one.

"Your turn, Captain," Talbert said. Bey took one last look at the devastation around him. He did not deserve to be rescued. He should have been one of the people roasting on the forecastle. He was tempted to go down with his ship. But the lieutenant, being the good guardsman that he was, would not leave without him.

Last thing I need is to be responsible for another death.

Bey slipped the harness on and was lifted to the chopper. The harness went back down and picked up Talbert, who spent the last moments aboard searching for any signs of the doc.

There was too much smoke and debris. What was perfectly visible was the waterline on the verge of swallowing the bridge and everything on it.

Talbert gave the signal to be hoisted. The cable pulled him up.

"Anyone else?" one of his crew asked.

"Not that I can see. Let's get these people aboard the *Sea Rock*, and come back for the other stragglers in the water."

When Trevor Zenner opened his eyes, he was underwater, surrounded by wreckage. The last thing he remembered was lying on the deck after falling off the ladder. The moment he recovered, he inexplicably went into a spasm before blacking out.

A few strokes returned him to the surface. The *Vandervoort* and some wreckage were all around him. Like the *Titanic*, it was consumed by the ocean, the bow moments from disappearing from view.

He looked to the sky. A single helicopter glided above him. Mark waved and shouted, but the bird had already shrunk in the distance.

"Stupid assholes! You leaving me here?!"

Feeling the creeping sensation that a predator was closing in on him, he continued waving. Like the dolphin he sacrificed in the pursuit of 'science', he was helpless to escape what was coming.

He was alone in the water, abandoned.

With fatigue setting in, Trevor clung to a piece of wreckage. It didn't do him much good. The destroyer's stern struck the bottom. Now balancing on its keel, it slowly fell forward. Over the course of a minute, its front section was devoured by the Atlantic.

The vacuum pulled Trevor down with it.

His final words were muffled by the water. They were simply incoherent, panicked shouts, cursing the people who seemingly abandoned him, cursing nature for not adhering to his plan. It was wasted energy, doing nothing except drawing the attention of an enormous shark.

The last curse word was not one of panic, but spiteful recognition of his fate.

"Fuck…"

O'Brien closed his jaws over the bite-sized scientist and swallowed him whole.

The fish continued circling, its intended target nowhere in sight. In following the soundwaves of potential prey, it detected the scent of a lifelong adversary. For years, it battled the tentacled species, killing many of the smaller ones. Now, one had risen to this new world.

Its very presence was a threat. The scent of the dead megalodon combined with that of ammonia proved that this enemy species was on a warpath. The shark moved west, detecting vibrations and the scent of ammonia.

O'Brien followed the path. No longer was he interested in whale calls. He was out for bloodshed.

CHAPTER 27

Drill was outmatched. Usually the one who did the chasing, he was now experiencing what it was like to be *chased*. Each time he turned, he was intercepted by one of the triplets. It was less of a fight, and more of a series of brief tussles between chases around the boat.

Lieutenant Commander Jim Davidson would have considered it humorous had it been a different scenario. He had ordered for the vessel to move east and assist with the rescue efforts. The efforts to move the ship were hindered by the megs, who were body-slamming each other into the bow.

Caudal fins flapped over water, the lobes bending with each motion. Lids closed over the white eyes whenever jaws parted for a bite.

They must be able to see, Davidson thought. All this time, he was curious if the sharks were blind, or if that was how the eyes naturally looked. If they could see, they probably had greater eyesight than the average fish, considering they were adept to seeing in the dark.

"Whoa!" He raised a hand over his face to protect it from a wall of water. Dash had charged Drill, who was being held in place by Webb and Bruce. Drill rolled across the surface, once again thumping against the cutter.

He submerged a few feet and raced east, the tip of his caudal fin barely visible. Like a squadron of fighter jets, the triplets pursued.

"Great. Just great," Davidson said. "They're going straight for the *Vandervoort*. There's still men in the water over there."

"Bogey's heading west. I repeat, bogey just turned west. Richard Denning, be on the lookout."

A snarling Jim Davidson unclipped his radio. "Bogey? Which bogey? We've got like a dozen bogeys around this island. Quit with this bogey bullshit and address the damn sharks by name."

A few seconds of empty airwaves followed. "O'Brien. Tracking shows him headed in your direction. He's still a couple miles out, but is moving fast."

"Sir?!"

Davidson turned to the petty officer third class, who operated the sonar. "Yes?"

"We have a bogey on approach."

Davidson stepped behind him, tempted to backhand the officer. "You too? Is bogey the popular word today? WHICH creature?"

"I… I don't know. There's no tag."

Davidson watched the screen. His anger converted into alarm. Something huge was moving under the water and heading straight for them.

He looked through the glass at the sharks. Both Drill and the triplets had stopped abruptly, as if they had come across an impassible barrier.

Drill, the ferocious brawler of the megs, turned to his left and darted north. The triplets fanned out, ready to give their new visitor a toothy welcome.

"It's closing in fast," the petty officer third class said.

Perspiration mixed with the seawater droplets on Davidson's brow. "Goddamnit, it's the Kraken."

As if it heard him, the beast emerged on the surface. Cruising through the shallow waters on Cielo Nublado's north side, it was on a direct course for the *Richard Denning*.

"Fire the MK-38. Kill the bastard."

The weapon was armed and ready to go. Its operator rotated the gun two degrees starboard, then centered it on the oncoming biological projectile. Rapid booms thundered from the forecastle.

The first few shots fell short, striking the water in its path. The next two plunged into the mantle, snapping one of its spines and drawing blood. The Kraken's response was instant. A stream of water from its siphon pushed the creature out of the path of bullets.

Bypassing the sharks, it continued on its objective to eliminate the human vessel.

"Rotate barrel ten degrees starboard." The order was obsolete as soon as it left Davidson's lips. The beast was already coming around the port side. "Full left rudder." Again, it was already obsolete. The Kraken paused momentarily, filled itself with water, then circled behind the *Richard Denning*. Safe from the Bushmaster autocannon and fueled by pain, it started its attack.

Fifty caliber machine guns greeted its tentacles. It was the same retaliation the Kraken faced during its first encounter with one of these floating machines several days ago. As it learned then, the best course of action was to absorb the pain and eliminate the hostiles.

Four tentacles secured a hole on the deck and pulled the Kraken aboard. The *Richard Denning* tilted astern, taking a similar appearance to its Navy counterpart. One of the tentacles slapped down on one of the machine-gunners, pancaking him to the deck. The other was constricted in the tip of another arm and fed into its beak. Even the constant suctioning sound of tentacles and the squelchy vibrations from its mantle could not block out the *crunch* and *splatter* of the man being reduced to pulp.

Davidson stepped outside, and was immediately forced to cling to the guardrail to prevent from reeling aft. "Son of a..." Seeing the beast clinging to the cutter, he turned his eyes to the skies. "We need some of those Seahawks over here."

Another crewman was snatched and gifted to the beak, his screams peaking with a *crunch!*

More tentacles stretched the length of the deck, stopping a couple meters short of the bridge.

Davidson noticed the odd way the Kraken leaned back. Its front arms quickly recoiled, then danced to the side. The creature was alarmed. Frantic, even.

Behind it, three caudal fins were slashing the water. The triplets had bitten one of its back tentacles, which were still in the water, astern. Like canines, they tugged on the ropy appendages.

Shifting its attention from the cutter to the fish, the Kraken fell backward into the water. The cutter leveled out, teetering to and fro.

"All ahead full," Davidson ordered. "Put some distance between us and the target, then circle to port. Gunner, rotate eighty degrees left. Fire as soon as you see the damn thing."

The fight was on. Dash maintained his hold on the tentacle while his brothers went after the mantle. Drawn by the blood which spilled from the bullet injuries, they went for the chink in the armor.

Bruce went for the first bite. His teeth never reached the target. In his attack, his snout struck one of the spines, which sank over a foot deep into his snout. Webb found a more barren area to attack. His jaws closed over a section of flesh. The meat folded, but the calloused tissue held its own against the six-inch teeth. It was not as soft as the meat on the tentacles.

Like the heads of a hydra, the tentacles rushed to the Kraken's defense. Two of them swarmed Dash's head, prying his jaws from their companion.

At the same time, three other arms went after Webb. One wrapped around his caudal fin, another constricting his neck. Hooks pierced his flesh, securing its hold. Like a saltwater fisherman holding a white marlin to a camera crew, the Kraken held the shark in front of its eyes. Webb wriggled, outmuscled by his captors, as was his brother.

The Kraken did not waste another moment. It pulled Webb to its mouth, its hold tightening. The closer Webb got, the more desperate he became. He snapped his jaws, twisted his body, tried lashing his tail… all of which amounted to nothing. His last movement was convulsion. The tip of the upper jaw popped his right eye, the lower jaw sinking into the top of his head. The beak closed, their tips meeting inside the orbital region of its skull.

Once the fish went limp, the Kraken tossed it aside. Now, it was the other's turn.

More tentacles wrapped around Dash, prodding his body with their hooks. The shark, still struggling to free himself, was brought to the beak. The bony maw was already clicking, thirsty for the taste of meg blood. Pieces of Webb's flesh dangled like ribbons from the curved tips.

There was a bite followed by pain.

The Kraken lurched backward, losing its hold on Dash. Bruce, having sunk over a hundred feet, ascended like a rocket and stabbed dozens of serrated teeth into the webbing between two of the rear tentacles. Soft as the arms themselves, his jaws drew blood.

True to his name, Dash hastened out of reach. Pumping water through his gills, he regained his strength.

During that time, his brother continued the assault. But the fish was young, and fighting a battle against an opponent who was older, stronger, had more experience, and a greater arsenal of weaponry. The rule of combat was to beware of the old in a world where most die young. This was true both in human warfare and in nature.

Despite his attempts to maintain his grip, Bruce was pried loose. Tentacles looped around his body, obscuring everything except his caudal fin and head. His jaw chomped seawater in a fruitless attempt to get some circulation over his gills.

The pressure mounted. The Kraken did not bother with biting this foe. There was a strange satisfaction in tightening its clasp. Like a closing fist, the tentacles squeezed. Now Bruce's jaws were open against his will, for his throat was compressed.

Three hundred feet away, Dash had regained his strength. The enemy was preoccupied, its back to him. As Bruce had done at the start of the fight, he detected the weakness in its mantle. A good bite at the right angle would allow his teeth to enter the slit and pierce interior layers of tissue. Then the fish would simply have to thrash back and forth to enlarge the wound. Once the hardened layer was split, it tore relatively easy, as the triplets had learned when battling smaller cephalopods in the deep.

The meg charged, expecting to close the distance with five swings of its tail. It only took two. Unbeknownst to Dash, the Kraken detected his movements. Having already been attacked from behind twice in this conflict, it was wise to his strategy.

Expelling a stream of seawater, it put itself on a collision course, dragging Bruce along.

Impact.

It was the equivalent to head-on collision between a semi-truck and a Dodge Ram. Dash was knocked out of the way with ease. Like a pin struck by a fourteen pound bowling ball, he was tossed head-over-fin to the side.

With the third member of this trinity stunned, the Kraken completed Bruce's execution. All eight arms constricted around the fish, folding its body in on itself. Organs imploded, cartilage compressed, all matter expelling through the only escape routes.

Bruce's eyes popped from his head, followed by blood, brains, and guts. The Kraken unclasped its arms and zipped away, leaving his crinkled body to sink for the last time.

The *Richard Denning* completed its roundabout, its commanding officer watching the ocean with binoculars. Sonar showed two objects in motion.

Only two?

Considering the size of one, it was evident that the triplets were outmatched. Blood in the water confirmed that the battle had consequences. One did not need to be a biologist to know that consequence was death.

Lieutenant Commander Jim Davidson was not void of honor. Had the triplets not attacked the octopus, it would have sunk his vessel and killed everyone aboard. No, the sharks did not pull it away out of the goodness of their hearts. But he did not care whether it was intentional or not. The results were the same. Now, the least he could do was avenge the ones who had been killed and save the survivor.

Then again, the bastards did attack the Red Nova. Jim Davidson, while compliant of Heston's plan, was unaware of the whole truth. Like many, he was a pawn in a scheme. Had he known the extent of the Admiral's plan, he would have never taken part.

As it turned out, it didn't matter. The Kraken could not be controlled. Violent and wicked, it was now on Davidson's list of threats to America. At least he could personally eradicate this one.

His gunner rotated the Bushmaster to twelve-o'clock. All they needed was for the thing to show its ugly face.

"What is that?" one of the crewmen said.

Davidson squinted to gain a visual on the anomaly. Up ahead, a dark purple cloud was filling the ocean.

"That's not blood…"

Dash was swimming on his side, his senses too jarred for him to realize he was turning upside down. The fish rotated, briefly inducing tonic immobility. Dash entered a sleeplike state, his muscles relaxing, their contractions becoming steadier. After a few moments, the shark was upright again.

His senses returned, his nostrils taking in the smell of his brothers' blood. The last of the triplets, he cruised in search of the beast that killed them.

The ocean had turned dark. That sunlight which Dash had grown used to over the course of a month had disappeared. A thick, murky substance filled the ocean, hindering both his eyes and smell. It was not here a moment ago, for he had easily picked up the scent of blood. Now that was erased. The only scent Dash could pick up was that of this stale cloud.

Swimming into it proved to be a mistake. He had entered a maze of fog. Every direction he turned only served to lead him into thicker fog. His sense of smell was jumbled. The only sense that functioned properly was his ability to sense water displacement.

There was movement to the right, enough to displace thousands of gallons of water. Dash altered course. With a slash of his tail, he fast-tracked to the source, ready to end this fight once and for all.

Yet again, he found himself lost in another thick cloud. This one was fresher, containing remnants of the ammonia-filled body that spewed it.

The shark looked up. Nothing. Left, right. Nothing. Down…

All eight tentacles lashed at once. Dash seized one in his mouth, drawing blood. It made no difference. The other seven arms slashed at him, raking his flesh with their claws.

Pumping water out its siphon, the Kraken drove the fish upward. They moved through dark water and emerged in bright sunlight.

Dash was thirty feet high, writhing like a bass on a fishing line before splashing down. At full strength, he managed to outmuscle the tentacles attempting to snag his neck and head. But like his brethren, they had him by the caudal fin. The hooks inserted their three foot lengths into his flesh.

The two beasts wrestled. Escape was impossible. All the shark could do now was angle his jaws to the left and bite the Kraken's face.

Chomp! Chomp!

As fast as Dash was, the Kraken's arms were faster. They lassoed his pectoral fins and neck, holding him back. Every bite fell short by several feet.

Small, rigid projectiles penetrated the surrounding waters. Still holding the meg, the Kraken turned its eye to the sound of gunshots, spotting the metal beast. Even after nearly being sunk, it had not fled the area. Instead, it was on the attack.

With Dash in tow, it backed away, but the vessel did not let up. The big weapon pounded its position, the projectiles falling a few meters short. It moved back again, refusing to give up its prize. Still, the floating adversary followed. Water spat all around it as projectiles hammered the ocean in search of cephalopod flesh.

The Kraken submerged, only to immediately rise back up. It had moved into shallower waters. In its current position, there was only a hundred feet of depth.

The Kraken knew its mantle could not withstand the razor-sharp stingers that big gun fired. It needed something to use as a shield. Something large enough to absorb the bullets.

Dash, still writhing with what little strength he had left, was hoisted vertically over the water. His jaws now pointed at the air, he felt the tentacles around his neck retract. The ones on his fins remained in place. Next was the feeling of flying forward.

It was an unnatural, confusing state, which spiked when pain was suddenly added to the mix.

Splat! Splat! Splat! Splat! Splat!

Multiple deep impacts shredded the shark's underside. Internal organs ruptured. Stomach contents spilled out. Blood surged from his mouth. Now, all strength was gone. The last of the triplets was moments from death, still held high by the Kraken while it raced at the enemy vessel.

Before death took its toll, Dash felt one final impalement…

"Shit! SHIT!" Davidson yelled. He could not believe it. That damn octopus was actually using the megalodon as a freaking *shield*!

How smart is this thing?!

That question was answered by the next attack. Within twenty feet of the bow, the Kraken threw the shark onto the deck like a Scottish caber. Ninety thousand pounds crashed onto the forecastle, its gun, and its handler. There was a brief scream, stifled by the sound of metal.

The fish was limp on the bow, its snout impaled on the barrel of the gun. Underneath it was the crushed body of the weapon, and the equally crushed crewman underneath it.

More weight tugged on the *Richard Denning*. Leaning forward, Davidson was helpless to do anything but watch while the Kraken climbed aboard his cutter for the second time. One of its tentacles pulled Dash's lifeless corpse off the forecastle and deposited him into the ocean like trash.

The Lieutenant Commander watched the fish disappear, subconsciously hoping it would spring back to life and come to the rescue again. Instead, he was forced to witness the tentacles tear the ship apart. The Kraken was completely on the forecastle. Tentacles ripped into the bridge. Two of them retracted, holding squirming crew members in their grips.

One of them was Petty Officer First Class Tom Elway. It held him in front of its eyes, watching with a childlike fascination as it slowly applied pressure.

No scream matched that of a man whose spinal column had just snapped. The end of his suffering came at the cost of his life.

Davidson never considered himself a religious person until now. At the very least, seeing this beast was a confirmation of the existence of hell. Nobody but the devil himself could conceive such a diabolical thing.

He retreated aft, where the remaining personnel were attempting to repair the rigid-hulled inflatable. Behind them, the creature finished its work on the bridge. Tentacles plunged into the exposed passageways, seeking out any sailors hiding below. One was found, grabbed, and spared the fate of being food. The Kraken opted for smashing him against the bulkheads instead. Davidson couldn't see it, but he could feel the repeated battering sounds under his feet.

"Hurry up!" a terrified crewmember shouted to the men deploying the inflatable. The small craft had been damaged in the initial attack, its hull and propellor compromised.

"It's busted up," one of them replied.

"Just push it into the water and maybe we can…"

The tentacle came down like a fist, reducing the crewmember into a red, gooey pile on a dented section of deck.

Davidson stared. The terror had subsided. Instead, he felt more tempted to laugh. He had retreated to the rear of the boat, as though there was anywhere to hide from this thing.

This thing sunk a destroyer, now two cutters, killed several megalodons, and yet I'm supposed to believe running away on this little inflatable boat is gonna save me.

"I got it!" one of the crewmen said. "The engine's working. Come on! Get in!" They deployed the boat and jumped in.

Davidson shrugged, checked out. "It's no use, gentlemen. You're only buying yourself a few extra moments."

The three men stared at him, and the rapidly approaching tentacles behind him.

"Forget him. He's lost it," one said. They gunned the engine and veered toward the island.

Accepting his fate, Davidson drew his last breath. He could practically taste the ammonia coming off those tentacles. The deck vibrated under its weight. Davidson tensed and closed his eyes.

Now, the terror had returned. "Come on, you prick! Get it over with!"

Impact came, not from sucker-layered arms, but water. A tidal wave of water, large enough to knock the Lieutenant Commander to his knees, covered the deck.

Davidson looked over his shoulder. The Kraken was no longer on the *Richard Denning.* Instead, it coursed through the water, speedily nearing the inflatable.

It had literally abandoned him in favor of chasing a fleeing target.

"Son of a bitch," he whispered. *I guess it's no fun killing someone if they're accepting.*

They had made a valiant effort in their escape, closing within five-hundred feet of the shore. Ultimately, they proved Davidson's point. The thing smacked the boat with one of its arms. The three men aboard were airborne. Two landed in the shallows, the third splattering on the shoreline. He was the lucky one. The other two were grabbed, squeezed, and delivered to the beak.

There was motion on shore. Marines had gathered with machine guns on their Humvees. Immediately, they started blasting away at the creature.

"Oh, no…" Davidson muttered. They didn't know they weren't safe on land.

CHAPTER 28

Nico followed the crowd out of Command Central, where they watched the beast mount the *Richard Denning* and reduce it to scrap. The triplets were dead, as were dozens of Coast Guard and Navy personnel.

Marines assembled on the north beach, some armed with M4 Carbines, others with M27 Infantry Automatic Rifles. Two Humvees pulled up to the dock. Water lapped several yards inland, pushed by a titanic force.

"Oh my God," Denise said.

The Kraken was coming ashore. A creature of incredible mass, its outstretched length surpassing the *Richard Denning*, it managed to move with the grace and speed of its much smaller modern day counterpart. A lifetime of living in crushing depths built strength matched only by its ferocity.

"Tell those men to clear out," Nico said to White.

The beach descended into chaos. The fifty-cals opened fire, the Humvee drivers not anticipating the Kraken's speed. Tentacles punched through the windshields and the drivers. It lifted both vehicles and smashed them into the sand.

A frenzy ensued. All eight limbs extended to their full lengths and slashed the annoying pests. Many marines stood their ground and paid the price. Many were launched skyward. Others were grabbed, either tossed into the beak or beaten into the ground.

Infantry bullets sparked pain, but inflicted no significant injury. Realizing this, the senior ranks barked orders, yelling for the men to withdraw. The ground forces backpedaled, still blasting away at the titan.

Tentacles slithered after them, their hooks cutting across the earth.

The beast was two hundred feet inland, its head perfectly upright, having mastered this new environment.

"Goddamnit! Where are the other choppers?" White said.

"Assisting in the rescue efforts. There are still dozens of men near the *Vandervoort*," the communications specialist said.

"Tell them to get their asses over here. Everyone else, evacuate to the west end of the island," White said. He turned to Denise, Nico, and Renny. "Get on your chopper. Get to safety."

Jeeps were zigzagging all over the beach area. Personnel piled into them, some reaching double the max capacity. White yelled out for one of the drivers, who brought his Jeep to the civilians.

"Take these people to the police helipad," he said. A crashing sound drew their eyes up the beach. The Kraken had grabbed one of the military

Jeeps and threw it into one of the business shops. The vehicle struck the roof, the impact throwing its passengers in all directions. The Jeep teetered on its engine, ultimately falling over the back of the property, where it landed on a full propane tank. The metal-on-metal collision induced a spark, which expanded into a fireball.

The Kraken backed away from the heat, searched the beach for new prey, its eyes settling on the large tent.

White pushed Denise into the vehicle. "The hell are you guys waiting for?!"

Nico and Renny joined her. The driver floored the pedal, veering left to avoid two other Jeeps that were fleeing. Doing so put them in the path of an oncoming Humvee full of marines. The armored vehicle swerved wide, avoiding collision, then immediately turned around after its driver saw what was chasing them. The gunner opened up on the target.

The impact of bullets further agitated the Kraken. Tentacles moved in arching rhythms, truly giving it the appearance of a colossal arachnoid dragging its abdomen across Cielo Nublado.

An explosive crash marked the end of that Humvee and the personnel inside. Shards of metal were scattered over the road as the beast slid over it, still in pursuit of the Jeeps.

The driver, as sweaty and jittery as his passengers, watched the Kraken in his rear-view mirror. "Holy Lord…"

"Eyes on the road!" Nico said. The driver looked forward just in time to see the '25 MPH' sign and the bend in the road right behind it. Still flooring the pedal, he cut the wheel. The Jeep went right, then teetered. It was a fight to keep the thing from flipping.

The vehicle leveled out, then rocked left and right while still going seventy-miles per hour. Each time the tires touched the road, the Jeep veered abruptly. All control was lost. By the time the driver realized this, they were off the road, straight at a flower shop. He spun the wheel to the right, reducing the head-on impact to a sideswipe.

They punched through the outdoor displays, grazing the front of the building. Turbulence rocked everyone in their seats. The driver's head whipped to the side and cracked the window.

Unconsciousness was instant. He slumped against the wheel, his forehead blaring the horn. Behind them, the Kraken was making the turn through the bend.

"I should've stayed with the chopper," Renny said. He moved to the front seat, shoved the unconscious Navy driver into the passenger seat, then took the wheel. "If we live, I'm updating my resumé to 'constantly saving people from killer octopus monsters'!"

Denise glanced at the oncoming beast. Its front arms were extended over seventy feet ahead of it, coming right for them.

"How 'bout you shut up and drive!"

Renny did just that.

The Jeep zipped forward. Tentacles found flower, dirt, and wreckage. They proceeded to attack the flower shop. Brick and mortar came apart, the structure's form and identity erased. The cephalopod pulled itself over the wreckage and continued the chase.

"Holy shit," Renny said, watching the creature in the rear-view mirror. Like the Navy sailor before him, he made the mistake of not watching the road.

"Eyes on the damn road!" Nico said.

Renny looked forward. There was a civilian in their path, staring past them, mouth agape.

Renny swerved past him, avoiding a very ugly impact. Nico looked through the window, then cursed when he recognized the guy standing out there. Dalton Mayberry, the café owner.

"That stupid idiot!" When the guy said he would never leave the island, he absolutely meant it. Now, the argument that there was no danger on land was crumbling under the Kraken's wrath.

Renny hit the brakes, allowing Nico to open the door. "Dalton! Get your ass in here! Hurry up!"

Dalton looked at him, at the monster, then at his shop where he had been hiding out. It was closer, his panic blinding him to the consequence of his decision. He went for the café, shutting the door behind him.

"Dalton, no!" Nico said. The creature was still coming. The man made his decision and sealed his fate. "Go."

The Kraken had to make a decision. Go after the land-based metal thing, or go after the one that hid inside the structure. Fascinated by the discovery of these habitats, and its ability to break them apart, it chose the latter.

Its arms lashed at the building, peeling parts of the walls and roof away. Inside, the structure was divided into separate columns, each one serving a purpose which the beast did not understand. Nor did it care to understand. As far as it was concerned, these structures now existed *only* to be torn apart.

In the rear of the building, it found the lone human hiding in the corner. He attempted to run. A useless effort, one that was quickly stopped. The Kraken ate the man, then went on to the next building. This one was twice as tall as the other. Size made no difference. It was just as easy to tear this one down.

Wreckage was pitched in all directions, causing damage to surrounding buildings. The Kraken scooped as much rubble out of the way as possible until it finally concluded there were no humans inside this one.

It went on to the next structure. Pieces of brick came down with the frequency of torrential rain. Black eyes searched for signs of life, with the intent of ending it.

Nothing.

So far…

"The thing's gone loco," Nico said. "Denise, is this normal?"

"Honey, I've only been studying deep water gigantic organisms for a little over a week," Denise said. "In other words, how the hell should I know?!"

"Good point," Nico said. They continued to watch while the Jeep gained distance. "What about present-day species?"

"They are more than capable of digging through crevices for crabs and other prey," Denise said. "It's usually a feeding behavior. This, though? It's similar, but it's different."

"Makes sense to me," Renny said. "It's a big guy. It needs to eat."

"It's not just that," Denise said. "It's an alpha predator. Sometimes, alpha predators seek to drive out rivals."

"Wait a sec…" Nico felt his pockets for his Excedrin bottle. This new development triggered a fresh headache. "You're saying this thing doesn't see us as food, but as a rival predator?"

"Alpha predators don't always have to be super big," Denise said. "Orcas are considered alpha predators, and they often feed on larger whales. I think the cephalopod views us in a similar manner. It recognizes we have technology, we're great in numbers, we're all over the land and the sea…"

"So, this thing's not gonna stop here," Renny said.

"It's gonna go on a goddamn killing spree," Nico said. Renny pulled the vehicle to the side to make way for three oncoming Humvees. Inside were the same marines speeding in from the police helipad. "Starting with these guys…"

****

Vince Heston was in the jail cell for no more than three minutes when one of the MPs let him back out.

"Pardon me, sir, but all forces are being ordered to evacuate this island." The MP took him by the arm and, with the assistance of a partner, led him through the hallway. Even with his hands cuffed behind his back, the Admiral walked with the stature of a man of his rank.

"How many casualties?" he said, speaking as though still in command.

The MP debated on whether to answer. The Admiral sounded sincere enough. "Lots, sir. Don't have a number yet, but the octopus has moved inland. We don't have heavy armor to combat it. The situation hasn't been contemplated."

"Escape route?"

"The airfield on the west. Got a chopper waiting."

"Understood. Well done, Corporal," Heston said. He let the two men lead him to the door. Heston got a brief glance of the outdoors. The other units had already departed. It was just him and the two MPs. "Sorry about this, gentlemen."

"Nobody could have predicted this, sir," one of them said.

That was tough for the Admiral to hear. The young, disciplined marine was compassionate toward the Admiral, even after all that was revealed. Either he did not know the full extent, or he had a really good poker face. OR, he agreed with Heston's intent. Either way, the Admiral was reluctant to follow through with his plan.

As a young Navy sailor, he had mastered the art of picking handcuffs. As an experienced officer, he could do it in his sleep without anyone noticing, as proven here.

His hands came free. He grabbed the nearest MP and slammed his head into the corner of the doorframe, knocking him out instantly. The other turned, his surprise causing him to hesitate—something Heston counted on. A kick to the shin put the marine on one knee. Heston got behind him and fastened a tight choke-hold. The marine struggled, then went limp. Heston, holding no grudge against these marines, lowered him gently. He took their handguns and spare ammo, then ran to the vehicle.

Instead of west, he went south. There were plenty of civilian boats left over, and they were easier to hotwire than cars.

First, he needed to get on his personal phone. With experience and rank came connections, and it was time to utilize them.

"Yeah... Tango-Charlie-Niner-Three. Send a chopper. Cielo Nublado, south waters. Look for a lone civilian vessel..."

****

Combat brought new discoveries for the Kraken. First, it had learned that the humans carried hand-held weapons which were capable of firing explosive rounds. One had struck its mantle, inducing pain. It was followed by a barrage of others. Individually, they only caused mild burns on its rock-hard flesh. Repeated blows, however, posed a threat.

This led to the second discovery. In its retaliation, it knocked a vehicle into a silver, cylinder-shaped object which was behind one of the buildings. It was the same thing which exploded back at the beach when hit by the Jeep. Whatever these objects were, they were combustible.

That knowledge came in handy when one of the flying vehicles arrived. Like its predecessors, it had learned to keep out of reach. What it did not seem to learn, however, was that the Kraken knew how to throw its own projectiles.

It found another cylinder object, pulled it from the concrete, and chucked it at the flyer. Bullets from its minigun struck the shell. The thing ignited, transforming into a tidal wave of fire which engulfed the target. It spiraled in midair, guns still blazing.

The resulting crash sparked a whole new explosion. Missiles and fuel erupted, smashing windows and shaking the earth.

With the aerial threat out of the way, the Kraken proceeded to wipe out the rest of the ground forces. It smashed another of their vehicles, forcing some of them to retreat into one of the buildings. They tried shooting their weapons through the little square holes, then retreated into the center once the arms began tearing the walls free.

The building came apart with ease. Tentacles seized the little prizes inside and delivered them to the beak.

Screeching tires alerted it to the last vehicle. The few surviving humans were fleeing.

As far as the Kraken was concerned, its objective was not complete. It would not be complete until all humans and megalodons were erased from its new territory. It had miles of ocean to clear. More death would spread the message to the rest of the species. Those who enter this region were subject to death.

It followed the vehicle through a series of roads, which ultimately led back to the beach where it came ashore. It snatched the vehicle, slowly constricted it while watching its inhabitants squirm in agony, then tossed it aside.

There was so much more to do. More humans to kill, more habitats to break apart, more vessels to sink.

One instinct overrode each of these objectives.

Looking out into the water, the cephalopod was encapsulated by a bloodlust as old as time.

Several hundred yards from shore, a singular dorsal fin rose. It was larger than the others, the flesh scarred from years of combat.

Once again, it was reunited with its worst enemy. Twice, they encountered each other in combat. The first occurred decades ago when both creatures were younger and smaller. Time did not obscure the memory. It remembered the taste of biting the flesh behind the dorsal fin, its hooks marking the upper edge of the fin while it held on. It remembered the pain of razor teeth severing one of its tentacles. It took two years for that arm to regenerate its full length.

These memories were front and center in their second, and most recent confrontation. The megalodon had increased significantly in size, but there was no doubt it was the same one. If the fish did not remember their feud cognitively, it did through instinct.

What would have been a fight to the death was cut short by a blow delivered from the heavens. A piece of rock, nearly hot as the sun, entered their world and drove them to the surface, ending their clash prematurely.

But life was full of opportunities, and today was a big one for the Kraken. It had killed the triplets. The human vessels were decimated. All that remained was the mature megalodon.

As soon as the Kraken entered the water, the dorsal fin turned. The fish had picked up its scent. It too, was seeking a fight.

The Kraken was happy to give it one.

CHAPTER 29

"Almost there. Let me guess, you guys expect me to fly you out too?" Renny said.

Nico prayed for the Excedrin to work fast. Renny's uncanny ability to be obnoxious even in the face of disaster was migraine inducing.

"Hey, if you'd rather stay here…"

"Yeeeah, no thanks. I think Kraken-zilla has sealed this island's fate. *Nobody* will ever wanna come back here."

The next turn brought them near the station. First they had to follow the road to the next intersection, passing the jail, then take another turn to the helipad.

Nico put his face to the window. The jail door was propped open. Something was sticking out through the opening.

A hand. Not something… some*one*.

"Pull over!"

The Jeep came to a screeching stop. Nico and Denise raced to the jail entrance. On the floor were two marines. They checked for a pulse. Both were alive.

One of them stirred.

"Relax, Marine," Nico said. "Take it slow. You've taken a pretty bad hit to the noggin."

Denise stepped further in. "Nico?"

He already knew what she was gonna point out. These were the two men who were escorting Heston. He gave the marine a moment to regain his senses. "Corporal, where's the Admiral?"

The Corporal looked around, then stared at the parking lot where their truck had been. "He escaped."

Constant transmissions were blasting through his radio. Nico grabbed it with the intent to alert White of the situation update. He didn't bother. It would have been a useless effort, for all military forces had bigger fish to fry. Literally.

"The big one's here. Two-hundred-fifty meters off shoreline."

"The octopus is going back in. I think it's going after it."

The next voice was White's. *"All units, be advised, Vice Admiral Jurgen is taking charge of this operation. He has dispatched a squadron of Seahawks from the carrier USS George H.W. Bush. They have been given instruction to shoot on sight any and all deep-sea biologics."*

Denise reached for the radio. Nico held it back. "There's nothing you can do, Denise."

"But the megs…"

"They're done taking chances," Nico said. "Blame Heston."

"The sharks haven't caused all of this destruction," Denise said. "They don't all need to be exterminated."

"Hey!" Renny shouted, waving from the Jeep. "Is there any chance we can continue this debate on the chopper?"

The obnoxious pilot had a valid point. Nico and Denise helped the marines to their feet. The second one was half-conscious, uncertain where he was or what was happening.

"I'll take care of him," the Corporal said. "You guys get out of here."

"We have another injured man with us," Denise said. "A sailor."

"Bring him to me. In a few minutes, this place will be teeming with medevacs. I'll send an alert."

The radio went off again. *"The Kraken's in the water! The shark's circling around. I think they're gonna fight!"*

****

Two titans, forced from decades of combat, stared each other in the eyes. Each recognized the threat the other posed. Both were experienced, had slain many members of the others' species, and knew that this current foe was among the highest of their ranks. Reaching such size and strength was not a common feat. Only the rarest specimens, gifted with superior genetics and a strong will to survive, did so.

The Kraken, though eager to engage, was extra careful this time. The two fights, especially the second, gave it vital knowledge of the shark's tactics and abilities. Patience and strategy were the key in this fight. The other megalodons were much smaller, thus easier to defeat by simply outmuscling them. This was not the case for the big one. O'Brien was not only bigger and stronger, but more experienced than the others. Holding him down and suffocating him would not be enough. He would shake loose. Worse, his bite applied pressure that could split rock. Those teeth would have to work to break through the mantle…but with enough pressure, they were more than capable.

Though experienced, the fish lacked one critical element. O'Brien was nowhere near as smart as the Kraken. His intelligence surpassed the smaller ones, allowing a wider range of comprehension, thus an ability to strategize. But it was nothing compared to the Kraken's intellect. He was an instinctual predator, first and foremost.

That instinct drove the megalodon to make the first move. Easily predictable.

Snapping jaws missed their target. Jet propelling, the Kraken darted to the left, then hooked around like an orbiting satellite. It tried to close in, but was forced to evade yet again. Size did not hinder O'Brien's speed, and like the Kraken, his eyesight was enhanced by the new environment. He watched the Kraken's trajectory, knew what it was attempting, and turned to intercept.

The fish pressed the attack. The Kraken continued evading. Each bite narrowly got closer. The Kraken needed to fill its mantle to jet propel, and at this rate, it could only draw in a small amount of water. There was no wearing down this shark.

Nor was it the plan.

They were now in deeper water. The Kraken's next evasion led it to breach. Again, it was a deliberate move. It searched the skies momentarily for more of the flying machines. It saw some in the distance, but they did not appear to be the warrior types.

O'Brien made his next move.

The Kraken, its mantle partially filled, jetted to the right. *Snap!* It gained seventy feet of distance, only to snap back like a rubber band. The fish had anticipated its move and acted accordingly.

Its jaws were clamped on one of its tentacles. Pain flowed through the cephalopod. Even after its considerations leading to the fight, it still underestimated its enemy's dexterity. The baiting tactic had run its course. It was time to fight.

The Kraken threw its other seven arms into action. They racked the megalodon's flesh, the hooks scraping its snout and gills. O'Brien's flesh was thicker than the others. Penetrating it required significant effort, especially when the shark was thrashing violently.

Each jerk of its head caused its teeth to saw at the tentacle. Every attempt to strangle the fish was futile. Being held by its mouth, the other tentacles were unable to reach the caudal fin.

The Kraken filled its mantle to the max, then expelled the water. It was successful in returning to the surface, but unsuccessful in freeing itself from those jaws. Dragging the megalodon resulted in greater pain and bloodshed.

O'Brien relished the taste of blood and flesh. His appetite went beyond sustenance. The Kraken's death meant supremacy of the seas. Eager to finish the job, the fish munched, shredding the limb, then yanked his head to the side.

The Kraken reeled backward, blood pumping from the stub where its arm had been. For the second time, it had lost a limb to the megalodon. The vengeful beast righted itself and lunged at the shark.

This time, it was O'Brien who evaded. The fish swiftly turned, bending its body to the max. The caudal fin smacked the cephalopod square in the face, knocking it backward a second time in a row. While the Kraken tumbled into the depths, the shark remained on the surface, dragging the severed tentacle.

Muscle tissue folded inward and was sealed by a natural paste secreted by the Kraken's tissue layers. Platelets hardened the stub, preventing further loss of blood.

Ready to retaliate, it ascended... only to be driven back down. O'Brien had ditched the tentacle in favor of finishing the job. Teeth pierced the Kraken's face just below the eyes. More pain followed when its mantle was driven into the bedrock. Sediment rose around the beasts, encasing them in a grey fog. Purple and red soon added to the mix.

Violent water currents twisted the clouds into strange shapes. Like spirits dancing to their gods, they twisted about.

Thrusts of O'Brien's caudal fin acted as a fan, blowing the Kraken's ink signature away. There would be no obscuring his vision. The shark had no intention of losing its foe.

Tentacles squirmed over the jaws. Two of them lassoed over the snout and pulled, while others tugged at the lower jaw. Hooks slowly sank into the flesh. Yet, the shark was unfazed. It sensed that these wounds were minor. No need to loosen its grip on measly pricks.

The Kraken's strength was matched by the shark's jaws. There was no prying them loose. Being held by its face, it could not angle its body to bite with its beak. Suffocating the fish would take too long at this rate. It was an identical scenario to their first encounter.

Memory went into use. The Kraken had freed itself, not through brute strength, but by finding the shark's weakness. The gills.

It thrust its clubs through the gill slits, baring its hooks to their full length. They plunged into the soft flesh inside, igniting sensitive nerves that sparked involuntary spasms.

O'Brien shook as though it had been zapped by an electric wire. His grip was lost, the Kraken free to go on the offensive.

It lunged, tackling the shark backward and driving it into the seabed. Feeling the slimy flesh pressing down on his underside, O'Brien swung his tail. The shark was swimming upside down, his back skidding against the sea floor, the Kraken riding his stomach.

The beak protruded, opened wide, and pressed into its flesh.

Feeling the tips about to cut into him, the shark corkscrewed. The winding motion slammed the Kraken onto its side. The shark continued racing along the bottom, dragging its opponent.

The Kraken held tight. A good bite with its beak would turn the tide of this fight. But O'Brien with his immense strength and stamina, was not making it easy. It took everything simply to hang on.

The mantle bumped against the uneven ground. Rocks and hills juddered its insides and scuffed its flesh. Still, it retained its grip. Its determination persevered, until the shark swam past an enormous rock.

All of a sudden, O'Brien was loose. When he turned around, he saw the cephalopod flailing on the seabed, having faceplanted violently on the side of the boulder. It was on its back, beak wide open, its senses frazzled. Ink spewed involuntarily, not enough to hide it from the meg.

Ironically enough, in spite of its heavy reliance on intelligence, it was the Kraken's primal instinct that protected it from the death blow. Sensing the vibrations of its attacker, it sucked in a thousand gallons of water and shot out of the way.

O'Brien smashed into the seabed, jogging his own senses momentarily. The shark leveled out and followed the scent of blood and vibrations of struggling motion. The Kraken was ascending. Retreating. Weakened.

The shark pursued.

His opponent had arrived at the water's surface, watching the world above. The tentacled fiend was more interested in everything above the ocean than the threat below. The shark felt no other vibrations nearby. There were no vessels on approach.

All it saw were three flying machines in the sky. The megalodon had seen these bizarre whirlybirds during its travels, but paid them no mind. They were always high above it, as indifferent as the fish in the sea.

He closed in on the Kraken.

Within fifty feet, the cephalopod turned, tentacles outstretched. The beast had exaggerated its injuries, tricking the fish into thinking its opponent was near death. Thirty seconds after its retreat, its senses had returned. Better yet, its plan was coming to fruition.

Its full mantle fired a stream of water with enough force to generate a current as narrow as a laser. It struck the shark right between the eyes, knocking his trajectory downward.

The Kraken threw itself onto the fish. Arms closed over the head and body, including the eyes.

O'Brien bit and slashed, neither of his weapons finding a target. He breached, the octopus clinging tight. Its mantle shifted, the beak unable to press onto the shark's back.

Numerous twists and turns followed, then a corkscrew maneuver. The tentacles pressed against the shark's flesh in its desperate attempt to cling tight. Next, O'Brien dove. Eight hundred feet of depth was crossed in a few short moments, ending with a collision into the sea floor. It was an impact that jarred both the shark and the octopus. Though briefly stunned, O'Brien had recovered the gift of sight. The hit had shifted the Kraken's tentacle which covered his right eye. Still, the beast clung to his body.

O'Brien put all of his energy into racing to the surface. The added weight required twice as much effort to ascend. O'Brien was relying on adrenaline at this point.

For the second time, they breached. The fish, determined to rid itself of the slimy fiend, tossed and turned.

Hooks sank into his flesh, flooding his nerves with pain signals. It was a prelude to the worst, which was now beginning. The Kraken pressed its mouth to the shark's back.

The pain tripled, reducing O'Brien's motions to a jumbled series of writhes and wiggles. In its hysteria, it failed to shake the creature loose. Only when it spotted an obstacle on the water's surface did it slow down. It was one of the metal beasts, operated by the humans.

The decision to slam into it was an impulsive one, but effective all the same. It dove under the vessel. In normal circumstances, it would have simply grazed the keel.

The Kraken, realizing it was on the verge of a headfirst, high velocity impact, let go and jetted backward. It had already suffered two major blows. A third could fracture the skull protecting its brain.

It looked to the sky. The flying things had arrived and were taking position. It then looked for the meg… a search which only lasted a split-second.

O'Brien charged its tentacled adversary, striking head-on. The Kraken raised its arms, then suffered the agony of teeth sinking deep into one of them. The shark pushed it backward, the water turning red with the blood of both titans.

The cephalopod monitored the flying machines. They were in position, those hot projectiles at the ready. Its plan was seconds away from backfiring.

****

"Affirmative. We've got both targets in sight. Missiles armed."
"Fire when ready."
The Hellhawk One pilot relayed the order to the other Seahawks in his squadron. He armed all four hellfire missiles, then put his finger to the trigger.
"Hellhawk Two, ready."
"Hellhawk Three, armed and ready."
"Fire."

****

The Kraken squirted ink, jetted streams of water, and clawed at the meg. Nothing worked. There was only one option left.

It pulled its injured arm with all of its might, suffering the torture of teeth slicing through the flesh. In that same moment, it inhaled the surrounding ocean. The tentacle severed, resulting in a cloud of blood.

The Kraken sped off.

O'Brien, more bloodthirsty than ever, sped after the retreating cephalopod. He dove down and turned west, putting all of his energy into his caudal fin. By the third stroke, he was stopped in his tracks.

All senses went haywire. The water turned scalding hot and violent. A shockwave, similar to the one which ravaged the depths, had hit him from above. The fish sank, his body pulsing with agony.

The Kraken had gained half a mile of distance in twenty-seconds. The blast of the explosion echoed through the ocean, followed by a tremendous but dwindling shockwave.

For a moment, it waited and searched for its enemy.

Nothing shared the ocean with it. The alpha megalodon was nowhere in sight.

Its plan was successful. The greatest obstacle to it becoming supreme ruler of the seas had been removed. Its campaign came at a cost. Two tentacles had been severed, and its body had taken several hits from the human weapons, including one which wounded its mantle. The beast would heal, but it needed to avoid the larger ships during that time.

That put the Kraken in a dilemma. Waiting would allow the humans to regroup. It needed to double down on its objective and strike fear into the heart of the species. By doing so, it would have to launch a preemptive strike at another of their habitats.

As it traveled west, it detected new vibrations. There was activity a few miles in this direction. The waters were gradually getting shallower, a sign that one of those above-water worlds was in this direction.

Driven by its strategy and an overwhelming impulse to kill, the Kraken progressed to its next target.

CHAPTER 30

It was not long after they arrived at the helipad when the air was filled with rescue choppers. The Coast Guard, Navy, Marine Corps, and Air Force had redirected much of their stateside resources to the situation.

"If I were to venture a guess, this is now all over the news," Renny said.

"You think?" Nico muttered. He looked around, cursing under his breath. "Damn, that admiral prick."

"You think he's close?" Denise asked.

"No. I think he's far. The guy's not dumb. The whole military is aware of his treachery now. He could be anywhere, especially in the midst of this chaos and confusion."

Several choppers were coming down to land. Most were headed to the airfields, while a couple Coast Guard vessels were descending to the police station. Medical vehicles sped into the lot area.

"Step back," Nico said. "They've got injured personnel on those choppers."

The trio stepped back and allowed the Navy and Coast Guard medical teams to do their work.

One of the choppers set down and immediately began unloading. Almost all of the passengers were Navy men, including one officer. Nico recognized the insignia on his shirt. That man was a captain. He waited for the officer to assist in unloading the injured personnel before approaching.

Nico raised a hand to get his attention. "Captain Bey, I presume?"

The captain, worn and despondent, looked at him. "Yes?"

"Any update on the situation? We heard missile strikes. Is the Kraken dead?"

"We don't know. Command Central reports that the big megalodon is still in the area, according to its tracker. Probably dead, because it hasn't moved anywhere."

"Where's Doctor Zenner?" Denise asked.

"Either under the destroyer wreckage, or inside the shark's gullet," Bey said. "Speaking of that jackass..." He turned to a couple of guardsmen who were removing the Porpoise from the chopper. "He made damn sure this dumb machine got saved."

Denise hurried to inspect it. "We can maybe put this to use."

"What for?" Bey said.

"To relocate the other megalodons. Get them far away from the coast."

"Not sure about that," Bey said. "The *Richard Denning* reported that the group broke up after a while, despite the fact that the signal was still going. I'm no marine biologist, but if I'm constantly being baited with the promise of a big steak, but no steak shows up, I eventually lose my patience. You can only promise a shark a whale for so long before it realizes it's being duped."

"Yeah, buddy?" Renny said. "Too bad you didn't consider that before you decided to use these sharks to start World War Three."

Bey raised his hands and stepped back. "World War Three? I don't know what you're—"

"Oh, shut up, Captain. We beat it out of the Admiral already," Renny said.

The captain seemed to shrink six inches. His natural defenses were up. He was caught and had no acquittal.

"I watched a docile shark goaded into a violent, rampaging machine, thanks to that asshat Dr. Zenner. I then watched a freaking octopus kill most of my crew, sink my ship, and take down several helicopters. These were men who trusted me to do right by them, and I failed. All I can do now is testify and set the record straight."

It was a response the trio wasn't expecting. It didn't let Bey off the hook for his involvement, but at least it was some semblance of decent character.

"Listen, if you can use your device to lure the sharks away, go ahead," Bey continued. "Just keep it safe, because we'll need it in the months of testimonies that are sure to come."

"No argument there," Nico said.

"I need to get a monitor to track the sharks," Denise said.

"I have Dr. Zenner's tablet," Bey said. He removed it from the chopper and passed it to her.

The device was still on, thankfully. The other sharks were heading east, away from the area of conflict. O'Brien was north of the island near the *Richard Denning's* location.

"I've got O'Brien's vitals. He's alive, but his heart rate's down. White blood count is up. Blood pressure spike. I think he's been jostled by the blast."

"Good. Maybe he'll drown," Nico said.

"Hey guys," Renny said, standing by the department helicopter. "I'd like to get out of here now. And Denise, I'm holding you to that seafood dinner."

Denise looked at the tablet, then at Nico.

He shook his head. "Let it die. There's nothing else we can do here. Let White take care of Heston. Renny, start refueling that thing, will ya?"

"You got it, boss. And hey, Doc. Don't be so sad. You realize what we just did? We freaking stopped a conflict that could've led to World War

Three. Feel good about yourself." He stepped over to the fuel station to bring a hose to the chopper. "At least the worst is over. It's gotta be."

CHAPTER 31

USCGC Cape Basin, one-half mile east of Islamorada.

"Sir, we've got something on sonar closing in rapidly from the east."

Lieutenant Commander Edward Mackey approached the radar tech. So much for the simple assignment. When his ship was assigned to guard the Keys, it seemed unlikely that any of the biologics would advance west due to the shallow waters.

"Get Headquarters on the line," he said.

"Key West Station, this is the *Cape Basin*. Come in."

"Go ahead."

Mackey took the radio. "Mackey speaking. We've got an unidentified bogey approaching from the east. Do we have any readings on the megalodons? My understanding is that they broke away from Cielo Nublado."

"White's last report indicated they were moving east and north."

"What about the Kraken?"

"Kraken's believed to be dead."

Mackey watched the thing on the radar screen. The thing was on the surface and coming right at them.

He stepped outside and raised a pair of binoculars. On the other side of the lenses were two black eyes gazing right back at him.

"Red alert. Notify all emergency services in the Keys. They need to start evac—"

The Kraken rammed the side of the boat, tilting it to the side. The beast had mastered the layout of the ships by now. Its injuries had heightened its resolve. It needed to eliminate this enemy fast and efficiently.

Tentacles plunged into the bridge, seizing Mackey and his crew. All arms found something to latch on to, then all at once, they pulled.

The *Cape Basin* tilted to starboard, its crew desperately trying to climb over the portside to stay above water. The capsizing of the vessel rendered their attempts useless.

It had no interest in eating this bunch. Satisfaction came from battering the sea, mashing their bodies until they were a string of body parts clouding the water.

The Kraken wrestled the cutter even after it had sunk. The bridge was completely torn away, the cavities now filling with water. The thumping of its engine came to a halt.

Once again, the Kraken was victorious.

Now at surface level, it continued east. By now, it was practically standing on its tentacles. The water was forty feet at most, less than half the lengths of its arms.

Up ahead was land. A few smaller boats were taking to the water. A blockade, which would suffer the same fate as their largest member.

The Kraken moved in for the attack.

****

Islamorada General Hospital

Carley Amburn felt as though she was watching a movie. Even considering her encounters with an eighty-foot killer shark, the sight of a monster octopus crawling onto the shore felt impossible. Yet, there it was on the screen, the very Kraken whose presence sparked the evacuation of her island. News footage played on Val's hospital television, intercut with the opinions of news anchors.

They watched as it crawled inland, battered buildings, and engaged with military forces before returning to the water. Next, the creature engaged in combat with a megalodon which dwarfed the one she encountered. The battle came to an explosive conclusion when Navy helicopters fired several missiles into the fray.

"My Lord," Valerie said. "And I thought I'd seen it all in my time."

Carley felt nauseous. She felt the world had flipped upside down. Too many major events were happening at once.

The news cut back to the anchors.

"We now have a new development regarding the confrontation with China. Both China and the U.S. have agreed to talks. This information is coinciding with reports that Admiral Vince Heston has been removed from his command, and that Vice Admiral Paul Jurgen is taking charge."

"I guess there's some good news for once," Val said. "The big monsters are dead. There's a chance we can actually *avoid* this bullshit in Asia. Good, because I didn't want to go out by nuclear fallout or by getting eaten."

"This just in. We have breaking news coverage. The Kraken has been spotted near the Keys. It has overturned the USCGC Cape Basin and is now moving in on Islamorada."

Valerie's fragile heart started racing. "Is this for real?"

Carley pulled on her shoes and raced for the doorway. Nurses were moving about in a panic. Family members were hounding them, shouting questions about transporting the patients.

"I need a stretcher! I can move my dad myself!"

"Are ambulances coming?"

"Will someone help me? I think my husband needs help. His heart monitor's going crazy."

The charge nurse raised her hands. "We have to prioritize those in the ER and in Critical Care."

The crowd erupted.

"The hell with this!" an angry husband shouted. "I'll get my wife out of here myself."

"Me too," someone else said.

The hallway descended into chaos. Carley retreated back into the room and turned to the television. News cameras were still in the air recording the Kraken's advance. Smaller Coast Guard response boats and two county sheriff patrol boats were intercepting the creature.

****

There were two different kinds of vessels, both smaller than the massive steel ones. Two red ones advanced from the left, both larger than the three green-and-white ones that joined the fray. The red vessels contained weaponry that was now very familiar to the Kraken. The green-and-white ones only contained handheld weapons.

Tiny pellets, whose impact were simultaneous to the cracking sounds of their launching, bombarded its flesh.

A slash of its tentacles capsized the nearest red boat. Even after it was overturned, the Kraken continued hammering, reducing it to a crumbled piece of metal.

The Kraken turned to the right. Two of the green-and-white ones were trying to flank it. Automatic weapons stung its mantle, inflicting minimal damage, but irritating the beast nonetheless.

Two tentacles wrapped around one of the vessels and squeezed, crushing it and the squealing men aboard. After tossing the crinkled pile of metal aside, it attacked the next one.

A swipe of one of its arms smacked the gunner right off the deck. The terrified helmsman looked behind him, saw that his partner was no longer on deck, then screamed when he saw the tentacles springing toward him. They struck with explosive impact, punching through the cockpit, down through the hull. They raised the skewered boat out of the water and displayed it to the two remaining enemies before smashing it into scrap.

The red boat continued the assault, its gun aiming for the eyes. Stinging pain caused the creature to lurch backward and raise its arms to shield its face. The damage was minimal, but it spurred the Kraken into swift response. It fell forward, angled its mantle at the opponent, then propelled itself like a torpedo. Its body rammed the red boat, bursting it into a hundred tiny fragments.

Repositioning itself back on its arms, the Kraken turned to the remaining boat. It had turned around to retreat, its gunner standing ready. The Kraken stood in place, letting the cowards make some distance. A retreating enemy was likely not a threat.

A *dead* enemy was guaranteed not to be a threat.

The beast assailed, snatching the boat out of the water, then allowed its beak to do the rest of the work. The front of the boat was no match for the bite power of its jaws. It spat the inedible fragments out.

With the sea defenses out of the way, the creature advanced onto the sandbar. Multiple humans were on the beach, watching in awe, then retreated in terror.

Tentacles attacked everything around them. The dock was ripped from its roots and broken into bits. Fleeing civilians were snatched and gifted to the beak. Even the vegetation wasn't spared.

As far as the Kraken was concerned, everything on this landmass belonged to the humans, and would be destroyed.

It pursued the crowd to a gathering of small structures, similar to the habitats it ravaged on the other island. Each building imploded under a single blow, the scraps brushed out of the way.

Up ahead were a few larger structures, densely populated with humans. Like a raging storm, the Kraken tore the buildings from the ground, revealing numerous humans hiding inside.

****

"Oh my God! Now it's attacking the Caribbean Resort! For everyone watching, this is not a hoax. This is live footage of the Kraken attacking Islamorada... Oh dear, it's now going after the Cheeca Lodge."

Carley had seen enough. It was obvious now that this beast would rampage through Islamorada just as it had done in Cielo Nublado. Emergency services were already strung out. It was everyone for their themselves at this point.

"Come on, Mom. We've gotta go."

"Hang on..."

"No, Mom. We *can't* hang on. We have to leave before that thing gets here."

"Carley..."

It was then when Carley realized her mother was not simply anxious. She was clutching her chest and breathing heavily. The monitors were reading irregular heartbeats and increased blood pressure.

"Oh God..." She took her mother's hand. "Mom, you'll be okay, I promise. Just hang on." She ran into the hall and yelled over the stampede of panicking people. "Nurse!"

Her voice was lost in the chaos. Shoving her way through the crowd, she reached the desk. The nurses were flabbergasted, some on the phone, others trying to assist with more critical patients. To their credit, it seemed everyone remained at their post.

"Nurse! Help. I think my mother's having a heart attack."

The nurse with the phone looked up at her in dismay. She waited for the person on the other line to finish his sentence then finally said, "Hey, I gotta go. We have a patient who might have to go into emergency surgery."

Carley could hear the voice shouting through the receiver. *"Are you kidding me? You realize what's happening right now? We have to clear the building."*

"I'm looking at her vitals right now on my screen. She's not going to make the trip."

"We've got maybe ten minutes before this hospital gets torn apart, either by the monster, or by the Air Force should they fire rockets at the damn thing. Your priority is to evacuate as many people as possible."

The nurse slammed the phone down. "Damn it."

"Heavenly Father, this can't be happening," Carley said, burying her face into her hands. "There's nothing we can do?"

"The OR and ER teams have been ordered to evacuate once they get their patients out," the nurse said. "Unless that thing is driven away, this hospital is going to be evacuated. If we can keep her stabilized, we can transfer her to the hospital in Key Largo, but all our flights are busy."

Carley pulled out her cell phone. "Hang on to that thought." She turned away, scrolled through her contacts, then tapped on *Renny*.

****

The police helicopter was fueled and ready, something Renny Jackman repeatedly reminded Nico and Denise of while they stood by, listening in on the Coast Guard radio reports.

"It's moving further inland. There're people all over the place. There's no way to shoot incendiaries without putting friendlies in danger."

"Copy that. We are redirecting the Sea Rock. Choppers are in the air."

"Guys," Renny said. Finally, Nico looked over at him. "It's not our problem anymore. You asked me to fuel up. Now…" He gestured at the helicopter. "May we go?"

To his relief, Nico and Denise made their way to the chopper. He smiled while standing at the door like a valet. "About damn time." His phone started buzzing. The name on the screen was Carley. He answered the call and put the phone on speaker.

"Renny? You there?"

"Yeah, Carley. I'm here. You and your mom out of dodge?"

"No, we're trapped in the hospital. That thing's making its way over to us, and my mom's heart is failing. The hospital staff is overwhelmed. We can get her to Key Largo, but there's no choppers available."

"Hang on. Take a deep breath," Renny said. He turned away, taking a deep breath of his own. *So much for that thing being dead.* He returned to the phone. "Hang on, Carley. We're back in Cielo Nublado… don't ask why. But don't worry, I'll come get you."

"Please hurry."

"Already double-timing it." Renny looked at his passengers. "Sorry guys, we're taking a detour. You're more than free to stay here, but I have to put on my cape and fly to the rescue."

"Knock it off, Renny. You know we're coming along."

"How will we get her though?" Denise asked. "That thing's ashore, and it hates helicopters. If we go anywhere near it, it'll come at us like a hound after a rabbit."

"Unless you have some special plan, we're just gonna have to fly over there and judge by eye," Renny said.

"Hang on a sec," Denise said. "There's one shot we have of drawing it away *and* killing it."

Nico and Renny stared, dreading her answer. Denise put her hand on the Porpoise.

"You want to lure the megalodons over to it?" Nico said.

"O'Brien, specifically."

Nico stepped out of the chopper and paced in a circle. "I knew it!" After a few laps, he turned to face her, arms thrown to the side. "Why?! Instead of one leviathan on the loose, you'd rather have two."

"It's not as complicated as that," Denise said. "There's no chance of the shark coming on land. But its presence can entice the Kraken back into the water."

"Isn't the thing dead already?" Renny asked.

"No. I still have a reading on his vitals," Denise said. "His heart rate is low. Probably got jarred during the missile strike."

"That's putting it mildly," Nico said.

"His tag does not indicate severe blood loss," Denise continued. "If we can get a boost to his heart, he might pull through."

"And you think he'll immediately follow whale calls to the Keys?" Renny said.

"He will if I adjust the acoustics," Denise said.

"Beg your pardon?"

"I can adjust the soundwaves to draw the shark to Islamorada. The Kraken itself is a silent beast, incapable of making sounds. BUT its actions make distinct soundwaves. Notably its jet propulsion. I can make adjustments to the device, apply it to the speakerphone we found on the drone, which we'll lower from the chopper as we lead the fish to the Keys."

Nico looked down and shut his eyes. The next few seconds were spent letting his desired outburst play out in his imagination.

"This is insane. How the hell do you plan to boost his heart?"

"I have my marine veterinary kit in the chopper," Denise said. "I can inject him with adrenaline."

"And where are we gonna get that? Happen to have some in your case?"

"No, but you said a bunch of people have left you keys to their shops. Does that include the hospital in case emergency medical supplies were required?"

Nico groaned. "Who'd ever guess that cooking you a pizza would lead you to insane ideas."

"That's a yes. We can use one of the Navy's underwater surveillance drones to apply the dosage." With Nico on the fence, Denise tried appealing to Renny. "It's the only way we can save Carley."

"Denise, this is NUTS!" Nico interjected. "Did you forget what you saw on the screen in Command Central? That shark is a killer. We watched it kill at least six sailors today alone. They're *all* killers, and should be destroyed. We revive that meg, it lives to kill someone else. None of them can be trusted, Denise. You saw what Albert did. You saw how violent he got."

"If I may…"

All three turned their attention to Captain Bey. He stepped into their circle, hands clasped over his midsection.

"Sorry, but I couldn't help overhearing. Albert indeed got aggressive, but not randomly. The meg was attacked by underwater drones which fired electrified darts. It took repeated attacks before the fish resorted to violence." He looked at Denise. "Fact is, it was *us* who turned it into a monster. Same with O'Brien. Yes, he has taken human life. But each occasion was due to Dr. Zenner's meddling. To my knowledge, the fish has never gone out of its way to attack anyone."

Silence overtook the group. Nico stared into the distance as he took this new information into consideration. It brought to mind how Denise was seemingly proven wrong about the triplets being nonviolent after the attack on the *Red Nova*. In fact, they were tame until spurred into attacking due to underwater soundwaves.

Renny bumped his fist against the chopper. "Hey, guys? I hate to interrupt this debate, but in case you forgot, Carley is in trouble and needs help *now*. Make a damn decision now, or I'll take off myself and leave your sorry asses here. You've got five seconds…"

Denise and Nico nearly wasted the countdown in awe of the demeanor they'd never before experienced from the pilot.

Reluctantly, Nico nodded at his ex-wife. "Don't make me regret this."

Denise turned to Bey. "You have access to any underwater drones?"

"There's a warehouse in town we've rented out," he said. "I'll take you there."

"Thanks. First, we need to make a quick stop at the hospital." She tapped her ex-husband on the face. "After this is over, I'll devote my time to something more important."

"Yeah? Like what? Giant prehistoric crabs?"

She smiled. "Us."

CHAPTER 32

Islamorada

Red as hell fire, the Kraken laid waste to the community, functioning as though it answered to nobody but the devil himself. Aircraft circled from above, attempting to line up a shot on the beast. Artillery was a no-go. As the creature had learned in its previous attacks, the humans would not risk firing on their own. With that in mind, it threw itself into large crowds.

One chopper peppered its mantle with three-round bursts from its M60. The beast reared on its hind tentacles, then pushed itself off the ground, tripling its height. In that moment, it lashed with its front tentacles.

The chopper was flipped upside down in midair. After a brief spiral, its fate was sealed with an explosive impact.

Lowering back to the ground, the Kraken continued on its rampage. It moved into the concrete lane in the center of the landmass. From here, countless vehicles were speeding onto a conduit which provided access off of the island over the water.

It followed a few of these vehicles, then stopped after arriving at a larger structure. People were fleeing the entrance onto the concrete lot in front of it. Many retreated right back inside after seeing the creature advance.

A few humans were in front, firing small handheld weapons in its direction. Unknowingly, they guaranteed the building's fate by further provoking its wrath.

****

Carley watched the cephalopod through Val's window. In the lot in front of it, hospital security and sheriff deputies were shooting at the creature.

"No, no, no. RUN!"

The defense line was wiped out in a single swipe from the Kraken's tentacle. It crossed through the lot, leaving a trail of death and rubble in its wake.

Hiding in this hospital was not an option. The building would be torn apart in minutes.

More gunshots echoed through the sky. Another helicopter lined up with the beast. The Kraken responded to the hits by facing the new threat.

Carley watched the chopper's positioning. Its gatling guns had ceased fire.

"What's happening?" the nurse said, unhooking Valerie from the machines.

"I think they're attempting a limited missile strike on the thing." Carley ran to the back of the room, grabbing her mother and the nurse. "Get down!"

A *boom* rocked the hospital.

Carley turned her eyes back to the window. She saw a wall of fire in the background, consuming the highway and the buildings on the other side. Gas tanks exploded in the blast zone, sending smaller *cracks* rocking the key.

In front of that wall of fire was the Kraken. A spurt of water was spilling from its siphon, winding down after a large spurt had been unleashed on the chopper.

Air support was dead. Ground units did not stand a chance.

On top of the fear was a sense of guilt. How could she have called Renny to this place? There was no way he would be able to get his chopper near the hospital without being battered out of the sky. She grabbed her phone, intent on updating him.

Two words at the top of the screen were the icing on the top of this horrible day. *No service.*

"Damn it." She sighed, and hugged her mother.

"It's gonna be fine," Valerie said.

"No, it won't, Mom."

Valerie smacked her on the jaw, catching her off guard. "Keep your chin up." She paused to cough, one hand on her chest. "You're my kid and I love you very much. Let's not spend these last few minutes panicking."

Welling up, Carley hugged her. Valerie wrapped an arm around her daughter's shoulders and squeezed.

"Also, that boyfriend of yours is probably working on some miracle."

Somehow, Carley mustered a smile. "Mom... you're absolutely insane. But I love you."

****

Cielo Nublado.

In front of Denise was the Navy's advanced surveillance drone, a large syringe used for injecting whales, and a role of duct tape. Fifty years of technological advancement and research, brought together by the simplest of tools ever invented.

She weaved the tape over the front of the device, securing the syringe to the front. By the time it was done, the thing had the appearance of a giant mosquito and a giant proboscis. In that syringe was enough adrenaline to put four rhinos into a frenzy.

"We're all set," she said.

On the beach was the police helicopter, positioned there by none other than Renny Jackman, who now waited for the biologist to bring her setup aboard.

Rear Admiral White stood in front of the remains of Command Central. In the past two minutes, he had been given a quick rundown of their plan.

"You guys absolutely sure this is the best course of action?"

"We need to get that damn octopus back in the water," Nico said.

"Assuming you can even lure the shark…"

"We will," Denise said. "I've adjusted the soundwaves on the Porpoise. We'll lower the speaker from the chopper and take O'Brien where we want him."

"Fine, but are you sure you'll get there in time?"

"We've already observed that this fish can go sixty miles an hour at attack speed," Denise said. "When you put together the adrenaline he's about to get and his hatred for the Kraken…"

"Okay, I get your point," White said. "Good luck."

"Thank you, sir." Denise brought the device into the chopper. Nico stepped in behind her, took a seat, and pulled the door shut.

"Chief?" White put his hand in the way, blocking the door momentarily.

"Yes?"

"Just wanted to say, I'm glad they let a local police chief in on this military operation."

Nico recalled their not-so-friendly encounter at the meeting in his briefing room two days prior. He nodded appreciatively, shook the Rear Admiral's hand, then shut the door.

Renny lifted the chopper and took them over the water.

"Radio's going nuts. Two more Navy choppers are down. There're rumblings about them launching cruise missiles at the bastard before it moves down along the Keys. We need to haul ass."

"O'Brien's eight-hundred feet down," Denise said. "Trust me, once he's awake, we'll be hauling ass alright."

"I don't get it," Nico said. "Sharks need to swim to get water over their gills. Why hasn't he drowned?"

"My readings show his blood-oxygen levels are low, but not depleted," Denise said. "He's clearly a more advanced—maybe more *evolved* member of the species. Maybe he's developed a way of pumping water through his mouth while immobile. Some modern day species are capable of that. Nurse sharks, tiger sharks, and reef sharks can switch between ram breathing and buccal breathing."

"What and what?" Renny asked.

"Moving forward and pumping," Nico said.

"Oh, cute. You remember all the science stuff your lady has taught you," Renny said. "How 'bout you be a good assistant and help lower the drone. Afterwards, you'll be in charge of handling the mic."

Nico lifted the loop of cable which held the mic and the fishing weight for keeping it submerged. "You know, you're awfully bossy when I'm not your chief."

"I guess I am," Renny said. He smiled. "It feels kinda… good!"

He brought the chopper over deeper waters, following Denise's navigation.

"Here!" she said. Renny stopped the chopper and lowered it to the surface. Nico slipped the drone into the water and watched it sink. Denise lifted the portable control module and steered the vehicle back and forth. Its camera transmitted to her screen, bringing to view a deceptively peaceful ocean, sparkly white from the sun's rays.

Those divine visuals gradually disappeared during the drone's descent into darkness. Its underbelly light came on, bringing the sea floor into view.

She drove it over a valley of rocks, debris, and death. To the west, she saw one of the triplets lying on its side. Its head was mangled, the body decorated by penetrating wounds. A shark that had the opportunity to kill Denise, yet it and its brothers passed her by. Only the influences of man and his technology brought out the worst in the world around him.

Veering left a few degrees, she found another body lying on its side. This one was double the size of the triplet. This one was fairly intact. Moving even. Its head, while mostly stiff, pumped its jaws every few seconds.

"Found him."

Nico clipped his harness on. Seeing the shark on that monitor unfolded the reality of what was ahead. They would be racing west at full speed, door open, and at low altitude.

"How's his heart rate?" Renny asked.

"Slowing down," Denise said.

"Then you better speed it up," he said.

The seriousness in his voice drove his point home. Denise guided the drone to the shark's mouth. It was open, gulping several hundred gallons of water to flow through its gills.

The suction nearly drew the drone right into its mouth. The jaws clamped shut.

"Whoa!" Denise veered the device away from it, skidding over the snout.

"Isn't that where you wanted to go?" Nico said.

"Not like that," Denise said. "If this drone got crushed, we're back to square one." She swung the drone back around. The jaws opened again. "Come on, big fella. Just lie still. You won't even feel this."

The drone neared the shark, whose snout quickly took up the entire screen. The eye moved, the tail fluttered, jaws parting.

"Holy!" She swerved again. The drone bumped off the meg's snout for the second time.

"Fantastic," Nico said. "It's near death, and it's still trying to eat the drone."

"It's been injured. Its senses are on heightened alert. It perceives everything as a threat."

They watched O'Brien flail against the ocean floor. His whipping tail pushed him several dozen yards up, only to quit. His energy fizzled out, his heart rate unable to get that much needed spark of life.

Nico watched the heart monitor on the tablet. *Bleep... Bleep... ... Bleep... Bleep... ... ...*

"Denise…"

She glanced at the straight line. "Oh, no."

It was do or die. For Carley, for *everyone* on Islamorada. She sped at the fish.

It lay on its back, jaws and eyelids shut. She cursed. *You stupid shark. The one time you need those nictitating membranes open, you had to roll against the rocks!*

"Can you get the needle through its skin?" Nico asked.

"Too thick," she said. She moved the drone down the length of O'Brien's neck. "The gills. I'll have to do it here."

"What's so bad about that?" Renny asked.

"Even a comparatively small needle like this will hurt like a son of a bitch." There was no choice. Or time.

She drove the drone through the gill slits, found a layer of soft, red flesh, then jammed the spear in.

… … … Bleep! Bleep! Bleep-Bleep-Bleep-Bleep-Bleep!

The screen went to black. The ocean below them began to swirl.

Anxiety got the better of Renny. He banked to starboard, an action which proved to be a wise one.

Two seconds after he moved, the shark breached.

O'Brien slammed itself against the water, pitching mountainous laps in all directions. His heart was racing and his neck stung as if bitten by one of the parasites from its home world. A combatant with no opponent, a predator without prey, but in serious need for both, he snapped his jaws and slashed his tail.

A wide-eyed Renny watched the fish, then glanced at Denise. "Well, Doc? You think he's revived?"

She harnessed herself into her seat. "Get ready. The real fun part's about to begin."

Nico held the weighted speaker. "How much distance should we put between him before I drop this?"

"At least a mile," Denise said.

Renny sped the chopper west at top speed, clearing the desired distance in less than thirty seconds.

Nico dropped the mic. Denise activated the Porpoise, sending signals of underwater suction and currents through the Atlantic.

She adjusted the tablet screen to show O'Brien's location. His blip was rapidly closing in on their location.

"Whoa!"

"What's 'whoa'?" Renny said. "Good 'whoa'? Bad 'whoa'?"

"Depends on whether we stay here," Nico said. "Double time it, Jackman! Go! Go! Go!"

Renny turned the chopper west and sped for Islamorada, dragging the speaker through the water.

CHAPTER 33

Carley repeated her prayers, offering her love and praise to the Lord, in preparation for the end. No longer did she seek a way out. She had accepted her fate, asking only for it to be quick and painless.

Like the devil it was, the Kraken made her misery as prolonged as possible by attacking the south end of the hospital first. Doing so did not provide any chance of escape, proven by the screams of those who raced out the doors. The tentacles were there, snatching anyone who attempted to make a break for it. The other arms went to work peeling apart the roof and walls.

Fear turned to anger.

Is it not enough, God, that I've accepted my circumstance? Does it really have to be drawn out? How much longer must my mother and I have to endure this terror?

Tremors shook the room. The windows cracked, then shattered completely. She could feel the floor levels beneath her beginning to crumble. Next, a section of the roof was torn free. The tentacle squiggled between them and the sky, its suckers baring their hooks like fangs.

If the visual and audible details were not enough misery for them to endure, there was the horrible smell. It invaded the building, teasing them of their killer's presence.

The tremors worsened as the beast shifted its weight. More of the building came apart on the south end, burying the poor souls on that side. The tentacle retracted, making way for the eye of the beast.

A big, bulging black eye with no hint of color peered into the hospital, searching for any human it could easily snatch.

Despite the temptation to shut her eyes and look away, Carley looked up at the thing. For the next few seconds, the Kraken seemed to watch them with a demented fascination. Perhaps it was the first time it witnessed humans huddling together. Maybe it was surprised that they weren't attempting to flee, as many of its victims had.

Its brief study of them ended. The tentacle tore another piece of the roof off, completely exposing Carley, Val, and the nurse.

Finally, Carley stood up. "Alright, whatcha waiting for?" She reached under her shirt, drew her department-issued Glock, and fired several rounds into those eyes.

The Kraken reeled backwards, its tentacles rolling backwards until they were pressed against its face. Like a child nursing a bruise, it kept its arms pressed there for several seconds before testing its vision.

Its sight was intact, the eyes only mildly injured. The wounds were microscopic in comparison to the creature's size. They would heal before the day was over. That sting, however, proved to be a great irritation. Just as the shooters on the boats had suffered for it, so would this latest offender.

The pistol quivered in Carley's grip. The thing was pissed off now. She questioned if it was a mistake to shoot it. Did she just guarantee herself an agonizing and frightening death?

She turned to face her mother. Val was wincing in pain, her color flushed, energy fading.

And somehow, the crazy woman managed to hang on.

"Kid, if you're wondering if you should put me out of my misery, you might wanna look over there first." She pointed past Carley to the east.

Carley looked. A single helicopter was quickly advancing at low altitude, heading right for the creature.

****

"Drop the speaker here," Denise said. "I'll keep the signal going, which'll keep O'Brien in the area long enough for us to lure the Kraken back to him."

Nico pulled the chopper's Carbine from its storage compartment and loaded a fresh magazine. "Something tells me that won't be hard." He tilted the muzzle at the burning helicopter wreckage spread across the key. The smell of charred metal and death entered the chopper.

Vehicles were racing north through the highway, oncoming traffic having come to an abrupt halt. The lanes were packed, the vehicles unable to turn around. Easy pickings for the Kraken should it choose to venture in that direction.

That was not as alarming as the situation at the hospital. The three-story building was in ruins. The Kraken had backed away mysteriously, its tentacles brushing over its face.

Its arms uncoiled and pulled back to the hospital. The arms reached for the mostly-intact north side of the building, specifically a section where the roof was completely torn free.

Renny lowered the altitude to a hundred feet and closed in to thirty-yards of the creature. Nico, secured with a harness, fired his rifle at the creature.

Every shot struck the mantle. In ten seconds, the entire mag was spent. Nico loaded a fresh one and resumed firing.

The bullets failed to inflict any major damage. Nico didn't intend them to. He just needed to get the damn thing's attention.

But the bastard was fixated on the hospital.

He looked at the thin streak of red on the top of its body. The creature's flesh had been punctured, either during the fight with the megs or with the *Richard Denning*. He concentrated his fire on the wound.

"Look over here, you big, ugly, sack of…"

The creature listed backward. It turned around speedily as though on a swivel.

Renny banked to starboard, then reversed the chopper to the beach area. "That's right, come this way."

The creature followed at frightening speed, toppling shops and trees in its violent pursuit.

Tentacles reached for the chopper, falling short by a few frustrating meters. It propped itself on its rear tentacles and lifted its mass, throwing its front arms out again for added length.

Renny ascended, wincing hard. The chopper jerked with the sound of impact on its underside. All three of its crew closed their eyes and awaited the fall. It never came.

Renny Jackman, the expert pilot with good instincts, had climbed just in time. The chopper had been hit from one of the clubs, but was still airborne, its engines still functional.

Finally, they were over open water.

****

The Kraken had fallen forward, still eager to take down the annoying mechanical pest. It crashed through an empty restaurant, wreckage flying hundreds of feet in all directions. The creature didn't bother inspecting the structure for any humans. It had its new target and was keen on bringing it down. Once in the water, it could refill its mantle and utilize its newly discovered means of blasting water through the air.

It stopped at the water's edge. In the span of a heartbeat, its interest in the chopper had disappeared. Now, its eyes were set on the huge dorsal fin moving several hundred feet out.

There was no mistaking its adversary. Somehow, the cursed megalodon had survived the human weapons and had followed it here to the landmass. There was only one logical reason for its arrival. The meg wanted to conclude their war, and the Kraken was more than happy to oblige.

It entered the water, crossed the sandbar, and progressed for the next battle—and it would ensure that this was the last bout between it and the meg.

O'Brien's belly was scraping the water. That did not hinder his efforts. This area was full of ammonia. The Kraken was here recently, meaning it was close.

His task concluded with new signals of water distortion and ammonia smells. The fish lifted his snout above the water. Pale eyes gazed at the oncoming cephalopod. It had spotted him, its motions those of an aggressive animal intent on combat.

O'Brien swam into deeper waters, impelling faster pursuit from the enemy. The Kraken was several body lengths behind him, using its ability to spit water to keep up.

Nearing waters with a depth of fifty feet, O'Brien turned around. His heart was racing, his gills throbbing, his temper red hot. He was not hungry. Food was the last thing on his mind. He wanted dominance. In his world, dominance could only be obtained through bloodshed.

Sensing its rival on the attack, the Kraken raised its remaining front tentacles.

O'Brien rushed the Kraken, crashing through the wall of defense. His snout smashed against its face with enough force to toss the cephalopod backward. On its back, the astounded Kraken flailed its arms over the water. The shark submerged, opened wide, and bit the rear of its mantle.

Those whirling arms increased in intensity when the shark thrashed the cephalopod left and right. Teeth sank into the hardened mantle, their notched edges threatening to saw at the flesh with each movement.

Left, right, up, down, the shark shook its enemy.

Tentacles tried clawing at the surrounding seabed in hopes of pulling the mass away from the jaws. The effort only resulted in both creatures being tugged. The Kraken shifted its appendages at the attacker. They lassoed, clawed, and lashed the fish. The attacks only strengthened his willingness to tear the mantle wide open.

O'Brien, still clenching tight, twisted to the right. Round and around, he whirled into a complete spin, the Kraken twirling with him. From high above, he resembled a gigantic drill bit boring into a brick.

The Kraken's world was becoming a blur. Its mind was frazzled, its arms separating from their target, its aggression now dissolving into panic. For the first time in decades, the Kraken feared for its life. In those years, it had suffered injuries, exercised caution over direct action, and assessed its threats before engaging. None of this was fear. It was part of the experience of being the dominant species in the ocean. It *always* knew it would emerge as the victor of each confrontation.

Until now.

Its mantle was on the verge of tearing. Once those teeth sunk deep enough, they would rip its body like tissue paper.

Unable to move away from the jaws, it attempted the reverse. Shooting water through its siphon, it drove itself into the meg, subsequently driving it backwards. They crossed the short depth at a forty-five degree angle. The shark slammed against the bottom, ejecting sand all around them. The tremor caused a parting in his jaws, freeing the cephalopod.

The Kraken righted itself and pushed up to the surface. It turned around, arms poised to attack.

Once again, the shark beat it to the punch. It crashed through its defenses, this time with open jaws. Rows of teeth came over its face. Eleven-inch teeth popped its left eye like a black cherry.

All six limbs grabbed the shark and pushed. Inch by inch, the teeth were removed from their penetrations, leaving rows of foot-long gashes, and a deflated bag of flesh that had been the Kraken's eye.

The beast parted its beak and tried to pull itself in for a bite of its own. Its effort was futile. The shark turned to the left, the caudal fin swinging wide. Had the Kraken not been blind on that side, it would have seen the tail coming at its face.

SMACK!

The Kraken spun to its right, crashing through several yards of ocean. Before it could right itself, the shark closed in again. Next was the pain of teeth intertwining over one of its tentacles.

****

They watched from high above, ensuring for their own peace of mind that the Kraken would not return to the shores. Huge waves rolled away from the fracas, each newer one a darker shade of red.

"O'Brien's got this under control," Nico said. He shared a quick gaze at Denise.

"I believe so too."

Nico attached his harness to the chopper's fast rope. "Get us to the hospital." He was halfway through the sentence when Renny sped the chopper inland. They crossed over a stretch of land decimated by the Kraken's wrath. Wreckage and bodies lay everywhere, survivors panicking in their attempts to reconcile with what just happened.

They flew to the breach of the hospital.

"There!" Renny said. "Someone's waving at us." After bringing the chopper closer, he recognized the woman waving a white bedsheet at them. "Thank God. She's alive."

He steadied the chopper where the roof had been. Nico tossed down the stepladder, then descended to the room.

"'Bout time you showed up," she said.

"Hey Carley. Glad I talked you into leaving Cielo Nublado?"

"Oh, don't get me started!" she said. "Renny said something about you guys getting a year's pay? Just for staying an extra day?!"

He grinned nervously. "To be fair, I didn't know they would do that." They turned to face her mother. Valerie was leaning up out of bed, helped by the nurse.

"Hang on, ma'am. We'll get you fixed up in no time." Nico looked up and waved at Denise, who tossed the fast rope and harness down to him. "You two get up there. She'll need your help pulling up Val. I'll clip this on in the meantime."

Carley and the nurse climbed the ladder into the chopper. For the first time, she was happy to be aboard this boring metal bird.

Renny looked back at her and winked. "Hey!"

"Oh, God, guys. Thanks so much," she said. Renny smiled, staring that way he did when he was expecting something. Right away, Carley realized what it was. *Fine, he's earned it.* She moved to the cockpit and hugged him. "Oh, my hero!"

"I knew it!"

She withdrew, punching his shoulder before heading back to pull Val up. "Just the one time. Doofus." She knelt alongside Denise with the fast rope. Her mother was harnessed and ready to go.

They pulled as quickly as they could. As they did, Nico climbed the ladder, arriving simultaneously with Val. He shut the door behind them and helped lay Val down.

"You'll be alright." He looked to the cockpit. "Punch it, Renny."

"Way ahead of ya."

The chopper swung around, heading east over open water before turning north.

Denise and Nico glanced out the window. The monsters were still engaged, the Kraken's movements distinct as those of a defeated foe unwilling to concede. Like the ancient samurai, it would choose death over defeat.

****

Repeated thrashes severed the tentacle, leaving the Kraken with five. O'Brien, still biting the limb, turned and slashed his caudal fin, striking the Kraken in the face with thunderous force.

It rolled backward, settling upright near the surface. It raised its stub in front of its good eye. Another injury, which would require extensive recovery. Angling its head, the Kraken watched the dorsal fin, which was gradually angling toward it.

O'Brien spat the arm, faced his opponent, then charged again.

Utilizing its siphon, the Kraken moved to the right, sweeping its arms to the left to counter the fish.

Caught in the tidal wave of tentacles, O'Brien rolled to his side, crashing upside down against the sand. Sweeping his caudal fin, O'Brien rocketed the short distance to the surface. There, he circled the injured Kraken.

It waited, bleeding and exhausted. Its arms were poised to counter the next attack. Being a fish, there were only so many ways its enemy could attack.

That was the Kraken's downfall, unbeknownst to it. With great intelligence came hubris. Assuming it was smarter than everything else in the sea, it had a habit of underestimating its opponent's intellect. In almost every case, it was correct in its assessment. Most of the regular sharks were incapable of critical thought.

O'Brien was no ordinary shark. There was more differentiating him from the others. While driven by instinct, his brain was larger, his mental capacity vaster. He wasn't as intelligent as the Kraken, but he didn't need to be. Especially when his opponent's battle plan was based around him being a thoughtless fish.

O'Brien charged.

The Kraken blew water, sidestepping to avoid the impact.

O'Brien veered left slightly, following the trajectory. In addition, he dove and immediately angled up. In a bounding leap, he crossed a hundred feet of water, countering the Kraken's defenses and coming down directly atop of its mantle.

Momentum and gravity drove the cephalopod to the bottom. The shark bit and thrashed.

The Kraken convulsed. The teeth pierced the bullet wound caused by the big ship.

The taste of blood spurred O'Brien on. He put all of his energy into the jaws, pushing his teeth deeper and deeper. Next, he slammed his foe face-first into the seabed. Clouds of silt burst all around them. He pulled back and smashed the Kraken again, grinding its smushed eye against the bottom.

Tentacles grabbed him and clawed him with their hooks. O'Brien ignored the assault, focusing all efforts on the mantle.

CRASH!

He slammed the Kraken a third time.

A fourth.

A fifth.

A sixth.

The clicks of a spasming beak filled the water. Billowing sand mixed with clouds of blood.

By the seventh impact, most of the tentacles had detached from the shark and were limply waving with the motions. Their last motion was convulsion. Nerves fired through the creature's body. Its mantle finally tore, gradually at first, then as easily as the thinnest invertebrate.

With a final shake, the mantle split wide open. Organs and intestines unraveled. Ink spewed involuntarily. The tentacles coiled, then unwound. Their color paled, as they sank to the bottom.

O'Brien took no chances. He inflicted his wrath on the Kraken until the mantle was nothing but a mound of shredded flesh.

The task was done. All he required now was sustenance to replenish the spent energy. Fortunately, there was plenty to eat from.

The mantle was even less recognizable by the time he was finished. After numerous mouthfuls, the megalodon was satisfied. Master of the sea, he turned around and migrated east, leaving a battered Kraken carcass in his wake.

CHAPTER 34

Key Largo, Florida.
Ocean Reef Medical Center.

Hospital waiting lobbies, hospital coffee and creamer, and the news—three things Nico absolutely hated on any *normal* day. Today, he may as well have been in a four-star hotel watching the NFL playoffs.

Denise's plan had worked. The Kraken was dead, its bloated remains now floating southeast. According to the reports, government officials had been dispatched to recover the remains for study. The operation was secondary, the bulk of resources directed to rescue and recovery efforts in Cielo Nublado and Islamorada.

Denise leaned over and rested her head on his shoulder. She held a cup of crappy coffee on her lap with the lactose-free creamer.

"It's not even noon yet. Talk about a hell of a morning."

"Tell me about it," Nico said. "You talked me into stopping the Admiral from getting us into a war with China. You didn't say anything about battling a big-ass octopus."

She smiled. "Well, I figured 'why not go the extra mile?'"

"That logic better apply to lunch," Renny said. He was sprawled out on the lobby sofa with a rag over his forehead.

"Here we go again," Denise said.

"Damn right," Renny said. "We're talking shrimp scampi, grilled salmon, buttered lobster tails, scallops, crispy cod, and *crab legs*! Lots and lots of crab legs."

"I'm amazed you can eat after today," Nico said. He looked at the television and the carnage all over Islamorada. "Hard to believe one creature, even one as big as the Kraken, was capable of so much destruction."

"And to think it's nothing compared to the devastation one *person* was about to cause," Denise said.

That statement sparked a thought in Nico's mind. He pulled out his phone and scrolled through the various news articles and broadcasts.

"What is it?" Denise asked.

"Nothing yet about the Admiral," Nico said. "If Silvia Remar had said something, it'd be all over the channels by now. Especially after what just occurred on my island."

"Maybe they wouldn't listen to her," Denise said.

"Or, she didn't bother."

"Who cares?" Renny said. "What are you gonna do? Hunt her down and chastise her for it?"

The good news arrived with Carley, who stepped into the lobby, completely spent.

Nico stood up. "What's the word, kid?"

Carley, completely exhausted, managed to smile. "They got her stabilized. Operation is going very well."

"Thank God." Nico was the first to exchange hugs with her. Then Denise and Renny.

"So, what's next for you?" Denise asked.

"I don't know," Carley said. "I think it's safe to assume nobody's going back to Cielo Nublado. My husband and I are thinking of moving north. Like we'd discussed after the eighty-footer attacked, somewhere dry sounds pretty nice. After finding out I almost got eaten this morning, he's pretty adamant about staying away from the ocean. Maybe find a country town somewhere."

"Ye-haw. Go for it, cowgirl," Renny said.

"That said, thanks guys. Seriously," Carley said. "You saved our lives."

Nico shrugged. "Well, it was the least I could do, since you pulled Denise and me off a sinking boat a while back."

"True! I guess we're even."

"Wait a second," Renny said. "What about me?! I saved your asses that day, too. In fact, I was the one flying the chopper."

"The fact we even got in the chopper was thanks to me, wise ass. As I recall, when we decided to look for him after he went missing, you were all like, 'For all I know, he's probably over at her boat wetting his whistle, if you know what I mean.'"

"That would've been preferable to what really happened," Nico said under his breath. Denise elbowed him in the ribs.

They welcomed the levity and the warmth of friendship it brought. Sorely, it had to come to an end. Carley was happy to move on, and everyone was happy for her, but good things could feel bittersweet.

"What about you guys?" she asked.

"Not sure yet," Renny said. "That said, I have time to make a decision. Thanks to the one-year's salary I'll be receiving. Too bad Nico talked you into leaving…"

"Yeah-yeah, rub it in," Carley said. She looked at Nico. "What about you guys?"

"Probably lots and lots of research," Denise said. "There's years of work that needs to be done. Lord knows what other lifeforms have emerged from the depths. Someone's got to travel around and study them."

Nico lowered his head. "I guess you're set in your ways."

"Of course..." she leaned her head on his shoulder again. "I need an assistant. Someone who's willing to stick around for a really, *really* long time."

He looked at her. "You asking me to travel the high seas with you? Go from cop to sailor?"

"More like researcher. Plus, I need someone knowledgeable in weaponry. Who knows what dangerous things we might come across?"

Nico smirked. "Not exactly what I had in mind when I was thinking of a change in pace... *but...*"

Denise pulled him in for a kiss.

Renny lay back down. "Blech!" He leaned up after his phone started buzzing. His face flushed after he saw his wife's name on the screen. "Oh, hell. I forgot to tell her I would miss my flight."

"So?" Denise said. "I think under the circumstances, she'll understand."

"That, or she'll feed me to the next sea monster that turns up."

Denise and Nico simultaneously leaned back in their seats.

"Oh, please. Don't tempt fate," Denise said. Next, it was her face that flushed. She leaned forward, "Oh, Jesus."

Nico put a hand on her shoulder. "What is it?"

"The thing that attacked Maxwell Island..."

"That electric eel thing?"

Denise nodded. "If it's bigger than the one O'Brien killed, it could cause more destruction than the Kraken."

"*That* much damage?" Nico sniggered in disbelief. "I'm sure it's dangerous, but *how* dangerous? The other one seemed to let out an electric pulse. Dangerous, but nothing the Coast Guard can't handle, I'm sure."

"Unless it's more mature," Denise said.

Nico's smile vanished. "More mature? What do you think that means? What kind of voltage would a mature giant electric eel be capable of?"

****

Cargo Ship USS Triumph.
Atlantic Ocean, three-hundred miles east of Savannah, Georgia.

It was nearing the end of an eighteen-day stretch across the Atlantic. It was the second trip for Billy Bates, the ship's newest deckhand. Even after near eighty days total at sea, he still could not get over the sight of the setting sun over the calm sea.

Most of the crew had gone below, the night shift performing their duties on deck. Billy didn't feel like sleeping. For much of the afternoon, he and another crewmate had been huddled near a radio, listening to reports of a sea monster attack on the Florida Keys.

It was as if mankind had entered a new age. An age of monsters.

The thought created a sense of danger. How safe was the ocean now? Would this continue to be a world in which man was allowed to inhabit?

Standing at Hold One, Billy looked down the length of the cargo ship. Over a thousand feet of steel, carrying twenty-one thousand TEUs—the equivalent of a forty-mile long train. The fact that such a machine could stand on water proved that man was truly the master of this domain.

Dusk shifted into night. There was no moon in the sky. Only the glow of the deck lights provided any visibility.

"Hey man," one of the night shift deckhands said. "Shouldn't you be in your bunk?"

"Not tired," Billy said.

"Still. Better get below."

Billy knew not to argue. He turned to walk toward Accommodations, passing stacks of huge containers on the way.

A flash of white reflected off the metal, gone as soon as it appeared.

He stopped, whipping to his left to look into the horizon. *Was that lightning I saw?* There were no reports of stormy weather in this area. The sky was cloudy, but not stormy before night set in.

For a count of ten, he waited. Nothing. He started to rationalize it as a figment of his imagination. Maybe someone on the structure panned a spotlight in his direction.

He continued on, stopping after three steps.

Another flash.

Billy looked into the water. Lightning strikes, traveling what appeared to be the length of the ocean. Like before, they vanished, encasing the Atlantic in darkness.

He stood frozen, questioning what he just saw. Lightning in itself wasn't peculiar. It was *where* the lightning was flashing that alarmed him.

Did I see what I think I saw? Should I say something? Again, he wondered if his imagination was going out of control.

"Did you see that?!" the deckhand shouted at him. Billy looked at him and nodded.

"It was *under* the water."

"Thank God," the deckhand said. He leaned forward, sweaty hands clutching the guardrail. "I thought I was the only one who noticed that."

"What's going on?" Billy said.

The ocean turned white. Nuclear white, blinding the world above.

Billy squinted and threw his hands over his face. Through the gaps, he managed to spot a singular streak of jagged light shooting from the glow. There was no mistaking its form. Electricity. *Lightning,* coming right at the *Triumph.*

A rolling *boom* echoed from under the ship. The deck lights burst into sparks. The deckhand spasmed violently, hands locked onto the rail.

Billy watched in horror as the man danced in place.

Another *boom* shook the vessel, pitching it to starboard. Billy's heart jumped into his throat after he recognized the sounds of screams in the chaos coming from behind him. He turned just in time to see another crewman fall into the water.

The white lights vanished. Alarms blared from within the ship. Several crewmen raced onto the deck, barking questions.

"What the hell's going on?!" one shouted.

"There's steam in the peak tank!" another shouted.

"Guys!" another yelled. "Get extinguishers. There's a fire in the engine room!"

"Did we hit something?"

"Injured man here!" One of the crew pointed at the deckhand, who had collapsed after his electrical jolt. They looked at Billy. "What happened? Did you see anything?!"

Billy stammered. "Lights?"

"Huh?"

"There's lights. We need…" He looked at the water. "A man fell overboard. Anyone have flashlights?"

Several crewmen aimed their flashlights into the water, guided by Billy's direction.

"I see him!" one shouted. The others focused their lights at the struggling man.

"What's that?" one said.

"A lifeline," another answered, approaching the edge with a donut.

"No. *That?*"

A shape took form beneath the crewman. Huge, thin teeth reflected the glow of the spotlights. Eyes, like those of a dragon, peered up at them. The snout, reptilian in shape, parted, revealing dozens of stake-like fangs.

In that moment, the jaws slammed shut over the crewman. Multiple stabbings and crushing pressure brought instant death. It lifted its head over the water, reared back, and swallowed. Next, it cruised down the length of the ship, its one-hundred-thirty-foot body on full display.

"A snake!" someone shouted.

"No! A dragon!"

"No…" Billy muttered. "An *eel*." He gulped. "An *electric* eel." He looked at the massive structure around him and the ocean it stood on. The engines stalled. The smell of burning fuel filled the air. This sanctuary, this proof of man's dominance over the ocean, was crippled from a single hit from the creature's electrical surge.

The thing submerged. Blinding flashes of light filled the ocean, immediately followed by a jagged bolt which hit the engine compartment. One million gallons of fuel ignited at once.

The next flash was one of fire.

The End

SEVEREDPRESS

facebook.com/severedpress
twitter.com/severedpress

CHECK OUT OTHER GREAT DEEP SEA THRILLERS

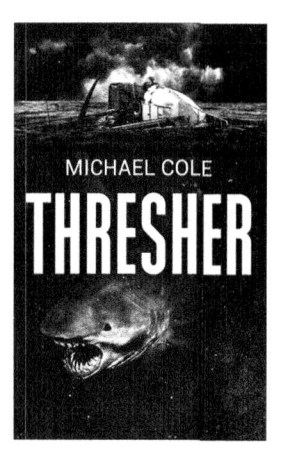

THRESHER
by Michael Cole

In the aftermath of a hurricane, a series of strange events plague the coastal waters off Florida. People go into the water and never return. Corpses of killer whales drift ashore, ravaged from enormous bite marks. A fishing trawler is found adrift, with a mysterious gash in its hull.

Transferred to the coastal town of Merit, police officer Leonard Riker uncovers the horrible reality of an enormous Thresher shark lurking off the coast. Forty feet in length, it has taken a territorial claim to the waters near the town harbor. Armed with three-inch teeth, a scythe-like caudal fin, and unmatched aggression, the beast seeks to kill anything sharing the waters.

THE GUILLOTINE
by Lucas Pederson

1,000 feet under the surface, Prehistoric Anthropologist, Ash Barrington, and his team are in the midst of a great archeological dig at the bottom of Lake Superior where they find a treasure trove of bones. Bones of dinosaurs that aren't supposed to be in this particular region. In their underwater facility, Infinity Moon, Ash and his team soon discover a series of underground tunnels. Upon exploring, they accidentally open an ice pocket, thawing the prehistoric creature trapped inside. Soon they are being attacked, the facility falling apart around them, by what Ash knows is a dunkleosteus and all those bones were from its prey. Now...Ash and his team are the prey and the creature will stop at nothing to get to them.

SEVERED PRESS

facebook.com/severedpress
twitter.com/severedpress

CHECK OUT OTHER GREAT DEEP SEA THRILLERS

THE BREACH
by Edward J. McFadden III

A Category 4 hurricane punched a quarter mile hole in Fire Island, exposing the Great South Bay to the ferocity of the Atlantic Ocean, and the current pulled something terrible through the new breach. A monstrosity of the past mixed with the present has been disturbed and it's found its way into the sheltered waters of Long Island's southern sea.

Nate Tanner lives in Stones Throw, Long Island. A disgraced SCPD detective lieutenant put out to pasture in the marine division because of his Navy background and experience with aquatic crime scenes, Tanner is assigned to hunt the creeper in the bay. But he and his team soon discover they're the ones being hunted.

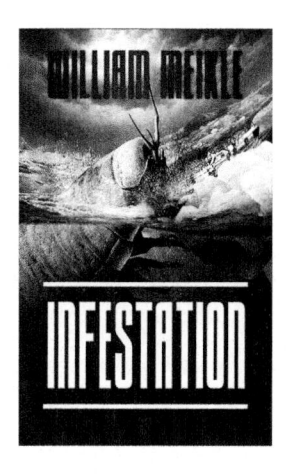

INFESTATION
by William Meikle

It was supposed to be a simple mission. A suspected Russian spy boat is in trouble in Canadian waters. Investigate and report are the orders.

But when Captain John Banks and his squad arrive, it is to find an empty vessel, and a scene of bloody mayhem.

Soon they are in a fight for their lives, for there are things in the icy seas off Baffin Island, scuttling, hungry things with a taste for human flesh.

They are swarming. And they are growing.

"Scotland's best Horror writer" - Ginger Nuts of Horror

"The premier storyteller of our time." - Famous Monsters of Filmland

SEVEREDPRESS

@severedpress
/severedpress

Check out other great
Sea Monster Novels!

Michael Cole
CREATURE OF LAKE SHADOW

It was supposed to be a simple bank robbery. Quick. Clean. Efficient. It was none of those. With police searching for them across the state, a band of criminals hide out in a desolate cabin on the frozen shore of Lake Shadow. Isolated, shrouded in thick forest, and haunted by a mysterious history, they thought it was the perfect place to hide. Tensions mount as they hear strange noises outside. Slain animals are found in the snow. Before long, they realize something is watching them. Something hungry, violent, and not of this world. In their attempt to escape, they found the Creature of Lake Shadow.

Matt James
SUB-ZERO

The only thing colder than the Antarctic air is the icy chill of death... Off the coast of McMurdo Station, in the frigid waters of the Southern Ocean, a new species of Antarctic octopus is unintentionally discovered. Specialists aboard a state-of-the-art DARPA research vessel aim to apply the animal's "sub-zero venom" to one of their projects: An experimental painkiller designed for soldiers on the front lines. All is going according to plan until the ship is caught in an intense storm. The retrofitted tanker is rocked, and the onboard laboratory is destroyed. Amid the chaos, the lead scientist is infected by a strange virus while conducting the specimen's dissection. The scientist didn't die in the accident. He changed.

SEVEREDPRESS

facebook.com/severedpress
twitter.com/severedpress

CHECK OUT OTHER GREAT DEEP SEA THRILLERS

SHARK: INFESTED WATERS
by P.K. Hawkins

For Simon, the trip was supposed to be a once in a lifetime gift: a journey to the Amazon River Basin, the land that he had dreamed about visiting since he was a child. His enthusiasm for the trip may be tempered by the poor conditions of the boat and their captain leading the tour, but most of the tourists think they can look the other way on it. Except things go wrong quickly. After a horrific accident, Simon and the other tourists find themselves trapped on a tiny island in the middle of the river. It's the rainy season, and the river is rising. The island is surrounded by hungry bull sharks that won't let them swim away. And worst of all, the sharks might not be the only blood-thirsty killers among them. It was supposed to be the trip of a lifetime. Instead, they'll be lucky if they make it out with their lives at all.

DARK WATERS
by Lucas Pederson

Jörmungandr is an ancient Norse sea monster. Thought to be purely a myth until a battleship is torn a part by one.

With his brother on that ship, former Navy Seal and deep-sea diver, Miles Raine, sets out on a personal vendetta against the creature and hopefully save his brother. Bringing with him his old Seal team, the Dagger Points, they embark on a mission that might very well be their last.

But what happens when the hunters become the hunted and the dark waters reveal more than a monster?

Printed in Great Britain
by Amazon